ONLY THE TRYING

Alex Cook

© Alex Cook 2019

Print ISBN: 978-1-54398-080-6

eBook ISBN: 978-1-54398-081-3

All rights reserved. This book or any portion thereof may not be reproduced or used in any manner whatsoever without the express written permission of the publisher except for the use of brief quotations in a book review.

CONTENTS

2007 / 2008: La Jolla 9
    Chapter 1— Tommie Smith 11
    Chapter 2— Señorita 20
    Chapter 3— Game Day (Act 1) 33
    Chapter 4— Game Day (Act 2) 40
    Chapter 5— Intermission: The End of the Innocence 51
    Chapter 6— Game Day (Act 3) 63
    Chapter 7— Game Day (Act 4) 72
    Chapter 8— Game Day (Act 5) 79
2008: Playa Ballena, Baja California Sur 85
    Chapter 9— Guns 'N' Roses 87
2008: The Columbia River Gorge 93
    Chapter 10— Bacon Waffles 95
    Chapter 11— I Think…It's Windy 102
    Chapter 12— The Gorge 108
    Chapter 13— Tell Me Something Good 113
2008: San Fransisco 135
    Chapter 14— Peaches and the Apple 137
    Chapter 15— Diary of a Mad Office Husband 146
    Chapter 16— Marinated 155
2009: Brazil 163
    Chapter 17— Rio 165
2009: Still Out West (Mostly) 171
    Chapter 18— Something Ain't Right 173
    Chapter 19— We're All Just Animals 184
    Chapter 20— Psycho Killer, Qu'est-ce Que C'est? 194
    Chapter 21— Stones and Bones 198
    Chapter 22— The Prodigal Son 213

Chapter 23— A Wolf at the Door 222
Chapter 24— The Trap 228
Chapter 25— Sprung... 238
Chapter 26— Across the Border.. 253
Chapter 27— Calexico... 268
Chapter 28— Dia de los Muertos 278
Chapter 29— The Devil You Know 285
Chapter 30— The Blank Canvas.. 293
Chapter 31— Piercing the Veil 323
Chapter 32— Squeezed.. 338
Chapter 33— Casting 350
Chapter 34— Leather Face.. 356
Chapter 35— Reginald Blundergusting.. 374
Chapter 36— Las Tres Hijas Restaurante 381
Chapter 37— Runaway Boys 423
Chapter 38— The Deschutes Pivot 433
Chapter 39— A Face with a View (or, Good for the Gander)....................... 439
Chapter 40— Back in the Rocking Chair... 450
Chapter 41— Donuts Are Meant to be Eaten 460
Chapter 42— Making Flippy Floppy (or, I Had a Flame but She Had a Fire)...470
Chapter 43— Grey Panthers 475
Chapter 44— Ithaca Bound 493
Chapter 45— Church on Time (or, Break Their Hearts and Have No Mercy) ..500
Chapter 46— T and HGH 512
Chapter 47— Castaway 517
Chapter 48— Cold Feet... 526
Chapter 49— The Dead... 534
Chapter 50— Procrastinundrum.. 546
Chapter 51— If the Horse Don't Pull, You Got to Carry the Load................ 551
Chapter 52— This Darkness Got to Give... 557
Chapter 53— 680 Steps 561
Chapter 54— Old Saint Hilary's 567
Chapter 55— Not Forsaken 572
Chapter 56— Dreams 576

It was the glowing skin that stretched across the valley at the small of her back—the tiny, golden hairs glistening in what little light she allowed when they raised themselves to the level of animals. He would trace first his fingers, then his lips; tasting the salt that accumulated at the crossroads. Working his way north or south, he would regularly pause for reflection—briefly considering the moment—before the hunger would again overtake him. Years later, when alone, he would often recall those moments with a pining clarity; realizing with conviction (and too late), that he had been in the fleeting presence of the Divine.

2007 / 2008
La Jolla

CHAPTER 1 —

Tommie Smith

Clay Barton meticulously painted the casing of the .44 Magnum hollow-point. Filling his nostrils were the fumes of a specific type of clear nail polish that in previous jobs had never failed him. His training in Panama had taught him that a coat of lacquer would make the cartridges waterproof, effectively protecting the internal primer and gunpowder from moisture contamination. After completing the sealing, he could then put the bullet into a powerhead and mount that small chamber on the tip of a spear. Mating the hollow-point with the speargun dramatically increased the killing power of the projectile. Over the years, he had used this technique during amphibious missions to protect his team from the curious predators that were known to be a danger to humans—mainly sharks and crocodiles. It was superstition that led him to always use the same brand of polish, like a baseball player who refuses to change his undershirt during a winning streak.

Every few minutes he would put down the tiny brush, roll his chair slightly left, and pick up a lighter and pipe. With his right hand he would push the flame into the small bowl of the pipe and then suck the ensuing marijuana smoke through the stem and deeply into his lungs. His heavy, longtime use had gotten him so used to the acrid burn of the weed that the assault of smoke on his olfactory and pulmonary systems went unnoticed. The only response the ritual triggered in his brain was a feeling of pleasant anticipation. As he worked his way through the cannabis and the cartridges, a sense of deep contentment seeped from his lungs. All of his real (and contemplated) trespasses were drifting towards inconsequential, along with his nearly constant paranoias. With a little more smoke he would soon be able to compartmentalize his current chore from the seriousness of what he intended to execute tomorrow. After three long pulls, he put down the drug paraphernalia and turned back to the bullets.

He preferred to use the large caliber hollow-point ammunition because it increased the tissue damage at the point of impact. The width of the bullethead expanded upon contact with skin, muscle, and bone, enlarging the wound circumference and elevating blood loss. The downside was a decrease in range and accuracy, especially when fired underwater, so he had to get close to his target if he wanted to ensure the bullet would achieve its maximum kill potential. In unimpeded air, a .44 bullet would travel over a mile, but water was nearly eight hundred times denser; hence the triggered hollow-point would begin to lose velocity after less than a meter in the ocean.

He finished the second cartridge and carefully laid it on the temporary rack he had created from toothpicks. He realized he was starting to get lightheaded from the nail polish but pushed on nonetheless as he needed to finish tonight. The third (and last) cartridge lay benignly next to the first two. He hoped he would need only one, but he was fastidious about his planning.

He fingered the handle of the tiny paint brush and stared at the bottle of nail polish. *I'm no different than any other highly trained professional*, he thought.

But then the little voice in his head reminded him of what he had become.

Except, of course, for the killing.

He heard the front door slam and flinched while grabbing for his holster. Checking his watch, he realized it was probably his girlfriend, Tory, returning from an afternoon surf session at Black's Beach. He checked and saw that the latch to his lab was secured. This information allowed his adrenal glands to stand down. His heart rate started returning to its previous, calm state.

"Tommie, are you home…?"

Clay reluctantly turned down Gnarls Barkley's "Crazy" on his iPod, which he had hooked up wirelessly to several speakers throughout the lab; he suspected he would be having an ongoing conversation through the walls. He pictured the partially neoprene-clad twenty-eight-year-old leaving puddles of seawater on the *saltillo* tiles of their rented bungalow. Soon she would put away her board and start heading for the bath. Forcing a smile into his voice, he hollered through the closed door:

"Tory…hi! I'm in my office! I'll be out in about ten minutes!"

He used the pseudonym Tommie Smith as a form of penance, like a religious zealot might wear a hair shirt. It reminded him of the incident, nearly three decades earlier, when his younger half brother, Paul, had been the victim of a brutal attack by two rogue policemen. The beating resulted in spinal cord damage; Paul had been wheelchair-bound ever since. Clay, the eldest, felt deeply and irrationally responsible for the accident. That night he had been chaperoning his two younger brothers…and it was their first shared time out on the town. Paul, who was half black, idolized Tommie Smith, a world-champion track athlete who had protested race inequality. Smith's iconic moment occurred when he and teammate John Carlos simultaneously displayed the controversial Black Power salute on the podium at the 1968 Mexico City Olympics. Every time someone called Clay by the assumed name, a mental image of his damaged brother got thrown up on his cerebral monitor. The recollection would inflict a jolt of shame upon his soul, like electricity running through an exposed wire attached to one's skin. Over time the scar tissue had grown thick, but the wound was so deep that any stimulus still elicited significant pain. That was the way he wanted it.

From the other side of the door, Tory started their regular evening dance.

"What are you thinkin' for dinner?"

"Pizza!"

"Really? Again? Tommie, you wanna feel like crap for the next two days?"

"Pepperoni and bacon!"

"Ugh…man, no way, I can't let you do that to us…anything but pizza!"

At the time of Paul's accident, Clay had been home on leave. He had been in the Navy for twenty-four months and had recently completed BUD/S training. He was only twenty-one years old and had yet to kill anyone. After Paul became paralyzed, Clay returned to his Special Ops team in Central America and struggled with the guilt. One of his symptoms was an increasing tolerance for high-risk behavior, and he started volunteering for the most challenging operations. His underwater ordinance training, combined with an overreaching military, found his commanders frequently selecting him. As a soldier, and more importantly a SEAL, his professional experiences started imposing a growing familiarity with death. Not the long-range, faceless, mass-butchering type of killing enabled by modern technology; but rather the timeless murdering that requires a messy, intimate extinguishing of another person's life.

2007 / 2008 - La Jolla

In the beginning, he thought he was okay with the killing. He wrapped himself in a patriotic flag of righteous violence, buying into the Manifest Destiny narrative delivered by his leaders. After several tours of duty, however, the rationalizations began to ring hollow. A spreading numbness changed his self-perceptions to that of a simple, skilled craftsman carrying out his trade. It was this somewhat nihilistic mindset that had defined his occupational approach ever since.

When Clay started with an A-Team, he was surprised by the intensity of the adrenaline high. The moments when he and his military brothers were hunting their prey brought about a clarity that Clay had never before experienced. He suspected that was what made them good—that for the most part the killing not only didn't repulse them but actually did the opposite: it inspired them. Over time the best operators developed a kind of psychopathy; in the worst cases, they became strangely attracted to the act of taking another person's life.

During this time, Clay also noticed the beginnings of a pattern. Regular struggles with the monotony of day-to-day routine, interrupted by brief, exhilarating moments when he and his teammates were operating as predators, in total focus mode. He worried that this rhythm was a sign that something was wrong in his head, but he told himself that this was what he was trained to do; he needed to either cope or get out. He reminded himself that to some extent he knew what he was getting into when he had enlisted. It wasn't until much, much later that he fully recognized the loss of sensitivity and accompanying mental damage that were part of the job. The silver lining, depending upon your perspective, was that without the acquired hardness, he never could've been effective for all those years.

His willingness to volunteer for difficult assignments placed him in rarified company. He participated in all the major operations enacted during his enlistment. Fighting the Marxist/Soviet proxies in the jungles of Central America served as his introduction. From there it was an easy jump to Grenada, to keep the insignificant Caribbean island from becoming a Cuban outpost. He was the only SEAL involved in that "invasion," and from his place as observer on a BGB the mission felt more like "Beach Blanket Bingo" than "Cuban Missile Crisis." After that, things started melding into one long, hot, sandy engagement: Air-dropped into Kuwait for a few weeks. Back to Panama (to evict Noriega). Flown to the Middle East for Operation Desert Shield and the ensuing Gulf War. Always following orders and always targeting poorly trained brown men armed with AK47s and insufficient degrees of conviction. In between, he would return to Panama and lose himself in a smoky haze of girls and self-medication.

Back in his lab, Clay offered Tory another dinner option.

"Sushi!" he called through the door.

"We just did that last week! Too much mercury!"

"Why don't you just pick a place?"

"C'mon, Tommie, don't do that! I'll go with whatever you want… I'm easy!"

Deciding not to reenlist after multiple tours, Clay got out when his commanding officers started making noises about promoting him to a desk job. In 1992, as he was preparing for the transition to the civilian world, the CIA came knocking, wanting him for their elite Special Operations Group. He was flattered and wary at the same time. The wariness resulted primarily from fourteen years of being underpaid by Uncle Sam. Concurrent with the CIA's courting, a private security company made overtures with a six-figure salary. The choice was a no-brainer. To him it seemed the only difference between his old job and the new was that the latter provided better pay and longer leave. He agreed to join Hightower Security, Inc., and started a new career as a mercenary. It was at that point that he buried the identity of Clay Barton and became Tommie Smith. He no longer cared about which song and dance the generals were selling for the politicians; instead, for Tommie Smith, it was all about the money.

Over time, as his reputation and his pay grew, he started to better understand the landscape. He became more careful about mission selection, paying particular attention to the mission's duration. Eventually, his connections were so well established that he cut out the middleman entirely, leaving Hightower and working solely as an independent contractor. Anonymous people came to him with jobs and he got to choose. Ten relatively productive years ensued, during which he was able to save nearly seven hundred grand.

Now he was thinking about retirement.

His occupation required a younger man's body. The demands placed on him were similar to those placed on professional athletes. He had the usual nicks and scars from shrapnel and bullet fragments, and he was in much better shape than most of his contemporaries—but most of his contemporaries were either dead or retired. It was obvious his explosive speed and strength were in decline; but what he most noticed was his inability to recover promptly. When deprived of food or sleep, his functionality suffered dramatically, especially if the jobs were physically demanding. Experience had allowed him to offset some of the physical loss, but he knew the clock was ticking. He noted that fewer of the more challenging jobs, in extreme environments, were coming his way. His decline in pay reflected that.

As he approached fifty years of age, he realized he was considered a liability for any work that involved being a member of a team. Eventually he was offered only the least desirable gigs: solo work for marginal employers. He found himself no longer fighting other professional soldiers but now forced to operate in the ethically conflicted civilian arena, where he was frequently asked to kill people in a surreptitious manner. When he reflected on his current situation, he realized he was disgusted by the dishonorable nature of his work and alarmed by how far from the main stage he had slid. But he needed the money. Being a soldier—and hence killing—were the only things he knew. He figured he had a year, two at best, which meant maybe one or two more jobs after the La Jolla gig, before he was done for good. He suspected he would need every penny of his savings if he wanted to keep living at the standard to which he had grown accustomed, especially with Alan Greenspan pushing interest rates towards zero. He fantasized about returning home, to be with his brothers and parents, as if nothing had changed over the last thirty years.

The third cartridge found its way into his grasp. *Yep,* he thought, *with any luck this is my last year.* He positioned the cartridge on the makeshift stand so he could encase it in the lacquer. *Finish tomorrow with no hiccups...one more job after that...and then I'm out.* Tory interrupted his thoughts: "Tommie!"

Clay momentarily ignored the voice outside of his locked door while he finished the last metal jacket then carefully placed it on the toothpicks to dry. He picked up the first cartridge, which was already dry, and considered its purpose.

"I'll be right out, Tory!"

He sensed her dripping feet walking down the hall, away from his office, and then heard the bathroom door close. He pictured her hands struggling to strip the wet suit from her lean curves, and, after clumsily bending over to pry the remaining grasping rubber from her ankles, she would likely leave the whole apparatus in a wet, sandy clump on the floor.

Once he heard the shower running, he carefully placed all of his tools in their customary positions. Then, he quietly unlocked the door. Before stepping out, he checked to make sure Tory wasn't in the hallway. After verifying the coast was clear, he backed out of his small workplace, reached in to turn off the lights, and then quickly closed and locked the door.

CHAPTER 2 —

Señorita

As the San Diego Metropolitan Transit bus rumbled towards the sea, Blanché Jackson Rochin watched the landscape gradually change from dusty, inland desert to verdant, crowded oceanfront. The drive was only twenty-two miles by private car, but for the working poor, the ninety-minute ride via public transportation (with multiple transfers) would have to do.

For three months now she had been making the tedious, weekly commute from her inland home in El Cajon to the foggy beaches of La Jolla. The routine had allowed her to identify each bus in the SDMT fleet by their physical characteristics. She called the beast that currently carried her "Stinky" because in certain parts of the vehicle riders were visited by a vague smell that implied the exhaust system wasn't fully isolated from the passenger compartment.

On the southwest corner of Interstate 8 and Interstate 5 resided a decaying elephant sanctuary, the staff of which would exercise the residents daily. During those periods some of the patients would hang their heads over the sanctuary wall, intermittently flapping their big ears while watching the traffic whiz by. From her window seat behind the driver (a spot she knew from experience suffered the least from the invading diesel fumes), Blanché would search to her left, through the smudged piece of safety glass, hoping to catch a glimpse of her wrinkled, grey friends. A feeling of youthful exuberance always overwhelmed her for the few moments when their worlds overlapped.

As far back as she could remember, Blanché had always loved elephants, particularly their articulated trunks, which to her seemed to have minds of their own. But she hadn't really understood them, not the elephants held behind the fence. She didn't actually see them as sentient beings, but more as caricatures—images from her childhood *Babar* or *Dumbo* books. She had been mesmerized as much by their out-of-placeness as anything else. Not just the continental displacement, but the incongruence of simple, dignified creatures positioned as they were at the busy, concrete convolution of a freeway exchange. As she flew by them in her modern conveyance, hurtling out of control to a place and life that seemed to be choosing her rather than the other way around, the elephants symbolized an earlier, less complicated time. It wasn't until several months later, when she recognized the sadness in their red-rimmed eyes, that she realized that they were prisoners as well, held captive, like her, by their circumstances.

Against her upper-class parents' wishes, and a little more than two years earlier, Blanché had gotten pregnant and then married—both acts resulting from a deep but sudden love for a young, beautiful Mexican man. They had met in Oaxaca while Blanché was on an exchange program from USC, apprenticing with an international human rights legal team. At the time she was pre-law, with aspirations to be an attorney. He was a *muy guapo* local student (but only part-time) and ran with a group of friends that intermingled with Blanché's social circle. They were introduced after dinner at an outdoor cafe and found commonality in their passionate critique of capitalism. The fertile combination of hormones, tequila, and a decadent chocolate *molé salsa* conspired to alleviate Blanché of her usual restraints, and she soon caught herself happily *in flagrante* with her new friend, Hector Rochin. He was equally smitten with his blond *gringa* acquaintance, and as a result, neither paid enough attention to the necessities of birth control.

When she called home to share the news of her pregnancy, she didn't ask for permission to keep the baby. Of course, she had concerns her parents might cut her off financially, but her worry wasn't so great as to force a reconsideration of her course of action. If she and Hector had to forge a new life on their own, they were up for the challenge. They believed in the surmounting power of love.

While she breathlessly explained to her college friends that she was "following her heart" and taking a break from college to become a wife and mom, her mother heard echoes from the past. She lobbied for completion of her daughter's education. In response, the twenty-year-old USC undergraduate assured her parents of her intent to return to college and get her degree, just not that year.

Eventually, from their home in Beverly Hills, the elder Jacksons accepted Blanché's decision. But they also made it clear that they would not be underwriting their only child's capriciousness. They would provide emotional support and a financial safety net, but the day-to-day adventure of moving forward with a child (and an incomplete education) was an experience the young couple would need to manage on their own. Blanché's father, in particular, felt struggle and sacrifice were necessary for the development of "character," a most underrated (and difficult to define) trait, in his experience. He also didn't want to incentivize his children to make decisions that neglected the accompanying responsibilities. What he failed to share with anyone, but which was obvious to everyone, was that he was pissed off by Blanché's willful detour, and hence refused to pay for a front row seat to what he privately called "a naive, romantic, and ill-informed, slow-motion train wreck." He couldn't understand why someone with the advantages of his DNA and resources would decide to raise a child with a stranger and no money. Given that Hector had no job skills, no savings, and limited ability with the English language, *padre* Jackson believed that most would concede he had a point.

Blanché would be the first to admit that the early months with her new husband were more of a struggle than she anticipated. Their relationship and finances were being stretched to the limits; she took the job in La Jolla because they needed the money. She worked as a live-in nanny, arriving at her employers' residence Friday by noon and leaving midday the following Monday. This schedule gave her three days working at the beach and four days in El Cajon with her husband and one-year-old daughter, Ella. Hector had found a job in the landscaping industry that required no documentation and paid ten dollars an hour. The young family shared an extra bedroom in Hector's cousin's house, which was cramped but affordable. They had been welcomed as family, but it was also made clear by the cousin's wife (Chita) that the arrangement was temporary. They would need to find independent living quarters.

Blanché paid Chita to watch baby Ella during the times she and Hector were working, but she got paid multiple times more by the family in La Jolla to watch their two children. It was a simple case of childcare arbitrage. Blanché and Hector had penciled out the numbers. If they were particularly disciplined, they could actually save enough to get their own, small, one-bedroom apartment in a slightly nicer neighborhood. The area they aspired to was shabby but safe, full of working-class immigrant families who looked out for each other. Drug and gang activity periodically filtered through, but it wasn't defining. Most importantly, the schools were decent, and cheap babysitting was in abundance. Blanché's plan was to continue her education at night, after things became a little less hectic, and work her way up the socioeconomic ladder like so many generations before her. In her mind, the La Jolla childcare gig was just temporary. This strategy gave her hope during those frequent times when Hector's ambitions seemed particularly absent. Blanché did her best to keep her frustrations from turning into spousal venting and had learned through previous failures to be especially vigilant when exhausted. She reminded herself of the cultural differences between she and her husband, and she hoped those differences would prove complementary rather than corrosive.

At first her new job had seemed great, but with the clarity of hindsight she could now see there had been warning signs from the beginning. The first had been Mrs. Aguilar's lack of involvement in the interview process. Blanché's introduction to the position had come via two men—initially, a formally dressed man introduced as Uncle Tony, then the handsome father of the two boys, Señor Aguilar. The first interrogation had taken less than twenty minutes, during which Tony verbally gathered information and photocopied Blanché's documents. The solemn man with the barrel chest and heavy Spanish accent then passed her on to Francisco Aguilar, the husband and man of the house, also dressed in suit and tie. Uncle Tony had respectfully referred to Aguilar as *Don* Francisco.

The next warning sign should have been the intensely detailed nature of the probing questions from Aguilar, the answers to which made obvious the precarious state of her and Hector's financial situation and residency status. The questioning had started as an inquiry into her Spanish surname, given her Anglo features; it became more politely invasive from there. By the end of the two-hour interview, she felt quite exposed, but Aguilar's Svengali-like style was such that she didn't feel uncomfortable. During the long bus ride back to the baking inlands, she reflected on his unusual ability to ask particularly intimate questions while still eliciting a feeling of trust, and even warmth. She considered that his bedside manner was that of a good family lawyer or doctor, despite his appearing to be only a decade older than Blanché.

A week later, Tony called and notified her that she had the job. The compensation would be weekly and in cash, if that was acceptable to her, and the amount he offered was far greater than she had hoped to negotiate. If ready, the family needed her to start the next Friday, at noon.

By Sunday night of her first weekend of work, Blanché thought things were a little strange at the Aguilar's beachfront estate; but the villa was so palatial that she ignored what she considered minor telltales. Back in El Cajon, her young family badly needed the money; her skills didn't provide her with many other employment options.

Uncle Tony appeared to be a bodyguard of some sort, and Señor Aguilar rarely interacted with the children—in fact Blanché rarely saw the mother or father. Blanché basically spent all day with the four- and six-year-old boys, corralling their tendencies to wander off and explore in a range of ever-growing concentric circles. They splashed in the tide pools, played games at the beach in front of the house, took afternoon naps, read books before bed, and generally led an idyllic life in a sublime setting. When she did interact with Señora Aguilar, she detected a general aloofness that made it clear the Latina woman was the *jefa*. Don Francisco and Uncle Tony were always warm and friendly to her during the infrequent times when their paths crossed.

Blanché's quarters were just slightly smaller than the shared bedroom in El Cajon, and the *en suite* bathroom, which she had all to herself, was a welcome upgrade from the crowded disaster of a loo back at her apartment. The finishes— especially the exquisite tile and stonework— were of a higher quality than the finishes she had enjoyed when growing up in Beverly Hills.

Naturally, there was delicious food, seemingly unlimited, which never required her involvement in preparation or clean up. She generally took her meals in the breakfast nook, with the boys and away from the adults. But she preferred things that way.

By the end of the first month, like a prisoner awaiting her upcoming parole, she started looking forward to her Friday morning commute to work at the beach. It was basically an opportunity to live in an environment similar to the privileged one in which she had been raised. Unlike when she was in El Cajon, her responsibilities in La Jolla didn't include the kitchen, laundry, or bedroom, and everyone that she interacted with generally looked and smelled good. Her weekend job came with temperate weather, splendid scenery, and, at first, impeccably mannered people.

She was self-aware enough to notice her emotional pattern, and feelings of guilt started accompanying her lack of enthusiasm for the long, hot return home to her real family on Mondays. She rationalized that her eroding sentiment, when it came to her husband and baby, was an acceptable trade-off, given her position as the family's main breadwinner. During one of her bus rides home, after doing some brief calculations in her head, she started entertaining ideas of a tangibly brighter future for her family. The Aguilars were paying her one thousand dollars a week, cash, and she was able to save a lot of it. That night, after getting showered, dinner made, and Ella settled in, she and her husband mixed up a pitcher of margaritas and binge watched *The Sopranos*. Despite her exhaustion, her optimistic mood translated into a degree of receptivity when her husband made some sly advances during a particularly salacious scene. She fell asleep feeling optimistic about their future.

Blanché remembered clearly the moment things started to change. At first the event didn't seem like a big deal. It was a glorious Saturday morning. The fog had just receded, and the city was sparkling eponymously. The boys were their usual energetic selves after their early breakfast, chasing each other around the house in a cacophonous, squealing melee. She suspected her attention would be needed to shepherd them to a calmer place and, in an effort to get ahead of the game, she dragged her body out of bed and started dressing. Having become relaxed with her position in the household, she was no longer as formal when it came to her workplace attire. This morning she favored comfort and ease over decorum. Naked except for her yoga pants, she was searching for her sports bra in a lower drawer when she felt a pair of eyes staring at her. Quickly straightening up and turning towards the presence, she saw Uncle Tony, dressed in suit and tie, with his ever-present earbud, staring at her from the doorway. He had quietly opened the door without her being aware…he couldn't have been there for more than a second or two. She immediately covered her breasts with her arm, while he slowly, far too slowly, stepped back out of sight, retreating into the hallway.

"*Señora necesita tu ayuda con los chicos.*"

From his new place in the hallway, he notified Blanché that *Doña* Aguilar had requested her assistance with the boys. There had been a gradual migration from English to Spanish during her daily interactions, as the Aguilars wanted her to speak English to the boys, but all the other conversations at the house seemed to prioritize Spanish.

"*Gracias*," Blanché answered while rushing across the room and closing the door.

It was the first time she had noticed the absence of a lock.

Things went slowly and quietly downhill from there, although sometimes she thought she was being paranoid. The random unwelcome touch in passing…the overly long stare that bordered on a leer. She felt like the whole male staff were in on it. Never anything too obvious, just enough to keep her feeling uncomfortable.

After the second month, in mid-December, Mr. Aguilar called her into his office on a Sunday night, after the boys had gone to bed. By now she suspected his involvement in some form of illegal activity, but she chose to ignore the evidence given her desire to keep the job. He traveled frequently with Uncle Tony at all hours of the night, and they both received late-night visitors with some regularity. When the suspicions would seep in against her wishes, she would beat them back by reminding herself that Francisco Aguilar might simply be a Mexican businessman—and, by the way, she had no obligation to play Nancy Drew.

Aguilar positioned her on one side of his desk, offering her a large leather chair while he moved to the other side then slid into a similarly indulgent piece of furniture. Since the Peeping Tom incident with Tony, she had started dressing in less formfitting outfits; today her oversized shift was more frumpy than shifty. The office was paneled in walnut, oozing a feeling of elegance and wealth, with faded, leather-bound books and a few pieces of Etruscan pottery inhabiting the shelves.

She sat politely, her ankles crossed, and let him lead.

"Mrs. Aguilar and I are very pleased with your performance so far."

He paused to let her acknowledge the compliment.

"Thank you, sir."

"How long has it been now, two months?"

"Yes sir, eight weeks as of last Friday."

"Oh no…you worry me, counting the days. I hope that's not a sign of discontent?"

He teased her with an exaggerated look of concern.

"No sir, I love it here."

"Good, good," he answered with a too-warm smile.

A pause as he lit a cigar. She noticed, but just barely, his Sinaloa roots when he pronounced certain syllables. Especially anything with an *r*.

"How is your baby—Erin, is it?" Again he rolled the *r* just slightly.

"Ella, yes, she is fine. This will be her first Christmas."

"And your husband, he is doing well? He is working?"

"Yes, he is really trying. But the language is hard for him. He has a full-time job in landscaping."

"Ah, a common starting point for many of us. I spent several years mowing lawns and washing dishes when I first came here. I hope he isn't too resentful of the time we steal his beautiful bride from him."

The last question came with a knowing grin.

"Yes sir…I mean, no sir, he understands how important this job is to our future. He is very grateful."

"Good, good."

Pausing to reach into his drawer, he pulled out a bottle of mezcal and two glasses.

"Señorita, would you join me in a family tradition? A taste of some smooth agave?"

"*Señora*," she corrected him politely. "*No gracias.*"

"Yes, of course…*Señora*…but we are celebrating."

"Excuse me, sir?"

"Oh my…did I forget to tell you? Your Christmas gift? We are raising your salary to twelve hundred dollars a week, and you will receive a bonus, in honor of the baby Jesus, of one week's pay. *Feliz Navidad!*"

Blanché's heart leapt into her throat. Christmas was going to be tight this year, with paying off student loans and Ella's medical bills; but she had found an apartment they could afford, if they could only come up with the first and last months' rent. That amount happened to be… twelve hundred dollars.

Blanché gulped. "Oh my God…thank you sir." *It's a sign*, she thought. *It's serendipity, my job here.* She took a moment to collect her thoughts, wanting to express how grateful she was but not wanting to encourage misinterpretation of her enthusiasm. "You can't imagine how appreciative I am for your generosity," she said.

She thought about her parents and how strongly they had doubted her decision. It was early yet, but she couldn't wait to prove them wrong. This was the first step in the process of pulling her young family up by their bootstraps.

"We should thank God, indeed," Aguilar responded. "It's been a good year."

He paused to pour and then continued.

"*Señorita*, it's important that you understand how important loyalty and service are to my family. If you are willing to work, and you are flexible, we will reward you. Handsomely."

She let the *Señorita* stand this time. He stopped pouring and stared into her eyes.

"Do you understand what I am saying?"

She wasn't sure she did, but she didn't want to appear disagreeable or stupid.

"Of course, *Señor* Aguilar."

"*Muy bien.*"

He finished pouring a double into each of the two glasses then slid one glass across the desk to within Blanché's reach.

"Perhaps you will reconsider?"

Not wanting to be rude, especially in light of her recent windfall, she decided to have just one. As she looked once again into his eyes, a *Jungle Book* image of Mowgli in the coils of Kaa flashed through her head, and she reminded herself to be careful.

"Perhaps just a sip, thank you, *Don* Francisco."

"Ah…there we go…thank you for humoring me."

Twenty minutes later, she had finished most of her mezcal and was feeling like she might have found a home. She was having a drink with her *guapo* boss, in a beautiful estate-by-the-sea…and making an after-tax annual wage of more than fifty thousand dollars. She actually loved her job and the two little boys she cared for. The thought of having another drink started toying with her, but she didn't want to jinx the moment, and so she started angling for a graceful exit. During a lull in the conversation, she considered getting up, but there was no sense of urgency. The warmth of the alcohol held her in a pliable place.

"*Señor*, may I take my leave and allow you to continue your work?"

"Of course, *Señorita*."

There it is again, she thought, the "*Señorita*"…

A moment later she was reaching for the handle of the study door when Aguilar interrupted her.

"Oh, one more thing, Blanché."

She turned and stood at attention, her back to the door.

"As you know, I hold a weekly poker game for some friends and business associates, every Saturday night."

She nodded in response.

"Next week, the girl who usually tends bar and serves us will not be available. Could you possibly stand in for her? We don't start until after the boys are in bed, usually around nine-thirty, so the job won't interrupt your daytime responsibilities. I should warn you, sometimes the games can go quite late, but I will pay you twenty dollars an hour, and the tips can be quite generous if the men like you."

He stopped to allow her to respond.

She was flattered by the invitation and excited about the money. The mezcal had put her in a place that welcomed the idea of a new adventure; but in the back of her mind she sensed a whisper of trepidation.

"Thank you for the opportunity, *Señor* Aguilar, but I don't think I would be a good choice. I have no experience as a bartender or waitress, and I don't know anything about card games."

Her response brought a frown to Aguilar's face.

"I would consider it a personal favor. It doesn't take a lot of experience, it's an informal"—he smiled—"and lazy group."

She looked uncertain.

"I've tried to find an alternate, but everyone is unavailable due to the holidays," he lied. Then he decided to set the hook and reel her in carefully. "Did I mention that last December, in the last game before Christmas, I believe the girl made more than five hundred dollars in tips?"

Despite her misgivings, Blanché thought about their earlier conversation. She agreed to fill in.

Her capitulation brought a warm smile to Aguilar's face.

"Thank you, *amiga*. We meet in the game room down at the pool *casita*. I will have Tony deliver the uniform to you. Please direct any questions you might have to him." He nodded. *"Buenas noches."*

He dismissed her with a smile then returned to some paperwork on his desk.

CHAPTER 3 —

Game Day (Act 1)

The pre-dawn darkness pressed into Clay as he sat silently in the rented, high-top Sprinter van. For six months his anticipation of this day's arrival had given him a sense of purpose, a *raison d'être*. He knew from experience that having meaningful work put him in a good mood…even if the work had moral complications.

Not that he realized it, but his body had recently begun increasing its testosterone-to-cortisol ratio. This had led to heightened levels of awareness and aggression similar to an athlete waiting for game day. But the only change Clay noticed was an irritability that made it difficult for him to be around others. Even with Tory. He generally found her very easygoing—good company, even—but lately he was only interested in her for sex. Naturally, she understood his compartmental needs and subsequently withdrew access.

As he glanced in the van's mirrors, habitually checking his perimeter, he felt good about the anonymity of the faded white rental. He thought it fit in seamlessly at the beach lot where it was currently parked—not too big, not too small; not too shiny, not too creepy—he didn't want anyone to remember seeing it. He methodically reviewed a checklist he had spent days preparing, reconsidering permutations should things go sideways.

A faint orange glow spread across the eastern horizon in time with the earth's rotation, chasing the darkness west while slowly bringing light to the city's daily procession. In response to the early morning chill, Clay pulled the hood of his worn Baja surf poncho over his beanie-covered head. Peering over the top of his clipboard, he noted with satisfaction the blanket of fog riding the ocean's surface and pushing up against the cliffs along the beach.

His was the only vehicle parked in the La Jolla Shores lot, and he let his mind wander for a second to ponder the intensity of the cold...it always seemed to peak just before first light.

The beeping from his G-Shock watch brought him back to the present. He quickly pressed a button on the Casio to silence the alarm.

Six-thirty.

He reached out to the dashboard for his partially gnawed Clif Bar. He shoved a chunk of the cool mint ingot into his mouth then added a swig of coffee from his thermos. Chocolate, coffee, mint...he savored the combination as he chewed the gooey mass into an even more moist and dispersed gooey mess; then he forced the mixture down his esophagus with another gulp of coffee. He knew he was in for a long twenty-four hours...he would need to mind his calories and hydration. If he successfully pulled off this mission he would record his biggest payday ever—*and* possibly be remembered as one of the solo greats within the clandestine industry.

Experience had taught him that the key to success was preparation and today he felt like he had a good, albeit outrageous, plan. Part of the beauty of his approach was the creative boldness of the whole thing. He had already spent months conducting surveillance—and he was highly confident nobody had seen him watching and listening. The neighbors all thought he was just a freelance photographer...an aging surfer who liked younger women. Given all the daily, human activity on the water, and the immature dating biases of the local men, he didn't seem unusual or out of place. His cover allowed him to wander around the beach community freely and at all hours, *with* his high-tech equipment. He would regularly load up his kayak or longboard and paddle out to take pictures.

At his rented, nine-hundred-square-foot home, which sat a few blocks off the beach, the only evidence of his profession was hidden in his "office." Although Tory technically lived with her divorced mother two miles away, she spent most nights at his place. She understood that the spare room was strictly off-limits.

His plan was to make a clean break from Tory (and San Diego) when he completed this job. He knew he would miss her sexual vitality, but he wasn't particularly impressed by her intelligence. For example, after completing a recent and strenuous lovemaking session, she had complained, without reason, about the shape, size, and firmness of her breasts. Recognizing the fishing expedition, he had accommodated her unspoken need for a compliment by insisting that her breasts were world class in every possible way (an observation that was not insincere). Then, in jest, he mentioned that during his time in Brazil, he had learned of a poultice made from minced jellyfish and diced papaya, mixed in equal parts, and that this concoction, if applied during certain lunar cycles, would make a woman's breasts both larger and firmer. He went into elaborate (and he thought, hilarious) detail about the preparation, application, and efficacy of the elixir, keeping a straight face while pushing the limits of ridiculousness in hopes that he would eventually cross into her zone of incredulity. Alas, he was forced to give up when he realized his ability to manufacture the absurd was exceeded by her gullibility—which was primarily induced, he believed, as a result of her rabid and selfish interest in the possibilities presented by an indigenous, Amazonian treatment that could keep certain parts of aging women (and tangentially, men) turgid. His conclusion was that humor was wasted not only on the humorless, but also on the self-absorbed.

The silver lining of Tory's self-centeredness was that after sleeping with Clay for three months, she still knew very little about him. Her lack of curiosity in other people allowed him to decide it wasn't necessary to kill her. The final data point in favor of her surviving their relationship came on the afternoon when he had rented the van (and before he painted the cartridges). For the first time in six months, Clay had shaved off his beard *and* gotten his hair cut…but Tory failed to notice any change in his appearance. Or, if she did, she didn't say anything.

He didn't realize that Tory's silence resulted from a preoccupation with developing a strategy on how best to dump him without causing a big scene. Dating a mature guy had been interesting, but she needed someone with a little more energy…someone whose demons didn't wake him up, screaming, in the early morning hours. She also wanted a family, and in her mind Tommie Smith wasn't marriage material. What had started as the mysterious, quiet type was now just plain spooky. Too many secrets. She didn't want to move back home with her mom; but sometimes a girl had to take one step backward to move ahead two. Of course she didn't realize it at the time, but the events of the next twenty-four hours would make the awkward break-up unnecessary.

Not aware of Tory's position, Clay felt a mild pang of guilt when he realized he would likely never see her again. And so the next morning he snuck out of bed early, stuffed anything incriminating or important into two large rucksacks, and walked around the corner of their home to where he had hidden the rental rig. Working off his pre-morning stiffness, he inserted all of his possessions into the van and then drove the few miles across town to where he sat now. Everything not in the bags would be left to the Gods.

Finished with his Clif Bar-cum-coffee sludge, Clay climbed into the cavernous rear of the windowless van. He carefully started gathering his SCUBA gear, including the speargun and the three bullet-tipped spears, and placed them to one side. He pulled on his black six-millimeter wetsuit, not because the water would be particularly cold, but because he might have to spend a lot of time fully immersed, and he knew hypothermia could negatively effect his coordination and judgment. Opening the van's rear doors from his position inside, he stepped out onto the sand-strewn pavement. His feet, hands, and head were bare, and he quickly turned to grab his ten-foot log. He wrestled the longboard out of the back and onto the sand in front of his Sprinter; then he returned to the van to grab a crab trap, complete with a thirty-foot tether line and bright orange buoy.

He carefully locked the van. In the vicinity of his parking lot, he knew there had lately been a lot of theft targeting cars and their contents. He couldn't afford to have a random break-in interrupt his detailed plans, so instead of just hiding the keys on one of his tires he placed them in a lock box which he in turn secured on the back door handle. Then he grabbed the crab trap and board, took a last casual look around, and started walking the one hundred yards across the beach, through the feeble, mist-filtered light. When his naked feet hit the sixty-two-degree water, an involuntary shiver sprinted through his body; he ignored it and pushed his board out through the ankle-biter shore break. As the water deepened, he lowered his chest and the square wire trap (with the buoy and the tether) onto the front of the board then paddled out through the modest, short-period swell. Through a few gaps in the fog he noted with satisfaction that the only other people in the water were a handful of surfers several hundred yards to the north, near the Scripps Pier, where the waves had more push. He paddled out about one hundred yards beyond the white water and dropped the trap. Patiently, he sat alone, waiting to see if anything might be different than what he had envisioned. With the fog he was sure that no one could be watching him, and after a few moments he felt comfortable that the crab pot was safely beyond the breakers, and not drifting. After saying a silent prayer to the surf god Huey, he pivoted the board and paddled back to the beach through the dark, empty waves.

A few minutes later he repeated the trip, but this time his board carried a mesh bag filled with his SCUBA gear, including the spear gun and the spears. When he reached the crab buoy, he took the SCUBA bag and a deep breath and dove about fifteen feet down. He knew that at ninety feet he could hold his breath for three minutes, but he didn't need to go that far down yet. He simply clipped the gear-filled mesh sack to a stationary carabiner attached to the tether on the crab trap then swam back up with minimal effort.

Upon resurfacing he mounted his surfboard and paddled the one hundred yards toward shore, into the empty lineup. He waited patiently, frequently turning in small circles as he watched first his orange buoy, then the swell, which eventually rolled into knee-high white water. After about forty-five minutes, when the sun was barely above the horizon, a few other beginner surfers started arriving in the parking lot: they pulled on rubber suits and paddled out into the mediocre surf. Clay knew that in a few hours the fog would disperse…that hundreds of people would be crowding this stretch of beach, engaged in the usual activities that California's coastline hosted every Saturday. Smiling with the knowledge that everything thus far was going as planned, he picked a particularly promising mid-thigh swell, turned and paddled thrice; then, when he felt the log sliding down the face of the wave, he leapt to his feet and rode the wave all the way to shore. With a grin he lifted the board under his arm and walked back to the Sprinter. Twenty minutes later he was tucked into a sleeping bag in the back, comforted by the ritual of working through his mental checklist. Before nodding off to the sounds of cars arriving in the lot, he remembered to once again set the alarm on his wrist.

CHAPTER 4 —

Game Day (Act 2)

The lieutenant in charge of Los Zetas's criminal activity in the Southwestern United States was sixty-two-year-old Victor Cortez. Victor had grown up in Long Beach, California, and had built a career by rising through the ranks of a regional crime organization, Los Nuevos Primos, with an expertise in the drug trade. Los Zetas was one of the newer and more powerful Mexican syndicates, and Victor had kept his role when the cartel had absorbed his smaller, more complacent group several years earlier. Cortez considered himself lucky to be alive, given Los Zetas's reputation for violence.

Los Zetas was started by deserters from the Mexican Special Forces who had exhibited a particularly entrepreneurial sensibility. When the well-established Gulf cartel had offered the soldiers a role as their enforcement arm at a hyperbolic pay raise, they had decided to switch sides, joining the bad guys. Having supposedly been trained by US and Israeli Special Forces, it wasn't long before their aggressive and expansive ambitions caused an internal conflict within the Gulf organization. Soon the forces that would eventually form the Zetas broke away (again) to operate as an independent cartel. Their brutal tactics were intended to instill fear, and they were successful in that regard. The ruthless gang usually expanded their territory by exterminating their competition;

so when they uncharacteristically proposed the acquisition of Victor's group, he and his partners quickly accepted.

Victor followed the same pre-dawn routine every Tuesday and Saturday. In fact, the greying criminal had been following this pattern ever since his wife had failed to return from a deep-sea fishing accident he had arranged. Of course the tale his men told was fictional, a narrative involving a heroic search for an inebriated, over-bored forty-three-year-old who had refused to wear a life jacket. Despite their suspicions, the police finally filed the case as an accidental drowning, given there was no corpse or evidence of wrongdoing. Everyone at the Cortez house seemed to be comfortable with this outcome, and the life insurance investigator was soon forced to reach the same conclusion—and pay a three-million-dollar settlement.

This Saturday, Victor's routine had actually started the previous night, when his men delivered a young woman he had chosen from an internet dating site. His tastes could be described as celebrity-centric; he usually picked a girl who bore a resemblance to a boyhood object of desire. That Friday night, he had chosen a Raquel Welch look-alike named Jo Tejada. Jo was nothing if not a professional, and despite being repelled by Victor's age-related sagginess and liberal application of cologne, she willingly got into character once one of Victor's men described her role. Her enthusiasm grew when she was given her costume, which was an authentic doe-skin bikini that approximated the iconic outfit that Ms. Welch had worn in the film *One Million Years B.C.*

Not only did Victor have the usual adolescent preoccupations with female sex symbols, but he also loved the board game *Risk*, and that night he had his date compete with him, in bed. Despite the indulgent presence of large amounts of champagne and chocolate-covered strawberries, Cortez was maniacally focused on winning. After several hours, Victor successfully controlled all of South America (at least on the game board) and was executing a blitzkrieg through Central America on his way to the United States. With a sloppy mouth full of strawberry, chocolate, and champagne, Jo told him with a defiant giggle (which harkened back to her community college drama training): "You and your uncivilized hordes will never violate the tender virtues of Lady Liberty!"

The spilling from her mouth and onto her bosom of both her taunting and the strawberry-infused champagne triggered deep within Victor's subconscious a complex psychological reaction, a subset of which sparked his already smoldering libido. Soon thereafter the board, the plastic armies, and the dice were all cast aside as Cortez acted out his adolescent fantasies on a voluptuous, well-cast Miss Tejada.

They both then fell asleep until just before dawn.

He awoke with a noticeable erection and a headache…an illogical combination that (since the start of his testosterone replacement therapy) frequently plagued him. At his request, Raquel stumbled to the kitchen for a container of freshly squeezed orange juice, with all the pulp. When she returned they both drank directly from the pitcher. He then had Raquel perform sticky, citrus-infused fellatio on him, after which she was dismissed.

Victor went back to sleep.

This time, when Victor awoke, it was to the sound of one of his men knocking on the bedroom door. The erection was gone, but he still had remnants of the headache.

"*Jefé*, the boat is ready."

One hour later, Cortez had shrugged off his hangover and was preparing for his regular Saturday morning swim across La Jolla Bay. His starting point was the cove at La Jolla Point. He had already climbed down the stairs from the low plateau above the beach; a Long Beach State sweatshirt protected his torso from the chill. When he reached the sand he handed the sweatshirt to one of his men (Jorge), tied the drawstring on his skintight suit, and waded through the tourists into the salty water. After fighting through the crowds of divers, SUPers, and casual bathers, he started settling into a rhythmic crawl stroke using alternate breathing. Every twenty strokes he would lift his head to confirm his bearing and avoid the kelp beds, but the infrequent water polo stroke never broke his cadence. Within five minutes he was on his own, with just a few other dedicated distance swimmers crossing his path sporadically. After twenty minutes he was about a mile out, had put even the other experienced swimmers in his wake, and was finally, comfortably, alone. This was the part he loved; the escape from his daily trepidations as he moved through the water with a comfort and efficiency that was partly genetic and partly earned from years of practice. A lifetime spent embracing the ocean had led to an instinctual understanding of the energy inherent in the swell, and he used the rolling corduroy to his advantage.

He was aware that most men were terrified of the unseen apparitions lurking beneath the ocean's surface; but for him that had never been a problem. The meditative calm that accompanied his tempo forced all of the other worries out of his head. He loved the feeling of the water passing along his skin as his body planed forward, as close to naked as regulation and decency would allow. That was one of the reasons he never wore goggles; they felt unnatural (and in the early days he couldn't afford them). So he swam with his eyes shut against the brine, opening them only when lifting his head to check his course.

Despite his moral shortcomings, to which Victor confessed every Sunday, he was quite dedicated to his biweekly swims. When he was growing up in Long Beach, his father (a longshoreman) had taught him all the strokes; and it was during those early years that he developed a passion for the ocean. It was this compulsion that kept him returning to the sea, and he was convinced that his swimming routine had allowed him to indulge his predilections in many other ways without completely destroying his health. The ocean was his recovery room.

He counted off another set of twenty strokes then lifted his head to target the beach between the Scripps Pier and the La Jolla Beach and Tennis Club. His body felt good. He was seriously considering round-tripping his way back to the cove if he felt this strong when he reached the beach.

Clay's head poked above the surface about a half mile out from where he had left his surfboard tied to the crab trap. The sun had now ascended well above the horizon but still remained low enough to cast a shimmering reflection on the surface of the sea. Underneath his vertically dangling body ran La Jolla Canyon, a sub-marine geologic feature that intersected with the Scripps Canyon about a mile out. From there it ran another thirty-two miles offshore, until it merged with the San Diego Trough at a depth of about thirty-two hundred feet. A chill ran up Clay's spine as he considered all the shadows gliding in the darkness underneath him, passing through the five-hundred-foot deep ravine. He could imagine their prehistoric brains, fully aware of his presence and trying to assess the quality of (to them) the rubber-encased meal. Quickly pushing the fears out of his mind, he took inventory and concluded he was feeling pretty good about his situation. The sun was at his back, the fog had lifted a few hundred feet, and he was still warm in his neoprene. With his body covered in black, including mask, gloves, and fins, he was effectively invisible as he bobbed between the small swells. The speargun was loaded with one of the explosive-tipped lances; he clutched it tightly in his left hand, just below the surface. He could see the flotilla heading in his direction, several hundred yards away. They were a few minutes later than usual but still well within the acceptable time limits of his plan. He noticed the diamond formation had followed the same protocol as always: Jorge, a monstrous man and head of security, surging through the water in his kayak a few yards ahead of the *jefe*; then the speed boat with two alert men slowly motoring to Cortez's left; finally another two kayaks closed ranks on Victor's right and rear. Surprise was absolutely necessary. Clay knew the men were all armed with pistols, and he had reason to believe the boat contained SCUBA gear as well as more sophisticated weaponry. He had to be quick with his attack, create a bit of confusion, and then, while the sun was in their eyes, somehow escape.

Making a few more vector calculations, he drew his free hand out of the water and checked his watch, pulled his mask down over his eyes, and stuck the SCUBA regulator into his mouth. As he slipped below the surface, his rebreather eliminated any bubbles from his exhalations, and he worked his way down and towards where he thought, in about two minutes, his target would pass. At about forty feet below the surface he knew he would be undetectable by the oncoming group. When he reached the estimated rendezvous point, he slowed, circled with his gun at the ready, and, when he was comfortable nothing dangerous was following him, started drifting towards the west.

About a minute later, Clay made visual contact with the hulls of the small fleet heading towards him, and started moving a few yards south to position himself directly under the speedboat. He knew the men in that vessel would have the best chance of seeing him, given their elevation above the water, and hence he wanted to stay out of sight by swimming as directly beneath them as possible. The motorboat was also his biggest and most obvious reference point, and he knew from his surveillance during the past six months that his target would always be a few yards to the south of the hull. He quickly ascended to a depth of about twenty-five feet, and started preparing for his shot.

As he began moving towards Cortez in the middle of the formation, Clay caught a glimpse of a shadow in his peripheral vision. He spun around. A twelve-foot juvenile great white had apparently been trailing him. Curious, it now cruised by his starboard flank. He watched intensely, finger on the speargun's trigger, as the huge fish glided slowly away. With the disturbing image of the open-mouthed, jagged-toothed creature still in his head, Clay worked methodically through his options. Time was of the essence…he had a limited supply of oxygen, and his escape routes were finite as well. His fear of sharks was reasonable, but not incapacitating. He knew that the likelihood of an attack on a diver, in the absence of provocation, was low. But he also knew juveniles were the most dangerous sharks, because they tended to use biting as an exploratory technique. Even a nibble from a juvenile great white would be devastating.

He focused on the predator for another thirty seconds, turning slowly, his gun poised. Sweeping his eyes in all directions, he saw no evidence of what Panamanian surfers called *El Dueño*—the landlord. By the time he decided to continue with his plan, the target entourage was fifty yards to his east. He had lost some of his advantage. He quickly porpoised his way back under the speedboat, verified from the hull positions that the formation hadn't changed, and then, with the spear loaded and aimed up at the surface, started moving to where the swimmer, Victor Cortez, should be.

Victor Cortez was happily reminiscing about the sex he had had earlier with Raquel and wondering if his Lycra Speedo had allowed retention of any of the orange juice residue previously coating his penis. He hoped it had. Reaching aggressively with each long stroke, his musculature was fully warmed. His bloodstream was distributing a potent cocktail of oxygen and calories mixed with dopamine, endorphins, and other "happy chemicals" throughout his body. From about fifteen feet directly beneath Victor, Clay freed the safety pin from the powerhead and aimed the speargun. As Cortez reached forward with his right hand, his head and torso rotated slightly left through the water, allowing his mouth to suck in a breath. Knowing he had only one opportunity, Clay released the .44 Magnum-tipped spear. The projectile shot accurately through the water: it simultaneously impaled and exploded inside Victor's chest cavity. The damage to Victor's internal organs was catastrophic…a portion of his heart was pulverized.

Clay dove towards the east, swimming at a forty-five-degree angle to the surface of the water, pulling the gun—and the dead lieutenant's body—with him. After two aggressive tugs, which effected a terrifying spasmodic action in Cortez's limp body, the gaping entry wound released the spear, liberating a fibrous amalgam of organic material: small, ugly bits of Cortez's intestine, cartilage, and blood. With relief Clay felt the resistance to his pulling give way. He then turned with all of his gear and dove straight down, towards the canyon. On his way down, at about fifty feet, two sharks, both about fifteen feet long, materialized from the blackness…they quickly torpedoed past Clay on their way to the surface. Their presence reminded Clay to load his second spear, just in case. He had many times seen how protein—*any* protein, but most especially blood—could quickly attract schools of predators…but to see three giant cartilaginous fish, all easily over ten feet in length, in the span of a few minutes? His nerves were jangled. *Was that just a coincidence?* he thought. *Or could they possibly have sensed food from that distance?*

Up on the water's surface, the bodyguards were frantic. They searched all around, peering into the water, trying to comprehend the attack on their boss. They unholstered their pistols and started firing indiscriminately at apparitions they believed swam in close proximity to Cortez's limp body. Jorge eventually ordered them to stop.

Within sixty seconds of Clay's attack the first shark hit Victor Cortez's body. It was more of an assessment than a full-on attack, but those subtleties were lost on the highly agitated crew. Jorge was trying to use his kayak to nudge the body over to the speedboat; but pistols began firing again. The ensuing bloodbath attracted more feeders. It took a tremendous amount of effort, but within two minutes the crew had fended off the sharks long enough to drag the corpse of Cortez from the water. Then they all boarded the speedboat and radioed for help.

Clay dove past one hundred feet. He moved rapidly away from the assassination…visibility was starting to get murky. His decades of experience hunting underwater had allowed him to develop techniques to keep his breathing and heart rate under control, but the inability to assess his opponents' location and tactics kept him on full alert. He had just poked a very capable hornet's nest, and he wanted to move away from the vicinity as quickly as possible, and without leaving a trace. Knowing that he had about an hour of oxygen in his tank—if he kept his metabolic functions at a relaxed level—motivated him to stay calm, execute his plan, and block out everything else.

He suspected the team at the surface would be using their sonar fish finder to try to pulse out his location; they would send down a diver or two to give chase. Also concerning was the likelihood that news of his attack might lead to an intense police presence on the beach. His plan hadn't included any uninvited predators, so he could only hope that the sharks would avoid him and add to the confusion at the surface. But there was no way to be sure.

At one hundred and twenty feet, he still couldn't see the bottom. But he was certain he was hovering over the canyon. He hadn't seen any other sharks for several minutes, so he decided the time had come to start his transformation to unarmed civilian. Peering into the abyss, he dropped the murder weapon with his two remaining explosive tipped spears. Then he checked the phosphorescent compass on his wrist. He started kicking strongly towards his entry point at the beach. Within a quarter of a mile the bottom had risen up to meet him. Soon, he found himself in around fifty feet of ocean. He slowly ascended to the surface. He took a quick glance around. His orange, crab pot buoy bobbed gently on the water, one hundred yards to the southeast. The flotilla of Cortez boats was barely visible during the brief moment he risked exposing himself. Up and down the coast, hundreds of people crowded the beach and swarmed the water; the closest were about two hundred and fifty yards away. He slipped back under the surface and started moving slowly in a zigzag pattern along the sea floor, steadily peeling off his gear, until all that remained was his tank, regulator, mask, and wetsuit. After dumping his tank and regulator, he surfaced. He took a moment to congratulate himself for being only twenty yards farther offshore than his buoy. Then he took a deep breath, dove down thirty feet to the bottom, and easily crawled the final yards to his crab pot. There, he completed his metamorphosis by removing and dropping his mask, and ascending via the tether. At the surface his longboard obediently waited where he had left it, tied to the buoy with a board leash. He allowed himself a small feeling of relief as he looked towards the shore: he was only one hundred yards from dozens of surfers bobbing up and down with the swell, most similarly clad in black rubber. He climbed on to his log and whispered a prayer of thanks to Huey (and a soft good-bye to the crab pot). Then he freed the orange buoy from its tether, attached the board leash to his ankle, and started paddling towards the lineup. A minute later he had paddled into the periphery of surfers. Pushing himself from a prone to a seated position on his board, he tried to quietly blend in.

"Oy, mate, where'd you come from?"

The Aussie voice caught him unawares. He spun to find a glaring, sunburned face. The Aussie was sitting on a shortboard, looking at him incredulously while guarding his position at the peak.

" Ahhh, man…busted…I, uh…had to take a dump…so…paddled out a few hundred meters to spare everyone the intestinal details… crazy time in TJ last night…dude….Montezuma is *definitely* taking his revenge."

Clay didn't want to continue the dialogue so instead pivoted, took a few hard paddles with the intention of letting the other surfers know he was going, and hopped to his feet on a knee-high mushball that he rode all the way to the sand.

With his board tucked under his arm, he nonchalantly walked right by a couple of agitated bicycle cops on his way to the Sprinter. That morning, when he had first walked to the water, he had a slight limp—the result from both an old knee injury and the weight of what he hoped to accomplish that day. This latest trip across the beach found gravity barely able to restrain him, as the satisfaction inherent in flawlessly executing a challenging plan had him in a buoyant mood. Not even sex made him feel as alive as he did when he was on a mission, hunting his fellow human beings.

Within a minute of leaving the surf he had reached the van. He loaded up the log, vacated his wetsuit, inhabited his jeans, and climbed into the driver's seat. He glanced at his watch while loading INXS into the CD player, happily noting that he was fifteen minutes ahead of schedule. As he pulled out of the parking lot, nodding his head to the beat as Michael Hutchence sang "Devil Inside," he allowed himself to consider that he just might pull it off.

CHAPTER 5 —

Intermission: The End of the Innocence

It was the uniform that triggered her anxiety, almost to the point of nausea as she slipped the diaphanous material over her body. After poking her head and arms through the appropriate holes, she reached for her glass of Chardonnay in an attempt to unjangle her nerves. Blanché had already tucked the boys into bed and now was scrambling in her small room to pull herself together for her Saturday night bartending gig. As she studied herself in the mirror (fastened to the back of the bathroom door), she realized that in any other context she would have loved the fit of the black, open back, Kate Spade minidress. The flowing poly-silk fabric draped her figure nicely, and, in combination with the flattering design, accentuated her strengths while disguising her weaknesses. It was maybe a half size too small, so she had to be brief with her undergarments. But she had to admit, the piece worked well on her.

Shimmying the last few inches into the tight frock, she padded barefoot into the bathroom to apply her makeup. She considered briefly the contradiction inherent in her lengthy makeover and her supposed abhorrence of the attention she would receive as a result, before brushing on her mascara. Fighting through the cognitive dissonance, she grabbed a pair of racy heels that she felt totally made the outfit.

The problem was associative. She wore the dress only when working for *Don* Francisco at the pool cabana poker games, and she dreaded the message the outfit implied. If she had been out with friends, to a place where she felt less vulnerable, she would have rocked the short gown with confidence, maybe even swagger. But at the card games, serving *Señor* Aguilar's guests, she felt like a silk-wrapped gazelle, hobbled and teetering, amidst a pride of lions, any of which could pounce at any moment.

Her original agreement to fill in temporarily had now become a regular Saturday role, as the other girl had never returned. The first night, four weeks previous, had been a challenge, given her inexperience; but by the end of the evening, as the last players cashed in their chips, she had survived unscathed…and learned a ton. Most of her time was spent behind the bar, watching the card game impassively; periodically she wandered over, waitress-like, to take drink and snack orders. After mixing the drinks (with the help of a barman's manual she had purchased for the occasion), she would then wade through the tobacco smoke to deliver the beverages.

All but one of the men had been pretty respectful—and even for the groper she had enough experience to gracefully pivot out of his grasp while laughing and peeling his lingering hand off of her bum. Despite her making light of it, she didn't like that the other men noticed and didn't seem to think their colleague's behavior was inappropriate. That night she had earned sixty dollars for her 9:30 to 12:30 shift. But the real money came with the tips, which at two hundred dollars were far below the expected half grand—but were still welcome. In hindsight she realized she was tired, and it had probably showed.

The next day, *Señor* Aguilar had asked in passing whether the evening had been too taxing. She politely mentioned that it was a late night, given her Sunday morning responsibilities, but that she was glad she had been able to help. He then asked if she would mind doing it again in the future if they needed a temporary replacement, to which she answered, "Sure." He closed the conversation by suggesting that if she tried a little harder, the tips would likely be better; then, without waiting for a response, he continued on his walk away from her.

Midway through the next week, Blanché was asked again to substitute, and, given her perpetual need for money and her relatively easy experience the prior Saturday, she acquiesced. The second engagement went better, as she boosted her energy level by nursing a couple of Red Bull-and-vodka cocktails throughout the evening (she recalled some friends in college calling them Vod Bombs). The caffeine and alcohol combo loosened her up a bit and made time fly, although she needed two cups of coffee the next morning before engaging with the two rambunctious boys. Her enthusiasm and relaxed demeanor led to a little more flirtatious give-and-take with the card players. By the end of the evening she had tallied up three hundred and sixty dollars in tips.

By the time the third Saturday rolled around she had already agreed to again play barmaid. She needed the money to furnish her young family's new apartment, and she was no longer intimidated by the role. In fact, she actually felt like she was starting to find her groove.

There were two new players that night, Beto and Martin. They both gave off an aura of confidence that bordered on machismo. When she thought no one was watching, Blanché found herself focusing on the younger of the two, Beto. She vacillated between attraction and repulsion. Her boss, Francisco Aguilar, treated all his guests with respect, but with these two his behavior seemed almost deferential. As the night wore on, it became apparent that they were celebrating Martin's birthday, and that the poker was just a distraction for the real party. Blanché was kept more than busy with all the tequila-toasting; she had even allowed herself to be coerced into joining the celebrants for a round or two. The combination of tequila and Vod Bombs had her feeling well lubricated, but she convinced herself she was still in control.

Two hours into the evening, the poker game found the largest pile of chips parked in front of Beto, the handsome, younger man whom Blanché found interesting. Throughout the evening she had caught herself silently rooting for him and was surprised by her efforts to grab his attention in brief, subtle ways. She hoped the others hadn't noticed. The more he ignored her, the more she was intrigued. She wouldn't have regularly entertained any notion of infidelity, but this evening had a sexual charge that was palpable, although not necessarily threatening. In the back of her mind she rationalized that her job description, and *Señor* Aguilar, encouraged her to flirt and have fun, and she was feeling quite good about the potential for decent tips on this, her third Saturday evening engagement.

Before she could even reflect on her growing competence as a server, Tony ushered in a gender-segregated group of about half a dozen men and two young women. The men appeared to be colleagues of the card players: the two groups greeted each other with familiarity. Blanché was struck by how lovely and revealingly dressed the women both appeared. It soon became apparent that their function was more lowbrow than high couture. One of the girls was darker skinned than everyone else in the room. She asked Blanché where the sound system was. After being pointed in the right direction, she capably slipped a CD into the player. A second later, the light accordions of the Ranchero music stopped, and with a twist of the volume, the speakers started ratcheting up the party vibe by pushing AC/DC's "You Shook Me All Night Long" into the farthest corners of the room. The card game screeched to a halt as the girls started working the room, mingling with the seated players, sipping from the men's drinks while making intimate small talk. Like kids on a scavenger hunt, it didn't take long for the professionals to discover the identity of the birthday boy. The attention of the room soon became riveted as the two girls double teamed Martin, delivering the obligatory lap dance intermingled with some interesting girl-on-girl naughtiness. After the performance, the evening started devolving into a boisterous bidding contest for attention from the two decreasingly attired girls. Blanché noted twinges of envy as Beto participated enthusiastically.

Before too long, *Señor* Aguilar asked Blanché to bring over a bottle of *Gran Centenario* from the bar. The men then started doing tequila shots from the belly button of the darker-skinned women, who gamely positioned herself horizontally on the card table. Things steadily became louder, to the point that Blanché felt she was at a frat party, with the incongruous fact that the guys were older and there was a lot of cash. At one point, two of the more animated men got carried away. They physically pulled Blanché out from her refuge behind the bar and, in Spanish, started auctioning off the rights to see her naked breasts. The other two women were getting the men all lathered up, aiding and abetting the bidding. It wasn't until the competitive process reached six hundred dollars that one of the restraining men noticed Blanché had started crying. He released his grip. With only one remaining man holding her impassively, she was able to shake free, run into the bathroom, and lock herself, weeping, in a stall.

As Blanché slowly tried to pull herself together the loud party continued outside the bathroom. She realized she had been terrified by how quickly the situation had spun out of her control, and hence how vulnerable she had felt. But now that she was in a seemingly safer spot, her brain couldn't help but wonder what a glimpse of her boobs would've been worth to these men. How slippery would that slope have been? She knew she thought of herself as different from the two women working in the other room, but she wasn't sure why, or where the line was drawn, or how money effected the positioning of that line.

Before she could reach any conclusions, the lighter-skinned girl burst into the bathroom, with Martin in tow.

"*Vamos, Hombre Grande…es el tiempo por un feliz cumpleaños recorder!*"

Blanché could catch only glimpses of the two as they passed by the crack between the stall door and the metal partition, but they seemed oblivious to her presence.

"*Por un* thousand *dolares, necesitas tener una pucha mágica, Señorita!*"

"No unsatisfied *clientes* yet."

"*Más que* one billion served?"

"Asshole!"

Blanché's Spanish was pretty good, but the South American accents and rapidity of the drunken Spanglish made it difficult for her to catch everything. Over the next few minutes, the sounds, smells, and items of clothing hitting the tile floor confirmed her suspicions. As the girl made all the right sounds, Blanché tried to be decent and give them privacy. In an effort to isolate and make herself invisible from the animal coarseness of it all, she closed her eyes and ears as tightly as possible—but the primal charge of sex caught her up in its strong tidal grasp, and she could not defend against its penetration into her clenched orifices. Seemingly just a moment after they started, it was over, and the urgent energy quickly vanished. In its wake spread an emptiness that amplified the zippering of pants, and the buckling of Martin's belt. The final denouement was marked by Martin's leather shoes hurrying out of the bathroom, leaving the young woman behind.

As the birthday boy rejoined the party, a cheer went up from the other side of the door, forcing Martin to smile and play the returning conqueror.

Back in the bathroom, Blanché heard the girl's voice.

"You think you're better than us, don't you?"

Blanché was afraid to speak. She could see a vertical slice of the girl's back through the crack in the stall. The whore was bent over at the sink, rinsing out her mouth as she washed her hands.

"I know you're in there, being all small and quiet, afraid to breathe because you think you might catch something."

Throwing her head back, she gargled water to clear her throat before spitting the mouthful back in the sink. She didn't need a response.

"They call you *la niñera con las tetas*...what do you do, watch his kids or something?"

The woman was now drying her face and hands with a paper towel and reapplying her lipstick.

"I used to be like you...good Catholic girl, babysitting for a few bucks, waiting for a good man to come claim me...plant his flag in my virgin territory."

She paused from the lipstick to giggle at the condescending metaphor. Growing up listening to Top 40 radio had given her an unconscious ability for wordplay, almost like someone who suffered from Tourette's. But instead of randomly blurting expletives she tossed out similes entangled with double entendres.

Blanché wanted to correct her, to tell her that she had already claimed a man, had a child, and was not *waiting* for anything; but she had heard that *these sorts* of people often carried weapons, and she was afraid that any type of provocation might incite a violent response. She really just wanted the whole distasteful interaction to go away.

When the young woman finished painting her lips, she twisted the crimson phallus back into its golden, metallic sheath. After hiding the small cylinder in her tiny purse, she wet another paper towel, wiped under her arms, and, without any sense of propriety, pulled down her G-string and wiped between her legs. Hesitating for a moment with her fingers in her crotch, she fished a condom out of her vagina.

"Fuckin' great!...Fuckin' rubber came off again. Fuck, fuck, fuck!... These things suck."

She wrapped the torn prophylactic in the wet paper towel and threw it into the garbage before continuing her questions. Blanché wondered about the size and hardness of the erection that had filled the condom just a few minutes earlier.

"So what do you do that makes you special? Read them bedtime stories? Wipe the shit from their hairless butts? Hold the boy's little dick so he don't pee all over the seat or floor?"

She released a laugh at her mental image of Blanché holding the little boy's penis.

The girl used the mirror to look at the thin metallic door separating the two. Blanché felt as if the barrier didn't exist as they locked eyes through the narrow slit.

"We're no different, you and me...I just take care of their needs when they get a little bigger."

She paused for a second to pop a breath mint in her mouth.

"And *I* get paid a lot more."

The hooker reached into her clutch and pulled out a fragrance that she dabbed strategically behind her ears.

"If you're going to sell your soul, you might as well get paid."

She then snorted something from a tube and followed that with a short, intense shiver. Taking a deep breath, she gathered herself.

"You're no better…you may be working up at the big house, and I may be out in the fields, but we're all on the same plantation."

Taking a last glance in the mirror, she adjusted her breasts then walked out of the bathroom and went back to work.

Blanché didn't realize how shallow her breathing had been until the door latch closed and she was alone. It was then that she realized her brain was screaming for oxygen. She stared at the door of the stall and blinked incredulously.

How dare she compare us?

She released a huge exhalation and followed it with a deep breath. A disturbing thought crept in.

Was I really holding my breath? Fearful it was contagious? The contamination of what that women was?

The invading perception was now spreading.

Were we really both on the same path, just at different points? Selling little pieces of ourselves…for what?

The tears started flowing again as the impossibility of her position started imposing itself on her. It was just that she felt so small…and the mountain felt so steep. After a few minutes of sniffling, she started reprimanding herself.

Wait, that's crazy…I'm a babysitter and she's a prostitute. What am I thinking?

She knew better than to feel sorry for herself, and she wrote off her emotional state as resulting from a combination of stress, sleep deprivation, and the Vod Bombs. Examining her dress for tear stains, she took another mind-clearing breath and committed to pulling herself together.

Five minutes later she escaped from the cabana bathroom relatively unnoticed. She was silently grateful for the hypnotic effect that the two dancers had on the men and discovered a renewed respect for the diversionary value of the well-tuned female body. Simultaneously intrigued by and fearful of the lurid, mating caricature on display in the pool house game room, she wondered how long the strippers could hold the audience's rapt attention. Leaning against the back wall, she had seen firsthand how quickly the pack could be redirected; after a few seconds, she decided not to test her luck. Casually sliding along the wall towards the door, she was able to maneuver herself out of the cabana's only entryway, up the pathway to the main house, and back to her living quarters.

Once she reached the sanctuary (relatively speaking) of her room, she slid the back of her wooden chair against the unlockable door. When she finally shimmied out of her uniform and slid under the covers of her bed, she did so with a racing mind, and a conflicted libido. Her head filled with alcohol and the vivid, immediate images of the evening's erotica, she quickly rubbed one out and was soon falling fitfully asleep.

It wasn't long before she found herself in a dream, traveling home on the San Diego transit bus she called Stinky. On this particular trip, instead of sitting in the safety of the front row, she was positioned in the middle of the nearly empty vehicle, where the diesel fumes were both intoxicating and asphyxiating. She looked over her shoulder to find the back few rows occupied by the participants from that night's party in the cabana, except the girls were totally naked and engaged with multiple partners, and periodically one of the sinners would interrupt their passion and beckon to her, siren-like.

Frozen in her seat, she was both fearful and mesmerized. After a few moments of hesitation, she stood up and started drifting towards the bacchanalia. When she stood so close that she could see the wine on their lips and sense the fecund emissions of the reproductive organs, the bus screeched to a standstill. The driver opened the doors with a hydraulic hiss. Stopping as if in a trance, Blanché performed an about-face and walked uncertainly up the aisle, steadying herself hand over hand on the backs of each new row of seats. When she reached the front alcove of the bus, she halted at the top of the steps, not sure whether to exit. She looked back to the driver for guidance, and with surprise saw her father at the wheel—offering her nothing and refusing to make eye contact as he examined the windshield. His eyes were rimmed red and bloodshot, as if he were tired, or maybe even had been crying. Not certain as to why, she was compelled to move away from her father and dismount, after which the doors vacuumed shut, and the bus sat idling.

In front of her she saw the large gates of the elephant sanctuary, and, after trying to access the facility via several locked doorways, she returned to the chained entrance and squeezed through the bars. Unsuccessfully searching for the elephants in all the outdoor areas of the asylum, she knew if she could find just one or two of the ancient beings she could embrace them—and they would accept her as one of their own. She started walking through the big barn-like facility, looking hopefully in the stalls; but with each unoccupied compartment she felt more lost. As she inspected each successive empty stall she picked up her pace, such that by the end of the long row she was hurrying to reach the last indifferent enclosure. When she rushed to the final doorway, hoping to find at least one inmate, she discovered with despair that it was vacant. They were all gone.

She walked back in what she thought was the direction of the front entrance, hoping to find her ride, but she had trouble retracing her steps. After several hours of walking in circles around the facility, the night grew dark and cold, and she noticed she was hungry and thirsty. A smiling man whom she thought was Beto but who had no clear face, offered her a hot dog and a Coke, but she thought he seemed slightly *off*, to the point of being mildly threatening. So she moved quickly away from him and committed once again to finding her way.

Shaking in response to the enveloping night, she rounded the same corner she had maneuvered several times that evening, but this time the front gate appeared. Beyond the gate she saw the bus, rumbling in place as if waiting for her. Stumbling in her high heels she rushed towards the bus and her dad, but something caught her attention in the periphery. She stopped and turned to see her reflection looking back at her in a mirrored window. Like Narcissus she forgot herself and spent a few minutes admiring the adult figure in the minidress and heels…until the mirror suddenly distorted the image and showed a grotesque version of herself. Chased from the self-absorption, she once again remembered her purpose. She hurried frantically towards the exit.

Kicking off her heels, she squeezed through the bars and ran down to the curb just as her father drove the bus away. She tried to call out to him but couldn't find the words; a cold wind blew an old newspaper against her naked shins. She sensed the paper contained some important information but couldn't make out the large print. By now she was really very cold and she cursed her clothes for being too skimpy to provide any real protection from the elements. All alone, she watched as the vehicle's taillights faded into the night. A tabby materialized and started purring figure eights around her calves. Not sure what to do next, she sat down on the curb, with the cat in her lap, and started to cry.

CHAPTER 6 —

Game Day (Act 3)

Clay knew how to take care of himself between engagements. Scheduling naps and meals was a requirement at his age, as he could no longer expect adrenaline to carry him through extended stretches that required physical and mental focus. He also didn't want to have to explain himself to anyone, so he had planned and prepackaged all of his meals, allowing him to eat in the solitude of the van.

His brief drive south, across town, led him to a shady, tree-lined street down near Bird Rock. After his extended time in the water, he was predictably ravenous. He guided the rig into an open spot parallel to the curb, between two houses. Climbing into the back, he then opened his rucksack, and fished out three peanut butter and jelly sandwiches. He had smeared a heavy layer of old-fashioned Jif peanut butter on each sandwich because, 1) he needed the calories; 2) it reminded him of his mom; 3) he liked the added salt and sugar; and 4) he thought the whole organic thing was a scam. The preserves he used were apricot, which he believed were one of the top three fruit spreads, strawberry and peach being the other two. He didn't count oddities like mango or jalapeño, because he didn't feel like they had enough appearances to qualify. (Of course, unlike most consumers, he knew that jalapeños were a fruit.) His one concession to the food snobbery he regularly eschewed was his choice of bread. He liked to use a high-fiber brand, and his current favorite, Ezekiel 4:9, was introduced to him by a Jewish soldier—and fellow mercenary—during a shared mission in the Levant. The Israeli mistakenly thought that the reference to the Old Testament meant the bread was kosher. Clay didn't care about whether or not it was blessed by a rabbi, he just liked that it kept his GI tract from seizing up. After inhaling the sandwiches, he washed the whole mess down with a quart of whole milk then climbed back into his unzipped, lightweight sleeping bag, where he fitfully dozed off.

Six hours later, for the third time that day, the Casio dragged him awake. The change in consciousness was welcome, however, as he had been having a terrifying dream that involved attending a final calculus exam undressed and unprepared. The proctor had morphed into a hungry great white at a particularly vulnerable time. As the shark-teacher chomped his way through each row of captive and unaware students, Clay frantically tried to grab his speargun, which lay on the ground, in a pool of bloody gore, just beyond his reach.

At precisely four P.M., Clay climbed out of his van, descending into the quiet residential neighborhood. He placed two magnetic rubber signs symmetrically on each side of the van. He then climbed back in to the Sprinter, put on a Swami's Pool Service uniform, and drove less than a minute to park in front of Francisco Aguilar's house. Grabbing an aluminum extension pole with a mesh net on the end, he pulled on a floppy bucket hat and walked through a side gate that he knew didn't always latch securely. With his head down, he did his best to remain invisible while using his peripheral vision and hearing to gather as much information as possible. He already knew minute details of the architectural layout and topography from his nighttime reconnaissance missions, drone surveillance, and visits to the city's Building & Permit

Department. His work had also confirmed that the security guard rotation was somewhat random, with the exception of the regular five-thirty Saturday afternoon shift change. Finally, he knew he would likely be challenged if noticed. An overgrown banana tree scraped at his uniform as he slipped around the house on a small trail delineated by stepping stones. The path followed the descending contour of the estate, towards the pool and the ocean. When he reached the chlorinated water, he started skimming the detritus with the mesh basket, slowly circling and observing, all the while hunched over and limping with a body language that conveyed non-threatening subservience.

"Hey! Pool guy! Where's Julio?"

One of the guards, Ricardo, had come up from the beach and noticed the unknown intruder cleaning the pool. The uniform matched, but the face didn't, so the security pro used a common trick intended to ferret out a conspirator. Clay was aware that the regular pool guy was named Bob, not Julio, and so avoided the trap while manifesting his best stammer.

"D-d-d-don't know n-n-n-no, Julio, but the head office s-s-sent me to start, and then B-b-b-bob'll b-b-b-be by later to check m-m-my w-w-w-work. I'm n-n-new, name's T-t-tom."

Ricardo's cousin had a bad stutter, and he compassionately recognized the similarities between this seemingly harmless, stooped pool maintenance man and his fearful, insecure cousin. The Swami employee had also correctly identified the normal pool guy's name, so Ricardo decided he could let his guard down a bit.

"You guys know that any new workers are supposed to be approved by Tony before they're allowed on the grounds."

Clay knew that each Swami worker was an independent contractor, and that the communication between management and the grounds crew wasn't always perfect. He also knew that Bob came between five and six o'clock on Saturdays, and so there was an inconsistency from the security detail's perspective on when they would see him, given the five-thirty shift change. If he was lucky, Bob wouldn't come until after five-thirty, when Ricardo (and Clay) had already left.

"I'll m-m-make sure t-t-to tell my b-b-bosses about the m-m-m-mistake. S-s-sorry."

Clay continued to clean the pool with his head down, hoping the interrogation was over. Ricardo thought for a moment, and then headed up to check and see if "Tom" had come in a Swami's rig. He stopped at the front gate, where he could clearly see *Swami's Pool Service* on the side of the Sprinter parked across the street. Satisfied that he had done sufficient diligence, he left the pool behind and headed in the direction of the main house, hoping to catch a glimpse of the *gringa* nanny as she was changing. Tony had told one of the more senior members of the security detail that she had an "amazing" rack, and that she liked "showing it off." That salacious tidbit had made the rounds; now the entire security detail was particularly alert to the possibility of catching a peek.

After Ricardo remained out of sight for a few minutes, Clay checked his watch. He had to get moving.

He collapsed the aluminum pole and limped back up the path to his van, checking to make sure Ricardo was still out of sight. On his way through the side gate, he made sure the latch didn't secure as he carefully closed it; then he headed to his rental. He threw the pole in the back and quickly drove the rig three blocks away, where he parked off the beaten path, on a dead end street. From under the front seat he grabbed a backpack that held a variety of essentials: pool chemicals, testing kit, respirator, small C-sized aluminum oxygen canister, a few tools, two liters of water, and three Clif bars. He climbed into the back and pulled a pistol, silencer, hunting knife, and spare magazine with cartridges out of a rucksack. After carefully secreting the pistol between his backside and his trousers' waist band, he wrapped the suppressor, full magazine, and hunting knife in a dirty old T-shirt and underwear and then placed the bundle at the bottom of his pack. Grabbing the keys to the van, he exited the Sprinter with the pack. He then peeled the magnetized pool service signs off the vehicle, threw them in the back, and hurriedly slammed the doors before locking them remotely.

Hustling Quasimodo-like back to the Aguilar estate, he let his shirttails flap in the breeze as he passed through the faulty gate and limped back down to the pool. He knew another guard would likely pass the area at any moment, and he didn't want to have to repeat the same song-and-dance that he had performed for Ricardo. When he got down to the pool, he positioned himself across from the small guest cabana so he could watch the front entryway for a few minutes. When he spotted the surveillance camera positioned outside the only door he congratulated himself for having anticipated its presence. He started pretending to test the pool water for acid and chlorine content, all the while preparing for his next move. Out of the corner of his eye he detected some movement, and he held up the testing kit so he could get a better look without appearing suspicious. Coming up from the ocean were the nanny and her charges, with the girl giving chase to the two shrieking boys. The trio passed him on the path about fifty yards away, heading uphill. Neither acknowledged the other's presence.

A few minutes later, his senses on full alert, his watch told him it was almost five o'clock. He decided it was time.

He got up from his position next to the pool, threw all of his equipment into his pack, limped over to the south side of the cabana (which was overgrown with mango and palm trees), and started acting like he was inspecting the pump and filter, both of which were housed in a small lean-to. After operating alone for less than five minutes, and having not detected any other cameras, he slipped through the partially open, solid-core wooden door that was the only entry point for the exterior poolside bathroom.

Staying in character despite being alone inside the small *baño*, Clay limped into the only stall, closed the door, and waited with a fiercely beating heart. After fifteen uninterrupted minutes, he felt comfortable that no one had seen him enter, and allowed himself a few deep breaths as he moved out of the stall. He then removed the uncomfortably located pistol from between his buttocks cheeks, locked the exterior door, and quickly went to work.

A few inches off the floor of the bathroom was an old-fashioned, decorative brass heating vent that was served by a central HVAC unit, which was dedicated to the pool house. Clay knew that if he could clear the passageway he would gain access to the interior of the pool house via another bathroom on the other side of wall. Pulling out his tools, he went to work on the vent hardware. Knowing he was exposed, Clay labored with a sense of urgency but knew he also had to work quietly. He paused periodically to listen for any sounds of approach into either bathroom that could interrupt his plan.

Within ten minutes he had removed the grill, pushed aside the ductwork, and started focusing (from the inside of the wall) on the vent that served the cabana bathroom on the other side of the ten-inch thick barrier. He was grateful for the oversized openings, which would allow him to crawl through the wall while causing minimal damage to the surrounding sheetrock. After establishing a passageway through the wall into the interior bathroom, he put all of his gear into his backpack, slid the sack and the towel hamper next to the hole, and prepared to squeeze his large frame through the gap. When everything was set, he started walking over to unlock the exterior bathroom door, so all would appear normal, when he heard someone twisting and pulling at the locked handle. He froze for a moment, wondering if he had time to free his pistol, a SIG Sauer P226, from the cotton swaddling in his pack. Deciding he didn't, he poised at the ready with his knife. Just as abruptly as it had started, the jerking stopped and a crying boy's voice faded into the distance.

"Is locked…Blaaannnchhhé! No let in! *Sméagol* need help! Hafta pee!"

Despite the context, Clay couldn't hold back a smile as he recognized the *Lord of the Rings* reference. He pictured a little boy holding his genitals, on the verge of tears, running back to the nanny who was already occupied with the older brother. He didn't know how far away they all were, but he did know he probably didn't have much time. He slid the dead bolt to an open position, took three, rapid, long steps to the far wall, and dropped to his knees. Silently praying that the trio didn't have access to the pool house, but simultaneously running through the available options if they did, he quickly shoved his bag through the opening in the wall and followed feet first on his stomach. His shoulders and the Swami's Pool Service shirt momentarily caught on the sheetrock that edged the square hole, but he reversed direction for a few inches, raised his arms over his head, and was then able to barely squeeze through. Before he completely wiggled into the interior bathroom, he used his extended hands to pull the wicker towel basket next to the displaced heating grate. He then simultaneously dragged the basket and the grate the small distance across the tile floor before carefully setting them into position, covering the hole.

As he began to extract his body from the old cramped room into the new palatial restroom, he still had his head partially stuck in the wall when he heard the door to his previous location swing open. Again, he stopped breathing.

"Robby, this door is fine….Are you sure you twisted the handle all the way?"

"I did! *Sméagol* swears he did!"

"Hm…Well, come here and let me help you with your trunks."

Clay lay motionless as he listened to the normal sounds of a babysitter helping a standing, young boy urinate into a toilet. When they were finished, he heard two sets of bare feet walk back across the tile and close the door on their way back to the pool.

With the adrenaline in Clay's body searching for an outlet, he involuntarily shivered against the cold tile floor. He realized, once again, how risky his plan was. He needed to get to a less exposed place as soon as possible. Pulling himself fully into the new bathroom, he replaced the grill hardware, stood up, and removed his shoes and socks. After stuffing his footwear on top of the fully loaded pack, he then climbed onto the vanity countertop and pushed up the square panel of wood in the ceiling that led to the crawl space.

Shouldering his pack, he pulled himself up in a manner that most would have found impressive for a middle-aged man—but that Clay felt was clumsy—and then scissor-kicked his way up into the rafters. He replaced the wooden ceiling panel and crawled along the joists a few feet before coming to a reinforced cross beam. He stopped and waited for his heart to stop pounding in his ears. He checked his watch, noting the time: 5:43. The day was far from over.

He allowed himself a feeling of accomplishment for making it this far. He had a few more small tasks before the set up would be complete, but he could execute those details from the comfort of his invisible perch, and he had nearly four hours to do so. For fifteen minutes he rested quietly, reviewing the plan in his head, before he allowed himself one of the Clif bars and some water. *One way or another,* he thought, *in seven hours it will all be over.*

CHAPTER 7 —

Game Day (Act 4)

The ceiling fan casually stirred the air as the men feinted and yielded through several hours of poker. The tone was greatly subdued compared to the previous Saturday's stripper-infused party. All six of the players had returned from the previous week's game, but the charged atmosphere of anticipation was absent. Tonight, early in the game, Blanché had been able to secretly examine Beto's face from behind the bar. She was at a loss as to what had caused her to previously feel attracted to him. She wrote it off as a bad case of beer goggles, or in her case, Vod Bomb-and-tequila goggles.

Throughout the week she had wanted to put the X-rated event as far behind her as possible; but despite her efforts to purge her mental hard drive, the night had left an impression. The interaction with the other women had been particularly troublesome, forcing her to reexamine a variety of her recent choices, including her decision to stay in her current role within the Aguilar household. It was primarily the outsized compensation for her unskilled labor that had her most concerned. Would there be a *quid pro quo*, she wondered? If so, when would it be collected?

She wanted to ignore the implications and rationalized internally that she was worth the elevated pay.

As usual, hiding under all the subterfuge was sex: a seemingly constant companion when men and women got together. She understood the biological imperative to reproduce, and all the complications and social inequities that accompanied traditional gender roles, but she hadn't closely examined all the ways her female instinct was driving her daily behavior....Had she really neglected the difficult path necessary to gain faculty and competence in a modern world? Had she instead chosen the well-trodden evolutionary path of depending on men for her survival?

Contemplating her current situation brought the conclusion that all of her power came from males whom she needed to keep happy. *Señor* Aguilar provided her with employment. His male children needed to like her or she would get fired. Her dad provided additional financial support in the form of a regular allowance. She depended on all of their kindnesses, and without them the quality of her day-to-day existence would decline significantly. The fact that the kindnesses were provided by non-strangers provided her no solace.

As her concerns kept nagging, she couldn't push aside the way she was packaging herself for the Saturday night poker guests. The tiny, tight clothes, the hobbling heels, the makeup, the coquettish laugh in response to their weak, unimaginative flirting. The whole intimate dance of reveal and withdraw, tempt and repel...it was like a carefully managed blowing on tinder to encourage a tiny spark to grow into a swollen conflagration.

It was obvious to her. At some level most women understood that embedded in the male kindling was a primal fire yearning to be released, and she wondered at her instinctively powerful drive to conjure that flame—despite the fact that she had no idea what to do with it when the fire overwhelmed her pyromania.

Why is it, she asked herself, *that when men follow their basic instincts it doesn't threaten their careers, but when women do the same it can be catastrophic?*

She suspected it had something to do with *calibration*.

The mental preoccupations (and another, long, sleep-deprived week) made it difficult to put on a happy face for the guests that night. After the previous Saturday's breakdown, she had done a little research on the vodka-and-Red Bull concoctions. She was worried about the influence the Vod Bombs had had on her emotional state. The internet informed her that in terms of physiological effects they were similar to two lines of cocaine. But she didn't want to give them up totally, because she felt they made her so much better at her job. She convinced herself that, like playing the underdressed airhead, it was also just a matter of *calibration*, and so she had set a limit of one. One Vod Bomb. Unfortunately she had reached her quota during the first half hour of her shift. The downside of her restraint was that now, two hours later, she was struggling to keep from nodding off. A quite insistent part of her was convinced one more Bomb would provide greater benefit than it would inflict damage.

As Blanché struggled with her inner voices, she also noted that a particularly low energy ebb had started to blanket the whole group. Despite the fact that he was winning, Francisco Aguilar, in particular, didn't seem to be animated. Blanché guessed (and hoped) it would be an early night.

The only time the conversation turned lively was when the topic of Victor Cortez came up. All of the men were competitors of Los Zetas in one way or another, so they strongly approved of his death. There was a normal sharing of rumors and hearsay; speculation was offered as to whether the attack had been driven by man or beast. Everyone knew about the sharks, but one of the card players had heard that Cortez's men had caught a glimpse of a SCUBA diver at the moment of attack. When this tidbit was offered, several of the men were incredulous that a diver could survive that far out with so many sharks. Aguilar offered that it may have been a hit carried out by Los Zetas against one of their own—an aging and incompetent lieutenant. The two older men at the table were noticeably uncomfortable with this observation. One of the younger men carried the conspiracy theory further by contemplating that the motive was to spark an inter-rival gang war. Always being the good host, Aguilar ratcheted down the tension by suggesting that regardless of the perpetrator, Cortez's death was good for all of them. He also couldn't help but boast that if the Zetas wanted a fight, he was prepared to give it to them. All the others mumbled their agreement.

Perched about eight feet above their heads, Clay was listening and watching. He was hidden between the joists and rafters, separated from the men at the poker table by only a thin wooden ceiling. Smiling with pride as he listened to the speculations below, he was pleased to hear about his brief celebrity; but as to the motive behind the hits, he was just as deeply in the dark as everyone else. He didn't even know who had ordered it, as all of his info came through intermediaries whom he had worked with for years, but whom he had never met.

If those intermediaries could compare notes, they would not have been pleased to learn that the man they knew as Tommie Smith had signed up for two jobs on the same day, and had neglected to hire a team for the bigger job. Clay had signed on for both missions because he loved a challenge and needed the money. He didn't know that he was starting to overestimate his abilities, given his three decades-long winning streak.

Before his right leg could fall asleep, he did his best sloth imitation and very slowly shifted his weight to his left, carefully avoiding creating any noise that might reveal his presence. Despite moving regularly—from seated, to kneeling, to all fours, to squatting, and finally to being hunched over in a standing position—the requirement of balancing on joists set sixteen inches apart was making him quite stiff. Before the upper-level criminals had started arriving at nine-thirty, he had been pretty mobile; but for the last two hours he had been much more restrained in his movements. After repositioning his weight, he again focused on the small screen he held in his hand.

Earlier that evening, after Tony had swept the room for surveillance gear, Clay had carefully drilled two quarter-inch diameter holes in the ceiling, contiguous to the light fixture that hung directly over the card table. To the casual observer the holes would never be detected, and even upon closer inspection it would be difficult to distinguish the small apertures from the busy-ness of the light fixture, fan, and patterned ceiling. Into one hole he had carefully fed some clear, plastic, surgical tubing until it was flush with the textured surface below. Attached to the other end of the surgical tubing was the aluminum cylinder he had brought in his pack. In lieu of highly concentrated oxygen, Clay had been able to obtain a mixture of nitrous oxide, oxygen, and sevoflurane from a veterinarian in Tijuana. He had never used the inhaled anesthetic before, so he wanted to give himself plenty of time to get all of his tools in place before administering the gas. Having been cross trained as a medic, he had used other general anesthetic agents twice when he was required to perform crude surgery (in remote battlefield conditions), and so he had some brief familiarity with methyl isopropyl ethers. In both cases the patients had died, but the wounds had been so traumatic that it was hard to decipher whether his own ineptitude had contributed to the outcome.

Through the other hole he had threaded a flexible articulating fiberscope with a fish-eyed camera lens on one end and a six-inch by four-inch monitor on the other. He had been watching through the snake camera for most of the last two hours, trying to discern any noticeable patterns that he could use to his benefit. The last details of the plan were finally falling into place. But he still wasn't sure what to do with the girl.

He knew the drug he was using would likely not render anyone unconscious, given the dispersal rate in the non-constrained environment. However, he felt there was a good chance the sevoflurane could help push the odds in his favor. Other than desflurane, sevoflurane was the most volatile anesthetic, with the fastest onset and offset time; it was used regularly during outpatient surgery on animals and people. He had picked sevoflurane because he read studies that showed it had particularly pronounced obtunding side effects; namely that exposure to sub-anesthetic levels caused significant memory loss, drowsiness, and slow reaction times. It was the latter two symptoms that he was most interested in inducing in his victims. He was hoping the tobacco smoke would disguise the slightly sweet smell of the gas, and he was depending on elevated blood alcohol levels to exacerbate psychomotor impairment in his targets.

He had waited until all seven (including the barmaid) had hit the head at least once before donning his half-mask respirator and deciding it was time. His watch told him it was 11:17. With an elevated heart rate, he reviewed his plans one last time, checked all of his tools, and then turned the knob that fully opened the valve on the gas tank. Unless something crazy happened, he was committed to action in fifteen minutes. In about thirty minutes the tank would be empty, and the anesthesia would start to wear off. He knew Tony and three other guards were wandering around outside; one of them would always be positioned in front of the pool house. Not sure whether the men inside were armed, he was certain the four guards outside were. The success of his plan depended on not attracting the professional guns wandering sentry-like *al fresco*—and that meant he had to be silent. He basically had a fifteen-minute window to drop down into the room, kill his targets, and then extract himself, all while keeping unusual noise to a minimum. Originally, he had felt his plan was good, given the circumstances; but he was starting to reassess the probabilities. From his hiding place, he realized the odds as to whether or not he would have to shoot his way out were even, at best.

CHAPTER 8 —

Game Day (Act 5)

It's funny, he thought. *No matter how many times I do this shit, it never gets boring.*

Like a spider, Clay had climbed down from the attic. He was now hiding in the corner, behind the bathroom door, getting ready to strike. He took three deep breaths through the respirator before glancing at his watch. 11:32. He was now only thirty feet and a few minutes away from the goal he had been working towards for the last six months. Sweat seeped from his armpits onto his pool uniform; he realized with alarm that his metabolic functions were skyrocketing.

This is insane, one against six…AND the four guards outside. And don't forget the girl…just my luck she's probably armed too…I only have fifteen rounds in my magazine! Shit! What the fuck am I doing here?

With the Sig squeezed tightly in both of his shaking hands, he was starting to fall apart. The suppressor-enhanced barrel twitched next to his right ear as he pointed it towards the ceiling. The urgency of his panic gained momentum as he thought about the impossibility of his plan. He was certain his breathing was being restricted by the gas mask that was partially covering his face, and he was moments away from ripping it off even though that would likely end up compromising his identity and what was left of his mental clarity.

It's not too late, he thought. *You don't have to die tonight. Just climb back up into your cozy nest and wait for a few hours, and then…sneak away…alive…when everything's quiet.*

Faced with serious existential angst, he definitely gave a shit now.

Before, when he was younger and part of a team, this never happened. The exigency of testosterone and the importance of his role within the unit made him unwaveringly committed. But now, when he was alone, older, and already had a good payday coming from this morning, his doubts were intensifying. He had bailed on two other jobs in the last two years and was starting to get a reputation as not only old, but also undependable.

Just as he made up his mind to retreat back up into the attic, the bathroom door swung open. In walked a large man whom the others called *El Oso*. He reported directly to Aguilar and was responsible for the distribution of drugs throughout the whole Inland Empire—everything east of LA County all the way to Arizona. After taking two steps to clear the doorway, he turned left and lumbered towards the bank of three urinals.

Clay sprang into action. He timed the firing so that the sound of the silenced pistol overlapped with the hydraulic sound coming from the door closing. Before the body with the exploded face could hit the floor, Clay had sprung forward to grab the man's bloodstained collar. With immense effort, he wrapped his gun hand around his victim's waist and wrestled to control the man's weight from behind. Focusing on the remainder of *El Oso*'s head, he let the corpse down easy, stomach first, allowing gravity to position the body on the floor with little to no sound. Skull and brain fragments, along with large quantities of blood, were splattered all over Clay and the bathroom tile, shocking him into a state that had carried him successfully through many firefights. He calmly and quickly wiped his Sig clean on the front of his trousers, and then headed to the door.

One down, five to go.

On the way to the door he ejected the magazine with thirteen remaining cartridges (one spent on *El Oso*'s head and one waiting in the chamber) and swapped it with the full magazine in his pocket, which held a fresh fifteen rounds. He now had sixteen bullets at the ready.

Over the years, Clay's job had periodically placed him in situations where he didn't have a clear advantage. If he could push past the fear, the ensuing moments of translucence and peacefulness brought out the best in him. His focus in those environments was somehow innate. He seemed to reach a zone that brought clarity and lacked hesitation. His mind floated above the fray, and his body took over. He became the opposite of a doctor who delivers life; he was a ghost who delivered death.

When he pulled open the bathroom door, at first no one looked up, as they expected the return of The Bear. That, plus the stupefying effect of the gas, was all the advantage he needed. The center of the round card table was twenty-five feet away. In three strides he had covered eight feet and fired three times, hitting the two men who were facing him and the one who was positioned in profile. He hit Francisco Aguilar in his left eye, and Martin in the center of his forehead. Both died instantly. Beto was starting to move, so Clay aimed for the rear of the confluence of his jawline and neck; he missed the cervical column by an inch or two. But the 9-millimeter bullet tore through the man's trachea and clipped his carotid artery. Twelve seconds later, Beto joined Martin and Aguilar, slumped lifelessly on the floor in a pool of blood. All three died relatively silently.

Clay had saved the final two men with their backs to him for last. Although they were the closest, they also were the most vulnerable. Their opportunities to find cover, or otherwise escape, were limited. They were already pivoting towards the source of the violence, though with the sevoflurane in their systems it took them a microsecond or two longer than it otherwise might. A grotesque caricature of death—a blood splattered phantom wearing a respirator and a Swami's pool uniform approached them with an upraised arm. Clay pulled the trigger before either victim could process what was happening…the suppressor released two forceful exhalations as the barrel spit the bullets towards the intended recipients. Both died instantly, bullets passing through their brains. He was left only to worry whether the gunshots had been heard outside the cabana.

There wasn't time to examine each body. Having seen the impact of the bullets on each of his six targets, Clay was reasonably certain each man was no longer alive. And, he had one more potential threat to consider—the girl. With eleven rounds left, he spun ninety degrees, expecting to find her behind the bar, aiming a gun at him.

She wasn't there.

Clay was momentarily relieved by the girl's absence. But he immediately became frantic.

Where is she…?

He kept his gun at the ready and spun around in a 360-degree crouch, checking the corners of the room, expecting to be attacked at any moment.

Nothing.

He took a moment to think. *Maybe she somehow snuck out and alerted the guards?*

Listening for any sign of movement, he heard nothing but his own breathing through the gas mask. He kept spinning in circles as he worked his way over to check behind the bar.

Maybe in the bathroom…? he wondered.

Slowly, he looked around the open end of the bar. She was on the floor. Keeping his gun pointed at her, Clay drew close enough to see she had nothing in her hands. He bent down to feel for a pulse.

He couldn't believe it! She was asleep.

The sevoflurane, he realized.

His mind quickly raced through the options. He had serious time constraints— he had to leave before he was discovered. But he thought about what the cartels would do to the girl if they found her left untouched amidst the room of bodies.

He'd been here before, he knew what he had had to do.

She's dead either way, he told himself. *It's just a matter of how fast and how much pain.*

But then a second thought occurred to him.

Maybe I can carry her out?

As he guesstimated her weight and the path back to his rig, he realized how crazy that plan was. Because even if he could pull it off… then what? The range of options quickly narrowed to one. He looked around frantically, trying to find an escape from the rising constriction in his throat. Then he aimed the gun at the girl's head, blocked his brain from considering her family, and said a prayer for both of them. He looked away, and…

Shit! Fuck! Fuckety Fuck! he realized. *I fuckin' can't do it!*

Keeping the gun in his hand, he drew the barrel away from the girl's head and scanned the area for something, anything else to come to mind. He grabbed a bottle of vodka, took a swig for fortification, and then quickly found some matches. As he moved from behind the bar, he tried to fight off the waves of conscience and self-loathing.

What are you doing? You know the rules—no witnesses, no loose ends.…

You're out of time, you fuckin' pussy! With increasing urgency he checked each of his victims, making sure they were dead. When he was about to check Aguilar, the *Don's* cell phone rang. Clay nearly jumped through the ceiling. Still, he had the presence of mind to fall to the floor, his heart pounding in his chest. With anticipation he pointed his gun at the front door.

Silence.

He jumped back to his feet.

Move! Move! Move!

He ran to the corner nearest the bathroom. He hurriedly emptied half the vodka on the sofa nestled there then wedged the bottle upside down between the cushions, allowing it to drain. As he dropped a lit match onto the couch, Beto's cell phone started playing *La Bamba,* and he heard voices outside the door. The couch combusted with a billowing black smoke that promptly started filling the room. Grabbing his pack, he raced into the bathroom, slid across the tiled floor, and frantically clawed his way through the wall to the exterior bathroom. Once through the wall, he quickly replaced the ventilation grates on both sides. He just needed a few minutes head start, and he didn't want to leave any easy clues as to his path of egress. Scrambling to his feet on the tile floor, he kept a grip on the Sig, shouldered his bag, and made his way to the last door. With his fingers wrapped around the doorknob, he whispered a quick prayer…

Please, Fortuna, keep smiling on me! One more break, and then I've got a chance!

Then, quietly but firmly, as the shouts of many voices rose at his back, he cracked open the door, took a deep breath, and slipped away, undetected, into the shadows of the surrounding trees.

2008
Playa Ballena, Baja California Sur

CHAPTER 9 —

Guns 'N' Roses

"This guy is driving me crazy," Keno moaned from his seated position as he peered into his computer. The internet speed was insufficient to send and receive even simple files, and the regular sips of his home-brewed, mint kombucha were only bringing modest relief from his growing frustration.

The responsibilities of his new position were invading every part of his life, including his attempted getaways to their new Baja vacation home.

Lola quietly sighed, playing along with their morning ritual.

"Which guy?"

From her studio she could see through the open door to the kitchen, where her husband sat, hunched over the computer in his lap, enslaved by his technology. Just over his shoulder, through the kitchen window, she glimpsed a breach. Her heart missed a beat as she watched the whale dance over the glassy, turquoise surface in the shimmering morning light. The scene reminded her of the majesty of the Sea of Cortez, and how lucky they were to be able to experience moments like this. The old man who had assumed control of her partner's body was oblivious.

"The satellite, internet, *non*-provider."

"What's the latest?" Lola asked politely, resenting the interruption to her morning creative process.

"He's an idiot."

"It *would* be nice to get some connectivity…be able to check on the boys," she empathized. She was simultaneously worried that Keno's early negativity would later resurface, igniting a spat about some non-related pittance.

"Yes, especially since they debit our credit card monthly for it."

She was fighting to be pleasant.

"How many days now?"

"Seventeen…no wifi, no service, no support, no options. Effin' Baja infrastructure."

He returned the computer to the kitchen table but his eyes remained tethered to the screen.

Lola paused from her painting, fighting the rising annoyance with her mate's predictable behavior. Ever since Trick had retired and Keno had taken over as managing partner, he had become more difficult to live with. He was more impatient with her and the boys, less loving in general, and always preoccupied with work. What used to be wonderful Baja breaks, where they could relax and focus on each other, had become extensions of his constant irritation with the world.

Deciding to change the morning ritual, she placed her brush on her easel and rose from her seat in her converted art studio. Keno continued his lamenting.

"I need to communicate with the office and write my quarterly client letter. I also need to pay some bills, check our portfolio, and make sure all is good with our assets."

And check on the Warriors, the Giants, and the 49ers—and *anything else in the sports world you can find*, she added silently as she moved across the room.

Knowing she loved their time in the Baja, Keno hoped that if he complained enough he might get Lola's help in resolving the connectivity issue.

"I just can't vacation in Baja anymore, Lola...the connectivity sucks too much. Now that Trick is gone, I have too many responsibilities back home."

The morning desert light played across the rose-colored *polido* floor as she barefooted into the kitchen.

"No hippie chick" be damned, she thought.

She glided casually and confidently to where Keno still sat slumped. Without breaking her rhythm she slid one leg over both of his, straddling his lap as her lower back nestled against the edge of the round wooden kitchen table. A slight, knowing smile poised on her full lips as she stared down at him. Her cut-off shorts simultaneously slid up her legs and pressed into her tanned, firm thighs as she rested her weight on him and leaned forward. No longer a nubile twenty-year-old, she still knew what was what. She now had his attention, as her threadbare, paint-splattered, decades-old Guns N' Roses T-shirt stretched across her strategically placed assets. Letting instinct shift his brain chemistry for the better, she prepared to lecture.

"Have you considered that we've done just fine without the intrawebs for most of our lives?"

"Hmm, uh…" was all he could muster as his thinking brain fought for control, the blood flow rapidly reorienting itself.

Lola talked down at Keno as she adjusted her hips provocatively.

"In fact, some of your best writing seems to happen when we've had long bouts of…no connectivity."

Unable to garner enough self-control for both eyes and hands, Keno chose the high road for his hands and let his eyes continue their shameless wallowing in Lola's close-range goodies. He welcomed the verbal medicine silently, given the sugary nature of the fully laden spoon with which it was being administered.

"So, maybe we could just wait patiently and let Baja be Baja on its own time? This isn't San Francisco, you know. It is, perhaps, California a hundred years ago….which is why we love it so…no?"

She leaned forward while pronouncing her last sentence, completing the muted lap dance with a kiss to the top of his head. She then unstraddled his steed and padded calmly back to her easel, confident in the adjustment she had left in her wake.

Keno waited a moment for the fog to clear from his wife's hit-and-run. After making some minor internal corrections, he picked up his laptop and started writing.

"You're the wind beneath my wings, you know."

He projected the words into her studio. Recognizing the sarcasm in his compliment, she absentmindedly mumbled back at him, hoping he would just move on.

"Whatever."

He understood her intent.

"I recently read that people who live in isolation lose their hearing more frequently."

Her paintbrush was already back to getting the details of a fishing boat just right, but she couldn't allow his poorly disguised jab to go unanswered. She used her diaphragm to push some words back at him.

"You know, as long as we're complaining about nits, you stole all the covers again last night. I was freezing. If you do it again—"

He interrupted her playfully.

"You'll do what?"

Taking her time, she considered the options and his vulnerabilities.

"I dunno...hmm...I know...I'll get someone to write a song about your privileged, white, male, homophobic, resource-grabbing, colonialist ways? Mebbe I'll hire someone like Tracy Chapman? I bet she'd do it... and then I'll have her play outside your office building every day during lunch...until everyone shuns you and you realize what a selfish capitalist pig you are and denounce your evil, money-grubbing ways..."

Impressed with her delivery of so many syllables without pausing for a breath, Keno decided to roll with her premise.

"You can do that? Hire a celebrity musician to slander people?"

"Everyone's for sale. Just a matter of price."

"Well then I think I'd rather have Pete Seeger...or maybe Woody Guthrie's boy...you know the 'Alice's Restaurant' guy?"

"Arlo. I think Pete's dead."

"No, I think Pete's still with us. I'm pretty sure he lives in Springsteen's pool house."

"Either way, your musician preferences just highlight your racist, sexist biases."

He took a minute before replying, so she would think she had the upper hand and let her guard down. Then he started the friendly taunting again knowing full well the provocative and insensitive nature of his word choice.

"I think you should come back and sit in my lap again...but only if you do it in blackface."

Lola put down her brush in mock shock before raising her voice a few decibels and one octave.

"Oh my god, you just said *blackface!* I think you might've killed a unicorn!"

"Or at least a politician."

If Lola could've frowned audibly, she would have. She checked her phone to make sure it wasn't capturing any of their conversation.

"Apparently you're irredeemable…or unconscionable…or wildly caffeinated…or all three."

"Let's leave our parents out of this."

"What…?"

It was obvious to both of them that the conversation had dwindled to an appropriate death. Even though neither could see the other, they shared a conspiratorial grin before reengaging in their isolated tasks. It was good to be understood.

2008
The Columbia River Gorge

CHAPTER 10 —

Bacon Waffles

The afternoon sun sparkled on the angry river as Keno sat in the passenger seat of the old Ford van. He was waiting for Trick to check the conditions while his stomach digested their recent breakfast. Every morning during the last week, the longtime friends had eaten at River Daze, a local restaurant where the menu offered waffles filled with chopped bacon. Keno already thought of most baked goods as butter delivery systems, so when the opportunity to add bacon and syrup presented itself he couldn't resist. Of course he had to wash the whole idyllic mess down with two pints of draft Blue Bus kombucha, because the lavender-and-peach flavor combination was just *too* good.

If he could've followed the meal with a nap, all would have been perfect. But instead, as had been the case all week during Keno's vacation visit to Hood River, Trick had a plan— mountain biking, snowboarding, or, today, kiteboarding. In some intense way they engaged their bodies with nature every day. Keno wasn't sure if they ate to power their exercise, or if they exercised so they could eat. He considered the possibility they might each have an eating disorder; but in their case, instead of inducing vomiting they rid their bodies of the extra calories through frenetic, masochistic activity. The shame of obesity was a cultural phenomenon that remained unquestioned by both of them. As he sat in the rig, Keno was sure that his digestive system knew what was coming. It started struggling with multiple tasks. Keno had happily forced the final bites of the waffle down his throat, but now his alimentary architecture needed to clear the decks and prepare for explosive movement. The protests came in a variety of uncomfortable manifestations, the most obvious being Keno's loud and frequent belching. Despite the input overload, he decided he needed some of the green tea he had brought in a thermos. Pouring the hot fluid into his mug, he immediately started the blowing ritual so he could more quickly ingest the familiar and calming beverage. At some deeper level he understood that it was all about the caffeine…specifically, its amazing ability to change *can't* to *can*.

Trick's plan for them to kite in the strong winds was freaking Keno out. It's not that he didn't think he was capable, it was more just a growing discomfort with outsized risks. This reticence to engage danger had started cropping up in his late thirties, and now, as he steadfastly marched through his forties, he was reluctantly gaining comfort with his loss of courage in the face of peril.

Not only did today's conditions imply an immediate threat to their physical safety, but there was also the apprehension he was already feeling about his next day's return to San Francisco. The thought of his inbox, overflowing with deferred responsibilities, left an outsized pit in his stomach. In general, the week with Trick had amplified Keno's misgivings about his job. The work had brought him life-altering financial success, but it had also left him feeling like he was being suffocated. He was reminded of his college roommate's father, who had opined, in his dry, Oxford accent that: "Making money is in-con-veeen-eee-ent…and making a lot of money requires tolerating significant in-con-veeeen-eee-ence."

At the time, he hadn't understood what his roommate's father had meant, but now it had become abundantly clear. By "inconvenience" he meant the inconvenience that comes with an all-consuming job.

He scolded himself.

First-world problems. You need to buck up, amigo.

Other than the vague mixed emotions about his job, it had otherwise been a really fun trip. But after six days he was beat (although he hated to admit it) and very much missed his family. If he could make it through today without collapsing, he would be able to go home with his pride intact, knowing he could still physically hang with Trick, even if just barely.

All week Trick had been deluging Keno's ears with vintage Dave Matthews Band, and Keno now had a loop stuck in his skull:

My head won't leave my head alone…

Further considering his Socratic tendencies merely invited secondary (and tertiary) thoughts of narcissism and infinite loops.

No new territory to be explored here, he reminded himself. *The absurdity of life, or not, and all the accompanying testimony.*

A new thought popped into his head; it involved a theory that exercise performed at a higher level than necessary was just another form of cutting—except exercise was socially acceptable. He considered the possibility that both were coping mechanisms used to escape from, or numb, the brain. Maybe the extreme sports he engaged in provided a facade of control by allowing him to choose when to inflict the pain, rather than just letting dumb luck decide? Not necessarily wanting to reach a conclusion, he knew that when he did push the limits it allowed him to ascend out of his soggy, trapped feelings, even if just for a moment. He wasn't sure there was a point to any of it except to try and feel good.

A blast of wind interrupted his intellectual navel gazing and brought his attention to the growing violence unfolding in front of him. The early caresses of air were now more insistent, as evidenced by the creaking suspension of the beater, white, Ford Econoline.

The wind had been building all day. It was now gusting over thirty-five knots, which ratcheted Keno's apprehension to a whole new level. He started reconsidering the potential consequences of the activity into which he was about to thrust his aging body. As the fears invaded and he struggled with self-doubt, he tried to talk himself onto the horse.

Steady, young man, you got this.

And then he marveled at Trick's unflappable optimism.

It takes a uniquely strong individual to see light where there is so much darkness....

He noted that the van and his flesh seemed to be headed in similar directions, despite his conscientious attempts to thwart the incoming tides of deterioration on his biology.

More darkness, he reprimanded.

He needed to focus on the task at hand. It was time for a mind-numbing injection of adrenaline, supercharged by the potential for serious injury.

But why? Just to get my stupid brain to focus on one thing? To temporarily shut down the endless concerns about past and future? Isn't there a better way—a way that doesn't require dancing on death's doorstep? He wondered if there wasn't a performance aspect to the whole thing.

Another burst of wind rocked the vehicle, reminding Keenan to be careful.

Reality presented itself through the passenger window.

"Grab your smallest kite," Trick told him. "It's blowing smoke, man."

The words redirected Keenan's attention. The Columbia River presented itself as an angry undulation through the van's dust-covered windshield. The frightening vision pushed all of his previous thoughts into insignificance. Nearly a mile across the inflamed water, on the Washington side of the gorge, he could clearly see the rust-colored cliffs biting deeply into the rushing current. Nearby, just a few car lengths from where he sat, a stretch of eroded basalt gradually led down the Oregon bank, serving as an interruption to the steady escarpment. For those with unusual obsessions—and the appropriate equipment—this crude ramp served as a pathway down into the chilly grey water.

The acidic taste of toasted rice languished in Keenan's mouth. Lately, when conditions warranted it, he had taken to adding a splash of *bacanoran mescal* to his green tea. Lola had bought a case of the fermented agave from a Sonoran rancher on their last trip south, and Keno had brought Trick a bottle as a gift.

Looking out the passenger side window, Keenan made eye contact with his excited compadre, noting the faint epithelial creases that formed around his eyes as they shone from his smooth, well-oiled face. The white teeth stood in contrast to his strongly pigmented skin. Keenan had a slight twinge of envy. His own light skin's loss of hydration and plasticity paled in comparison. He considered his friend's animated behavior in light of the current conditions.

"Come on, Keen-O, it's on!" Patrick's soft bass urged through the open window. Keno's brain tried to shift gears.

"Like Donkey Kong?" Keenan deadpanned, savoring the slight burn of the crude tequila on his gums and throat.

"Is there any other way?"

The familiar exchange led them to a warped, overzealous grin; it helped to relieve some of the tension. Old friends about to go at again.

There was something simultaneously comforting and invigorating about the moment. Above them strode the spring sun, aloft in a flawless blue sky, beginning its seasonal assertion over the lassitude of winter in a glittery brilliance of light, rock, and water.

His ruminating friend not moving fast enough, Trick recognized the smooth clay mug Keno was holding. It was a present he had brought over from Japan. He liked that his friend felt the gift warranted a regular place in his routine; however, right now he wanted his buddy to embrace more of the caffeine and less of the Buddha. He was anxious to get on the water.

"*Hermano*, put down that *sencha* and grab your kite gear. Man, you're turnin' Japanese with that stuff. *Listo, amigo.*"

As he pondered his forty-seven years, Keno continued to examine the meteorological carnage spreading across the Columbia River. It was becoming painfully obvious that he had come too lightly armed in the stimulant department. The westerly thermal winds were colliding with the rapidly flowing snowmelt, compelling bus-sized swell. With ten-foot wave peaks exploding in carpet bombs of spray across the river, visibility was limited.

Smoke on the water, indeed, Keno observed silently, simultaneously monitoring the tightening in his lower GI tract.

He allowed, briefly, that his age might be an impediment at some point in the day's activities.

"KEE-NO!"

Trick's bellowed admonishment finally broke the spell. Keenan came to life, putting down the mug and climbing into the rear of the van with his buddy. Gathering the smallest kite in his quiver, he looked for reassurance.

"Man, is my 6-meter gonna be small enough?"

The warm, consistent eleven-knot Baja days, when a 14-meter kite would lift him and his board gently across the Sea of Cortez, seemed like Kansas to Keno's flying monkey-threatened Oz right now.

"That's what I'm taking. Do you have anything smaller?"

"No."

"Then I guess it'll have to do, won't it?"

Keno was irked by his buddy's lack of concern about the conditions. Before he even realized what he was doing, he had turned his discomfort into a little verbal barb.

"Hey, what's with all the Dave Matthews? I thought you black guys just listened to Reggae or Snoop Doggety-Dogg?"

Trick briefly stopped assembling his gear, pointed sideways at his crotch and raised his eyebrows.

"Uhh…suck my huge Japanese dick? Bitch?"

Another blast of westerly wind rocked the van and focused Keno's worries on the now. As he finished gathering the gear, all of his regrets about yesterday and fears over tomorrow disappeared like spilt water in the sand.

CHAPTER 11 —

I Think...It's Windy

About twenty minutes earlier, Patrick Bowman had left Keno in the cab to reconnoiter the conditions. As he lowered his six-foot, two-inch frame from his toy-hauling Ford, he noted that what used to be cat-like was now lumbering. His right knee, victim of the football injury from so long ago, was complaining more than usual in the brisk spring air. He already had a good idea that the conditions were epic, based on the wind sensor readings from the IKitesurf website and the howling assault his rig had received as it approached the river corridor.

He didn't mind his friends calling him Trick, but he always introduced himself with the more formal *Patrick*. He didn't want to think in racial terms, but his Jamaican father and Japanese mother had given him a decent education as well as unusual features, and after forty-five years he had an impressive enough resume that he felt he ranked. In the Gorge, too many new acquaintances presumed a "hey brudda" casualness, which he found disrespectful. By initially insisting on *Patrick* he was often able to preclude the awkwardness.

He had to intentionally resist the thought that any perceived slight towards him was a function of his skin color, bleached dreadlocks, and a history charged with racial injustice. Having succeeded over the years by always choosing to find the positive in the world, he refused to wallow in the ugliness, though at different times the ugliness had been forced on him. He recognized his physical characteristics made him stand out, especially in this homogenous part of the world.

As he approached the unforgiving rocky launch spot at river's edge, his inability to maintain a normal gait, and the gritty feel of blowing sand abrading his exposed skin, further verified the wind's intensity. He noted the polished, ostrich egg-sized stones rolling underneath his sandals. The high desert environment just east of the Gorge was particularly unforgiving; the stunted shrubbery uniformly leaned away from the relentless bullying of the westerly winds. He knew the conditions were starting to push into the red zone, even for experienced kiters like he and Keno. Neither would be the first to suggest prudence.

A noise distracted him.

"Hey Trick! Whadaya think?"

The voice came from behind his right shoulder, a forced exhalation into the screaming wind. He turned away from the river and saw a young, familiar brown man. He was dressed in a black Slingshot Kite hoodie, worn jeans, and beater sandals. Trick first considered the intruder, twenty-year-old Scott Basulto, and then considered the question. Without thinking, and in the timeless tradition of posturing men, he offered the competitor nothing—or at least very little.

"I think," he said with a dismissive frown, "it's windy."

Trying to hide the hurt in his eyes, Basulto looked down while fading his smile.

As he said it, Trick realized it was a bad habit—the affected hard veneer to show the world he wasn't weak. He pushed his short dreadlocks back under his Patagonia hood and made a greater effort.

"I'll probably go with my 6, *hermano*. I'm gonna ride my strapped surfboard, and I'm carrying about two hundred nowadays, so...it may build, but my 6 is my smallest kite."

He shrugged and turned back to the river while delivering his last observation:

"Tough conditions."

Basulto respected Trick's relative position in the Gorge pecking order. His body language acknowledged the bone the older man had thrown him.

"Thanks, Trick, 'preciate it."

With a brief nod, Scott turned, and pushed his lean frame back through the wind. He was headed to his beat-up, red Toyota Tacoma, where he housed all of his gear and a mattress under the homemade canopy. He noted a few small groups of dispersed locals in worn, earth-tone, REI-appropriate gear, having what seemed like similar conversations about the conditions. Wool beanies and hipster facial hair proliferated. His radar picked out curves and longer hair under the wool and microfiber… he knew some of the stronger women kiters were in the house.

Basulto, the son of orchard workers, had grown up in the physically demanding farm belt of the upper Hood River Valley. Though he appreciated the information the Rastanese had just provided, he would've managed the situation fine without it. Most advanced kiters studied the local weather conditions obsessively. Anticipating the consistency, direction, and magnitude of the wind in different seasonal and geographic contexts was essential for one's survival. Trick had let Scott know his opinion on kite surface area and board type, for an experienced two-hundred-pound rider, in today's conditions. He had also told Basulto the wind was forecast to increase, so he should err to a smaller size when choosing his kite. All else being equal, stronger winds called for smaller kites, and vice versa.

Scott was one of the few kids who had successfully made the transition from the soccer fields of the apple and pear pickers to the high tech (and hence expensive) *gringo* playing fields of mountain and river. Recognized for his toughness, he worried over the bloody bandages that covered the friction blisters on his right palm and left big toe. Like all the local wind junkies, he had an inability to lay low when it was blowing. Constant gripping of his kite bars and rubbing by his foot straps had taken their toll. In response to his frequent kiting his forearms had evolved to a Popeye-like heft, and his back muscles reminded his current girlfriend of a flying squirrel. He knew the bandages would be washed down the river before he was five minutes into today's session, but he would deal with the bloody mess later, after the adrenaline gods had been paid.

He was at the stage in his learning curve where each day brought new breakthroughs—higher jumps, longer rail grabs, and bigger back and front rolls. Of course, that also meant harder collisions and bigger yard sales when things went badly. The river was softer than a concrete skate park, but a recent burst eardrum reminded him that big jumps could result in serious injury, even on the water. Although it hadn't yet registered in his young brain, Basulto was addicted to the adulation. He loved belonging with the "big boys" and being recognized for having the courage—and creativity—required to kite at a high level in the Gorge. Perhaps most importantly, kiting in these conditions required an intense focus that allowed him to escape from the daily vacillations between boredom and anxiety. The nagging injuries would go away with the wind, but for now he responded obediently, like the rest of the wolf pack, to its howling call.

As Trick and the other locals watched the boiling river with a combination of excitement and fear, they considered which weapons they would use to attack. Though a minor tribalistic vibe oscillated between groups, the level of hostility one generally felt among traditional surfers wasn't present. Kiteboarding involved a much larger playing field, as the river could carry fifty kiters at one launch spot, and everyone could enjoy the fun by rapidly spreading out, skipping over to different zones up and downwind. This was usually not the case with prone surfing. Trick recalled several bloody experiences, at good point breaks, where bones and boards had both been broken by jockeying surfers who became too aggressive within a small, well-established takeoff zone.

For today, Trick had decided to ride a NORTH WAM surfboard, five feet, ten inches in length, with about twenty-seven liters of flotation. Not unusually, it carried the garish artwork and bright colors that seemed geared to adolescent boys. Medieval creatures, various armaments, and cartoonishly voluptuous girls were typical in the surf-and-skate culture. Trick felt misaligned alongside these designs, but the board worked well in the swell and high wind, so he abided.

In general, board types could be split into two groups: Twin-tips and surfboards. Many of the younger riders, like Basulto, preferred twin-tip, or "bidirectional," boards that looked and performed more like skate, wake, or snowboards, and were symmetrical in shape. Twin-tips almost always had straps and allowed for the most flexibility in acrobatic tricks and jumping; but they were not as effective at riding waves, given their lower volume, or flotation. Twin-tip riders could do the stunts pioneered by wake, skate, and snowboarders, using wind as a means of propulsion, rather than a boat or gravity. They also tended to aggregate in shallower, flat water conditions, often with accessibility to apparatus like ramps and sliders.

The second group, kite-specific surfboards, also called "directional" boards, were similar to regular performance short boards but had several extra layers of fiberglass to add strength. The aerial tricks of kiting required a stronger platform. Surfboards generally had greater flotation than twin-tips, and this greater buoyancy could be used to support heavier riders or allow for smaller kites. Surfboards came in many sizes, some with—and some without—straps. Those with straps provided for greater control, especially when "boosting" or "hucking big air," terms synonymous with jumping. Trick had decided to ride his surfboard with straps today, because that set up would enhance his ability to fly—and safely land—jumps that could reach over forty feet in height. Surfboards without straps allowed for different types of tricks and greater freedom in foot placement.

In the Gorge, there was a contingent of older locals who rode strapless surfboards as a commitment to what they saw as a more pure form of wave riding. For this group, carving swell faces with panache was more important than boosting. Most of these men and women had sailed the river for decades as windsurfers; they felt a bit entitled. Many had grey seeping into their hair, and the men generally sprouted a constantly changing assortment of soul patches, goatees, and other indications of resistance to the inevitable decline of youth. Keno and Trick were distantly attached to the strapless gang, but they valued their independence more than any feeling of belonging. Basulto was too young to be remotely affiliated with the strapless gang. He hung mostly with the twin-tip crew.

Though not a precise science, triangulating which gear to use in specific conditions was essential to enjoying a successful session. Basulto already knew his own ability and weight, so he now had all the inputs to help deduce which board and kite he would choose. He decided to take his twin-tip and rig a five-square-meter kite. He was hoping to pull off a particularly acrobatic session that would further enhance his growing reputation as a charger.

Keno and Trick were more focused on survival.

CHAPTER 12 —

The Gorge

The geological feature that separates Oregon from Washington is the Columbia River. This great waterway is sourced at Columbia Lake in Western Canada, but it doesn't really become mighty until joined by the Snake River in Eastern Washington. The headwaters of the Snake lie in Yellowstone National Park, and, as the name implies, that river undulates over one thousand miles through Wyoming and Idaho before finally pushing into Washington. The Snake and the Columbia drain a basin that covers parts of six states. From the point where the Snake selflessly marries the Columbia (and gives up its name), the cohabitating waters head south and west in a long, meandering journey until they ultimately dump more water into the Pacific than any other North American river.

Geologists believe that between ten thousand and fifteen thousand years ago, during a series of mini-ice ages, multiple, massive floods were released from an enormous lake that sat over what is now Missoula, Montana. Glacial Lake Missoula was about two thousand feet deep and held as much water as Lake Ontario and Lake Erie combined. When it was full, the lake surface sat about four thousand feet above sea level. Encroaching and receding ice dams caused repeated cataclysmic releases of the contents of this huge lake, which eventually drained along the modern course of the Columbia River. With the force of sixty Amazon Rivers, or ten times the flow of all the world's rivers *combined*, the deluge washed over much of Eastern Washington; it eventually followed the more defined path of the Columbia. Along the way, this avalanche of water was forced through an eroded corridor in the Cascade Mountain Range as it pressed west to the sea. Gravity pushed the moving lake through the narrow passageway, and a phenomenon of biblical proportions ensued. The river swelled over its banks, accelerating and rising in ferocity, and peaking at nearly nine hundred feet high and fifty-five miles per hour. The torrent carried blocks of ice and granite the size of city buses, scouring the earth in a series of rapid and deadly erosions. Indigenous tribes who fished for salmon along the riverbanks received no warning. They were annihilated. This violent passage through the Cascade Mountain Range resulted in an eighty-five mile stretch of vertical waterfalls, obsidian cliffs, steep riverbanks, and limited topsoil that is now known as the Columbia River Gorge. In 1986, this run was named a National Scenic Area, which places it somewhere between a National Park and a National Forest in terms of environmental protections.

The Gorge is a Mecca for recreation enthusiasts. The extreme vertical nature of the topography allows for a variety of challenging conditions. Year round glaciers cap Mt. Hood and Mt. Adams, both of which rise to over ten thousand feet and straddle the Columbia River south to north like Siamese twins. Steep tributaries present great opportunities for fearless kayakers to challenge themselves and their equipment. National and state parks and forests are omnipresent, providing a dense arboreal feast of evergreens and perennials. Fishing for sturgeon, trout, and steelhead is uncrowded and of a high quality. Mountain biking and road biking are extreme. Downwind stand up paddling (SUP) is world class, hang gliding and paragliding opportunities are abundant, and a small rock-climbing contingent enjoys the local options. In the winter, outdoor adventurers embrace all forms of snow and ice activities. Mt. Hood is one of the most climbed and picturesque peaks in the world and hosts Olympic alpine teams who train year-round on the glaciers.

The locals committed to intensely exploring the recreational opportunities of this area are often called *Gorge Rats*. This term could be used pejoratively or as a compliment, depending upon the context. Locals take pride in their single-minded focus, outdoor capabilities, and rugged independence. The local Gorge summer trifecta consists of (1) a sunrise snowboard carve on the glaciers of Mt. Hood; (2) midday mountain biking on the groomed labyrinth of trails in Post Canyon; and (3) catching the late afternoon kite or sailboard session on the river. Gorge Rats are infamous for prowling late-night watering holes in search of an attractive companion to help them complete the rare, four-sport day.

At the center of this recreation melee is the town of Hood River, Oregon, so named because it sits at the confluence of the Hood and Columbia Rivers. Like the western cities of Moab and Durango, Hood River's economy was founded on natural resources. Originally a fishing and timber town, Hood River's founding industries were crippled by hydroelectric dams and government-mandated protection for the spotted owl. Apple and pear orchards took over during the last century, and the recreational tourism industry has kicked in more recently. Of course, yoga studios, artisan beer and coffee spots, and store fronts loaded with super high end equipment proliferate. Locals judge people not by the value of their cars, but by the value of the gear on top of their cars. In the summers, downtown Hood River bursts with a healthy mix of adrenaline, kombucha, Jonagolds, carbon fiber, caffeine, Native American-caught salmon, chainsaws, and namaste. To the north, just across the river in Washington, Klickitat County is home to innovative leaders in both the drone and cannabis industries.

Despite all these great distractions, it's the wind that makes the Gorge unique. On the western side of the Cascade Mountains the cool Pacific Ocean marine layer dominates, while to the east, the high desert reigns supreme. As the desert heats up, the air rises, causing a low pressure environment. The pressure differential between the west and east sides of the mountains sucks the cool moist layer against the western flank of the Cascades, with the Gorge serving as the only gap through which the air can flow. This marine layer gets accelerated through the gap, via the Gorge, as if through a funnel. In the summer, daily winds of at least twenty miles per hour can be expected, with gusts over fifty miles per hour not unheard of. These conditions attract enthusiasts from around the world, as the Gorge is one of the premier wind destinations on the planet.

During the spring snowmelt, when floodgates run wide open, the downriver current from a hydroelectric dam can run as swiftly as six miles per hour. At that pace, a passive floating object will move a mile downriver in ten minutes. If plagued by inattention or equipment failure, experienced kiters and windsurfers can find themselves miles away from their launch sites. Other challenges include huge river barges carrying loads of inland wheat, timber, or coal. These vessels have limited steering or braking capabilities, and hence have captured thousands of dollars of gear on their bows and in their propellers. In most instances, the Gorge is not a place for novices.

Springtime on the Columbia River means even more intense conditions than usual. Many visiting sailors who might be comfortable with high winds at their local spots will find the conditions overwhelming, with the launch at Rufus providing its own set of problems. Keno and Trick knew that the violent, gusting wind meant everything would be bigger and faster, reducing their margins for error significantly. Moreover, it had been a late spring in the Pacific Northwest, and hence the river temperature was still influenced heavily by glacier melt. Too much time in the water could lead to hypothermia. Out of the water, the fifty-six-degree air with fifty-mile-per-hour gusts of wind were no treat either.

If not done correctly, landing in the water after flying in a fifty-yard parabolic arc could inflict real damage. Hitting foreign objects such as rocks, boats, logs, or other kiters could mean death. Keno and Trick understood the risks, but felt the high was worth it. They had honed their skills on this river over hundreds of hours, and they felt that what could be life-threatening for some was dramatically less so for them. The Gorge was a challenging place to play and attracted the most robust athletes. A certain pride came with surviving what most outsiders would find to be impossible conditions.

CHAPTER 13 —

Tell Me Something Good

Trick's van was parked at Rufus along with a handful of other recreation rigs. Converted vans and Subaru Outbacks dominated the lineup. Rufus was the name shared by both the launch site and the nearby rock pile of a town. The hamlet was not much more than a truck stop and dive BBQ grill. It was located about two hours east of Portland on I-84, in rural north-central Oregon. As far as anyone knew, Chaka Khan had never visited.

Both sides of the river had similar landscapes. The long stretches of rocky soil, winter wheat fields, abandoned silos, random vineyards, and a greying population appeared indifferent to which state claimed them. The ridge tops were planted with massive turbines used to capture and convert the perennial, omnipresent wind. The monoliths would then feed their electricity into the southbound grid to nourish an insatiable California.

As Keno and Trick started gathering their gear from the back of the trusty van, the usual banter arose amidst the tense atmosphere. While he strapped his bar and lines to his kite backpack, Keno started with the nervous questions as a way to steady himself.

"Brother, you gonna wear gloves?"

Trick was struggling into his thick, five-millimeter wetsuit, hoping to build some core heat. Keno was already fully encased in rubber. Rivulets of sweat had started rolling down his forehead as a result of the effort.

"Fuck yeah…the water's in the high forties, wind'll be gusting to fifty…Shit, man, I'm wearing hood and booties too."

Keno tried to hide his fear with some teasing levity.

"Barometric pressure and water depth…?"

Trick front-zipped his wetsuit horizontally across his chest and hoisted his kite pack onto his back. Then he turned to his friend with a playful smile and an upraised hand.

"The whole flock, bag."

The gesture included an inward-facing palm, with fingers floating to the sky. Trick was giving it back to Keno with a plurality of "the finger" and a shortened reference to his friend's doucheness. After nearly three decades, they had developed a shorthand dialect that worked for them.

Keno shouldered his gear and offered the kiters' overused high-wind joke.

"It's really nukin' out there, man, I may just tie lines to my bandanna and hold on."

"Never heard that one. Funny. Really."

"Strapped or strapless?"

"The swell is huge…the dam is spilling massive current and the wind'll keep building…I'm going strapped. Just want more control."

"Don't tell Lola I'm not wearin' a helmet," begged Keno, not expecting to get any support.

"Okay, but…*hermano*, I'm not lyin' if she asks. That woman is telepathic."

Keno recognized the irony embedded in the conversation. As the wrinkles kept spreading, using adolescent nicknames and sport-specific slang seemed a bit undignified. But he also felt aging could be slowed with the right attitude, and at this point, when it came to his physiology, he was just trying to keep user error from accelerating long-term system failure. Although he still liked to push the limits, he was gradually recognizing that those limits were closing in on him. Whether caused by a normal decline in testosterone levels, or a greater love for the life he had built, he was finding less thrill in riding the dragon. His mind flashed back to about a year ago when he had been involved in a gnarly, mid-river crash that rendered him unconscious. Luckily, he had woken up a few seconds later. Unluckily, he was underwater, peering dreamily up at the surface. The rescue by the sheriff's boat…the trip to the emergency room…the concussion…the two-hour loss of memory…it had all underscored the import of the lesson.

If that wasn't a vivid reminder of my fragile mortality, Keno thought now, preparing to venture on to the river once more, *what was?*

Shaking off his doubts one last time (he hoped), Keno joined Trick in double-checking all their gear. When they were comfortable everything was in order, they loaded up their kites, bars, pumps, and boards for the short walk to the launch site. Their specialized, ultra-tough sunglasses added a surreal, aqua tint to the burnt, sandy surroundings. Even though good kiters spend only a small amount of time looking up at their kites, Keno and Trick knew eye protection was imperative. There were brief moments when their wind engines were hard against the sun and visual confirmation was necessary.

Three minutes later they were situated in the lee of a rocky berm. The two men carefully placed their boards nose first into the gusts, making sure not to leave any edges exposed to the wind's prying fingers. They then unfurled their kites and got to work inflating the bladders that supported the outline of their flying devices. Standing on the horizontal feet of their plastic, knee-high pump barrels, they secured the leading edge of the deflated kite canopies to a line attached to the pump then inserted the nozzle into the kite's inflation valve. The kites had a wingspan of over ten feet, and without the weight of the standing men even a light gust could grab and send the colorful, fabric contraptions tumbling downwind.

As they started the precarious process of manually pumping air into the kite bladders, they watched the few kiters who were already out on the water. In the high wind the small kites were difficult to control, whipping around like wasps tethered to a string. Foot pressure from the wind riders forced the fins and rails of the boards to dig into the water, which kept the sailors on a tack perpendicular to the wind. Periodically, a wind gust would overwhelm the rider's ability to control their tiny vessel, and they would go skipping downwind, trying frantically to depower their kites and edge their boards. As the intrepid kiters flew up onto the faces of the enormous rolling corduroy, sailors and rigs would be catapulted in spectacular ascensions, both voluntary and involuntary.

As Keno and Trick rhythmically pushed more air through the one-way valves, the kites began to flutter in the wind. The continued pushing and pulling of pump handles started bringing the wings to a full "C-shape," and the heat building up in their wet suits promoted the warming of their muscles. Scattered around them were a handful of other intrepid Gorge Rats who were similarly engaged.

Keno and Trick each drove the pistons through their pump cylinders about thirty-five times. As the pressure in the inflatable bladders approached 10 PSI, the kites began to fully roar to life. Like young, untamed dragons, the kites now demanded to be released from their tethers so they could soar on the surrounding gusts. Keno carefully removed the pump nozzle, sealed off the inflation valve, and inverted the kite flat on the ground, facing into the wind. He further hobbled his beast by placing a softball-sized rock on the canopy. After considering the surrounding terrain, he carefully laid out and attached four twenty-meter lines to the front and back points of the leading-edge bladder of his kite. These six-hundred-pound-test, polyethylene Spectra lines were about the diameter of a large toothpick, and were attached to the kite on one end and Keno's control bar on the other. The control bar was a simple, twenty-inch molded plastic and metal baton that was used to control the kite. When the kites were flying, a pull on the right side of the bar moved the wing right, and a pull left moved it left: just like the handlebars on a bike. Trick and Keno mirrored each other's actions as both men raced to complete the rigging process first. It was a competition neither would ever acknowledge.

Unusually, Keno was the first to get his rig ready for launch. Happily, he broke the silence.

"Hey Trick, how about a toss?"

"Yep," the big man replied, begrudgingly accepting his defeat.

Halting his rigging efforts, Trick prepared to launch his buddy's green-and-blue Cabrinha kite. Both men knew this next step was fraught with risk, despite having successfully executed it hundreds of times.

Kites are designed to perform in a quarter sphere of air that opens towards the wind. When teaching newbies, Trick compared this "power window" to the shape of the Sydney Opera house. The more perpendicular the kite canopy sat relative to the wind direction, the more power it would generate. The edge of the power window delineated a rainbow ("The edge of the opera house opening," Trick noted to the newbies). The flat bottom of the rainbow arch sat on the surface of the water. The above-water portion of the arch was where the kite was the most stable, and where it generated the least amount of power while still aloft. Directly over the kiter's head, at twelve o'clock, was the point in the power window with the least pull on the kiter…but it also could be dangerous if there was a lull in the wind: the kite could "Hindenburg" out of the sky, dropping to the water like a stone. Also, any sudden move through the power window could generate significant pull on the kiter. Maneuvering the kite appropriately, guiding it nimbly, at different speeds and angles through the power window ("The theoretical surface of the opera house opening," Trick noted), was how the sailor could generate more or less lift from varying kite directions.

The control bar was attached to a harness secured around the rider's waist. The harness helped to make kiting accessible to a broad population: it allowed body weight rather than solely upper body strength to be used to counter the pull of the kite. Sound core strength and a solid fitness level were helpful when learning, but not required. Gorge Rats often had unusually robust strength-to-weight ratios, as years of battling the elements had whittled their bodies into efficient machines.

While Trick grabbed the leading edge bladder of the Cabrinha and lifted it off the ground, Keno secured his bar and lines to his harness and double-checked his attachment points. A clear nod between the two friends started a tandem move to the water's edge, with the lines cutting through the wind perpendicularly. As Trick reached the edge of the river, he struggled to control the kite as he lifted it above his chest to get it to launch position. Keno did one more safety check then slowly walked backwards, away from his friend, taking out any slack in the lines.

The wind was particularly gusty, swirling at the river's embankment. It added to the perils of launching. A shifting wind could cause a dramatic increase in the power entrapped by the kite, which could drag riders across rocky terrain, or into other life-threatening predicaments. Today, the howling wind was far too loud to allow for verbal communication. As they exchanged a thumbs-up, Trick waited for a gust to lift the kite vertically out of his hands. Keno leaned back, preparing for the pull on his lines. Today the gusts were omnipresent: the big man promptly released the screaming hornet into the wind. Keno controlled the launch. The kite pulled him forward, allowing him to bound across the rocky berm—bouncing towards Trick and the river in huge steps—defying gravity as if he were walking on the moon. As Keno passed Trick, his friend handed him his board with a relieved smile, and Keno hurried into the icy, frothy river. Floating in a seated position in several feet of water with his back to the wind, he quickly secured the board by inserting his feet into the padded foot straps. As he briefly drifted downwind, he quickly dropped his kite from twelve o'clock to ten. The wing pulled him up and across the river surface. He rapidly gained speed, heading north, towards Washington, skipping over the tops of the waves as if Newton had been a fraud.

Keno approached twenty miles per hour as he neared the middle of the river. He noticed a particularly attractive swell forming as it moved towards him. He glanced around to make sure the area was clear—then made the decision: *Go!*

As his heart rate increased, Keno steered aggressively up the watery ramp. At the peak, he simultaneously sent his kite directly overhead (for added lift) while pushing off with his feet into the cresting wave. In his brain, everything slowed as he soared above the violence and lofted into the silent world of flight. The kite boosted him up: ten…twenty…thirty feet. The surreal scene of flickering sun, water, and rock mixed with his surging adrenaline. This brief, peaceful moment was why he kited, his mind focused solely on the present as he soared like a bird. A few seconds later, his body weight reestablished its dominance over the lift that had been generated by kite and wind, and he began a downward drift. It was important he move out of his dream state as landing became the priority. Steering his kite back to eleven o'clock, he maintained a full crouch, keeping the nose of his board elevated. He spotted his landing forty feet downwind. A few seconds later he came down lightly, his back leg absorbing most of the shock through the tail of the board. He steered his rig back to a broad reach then hungrily began his search upwind for the next ramp.

Onshore, preparing to launch, Trick smiled as he watched the episode unfold. He looked at his yellow-and-black Naish kite, which Basulto held overhead, and gave the thumbs up. The young Latino nodded, waited for a gust, then tossed the frantic *abeja* to freedom. Trick rushed into the icy waters, slipped his feet into the straps, and with a flick of his kite took off after his pasty, neoprene-clad friend.

For the next three hours they chased each other across the river, holding on to their kites and edging their boards with all their might to keep from getting blown off the water. They carved up and down the rolling river swell, slashing both the faces and backs of the cresting waves as they gouged buckets of spray from the undulating half-pipes. Every few minutes or so they would find the magical combination of gust and ramp that would launch them skyward to freedom. With wind sensors on nearby silos peaking at fifty miles per hour, it was the strongest wind they had ever kited.

As the sun approached the orange splattered western horizon, Keno worked his way upwind. He and Trick were the last of a half dozen or so kiters still on the river. They were both starting to make small mistakes… Keno knew from experience this was an indication of fatigue. To show he was done, Keno finally caught Trick's attention and drew his finger across his throat. Trick replied with a thumbs-up, signaling his understanding.

They both made it back to the Rufus launch site about a mile upriver, and with the help of some fellow kiters, they safely landed their kites on the same leeward rocky embankment where they had inflated.

Happily back onshore, they wrapped up their gear in silence, drained, but with a strong feeling of satisfaction. They shared an understated communion with the few other kiters who were also knocking down their kites. The talk was devoid of posturing. They all knew they had just walked the walk.

Thirty minutes later, Trick and Keno had loaded all their gear, exchanged rubber for cotton, and were in the van heading west to Portland. As they chugged up the freeway on-ramp, Trick plugged in his iPod and selected "This Must Be the Place (Naive Melody)" by Talking Heads. Pushing the old rig hard, Trick merged onto the empty freeway, which ran alongside the river. His voice competing with the ferocious headwind roaring into every nook and crevice of the vehicle, David Byrne poetically explored the yearning for place.

Home...

...is where I want to be.

Lift me up and turn me 'round...

Trick worked to get the groaning Ford up to sixty-five miles per hour while nodding his head to the beat.

"Awww, man...twenty-five years and this song still speaks to me."

Keno reached over and cranked the volume.

"Soooo good," he agreed.

To their right, the river was a blazing serpent winding through a landscape gilded by the setting sun. The wind was ripping effervescent scales off of the serpent's back and spraying them across the scene in a display of exquisite violence. Keno and Trick had wandered into this melee, immersed themselves to the point of belonging in a way that few humans could ever understand, and then successfully exited it with a slightly stronger sense of what it meant to be alive.

I love the passing of time…

As their adrenaline began to wear off, they looked at each other and started giggling. The significance of what they had just accomplished was starting to register, and they both never wanted to leave. Keno reached back into the cooler, grabbed two bottles of home-brewed kombucha, twisted off the tops, and handed one to his buddy.

Trick held up his bottle in a toast.

"*Salud, amigo.*"

Keno smiled in return, but other thoughts were already invading as he began to lose his grasp on just *being*.

At that moment he realized it was always just temporary.

He reached over and gave the volume knob a slight counterclockwise turn.

"Hey man, do you ever *really* listen to the lyrics?"

Trick looked at him quizzically.

"Yeah…I mean…I think so…whadaya mean?"

"The title says it all, brother."

" 'This Must Be the Place'…or 'Naive Melody'?"

"Both."

Trick decided to just let it sit for a while and listen to the song. He guessed Keno would continue when he was ready.

Home...

...is where I want to be.

But I guess I'm already there...

Keno took a sip from his drink and stared out the window. A moment later he looked back at his buddy, hoping for some evidence he was trying.

"Don't you get it? It's about the universal search for home...to belong...in a place."

Keno looked at Trick for affirmation but instead got a mixture of curiosity and surprise.

"Uhhh pretty obvious...right?"

Keno continued.

"But there is no *physical* place...home is a state of mind...a metaphor for peace or contentment...and it is childish...*naive*...to keep searching for a physical place..."

Keno was searching for the words to complete his thought...

" ...where things are good all the time, because...like *The Big Rock Candy Mountain*...it doesn't exist."

"But there are definitely places where I feel better...where I feel like I belong."

"True...you ascribe good feelings to a place...but incorrectly... because it's more about who you're with, what you're doing...how you perceive that moment...and it's all fleeting...even life itself."

Trick had to give the concept a little more thought.

"That's pretty deep, man."

"Now you're fuckin' with me."

"No, seriously…some deep feces. Kinda like Thomas Wolfe's book, *You Can't Go Home Again*.

"Right?"

I come home
She lifted up her wings
I guess that this must be the place…

"Now he's saying any time you can find love, that's home?"

"I think so…but that's just one example of home not being a physical place…it's more of a perception."

"Wait…so, we crave returning to the physical place, 'cuz we think that was the source of our happiness, but it was really just an experience… and that experience is temporary?"

"That's my guess."

"But there are clearly some special, physical locations? Like Rufus today?"

Keno shrugged, giving it some thought.

I'm just an animal looking for a home and
Share the same space for a minute or two…

"Probably…maybe…I don't know. Go out to Rufus sometime, alone, when there's no wind and tell me how special it is?"

Trick finished his kombucha and handed the empty to Keno.

And you love me 'til my heart stops;
Love me 'til I'm dead…

"Another, my brother?"

"Man, I think I need something stronger for this conversation."

Keno fished around in the ice and pulled out an Abita Purple Haze. He grabbed a bottle opener from between the seats, popped the top, and handed Trick the ice-cold beer. They drove on in silence, listening to the music and thinking about life as the raspberry wheat beer worked its magic. After about twenty minutes, Keno broke the silence.

"Hey man, you ever wonder why we do it?"

Keno finished his kombucha and repeated the opening procedure on another Purple Haze. Like a volatile girlfriend, he and alcohol had a history. In his mind, before he started, he set his limit at two.

Trick took a long pull before answering. He was pretty sure it would help, given Keno's recent introspective ruminations.

"Do what?"

"Kiteboarding, surfing, snowboarding, mountain biking…beating our bodies up with all the crazy physical activity?"

"You mean, why do we waste so much effort and money on totally unproductive activities and ridiculously expensive equipment?"

"Exactly."

Trick was simultaneously driving and trying to dial up some vintage Bachman-Turner Overdrive on his iPod. He knew Keno's question about motive was somewhat rhetorical and therefore his buddy already had an answer he wanted to share, but a beer-induced soliloquy drifted into his head, and he decided to override the filter and front run Keno's plan.

"Are you worried that our extreme form of exercise may not be a healthy coping mechanism? All just a form of masturbation? A technology-aided, sacrilegious spewing of metaphorical spunk all over the virginal face of Mother Nature?"

Keno fought unsuccessfully to keep from spraying his mouthful of beer all over the dashboard, then turned, sputtering, to his friend.

"Whoa, Dude…what the fuck…where'd *that* come from?"

Trick laughed.

"What, you think you're the only one who has weird, inappropriate thoughts? I just don't feel the need to share them all the time."

"*Touché*." Keno chuckled. "By the way…no way Mother Nature is a virgin."

"That's a rabbit hole I'd rather not chase you down. By the way, I think of it more as meditation for fidgeters."

"What?"

"All of our crazy recreation."

"Meditation for fidgeters…that's clever."

"It's working out okay."

"What?"

"Being clever…*By the way*, you will be cleaning that shit up."

"What are you talking about?"

"Tyler Durden and the beer you spewed all over my rig and your junk."

Looking down, Keno saw that not only had he sprayed beer all over the dashboard, but the Abita bottle between his legs had been misbehaving in a particularly embarrassing way. He sighed in resignation.

"Whatever."

Trick threw more beer down his throat and managed to dribble some down the front of his sweatshirt.

"Dude, you *whatevered* me! How weak."

He wiped his mouth with his sleeve then returned to Keno's inquiry.

"Okay, your question was, 'Why do we do it?'"

"Yeah...but now I'm a little scared about what twisted shit you'll come up with next."

Trick grinned. The beer was further infiltrating. They didn't drink a lot, so when they did it worked.

"What, brother-man, not liking your own medicine?"

Keno stared back at him.

"Still waiting."

"Okay, man, let's see...How about...we do it for fun, health, endorphins, adrenaline...the challenge...feelings of accomplishment? Pick any or all of the above."

Keno smiled. He had been waiting to share his pearl, wanting to tie it all back in to the Talking Heads.

"Thanks for accommodating me...probably different reasons for different people...but for me, I think I'm just trying to find a little slice of peace and maybe even some joy...you know, adding a little color to the blank canvas of existence?"

Trick was nodding with understanding and in time to "Takin' Care of Business."

"Ahhh...now I get it. You go kiting because...for a moment...it takes you *home*."

Keno smiled. It was good to be understood.

"Yes, but just like beer"—Keno held up his bottle and clinked Trick's—"if I do it too much it stops working."

"Oh, baaaallllance...what a novel concept."

"Smart ass."

"You deserve it for all the proselytizing."

They both laughed, Keno a bit less heartily.

Trick checked all of his mirrors to make sure no other cars were around before taking another big gulp. Keno followed suit and then sang along with the stereo—poorly but with enthusiasm: *"You get up every morning from your alarm clock's warning—"*

Trick joined in with even more volume and less skill: *"—Take the 8:15 in to the city…"*

When the song ended a moment later, Trick had another thought.

"Hey, man, how do you know it's not just a buncha chemicals making you feel good? You know, *home* may just be those moments when your brain is soaking in serotonin and dopamine?"

"Or alcohol or THC? Caffeine or nicotine?"

"Exactly."

"What the fuck do I know?"

A pregnant pause, then Trick followed-up with their inside joke:

"But there's one thing I *do* know…"

"There's a lot of ruins in Mesopotamia?"

"Nope. 'Damn, this Purple Haze tastes good.' "

Another pause. Keno looked disappointed that he was left hanging with the B-52's.

Trick gave him a big, patronizing grin.

"You know, Keno, not everything's a song lyric."

About thirty minutes later they hit Hood River and Trick pulled off the freeway to get some gas. They were each nursing their second beer and enjoying a continuation of the meandering, philosophical dialogue. As the Ford shepherded them to the pumps, one of their Gorge Rat buddies came over to serve them.

"Hey Trick, whadaya need?"

"Gerry!" Trick extended his fist and bumped that of the station attendant. "I didn't know you worked here?"

"Yeah, bro…flexible hours. That desk job, man, just too harsh, brudda, ya know? Always gettin' in the way of my kiting, man."

"Workin' for the man…not for everyone, amigo."

"Right on, man. Just gotta keep on paddlin'."

Trick guessed Gerry would likely be back begging for his white collar gig when winter approached—if he wasn't smoking too much weed. He was supposedly a decent aeronautical engineer; if he could keep his pee clean, the drone manufacturer across the river was always hiring.

"Can you please fill it up with regular, my brother? Here's my card."

"Yeah, Trick, no problem, man."

Gerry took the card and walked away to do his job. Trick looked over at Keno's raised eyebrows.

"The Gorge does funny things to people."

"I smell that."

Parked at the pump in front of them was a red Toyota 4Runner. The SUV was covered in mud and had a variety of boards and bikes hanging out of the back and off of the roof. A DaKine pad protected the car's tailgate from all of the dangling equipment. In the dying light, Keno could barely make out the bumper sticker just above the tailpipe.

Kiteboarding ruined my life.

Later, as they pulled back onto the freeway, Keno recalled a joke he had overheard recently at River Daze.

"What do you call a snowboarder without a girlfriend?"

Trick laughed, as he had heard the riddle a week earlier.

"Homeless?"

Forty minutes later Trick arrived at the Portland Airport Sheraton. The lively conversation and cocktails had made the time fly. As Trick pulled under the guest overhang, the burden of real world responsibilities returned to roost on Keno's shoulders. His biggest concern was his job. He didn't mind the real estate investing and development part, and he even enjoyed managing his team; but having to deal with the seemingly endless demands of clients and investors was an effort that he found extremely taxing. The issue had been nagging at him for a while and had been exacerbated a couple of weeks earlier. A large client had called Keno's home number in the middle of the night insisting on sharing an idea for increasing the occupancy of an office building in which they were jointly invested. Few people respond well to pre-dawn phone calls, but Lola in particular had had enough of the intrusions. After he hung up, with eye mask pushed up on her forehead, Lola read her husband the riot act, reminding him about the need to establish business and personal boundaries. Keno had meekly agreed with her. The problem was implementation. He had struggled with how and where to draw the line and was hoping Trick might be able to help.

"Hey Trick…how did you deal with all the bullshit questions from clients? The constant need for more transparency and detail? At all hours of the day and night? It's total make-work and a real invasion of Lola's and my privacy."

Trick's eyes grabbed Keno with a solemn look that showed his alarm. He then calmed himself while collecting his thoughts and taking a deep breath. They shared some common financial ground in this area, as Trick was still a significant shareholder in their partnership.

"Keno, you know I always welcomed that sort of inquiry. I welcomed it because we ran an ethical, attention-to-detail business, and I anticipated our investors' and clients' needs. I *wanted* their questions because it gave me a chance to show my investors that we were good stewards of their capital, and that we were deserving of their trust."

Trick paused for emphasis before continuing.

"Keno, I told you this before…you need to never lose sight of the importance of respecting your capital base. Entrepreneurs around the world are dying for money, and you think the guys who give us money are a burden? Please, please, please, never forget, a stable capital base is a luxury…we worked long and hard to obtain those relationships."

Keno felt chastened. He realized how entitled the question had sounded. He now wished he hadn't complained to Trick, even though they were friends. It was obvious that despite his desire to move out from Trick's shadow, he still needed a swift kick from his business mentor every now and then. Keno wanted to move away from the embarrassing moment.

"Of course you're right, man, I'm…I'm…just feeling so stretched right now."

Trick was concerned.

"Things good at home?…The boys?…Lola?"

"I think so, mostly."

Trick raised his eyebrows.

"Do we need to talk?"

No way was Keno gonna show weakness twice in one day.

"Nah, thanks. I'm the quarterback now, I got this."

Trick smiled in support, knowing something still lurked, but also knowing Keno wasn't ready to discuss it. Reaching his hand out he squeezed his buddy's shoulder.

"I know you do, brother. It's a heavy load, but I know you're strong."

Keno nodded back with a half smile. It was Sunday evening and he needed to make the standing, 8 o'clock Monday conference call in his downtown San Francisco office. To do so his assistant had him booked on an early morning flight. Already he was feeling guilty about his time away from his job and family. A quick mental image of a resentful Lola being overrun by their two teenage boys only increased his anxiety. He grabbed his overnight bag and hopped out of the van.

"Hey man, thanks for letting me stow my gear at your place. Great trip…really mean it, Trick. Thanks for everything, *amigo*."

Trick looked out the open passenger window, involuntarily shivering in the Portland fog.

"*No problema, amigo*. It's been a blast, I miss you, buddy. Let's not let another year pass this time, eh?"

"Sounds good."

Trick extended a long arm. Keno responded similarly, and they shook hands through the open window.

Before letting go, Trick pulled his buddy closer and offered a parting wish.

"I hope you find what you're looking for, my friend."

"What do you mean?" Keno responded quizzically.

"Home."

"Uh, ya…me too," Keno offered mindlessly, not really sure why Trick felt he was lost.

As Trick pulled away, Keno headed towards the hotel entry, but stopped to listen when he heard the big man's singing wafting out of the open windows: "*I'm just takin' care of business…and workin' over-time!*"

Keno smiled at the taunting as Trick's old white van started meandering slowly back towards the Gorge. With a small explosion of smoke, the rig began crop-dusting everything in its wake, spreading a burping haze of exhaust. "Rub it in…self-employed…asshole," he whispered to himself with a strange combination of envy and amusement.

He turned to hustle into the hotel, hoping to hit the sack before it got too late. At four o'clock the next morning, the wake-up call would come hard and fast.

That night, as Keno tossed and turned on his over-starched hotel pillow, the anxieties started haunting. As the managing partner of a real estate business he had cofounded with Trick, there was so much he was expected to control, but really couldn't. As the worries kept spinning, his mental to-do list got impossibly long, and thoughts of his San Francisco reentry were pushing him towards a panic attack. Around one A.M. the fatigue and beer finally overwhelmed Mr. Scary, and his mind started winding down. He teetered between sleep and consciousness as the concerns slowly loosened their grasp.

Ever since Trick had dropped him off, he had been searching for a quote—from T.S. Eliot he thought, though he wasn't quite sure. Just before the fog enveloped him completely, it fluttered in, quietly, landing like a butterfly on his pillow.

For us, there is only the trying.
The rest is not our business.

By the time the alarm sounded the next morning he had already forgotten it.

2008
San Fransisco

CHAPTER 14 —

Peaches and the Apple

A sweaty Lola Barton stifled her gasping affirmations into the pillow as her panting lover increased his intensity. Wolfgang had stopped the languid kissing on the back of her neck and moved his grasp from her breasts to assume a more assertive position—one hand controlling her left hip and the other intertwined with, and pulling on, her thick, sun-caressed brown hair. His breathing devolved to grunting as he extended to a more upright posture and increased his pounding into her from behind. She arched her back, responding in kind, and guided him with her guttural noises to a deeper spot as she felt a tingling ferocity growing between her legs.

Lola had not intended for it to go this far. What had started as a somewhat innocent and curiosity-based exploration on Facebook, during a moment of loneliness, had grown into this heaving mosh of naughty infidelity. The one boy who had broken her heart nearly thirty years ago. She had just wanted to know where he was, what he was doing, maybe even show him what he was missing.

What was the harm in that?

Her Mediterranean skin and commitment to good nutrition and yoga had allowed her to age well. After nursing both of her children, she had arranged for some doctor-assisted breast tidying…which also happened to help keep the men noticing. She had been raised to think cosmetic surgery was cheating, but when compared to the Marin crowd, she felt virtuous, given she had not yet had any work done from the neck up.

She had never planned to initiate a physical relationship, just a little reassurance from a previously skeptical, independent source. His profile and photos were intriguing. He was divorced, two grown kids, and seemed to have successfully joined the family construction business. It couldn't hurt to learn more, she reasoned, so she clicked on the "Friend" icon.

No one can have too many "friends"—right? she thought.

She was sure she would be judicious enough to draw a line, if necessary.

Jesus, I'm married with two teenage sons! she told herself. *I'm not gonna do anything stupid!*

It started as a distraction, a bit of flirting and controlled keyboard interaction. The next step down the slippery road coincided with a Wolfgang business trip that was suspiciously scheduled when Keenan was out of town. After dinner and a few drinks, the ground around Lola felt a bit less stable. As Wolfgang drove her home (to save her the cab fare) the chemistry reignited, and her fortitude waned.

It soon became apparent that her fragile conviction had been dissolved by the sambuca—as evidenced by her current, selfish focus on Wolfgang's demanding cadence. Days later, she would wonder at the justifications people could make for a brief respite from the burdens of the human condition.

After they were done, she fought against the remorse. She knew it wasn't fair to him. The usual contradictions inherent in short- and long-term contentment. Narcissism and empathy. She tried on a few of the rationalizations, but they didn't seem to fit as well as they had prior to the sex, when the hunger was at its greatest.

So pathetic, she silently flogged herself.

She cared deeply for her husband, and their life. But apparently it wasn't enough. Longing for attention (and intensity), she wanted to once more feel the high of a new infatuation. The oxytocin rush. Her life was good, but she yearned for the intoxication that came with knowing a man was totally focused on *her*; that he physically (and voraciously) wanted *her*. And she also wanted the power that a woman enjoyed from that knowledge. She wanted to share her thoughts with a new and attentive mind, and hear new ideas and perspectives in an intimate setting. But at the back of her head she knew the truth—that what she really wanted was long gone—and therefore this whole tryst was just a futile confirmation of the inaccessibility of one's spent youth. Her medical studies had taught her that the dopamine receptors in her brain were no longer mainlining the pleasure responses to the same degree as they had in adolescence. It wasn't that previously exciting experiences didn't still feel good; it was more that the same experiences felt less acute, as though someone had thrown a thin, moist blanket over the whole thing. Of course, the predictability of it all didn't help.

She separated from Wolfgang and made the obligatory post-coitus bathroom trip. At least she wouldn't get pregnant or a venereal disease, she reasoned, thinking of the condom, and what it meant that he had brought one.

The prophylactic made her flash to a time long past: Back at NYU, indulging in irresponsible acts of truancy. Lazy days filled with books, naps, and sex, and nights dancing to the impossibly vibrant and hypnotic sounds of Ska bands like the Police, the English Beat, and Talking Heads. New York City was hosting a Disco-annihilating British Invasion, and the hipness of it all was exhilarating to the early adopters. Lola embraced this New Wave with an adolescent vigor and outlaw carelessness. Going braless with skimpy underthings, miniskirts, and tight tops was *de rigueur*, and the boys were always frothing. The world seemed so new, big and full of promise, and Wolfgang Dalman was seemingly always a step ahead as they both grabbed big handfuls of life. Tall, slim, and from a wealthy Argentinian family, he was mysterious bordering on dangerous, with an easy laugh, strong features, and a way of moving in space that was captivating. He spoke English with an Oxford accent he had inherited from his British boarding school days. Women were mesmerized by the things coming from his full Latin-Aryan crossbred lips. Academics seemed to come easily to him, though he responded to his potential with a lazy shrug.

They hooked up early in her junior year, fall semester, at a campus party. She remembers dancing to UB40's "Red Red Wine" with a nondescript partner. Just a warm-up for her, a chance to start chumming the waters. As the song finished, she thanked her partner and headed back to her girlfriends. Just then the DJ decided to take it up a few notches, unleashing Fishbone's "Party at Ground Zero" on the smoldering crowd. A *cabron* silhouette grabbed her as she was coming off the floor. He was a fifth-year senior and, like her, had a streak of the exhibitionist. She had noticed him before, but he was always with a high-wattage member of the competition.

With raised eyebrows her new acquaintance nodded towards the dance floor. It was more of a challenge than a question, and there was an instantaneous, silent exchange.

Can you hang?

Better strap in, pretty boy....

They tore into the Fishbone speed-Ska anthem like two voracious carnivores attacking raw meat. Three songs later the Beat's "Save It for Later" was caressing the room…and she was falling hard. Her partner's shirt was soaked with sweat, and his smile revealed he was nowhere close to done. After they skated through the Specials' "Free Nelson Mandela," and the Violent Femmes' "Blister in the Sun" she was so hot her mascara was running in time with her heart, and her libido. She was nitro to his glycerin. They became inseparable.

Given the risks they took, Lola still doesn't know how she didn't get pregnant. It was probably her terrible diet, combined with all the dancing she did, that kept her fat levels low and led to an irregular menstrual cycle. Amazingly, she kept a C cup attached to those ribs.

Lola remembers a magical, summer night at a formal reception in a suite at the Carlyle. Wolfgang's parents were hosting. After meeting the parents, she and Wolfgang rendezvoused in secret out on the balcony, both well lubricated with long gulps of Mumm's. She, bent over the iron railing, Ann Taylor skirt bunched up around her waist. He, trousers and boxers draped over his Bruno Magli's, pumping frantically in an effort to put out the fire. The shimmering lights from moon and city bathed them while the lingering tastes of champagne and oysters intermingled with the noticeable smell of humid coupling. The thought of being watched only added to the intensity.

And she wasn't just passively receiving. In November, the night before she introduced him to her family over a traditional Thanksgiving dinner, she attacked him in the CBGB loo after a particularly inspired performance by Talking Heads front man David Byrne. For her, "Burning Down the House" still conjured images of an incredulously excited Wolfgang looking up at her as she lowered herself onto him in the impossibly narrow stall, exposed teenage bum indifferent to the buzz of the bladder-swollen lines of drunken club-goers beyond the thin, graffiti-covered, metal door.

Over the Christmas holiday he flew back to his family's compound in Miami, and she went home to her parent's place in Westchester County. The phone calls became awkward and unenthusiastic on his end, and she sensed something was wrong. By the time they returned to school in January, his ADD had led him to a spicy Chilean copper heiress he had met in South Beach. She was devastated.

For two semesters she struggled to right what had been a smooth-sailing academic ship. It nearly capsized as her pre-med plans vacated the premises. She was sure they were meant for each other, and that she could do something to get him to recognize that truth. He wasn't ready for any real commitment, and at least had the decency to not take advantage of her sexually. At the time she didn't see it that way. She floundered, cataloguing her deficiencies and wallowing in depression as her overtures were rebuffed. Everything paled when compared to the intensity of her time with Wolfgang. She was sure she would never recover.

About six months later the salve of time gradually started taking hold, and the nadir passed. The new emotional tissue proved impressively resilient—she would never allow herself to get hurt like that again. Despondent, she graduated with a deflated GPA and a degree in psychology, and soon thereafter headed west. She needed a break from New York and "the Wolfgang experience," and California seemed to be where people went to leave things behind. Over the years, she had regularly wondered what her former flame was doing, but she hadn't intended such an intimate reacquaintance after nearly three decades of separation.

Wolfgang was savoring the tastes and scents he hadn't realized he had missed. He recalled having a great time with Lola in college—remembering her as being fresh, smart…so full of energy…fearless in the pit as they had held their ground dancing into the morning. And, she actually looked better now....Why hadn't he closed the deal back at NYU?

He realized his misjudgment had been a function of an abundance of options. He had met Lola at a time when he had many promising leads in the female department, and few ambitions in the responsibility department. It was a time when he was floating from one experience to the next.

Six years after graduating, he had married a feisty WASP lawyer from Palm Beach. His parents had rejoiced at his maturing. Unfortunately, despite his sincere efforts, his propensity for polygyny had remained. More than a decade later his marriage collapsed and he watched ten years of his life get flushed away in an unremarkable effluence of distrust and ambivalence. Both combatants were exhausted from resentment and time. The holy triumvirate of marriage, career, and parenthood, all simultaneously demanding what seemed to be an infinite amount of energy, had finally taken its toll. Wolfgang's early infidelities merely served as the smoldering *coup de grace*.

As he sat in bed, waiting for Lola, he luxuriated in the fertile smell of copulation and wondered when Lola's bed had last hosted conjugal sex. He pondered his next move...he didn't want to misplay this.

Lola came out of the bathroom with a towel wrapped around her essentials, noting with alarm the shamefully obvious smell of sex. She had already made up her mind.

"Wolfgang, I'm really sorry," she said, "but this was a mistake."

He couldn't believe his ears, as he had already planned out the next few decades. It was so clear to him now: *She was the one!*

His mind raced as he struggled with the contradiction posed by her words (on the one hand) and their just completed diddling (on the other hand). Replaying her physical and verbal exclamations brought forth a salacious recollection.

She clearly enjoyed it, he thought to himself. *Right?*

He decided to work towards a stay of execution…see if he could buy himself some time until she got over the guilt. "Maybe you're right…but can we at least admit that something powerful just happened?"

Lola just wanted him gone, but there was no need to make it personal. In fact, she considered that approach might make the whole thing even messier than it already was. She tried to appeal to his sense of morality.

"Wolfgang, none of that matters. I took an oath, I said the words, and it means…meant…something to me."

Wolfgang interpreted the uncertainty inherent in her phrasing as a lack of conviction.

"So we both acknowledge that there is something powerful, even magical, that draws us together? Serendipity? Life is so short…I miss sharing our thoughts together. Can we at least be distant friends?"

The words struck a chord. Someone who valued her thoughts, her ideas? God she missed that!

She entertained a brief "what if" moment then returned to the task at hand. In this case the end justified the means. "What time is it?" she said, knowing the answer perfectly well.

He looked at his Rolex Mariner.

"Almost ten."

"Oh my God!" she said in an affected panic. "Wolfgang, you've got to grab your things and go. My boys will be home any minute."

His naked body now out of bed, he stepped towards her and confidently reached for her towel. She slapped his hand away firmly—

and without a smile.

"No!" she yelled. *"Now!"*

For a fleeting moment neither moved. Wolfgang sensed her fear, and Lola sensed Wolfgang's hunger. They both knew he could easily overpower her if he chose. At NYU they had sometimes explored games of control during their lovemaking sessions. At the time, the role playing had brought increased excitement to their intimacy, and at that moment (in the Barton's bedroom), they both latched onto the memory. During the brief pause a tremor passed between them. Then Wolfgang shared a benign smile, and the moment was gone.

He bent over quickly, grabbing his clothes, then slipping into his shirt and trousers. Lola collected his shoes and socks then hustled him towards the door, handing them to him across the threshold. As she urgently closed the door on him, he made known his intentions.

"I'll contact you…don't worry, I'll be discreet."

She whispered without conviction as she turned the dead bolt.

"Please don't."

On the other side of the door she heard him struggling into his boots. She looked at her hand shivering on the doorknob while she waited for him to leave. *What am I doing?* she thought. *Keenan will be home tomorrow.* The words stuck in her mind. *MY HUSBAND WILL BE HOME TOMORROW! This has to stop. Now!*

She heard Wolfgang turn and walk away. Her heartbeat finally started to slow. She removed her hand from the doorknob…and the physical temptation receded. She steadied her emotions, but she couldn't stop the words that kept playing in her head. *The heart*, she knew, *wants what it wants.*

CHAPTER 15 —

Diary of a Mad Office Husband

The San Francisco-based Alaska Airlines flight attendant had taken a shine to Keno. He was physically exhausted but happily tucked in to his upgraded first class seat, enjoying a cold beer and a cheeseburger. Usually not one to drink in the morning, he was still at a stage in his life where he couldn't turn down free liquor. He knew indulging his appreciation for alcohol was wrong, but his appreciation for a beverage offered *gratis* overruled his common sense, and his mind greased the skids by rationalizing that the potent potable would aid his body's recovery from injury. As evidence, his brain presented the stiffness in his hip, a likely victim of the previous day's kite session.

After the one-week vacation from his family, he now had a strong yearning. Like Odysseus nearly home to Penelope, his exhaustion increased his tunnel vision. He rarely spent more than a few nights away from home, but when he did he noticed a pattern. At first he would wallow in his freedom, grateful for the unconstrained time away from his wife and the boys. However, after a few days, he would start to view his family, and Lola, from a different perspective. All of the small, daily, petty annoyances would start to fade, and he would consider their relationship in a new, much more sacred light.

"Mr. Barton…" The young Alaska Airlines flight attendant engaged

Keno with her silky voice. "Is there anything else I can do to make your flight more pleasurable?"

She smiled into his eyes with a warmth he fell for immediately. After casually clearing the empty beer bottle from his tray, she reached over him and reclined his seat. When she finally got him all settled, the siren reached into his lap with a deft touch to smooth his blanket and make sure his seat belt was firmly fastened.

Oh yes, Keenan thought, *there is so much more you can do to make my flight more pleasurable....*

He nodded to her gratefully. "Thanks for everything. I'm perfect."

The flight attendant smiled then receded into the darkness, leaving behind a pleasant scent. *She is so good at what she does,* he thought. *Am I really falling in love?* He again caught a whiff of her scent, sensing its charged aura. *Unbelievable!* he thought, still lashed to the mast. *I am so easily manipulated.* The beer and burger had set him up nicely for the two-hour flight to San Francisco; soon his thoughts drifted back to his wife and their enduring relationship. He often contemplated the power of their physical chemistry, and he was grateful for her commitment. Looking forward to a continuation of his exploration into that subject later that evening, he hoped Lola would be receptive. He drifted to sleep with a smile on his face and didn't wake up until the plane's wheels kissed the SFO tarmac.

As he hustled to the parking lot to grab his BMW, he felt that he was being sucked back into the rapidly flowing circulatory system of the big city. Despite a brilliant, bluebird spring morning, he felt his stress levels beginning to rise significantly.

The morning traffic was the usual mess. He fought tooth and nail to try and get to his office in time for the eight o'clock meeting. His cortisol levels increased as he anticipated the hyper-frenetic schedule that would be his punishment for all the responsibility he had abandoned during the previous week. Adding to his consternation were the selfish jerks (newly minted tech billionaires, he was sure) who would take any risk with their racy status symbols to gain a single car length. He boiled as the traffic crawled north past Candlestick Park, his sense of urgency frustrated by the densely packed roadway. Several times he was forced to lock and load his custom, onboard, asshole-vaporizing cannon, but he never actually pulled the trigger on his fantasy. It's not that he felt death was too severe a penalty for the aggressive drivers but more a desire to decrease collateral damage to the surrounding civilian population. In a few more hours the perspective he had gained from his time in the Gorge would be fully supplanted by the return to his role as a commercial mercenary.

In the lobby of his building he took the escalator steps two at a time while quickly knotting his necktie. He picked up his first green tea (brewed hot and then poured over a large plastic cup of ice) while recognizing that his shoes needed a shine. He wondered which rebellious part of his brain convinced the other parts that a five A.M. Monday beer made sense. By the time he walked into the crowded Bowman, Barton & Jones conference room (exchanging greetings along the way) his senses were on full alert. A smile pushed its way to his lips as he heard the booming, gravelly voice of his LA partner, Michael "Pee Wee" Jones, projecting out of the speakerphone. A rhinoceros of a man, Pee Wee was delivering the punch line to some inappropriate joke he had heard over the weekend.

"Oh, I forgot, your brother has the car tonight!"

Despite being the boss, and not having heard the whole joke, Keno laughed heartily. Like most humans, he wanted to belong, and Pee Wee had a way that brought people together. Out of the blue, he realized that this quality was called *leadership*—having the skill to aggregate people for the completion of a task—and he wondered if it was learned or innate. Then, given all of the other important matters on his plate, he wondered why he wondered.

Come on Keno he chastised himself. *Focus, buddy, we got shit to do.*

As Keno took an internal inventory he realized there were conflicts. The math was easy: he was operating on just under three hours of sleep, which meant he was about five short of what history told him he generally needed. But there were other issues as well. His head was already throbbing, and a painful stabbing in his neck had materialized during the morning flight. Of course the beer he had self-prescribed had done nothing to loosen up his hip. He had a business to run, which meant herding a school of overly ambitious sharks, any of which could turn and bite if they sensed a weakness. Visualizing the full jar of ibuprofen in his desk drawer provided some solace, as did sucking in another mouthful from the straw that ran into the clear plastic cup full of green tea, sugar, and ice. Caffeine would necessarily be part of his strategy, but not being a coffee drinker meant using alternative sources.

He wondered what Trick was doing at that moment. Then he recalled the former Managing Partner no longer woke up to an alarm.

Probably still asleep, the bastard. He begrudgingly acknowledged that he was seriously jealous. *Shit, he probably doesn't even know what day it is….I should have retired with him and moved up to the Gorge. What am I doing here in this multi-story, steel, concrete and glass HVAC coffin?*

He answered his own question:

Suffocating. Trading your life's blood—your soul—for money. Why? So your family can have an indulged, entitled existence…that's why, you idiot.

Mick Jagger taunted him from left field:

I'll never beeee

your beast of burden.

My back is broooad

but it's a-hurtin'.

All I want

is for you to make

love

to meeee…

Was it really all that simple? Men and women? A well-disguised, culturally negotiated trade of sex for money?

He pleaded with his brain to allocate some resources to the task at hand.

Let's focus, big boy! Really! Stop fucking around! It's showtime!

Then his mutinous mind conjured a video of his seventeen-year old self. He was with a group of his Florida high school buddies, partying in drunken rebellion and gleefully hollering the lyrics of "Beast of Burden." Of course, the soundtrack included the expected adolescent insertion of naughty words.

All I want

is you to fuck

the hell outta me…

The image didn't inspire confidence. It seemed his fatigued condition was making it difficult for him to transition to the leadership role his title demanded. The whimsical, inner, little man had taken over the control center and was in a sophomoric mood. His eyes wandered to the shapely intern who occupied both the space immediately across the conference table from him and a sheer silk blouse.

Amidst the seemingly out-of-control, whirling, cerebral images, he noted the watch on his wrist said 7:59. Being the punctual sort, he gathered his energy and loudly cleared his throat. The room became silent and everyone allocated their full attention to him.

Wow! He looked around the conference table, impressed. *I'd forgotten about this part!* The power he carried over all the well-groomed professionals in the room was invigorating.

He launched into his routine from pure habit, mixing the usual enthusiasm and metaphor that ignored the reality of his shaky foundations.

"Good morning, everyone! Welcome, Pee Wee and Los Angeles. It's good to be back in the saddle. I'm a little out of the loop, but I'm well rested and ready to hit the ground running. So let's go around the table and hear what everyone's working on. Pee Wee, let's start with LA."

With that intro the morning spotlight moved off of Keno and onto Pee Wee; but Keno still needed to pay attention. As the managing partner, he was expected to understand all the details of the firm's projects.

"Roger that boss-man. Jimmy, you want to catch Keno and San Fran up on the Miracle Mile hotel repositioning?"

For the next ten minutes, Jim Gupta talked about the nuances of the capital structure and design features of a project their partnership controlled on Wilshire Boulevard. His facile use of technical language implied a competency that was unfortunately overwhelmed by the boring content and his monotone delivery.

About three minutes into Jimmy's update, Keno interrupted on an obscure point.

"Tell me more about the fixed-to-floating reset at the end of year two? What are the covenants and what's the benchmark?"

He did it partially because he felt clarification was necessary, but he barely listened to the answer. It was important for the team to know he was on top of his game, paying attention, and that at any moment he might call them out. Keno felt an environment of mutual respect fostered his colleagues' best performance, but he also knew fear could be a great short-term motivator. The real reason he had interrupted, however, was his need for an interaction to keep him awake. No one feared, or even respected, a low-energy colleague who fell asleep in meetings. It just wasn't a part of their culture.

By the 8:15 mark, Keno was fighting to keep his eyes open. At 8:22, his tea was empty and what he called "helicopter head syndrome" was threatening. It was early, not even thirty minutes into the morning call, and he was already in serious trouble. At 8:45, he was barely holding on. They were three-quarters of the way through, and he was surreptitiously timing how long he could hold his breath (another trick he had developed to stay awake during long, boring meetings). His personal record of one minute and twenty seconds wasn't challenged. Clearly he was running out of weapons. He had already interrupted the call with four questions, which had put him close to the fine line that delineated "insight" and "nuisance."

As he vacillated between semi-consciousness and alarm, he realized he was exhausted. Not exhausted as in "I was out late drinking last night," but the type of exhaustion that comes from a decade of fourteen-hour workdays and coming home to change diapers and pay bills, all while averaging just six hours of sleep a night.

"Our projections show an IRR of greater than thirty percent in the base case scenario…"

Poised to ask another question, he thought better of it and instead considered his younger son, Gus, who was struggling in school. He had always been a top student, but lately he had started acting up in class, and his grades were suffering. More and more, it seemed, Gus would lock himself alone in his room for hours, playing video games, or practicing his guitar. Any attempt by Lola to intervene and redirect was met with a stubborn recalcitrance. Two weeks ago, in exasperation, Lola had asked Keno to get involved. He had taken a firm stand with the sixteen-year old, and his well-intended direction had devolved quickly into a shouting match. Keno, in a fit of frustration—and after being forced to consume a particularly long barrage of verbal disrespect—failed to restrain himself from physically grabbing and shaking his boy by the arm.

"Mr. Barton, if you look at the cap table displayed on Graph 4a..."

Keno hadn't been paying attention, but when he heard his name he snapped to the alert.

"Yes, I'm sorry, Fred. Which page, again?"

His neighbor at the table—a young, former tennis professional named Milton—slid a handout to his boss. Keno glanced at the graph and mouthed "thank you."

After focusing on the presentation for a minute or two, his mind started slipping again. The fog and his worries reinvaded, and soon his thoughts drifted to a prayer he had learned as a child...a verse he had pruned years ago and onto which he had grafted a final sentence to include Lola. The message may have been a bit dramatic (given the lack of existential threat), but so was much of organized religion, and the cadence of the verse often comforted him. Wondering why he remembered it, he recalled that it might have been his dad's favorite, which reminded him of his family. He realized he hadn't seen his older brother Clay in over twenty-five years, and his dad for at least five. He wondered where Clay was, what he was doing, or if he was even alive. He thought their mom might've heard from him a few years ago, but he wasn't sure. As the droning of the conference call dwindled to white noise, the images of his family left him with a strong sense that something was missing, like an amputee yearning for a phantom limb. He whispered the prayer silently, under his breath, hoping for an end to his modern odyssey.

O Lord,

support us all the day long,

until the shadows lengthen

and the evening comes,

and the busy world lies hushed,

and the fever of life is over,

and our work is done.

And then

let me make it home safely

and lay down with

my beautiful wife.

CHAPTER 16 —

Marinated

Like the Titanic and New York City, Keno's plans for a grand coupling with Lola were not meant to be. He came home exhausted and immediately defaulted to the activity that took the least amount of effort: the Golden State Warriors were playing the Los Angeles Lakers on TV, and he plopped down in his favorite chair to watch Kobe Bryant battle Baron Davis on the basketball court.

Lola, feeling contrite after the previous night's infidelity, had been able to convince herself that her tryst with Wolfgang was merely a one-time lapse in judgment. The review process had been intense, but after several hours of self-examination (and guilt), she decided that her marriage was on solid ground, and her experience with Wolfgang should be left alone to fade into the distance as rapidly as possible. It was the best result for all parties, as she didn't feel confessing her sin to Keno would accomplish anything. She worried that Wolfgang's threats to follow up would cause complications; but she was sure that if she ignored him he would soon lose interest, just as he had done in college. She hadn't been unfaithful before and didn't plan on repeating the mistake. Besides, she rationalized, in France her rendezvous with Wolfgang would be considered part of a full life, even *de rigueur*.

When Keno first arrived home, she had been fully occupied in the kitchen, working to separate herself from the previous night's miscalculation. After briefly accepting his initial efforts at affection, she deflected him from her workspace so she could attend to the marinade. She was preparing her signature dish: smoked baby back pork ribs, with sides of mashed potatoes and sautéed spinach, and a dessert of German chocolate cake (which she had made from scratch). She used a proprietary chili rub for the meat, which she knew was her family's favorite. The spinach had come from her garden. It was the first harvest of a spring crop that she had barely salvaged from the caterpillars. Her goal was to take care of her family's stomachs and then see what popped up with her husband. It would be the first step in her penance; she had been planning and working all day towards this redemption.

During the first quarter, their two boys, Gus and Sam, wandered in independently and joined their dad in front of the TV. They all enjoyed basketball. Keno had raised them on San Francisco Bay Area sports teams. At halftime, the three got up and followed their noses into the kitchen, looking for the origin of the mouthwatering smells. Lola gave them a fifteen-minute warning—it was already eight P.M.—and sent them back out with a tray of *crudités* and chips. Within a half hour the boys had finished the appetizers and were somewhat sated. The third quarter had just ended, and the Warriors were holding their own against the juggernaut Lakers.

Midway through the fourth period, Keno opened his third beer and was engaged in a seemingly contradictory pattern of nodding off and getting more involved in what was turning out to be a barn burner of a game.

About fifty minutes after the first fifteen-minute warning, Lola had everything just right and was excited about the meal. She had been nibbling and testing for hours…this time, she felt, she had outdone herself. The table was loaded with plates piled with ribs and fixin's. In particular, the garlic mashed potatoes were weighed down by an extra stick of butter. Excited to share her efforts, she couldn't wait to see her family's faces as they dug into her multi-hour creation.

"Boys, dinner is ready!"

The Barton men heard their matriarch, but they had lost their sense of urgency in terms of appetite as a result of the snacking. Also, the game was down to the last few minutes. There had been twelve lead changes in the fourth quarter alone, and the sense of community between the father and his sons had grown strong. They all were loudly cheering every time something favorable happened for the Warriors.

Anything less than a rabid scramble to the table would have been disappointing for Lola, so the absence of any interest at all set her on a dark course. She couldn't care less about televised sports and had no understanding of the hypnotic nature the activity had over men. Fighting her rising anger, she reasoned that maybe they hadn't heard her. With a few more decibels she gave her family a chance to redeem themselves.

"Keno! Gus! Sam! The ribs are getting cold!"

With thirty seconds left in an extremely tight game, the guys were not about to vacate their spots; but they knew this was challenging territory. Keno tried to manage a compromise.

"Thanks, honey…almost over, we'll be right there!"

Lola made some minor adjustments to the presentation of her feast. Then, after waiting for five minutes, she sat down alone at the table, fuming. She started playing the negative marital tapes that were most recent and hence particularly accessible.

Why do I even try with him? He doesn't respect me…and now he's teaching my children the same insensitive behavior! Why do I even care? He obviously doesn't care about me. Just because I don't get a paycheck, they all think I have no value. He has no idea how much work goes into maintaining this house and raising his children. After going for a weeklong vacation with his BOYFRIEND, he comes home and doesn't even show any interest in what I'm doing. And I'm doing it for him! I'm just a cook and a vagina to him—he couldn't care less about who I really am, about what's going on in my head. What's the point in hanging around as an unappreciated slave?

Pissed off, she committed to making some changes.

In the family room, the game had gone into overtime, and the trio had forgotten about the cooling meal. By the time the Warriors had squeaked out the win, Lola had finished her dinner and was clearing her plate. When her men walked into the kitchen, glowing from the victory in which they had only vicariously participated, it was late—a bit past nine-thirty—and Lola was livid. They all knew the symptoms; now they wondered how best to avoid the eruption. The sons each grabbed a loaded plate, mumbled something about homework and gratitude, and then hustled up to their rooms. Keno sat down in front of the last remaining plate full of food, and started attacking the ribs. As of yet, he did not realize the magnitude of his transgression. He was hoping to make up for lost time with enthusiasm.

"God, this is great, Lola! Sorry, we were a little late, the game went to overtime—and we won!"

Lola wasn't having any of it.

"It was meant to be eaten warm," she replied icily.

Keno's calibration of the situation was impaired by the circumstances, and he was having difficulty picking up the obvious signals. He was nothing if not persistent; but of course, timing is everything.

"And there's chocolate cake for dessert? I am the *luckiest* man. When did you have time to do all this?"

The ancient cycle of insensitive behavior interpreted as offensive behavior that in turn leads to hurt feelings and, soon thereafter, anger, was already complete. Now it was Lola's turn. She effortlessly moved to the next step, retaliation. Her husband had been a lout many times before, so she was well practiced regarding which buttons to push.

"Is that your fourth beer?"

It was. But Keno didn't take the question as being arithmetic in nature. His enthusiasm immediately cooled.

"I'm not sure, I haven't been counting. Is there a problem?"

"You know I don't find you particularly endearing when you drink."

How quickly the mind can turn from charitable to inhospitable, especially when bathed in alcohol! The fact that he worked much harder than she and therefore deserved his minor, infrequent indulgences was so apparent to him that he became indignant when presented with any other possibility. This oft-repeated train of thought started him marveling at the degree of ingratitude that the women in Marin displayed when it came to understanding their level of good fortune. What at one time had been opulent had quickly become routine, as the microcosm of wealthy women competed for status and pole position. Of course the whole thing required money, and that meant tremendous and ongoing pressure on the husbands, who were expected to fund the ridiculous arms race. The newer women to Marin County were quickly indoctrinated to the process, and Keno often chided Lola to try and remember from whence they came. He had even developed a term for the growing requirement for luxury. It popped into his mind at just that moment:

Marinated.

He let the juicy word sizzle in his mind for a moment then savored the definition:

: An adjective describing a Marin resident (usually female) who, as a result of exposure to other Marin residents with similar perspectives, loses the sense of her relative good fortune.

Keno silently used the word in a sentence.

Lola is so fuckin' **marinated***.*

Of course Lola was aware of his thesis, and his one-word summary for same. (How could she not be, given that he reminded her of it so regularly!) She not only disagreed with his premise but hated even the mildest suggestion that she was one of the afflicted.

Now it was his turn, and he was equally adept with the stiletto in tight quarters.

"How were the tennis and golf lessons this week? I noticed we have new curtains? I don't recall discussing the costs?"

The difference between *intelligent* and *thoughtful* became clear as the two well-educated spouses tore into each other in the predictable way. The discussion proceeded loudly into a grown-up version of the preschool escalation of "Am not! Are too!"

The pointless yelling finally petered out when Lola, on the verge of tears, said she was going to bed.

Keno also deeply wanted to go to bed, but now he couldn't, because doing so would imply he wasn't angry with Lola. So he returned to the scene of his original crime and clicked on ESPN. After thirty minutes of SportsCenter, where he got to listen to multiple opinions on the Warriors game he had just watched, he drained his fifth beer, turned off the tube, and headed upstairs with irrational hopes of enjoying some makeup sex.

Aware that too much drink can impair some men—and recalling, vaguely, his own sordid history with alcohol—he noted with satisfaction his significant degree of intoxication. He had always been a quick-release kind of guy and had found that the numbness that accompanied significant alcohol consumption usually gave him more staying power, with no wilting side effects. The term he coined to describe this condition was "beerection," and his head carried a lasting vision of pleasing his wife as he ascended to their bedroom. In his oblivious wake was a messy kitchen that included five empty beer bottles and a sink full of dishes.

Struggling to fall asleep, Lola had been tossing and turning for twenty minutes until the emotional drama of the previous thirty-six hours finally caught up with her. Giving in to exhaustion, she started drifting into the pleasant zone that preceded *fully unconscious* when the hands started reaching for her. Despite not feeling the least bit amorous, she worried that she may have overdone it in her earlier criticisms of her husband; so she didn't immediately shoo him away.

For his part, Keno was similarly exhausted. But his biology responded to his weariness in a wholly different way. Like a stressed plant prematurely forced to seed, Keno's extreme fatigue was pushing his reproductive needs front and center. The alcohol amplified this need. It not only impaired his judgment but also stoked his libido. He was certain he just needed to grease the skids a bit, deliver a good tongue-lashing to the man in the gondola, and then the gates to Lola's secret garden would magically unfold.

Feigning sleep, Lola allowed Keno's efforts to proceed unimpeded—but also unaided. She was mildly curious as to whether his oral skills were up to the challenge of reversing her current emotional state, but mostly she enjoyed the feeling of power that came when she had a man's attention focused solely on her needs.

Unfortunately (for Keno) his wife still bore enough resentment towards him from his earlier *faux pas* that it wasn't likely she would respond to his efforts. Unlike him, she generally needed more than physical stimulation to be aroused, and the receptors in her brain had yet to receive the necessary neural stimulation engendered by proper foreplay. The more he attacked her pearl with a sense of urgency the more she withdrew, all the while inwardly criticizing his lack of awareness and sensitivity.

Keno's well-developed persistence kept him pushing, which in this instance served only to solidify Lola's intransigence. It wasn't that she always found his "battering ram" approach off-putting. In fact, when she was in the right mood and had advance notice, his single-minded focus could be quite welcome. However, there were times when a gentleman came to visit that she preferred a lighter, more delicate touch; some light courting in the form of a handwritten note, and perhaps a small gift. Maybe even some gentle exploring around the perimeter of the house, including some appreciation of, and attention to, her flower and vegetable beds, before showing up on her front doorstep and demanding entrance.

After ten minutes of Keno's pointless inquiry, Lola found herself unfairly comparing her husband's crude efforts to the subtle nuance that Wolfgang had visited upon her barely twenty-four hours earlier. With that vision planted, she was at least good enough to recognize it unfair to allow Keno to go on with the burrowing, but not so good as to offer an explanation to soften his humiliation. She denied her husband access by rolling onto her stomach and promptly falling asleep. Evicted from what was now the pit of despair, Keno had little choice but to follow her lead, climb his head up to the pillow, and, a minute later, collapse into unconsciousness. His dentist would have been aghast at the seafood stew that was left to ferment overnight in his mouth. Addressing his disappointment and outsized libido would have to be accomplished in the morning.

2009
Brazil

CHAPTER 17 —

Rio

Wolfgang woke up sweating profusely. Not sure where he was, he seemed to be swimming in what appeared to be fish scales. It was as if he had spent the night canoodling with an overgrown trout that had left evidence of their intimacy sprayed across the bedding. Desperate to bring his body temperature down, he kicked at the heavy duvet that covered him. His heart rate immediately decelerated as cool air replaced the furnace that had developed under the sheets. He flung his fist in a desperate roundhouse to try and punch whomever was wielding the mallet that was rhythmically tapping his cement-filled head just above the left ear. Coming up empty, he recognized the symptoms of a hangover and considered opening an eye…his mind declined the invitation. The morning filtered delicately through both the closed lace curtains and his eyelids, but if he opened either he feared the mallet would grow into a jackhammer. He rolled his face away from the intruding morning and warily, slowly, allowed the world access to one eye.

What is *this?*

Even in his dysfunctional state he could discern a delectable tidbit when it stared him in the face, although this tidbit was asleep.

Perhaps a mermaid? His brain was trying to solve the mystery of the fish scales. Not wanting to wake the creature, he slowly lifted the covers and took a peak.

Definitely not a mermaid, he thought. But he was not displeased in the least with the view of the naked lower half of the woman snuggled against him in the bed.

The mist started clearing when he finally spotted the shiny bodysuit hanging from the bedpost nearest the woman's head.

Aha…sequins…not scales!

He recalled that he had met the girl at a Carnaval party the night before. The state of his bed linens made it clear that the removal of her skimpy costume had been done with haste—and aggression. He wondered if the torn remnant of the girl's sequined outfit would adequately cover her curves when she went on her way. But he became puzzled by the presence of several garish plumes randomly decorating the furniture. The pieces of the concupiscent puzzle further came together when his gaze fell upon a bedraggled headdress tossed askew on the carpet.

He recalled her performance at Carnaval the night before. Balanced on a pair of six-inch heels, nearly naked, engaged in a frenzied samba that had captured the attention of nearly every pair of eyes in the audience. She had been the object of fierce attention after she descended from the stage to mingle with the crowd…but Wolfgang had eventually emerged victorious in the competition for her affection. A flash of pride surged through him.

Yep, he assured himself, *still got it.*

As soon as the self-congratulatory thought arrived, it vanished with the humiliating memory of his inability to consummate the seduction.

Whatever "it" is… he acknowledged, amending his previous assessment.

Despite his best efforts, his ability to maintain sexual viability was now fleeting—except with Lola. Even his attempts at self-pleasure were unsuccessful unless he fantasized about his married obsession. She was in his head, pestering him like a bad case of tinnitus—seemingly impossible to cure and pushing him well past a simple preoccupation. He suspected that without a remedy he would soon go insane but was worried about his ability to self-diagnose. *Can crazy people identify the moment their judgment has gone wanting?* He skeptically wondered. *If your faculties are faulty how do you know you're unhinged?* Considering the parallels between himself and Van Gogh he regularly used his fingers to take an anxious inventory of his ears. Finding them both intact always brought a reassuring flush of relief. Despite the perturbances, there was, however, a silver lining. Whenever Lola materialized in his thoughts she brought with her a jolt of elation. The result was an ongoing emotional state that teeter-tottered between anticipation and dread. The feelings were amplified by Lola's total control over the timing of their infrequent meetings.

He had tried to separate from her, but the vision of her underneath him haunted him daily. This fixation had been going on ever since the reunion in her bedroom nearly a year ago. The luscious papaya currently unwrapped in his bed was just one in a long line of ineffective attempts to displace her. As soon as the hoped-for antidotes opened their mouths, the weight of their inane utterances would droop his arousal like gravity on a wingless bird. It was maddening in instances like the most recent, when all the important visual factors were in place but his architecture still wouldn't comply.

Contrarily, with Lola he was robust…a stallion with a doctorate in female anatomy. He read her like a book and could fulfill her needs before she even knew what was missing. Unfortunately (for him) she only allowed access when things seemed to be going particularly poorly at home, which meant Wolfgang had enjoyed only two sessions with his *preferida* since the first.

She's definitely the one, he thought, getting out of bed to begin searching for his clothes. *But how to convince her of that fact before I go crazy?*

As he went around the room to find his things, his mind started the regular imagining of a life where Lola was his...which in turn got the wheels turning *vis-à-vis* how next to communicate with her in a manner that didn't threaten his fragile access. It had been several months now... he badly needed a fix. He looked again at the gorgeous creature who had slept next to him, noting with disbelief that he felt only indifference. Laughing inwardly at the absurdity of his predicament, he realized that he might as well have been a celiac and she an eclair. Lola had become his compulsion, nothing else could hold his attention. The more Lola pushed him away, the more irrational his hunger became. Gathering his watch and wallet (which he found, oddly, under his pillow), he started working his way into his clothes while formulating a serious plan.

Something else was nagging him. Looking down at the crook of his arm, he saw a tiny, pink, prick mark...and then he remembered the speedball. A trickle of guilt and shame violated his defenses as he replayed the telephone call with his father the day before. Wolfgang was supposed to have resolved a family real estate deal in Miami but had been procrastinating. The only son had been clamoring for more power within the company, so the father had given the assignment as a test. Wolfgang believed that in his father's eyes, his whole life had been one long, miserable failure, and the predictable conversation had left both generations disappointed and angry. It seemed that Wolfgang was incapable of reaching the level of functionality that his German-born father expected. The pattern of their interactions incited a shared frustration. His father's telephonic insult still rang harshly in the younger Dalman's head:

"You have the perseverance of an ice cube in the Sahara!"

After hanging up on his disapproving father, Wolfgang irrationally decided he didn't need the money or the corporate job and would do just fine living independently.

Fuckin' Nazis, he thought, walking away from the phone. *Who cares about their blood money!*

His last stint in rehab had left him feeling that he was done with intravenous tampering, but he began the search to reintroduce the drugs into his veins, just to spite the patriarch. After finding a dealer and numbing his senses to his father's rejection, he ventured out into the night in search of companionship—which was how he ended up with the girl in his hotel bed.

He looked again at his intended sexual companion and thought of Lola.

If Lola were here, she'd see what a demanding asshole my dad is…she would understand.

Before he crept out the door he scanned the room for forgotten items. With his anger and hangover still boiling, he again noticed the sequined piece of spandex hanging near the sleeping girl's head. A picture from the night before flashed into his brain. Checking in to the hotel, the Samba Princess, wearing only the sequins underneath, wrapped in his linen sports coat for modesty and warmth. As he slipped into the lithe jacket, he realized that the only clothing the girl would have was the feathered headdress and the torn one-piece outfit. Holding that thought, and in a state of misplaced rage, he quietly liberated the skimpy garment from the bedpost and folded the costume into his coat pocket, leaving her just the plumes. The thought of her panic as she tried to negotiate her way home, abandoned and without any clothing, money, or ID, left him with a perverse feeling of comically sadistic pleasure. He eased out of the hotel room quietly, making sure to control the latch before exiting fully. The bounce in his step as he fled down the hall reminded the hotel maid of a golden retriever puppy chasing after a ball.

2009
Still Out West (Mostly)

CHAPTER 18 —

Something Ain't Right

Aloysius Barton wasn't sure how it had entered, although he recalled that it had often been very clever. Things had been going so well for so long, he had almost forgotten that the demon existed. Like the chicken pox from his childhood, he realized it had probably never been purged but instead had been lying dormant, waiting for its opportunity. He thought of it as a demon, but it could more accurately be described as a *malaise*, or depression, the symptoms of which included a heightened awareness of his worries, which grew with each tightening breath. Simultaneous to the increasing prominence of his fears was the increasing subjugation of his blessings to the point of insignificance. This negativity, if unattended, had a history of quickly overrunning all of his well-laid defenses, exposing the pointlessness of the civilizing fight against the tireless forces of entropy and decay.

Like a forlorn lover, he stared longingly out his office window, gazing at an imaginary forest embedded in the reality of the empty, red Arizona moonscape. For no identifiable reason he was missing deciduous trees, especially the quaking aspen. A mental vision of a languid, cool river meandering lazily through a shade canopy of cottonwoods effected a sense of longing that was bordering on obsession. Insects hovered lightly over the surface of the gurgling water as he waded over some small rocks along the bank, working his fly rod in the late afternoon sun. The fantasy made it clear that he was fed up with the oppressive Arizona heat…the lack of water and greenery…the monotony of no seasons. Being aware that he had often taken the opposite position when in cooler climes wasn't enough to shake his commitment to half emptiness.

Like a child, he couldn't resist fidgeting regularly in his leather-covered chair; but, unlike a toddler, his restlessness resulted from a discomfiting invasion of anxiety, cynicism, and gloom.

As he stood looking out the window, a slumping form walked into his field of vision; the intruder triggered a whole new barrage of sensations. Sylvester Wright was their oldest masseuse. He suffered from what Aloysius had unprofessionally diagnosed as Short Period Iterative Narrative Shifting (SPINS). The paunchy, bearded, sixty-eight-year-old could oscillate through a dizzying array of convictions about a variety of issues, all within a one-hour therapy session. He regularly contradicted himself during these breathless, manic monologues, as if his empathy was so great it disallowed any long-term commitment to one point of view. He would even go so far as to acknowledge an equivocation before launching into another verbal display of his inability to form a lasting judgment. Despite the peculiarities of his brain, his hands were extensions of the divine, and his clients regularly professed to be the recipients of physiological miracles after their time on his massage table.

Sylvester's particularly complex set of characteristics would be interesting to manage were it spread out among several employees; when embodied in one it was maddening. Aloysius had, on many mornings, been the victim of a vehement and considered presentation from Sylvester addressing why he (Sylvester) was underpaid and mistreated, only to have the masseuse show up after lunch and provide an equally passionate discourse on how grateful he was for his job. The disorder (SPINS) seemed to be triggered by stress, particularly financial: Aloysius noticed a pattern that mirrored the Wellness Center's two-week pay cycle.

As Sylvester spread his counterproductivity to those around him, it triggered in Aloysius a mental aggregation and exaggeration of all the dysfunction which was currently a part of his life, starting with his children. During these times he would become particularly frustrated by the seemingly endless stream of problems (which for some reason others neglected) that he knew (resentfully) would eventually fall into his lap. He often wondered why people didn't just grow up and take care of their shit—but seven decades of experience had led him to believe that the likelihood of that happening was slim. This revelation made him consider switching sides and joining the irresponsible. He recalled that his time on the opposing team (during his younger years) seemed to have been a lot more fun.

As a result of his growing negativity and resignation, his office had recently felt more like a prison. When he first started, his legal work on behalf of impoverished and detained immigrants had seemed noble and invigorating, but now he just felt like a turnstile operator in a never-ending tragedy. The non-stop evidence of injustice was overwhelming his coping mechanisms. Not only that, but the daily and inappropriate hopes of his clients placed a burden of responsibility that was literally crushing the life out of him.

Not unusually, the malaise had started as a physical symptom, this time a tightness in his lower back. He couldn't pinpoint a specific catalyst, it just randomly materialized one week while his regular afternoon yoga class was winding down. Like a bad smell, he resented its presence. That night at dinner, his romantic partner, Lilly, had commented that he seemed to be in pain. Aloysius took the comment as a criticism, although it wasn't intended as such. For some strange reason he felt that his natural state was perfection, and therefore any problem could only logically result from self-mismanagement. This twisted rationale led to a sort of resistance to admitting that anything was wrong. While pushing his brussels sprouts around on his plate, he reluctantly confirmed that his back was bothering him. Lilly's predictable, know-it-all insistence that his physical ailment was a manifestation of some inner turmoil merely increased his irritation, despite the fact that she offered no scientific support for her diagnosis. As stated earlier, he had trouble acknowledging his own weaknesses, and he particularly didn't like other people volunteering advice about them. It didn't help that Lilly was probably right. The fact of the matter was he just wanted to be cranky, because, for some reason, a more civilized posture seemed too difficult.

His nearly full-time home was Desert Lilly's Health and Wellness Center, located in Carefree, Arizona. Lilly Stein, his "partner," was the proprietor, and he had provided the start-up funding. The center had been reasonably successful since inception, mainly as a result of Lilly's maniacal planning and oversight. She brought an attention to detail to her business that permeated nearly every part of the operation. Aloysius helped out on the management side when needed.

With generous pay and consistent communication, Lilly had been able to attract high-quality staff, and Skye Redbird had been one of Aloysius' favorites. Despite her name, Skye was quite matter-of-fact when discussing the benefits of yoga, matching her academic intellect with her graceful comportment. He reveled in her pronounced but not overly soft curves, supported by a tawny musculature that she carried well on her petite frame.

Aloysius no longer looked at younger women through an inexperienced lens. At sixty-nine years of age, and with an adult daughter and two grandchildren, he had lived long enough to see past the physical attractions that accompanied a relationship with a budding woman. Just the same, and even though the hormones were no longer running the show, he could still admire the innate beauty inherent in the well-proportioned female construct.

After a few days of agony, he tentatively returned to Skye with his ailing back and hopes of relief. The lumbar pain had made sleep difficult, and that deprivation had intensified his depression. As he waited outside for the class to start, he noticed he had no patience for the usual small talk of the milling yogis. He wondered whether he should have come. A moment later, Skye greeted him personally as she opened the studio doors then invited everyone in.

Soon class was underway. Al's back started to loosen up. As Skye started working the class through a series of sun salutations, the endorphins started to kick in, and Aloysius was struck by the similarity of his current feelings to those he experienced when swimming or doing basic calisthenics. This thought crystallized into the cynical notion that yoga was just a stretching class, gussied up with tight clothes and a dollop of dime-store mysticism, then marketed to those consumers who found unvarnished sweat and effort repugnant. He considered that the chemical "high" of rudimentary exercise was being packaged as enlightenment and sold at a significant premium. It followed that Desert Lilly's was just a scheme to defraud (mostly) irrational women who were burdened with too much money. With a weird mix of horror and humor he concluded that Lilly's and his wellness business was to exercise as lipstick was to a pig. Stuck on this revelation (despite his efforts to shake it) he decided he could no longer stomach the duplicity. He impulsively vowed to never visit another yoga studio. In a gesture to prove his commitment, he prematurely ejected himself from Skye's class as she cued the transition from Proud Warrior to Down Dog. His back was not appreciative.

As he limped out into the stifling heat, he again became obsessed with the idea of sitting within a clonal grove of aspen (which he knew to be from the same genus as poplars, the most common tree in North America). He considered the possibility that dementia might be clouding his judgment; nonetheless, he climbed into his silver 1973 300D Mercedes—and headed north. Romanticizing about root-connected trees, he visualized the white bark peeling intermittently to reveal the black underside…the leaves trembling delicately and in unison with the wind. As he sped away from the wellness center, he clumsily (and dangerously) stripped down to his skivvies while tossing the reviled yoga shorts and shirt out the window. He decided to keep his leather Birkenstocks being that his feet were quite sensitive. Habit led him east, down the Carefree Highway, and then north on US93. He was nearly an hour into his drive before he realized he was heading to Las Vegas. As the sun set over his left shoulder he rolled down the windows (but kept the air conditioning on), cranked up Harry Nilsson's *Everybody's Talkin'*, and let the twilight desert air consecrate his skin. Habit dictated he reach under the seat for his bottle of Stoly—he just wanted to pour a little accelerant onto his liberational high—but his search came up empty. He had cut that friend off years ago.

About two hours into his getaway, on the near horizon, he saw a small, straggly grove of what appeared to be aspen. The shivering trees were surrounding a simple weathered outpost. It wasn't until he was pulling into the dusty roadside parking area (and saw the fatigued sign announcing The Quaking Aspen Bar and Grill) that he realized the demon had tricked him.

A classic bait and switch, he thought, shaking his head in disbelief.

He now recognized the manipulation: subconsciously hiding his yearning in a seemingly harmless thicket of trees, and then, once he had been coerced into driving into the right context, quickly shifting the desire to the original intended.

God, he admired, *this demon is fucking tricky.*

But by now he was nearly done for. He could almost taste the sweet, icy cold carbonation…his first beer in years. He was rapidly losing control and was primed, zombie-like, for escape.

As he looked through his dusty windshield at the old wooden single-story structure, he made a last-gasp attempt to claw his way out of the pit. He forced himself to consider what he was about to throw away: Loving relationships. A successful legal practice. His health. But the malaise was strong and knew the terrain. It quickly countered by focusing his attention on the welcoming neon beer signs calling from faded windows.

Then the inner demon highlighted the lack of appreciation Al had received for the sacrifices made for his children, the women in his life, and his *pro bono* immigration clients. The tug of war continued as the demon focused on the utter futility of it all: What's the point of even trying (the demon seemed to be asking) if no one recognizes the effort?

All too soon, the beast reminded Aloysius, it would be over…his so-called "loved ones" would briefly and insufficiently eulogize him at an under-attended wake. They would then box up his bony remains and send the whole package inside a fifteen-hundred-degree (Fahrenheit) cremation chamber, after which he would reside in an urn on someone's mantel—or more likely in his least-resistant offspring's attic—to commune with the cobwebs and dust while never being considered again.

He noticed his quite dry throat and happily visualized remedying the situation in the Quaking Aspen.

His funk reappeared as he recognized the limitations that accompanied his current degree of undress. Searching his immediate surroundings for a solution to his wardrobe shortcomings, his outlook improved with the recollection of a Halloween Elvis costume he had never returned. He believed the costume was currently resting, unoccupied, in the trunk.

Yet another benefit of procrastination, the demon reminded.

As he watched the sun set, waiting for the cover of night to reinvigorate the King, he fought one last time to regain his strength. Feelings of gratitude imbued him as he considered the chocolate cake Lilly had recently baked for his birthday. As he thought about his daughter, Scout, her recent struggles with PTSD and addiction, and how strongly she needed his loving stability, he felt relevant…even necessary. The counterattack was working, and he continued to count his blessings.

Maybe I shouldn't do this. The thought came to him as he observed the first of the evening's stars glittering overhead in the desert sky. *It's not too late to just drive home and join Lilly for a quiet dinner.*

The demon, alert to this flanking move, adjusted its strategy and offered a compromise:

How about just a short excursion inside? A single beer and a chaser, after which you'll be free to return to your former do-gooder life of sobriety and health. What's the harm in that?

Aloysius was uncertain…*were* they stars, or just smudges on his windshield? To make the choice easier, the beast reminded its host of the perpetual disappointment that surrounded them both and that, like a dystopic noose, grew a little tighter every day.

You and me, the demon said, *we need—we deserve—a break from the incessant burden of existence…the need to maintain a positive mental attitude. And, by the way, aren't we really thirsty?*

Aloysius cleaned the smudges with his hand; the final fall was easy. He capitulated, gleefully embracing the rationalizations that his nemesis coauthored. Hidden by the growing darkness and his willingness to self-deceive, he slipped out of the front seat. *Why should I be the steadfast Dutch boy, finger in the dike, suffering alone through the cold night?* He made his way to the trunk of the car and slipped the Elvis costume from out of the back. *For that matter, why should all the world around me get to enjoy the carnal pleasures of bacon* and *a bump with interesting company?* By working his way through the challenges of zipper and Velcro, he quickly finalized the King's resurrection.

A few moments later, Aloysius strode from the Mercedes, his back pain receding with the twilight. As he readjusted the belt buckle on his seventies Elvis jumpsuit, he noticed his mood elevating in anticipation of the oncoming adventure. He thought himself nearly cheerful as he simultaneously reached for the brass door handle and remembered that at least one of his children (Keenan) had achieved professional and material success. This recognition gave him a small but legitimate data point, which in his mind substantiated his worth as a parent and warranted the soon-to-be-enjoyed alcohol.

Inside, the tired, sparse crowd turned as one to assess the intruding, messianic Elvis. Sporting cape and sandals, Aloysius strode dramatically across the threshold. Upon noting the limited number of patrons, he decided that if things went well, generosity might be in order. He loved attention—and he wasn't above paying for it.

All of the occupants wondered about his outfit. One large, dirty diamond miner nearly made a snide comment. But he thought better of it and returned to his drink. The establishment was situated in the "live and let live" rural Nevada desert, Libertarian country. They had all seen much stranger.

Behind the rough-hewn bar worked the proprietor, Colonel Barnaby Sampson Ahabito, a one-eyed former lion tamer. His rank was self-granted, for theatrical purposes, and therefore not a certifiable military credential or a sign of any real accomplishment. Several years ago, the retired circus performer had lost half of his vision in a single swipe of a paw belonging to a constipated African lion (upon whom the Colonel had been attempting to administer an olive oil enema). The macabre tragedy had taken place on a lazy Iowa afternoon, during a multiday summer engagement in the heartland. The ensuing riot of blood and gore allowed the ferocious feline to groggily stumble off into a nearby cornfield, after which the local Waterloo security officers gave unenthusiastic chase. In hindsight it was obvious that the large cat had been insufficiently anesthetized.

After the accident (and a reasonable time for recovery), circus management had let Colonel Ahabito make a go of it as a clown; but it soon became apparent that the Colonel didn't have the right stuff. And so he took his meager savings (and mutilated face) to the desert, where he promptly bought The Quaking Aspen. Tonight, Colonel BS (as the regulars liked to call him) had decided to forego the eye patch. The awkward reaction his disfigurement inevitably elicited from his customers provided some comic relief from the nightly monotony of slinging drinks. Like Pi's tiger, the lion was never recovered.

Aloysius grabbed a seat at the bar next to the diamond miner. He warmly asked Colonel BS for a beer and a bump, and coolly neglected to effect the alarmed response the barkeep was hoping for.

Jokers and clowns were working their way out of the dated jukebox, and the caped Elvis noted the appropriateness of the lyrics. Gerry Rafferty's feelings of entrapment in an absurd world seemed perfect for the current situation…

> …*Trying to make some sense of it all,*
> *But I can see it makes no sense at all…*

About thirty minutes later, as he ordered his third boilermaker, Aloysius loudly let Colonel BS know that the next round was on him. There were only six other patrons, so the gesture wasn't too extravagant. A warm glow was spreading throughout his body as it sat confined within his Elvis costume, and he hoped the free drinks would broaden the pleasant circulation to include his new companions.

A wary lizard watched the sad crew from the rafters. The quiet reptile happily chewed through his fifth fly of the hour. Its daily nutritional needs were now met.

For Aloysius, with the temporary exceptions of his costume and his blood alcohol level, nothing had changed but the hands on the clock.

CHAPTER 19 —

We're All Just Animals

He knew he shouldn't, that it would be incredibly wrong in any civilized culture, but like a bear in the woods he was also extremely curious. As with eating boogers, picking scabs, and the urge to reproduce, he had an instinctual need that ran aggressively in the face of social convention.

The effort had been monumental, as evidenced by his bulging heart, which was only now starting to recede back into his chest. As he took a furtive look around, the rapidly cooling sweat on his brow also implied a just-completed Herculean task. He really, really needed to see it…of its epic nature he was that confident. Of course, the potential for record-breaking size made sense, given the circumstances. With the creative process over, the artificially conditioned air was beginning to circulate the olfactory evidence of its external independence.

If he were at home, alone, he could just stand up, over the warm porcelain seat and look behind him. But of course he was quite removed from Carefree, and his current setting had made the whole evacuation much more complicated. Here in the crowded cell, his posterior skin had had to tolerate the chilled stainless steel, his jumpsuit bunched around his ankles, leaving his whole, saggy personage exposed for viewing. Out of politeness, the diaspora inhabiting the Clark County Detention Center had mostly averted their eyes. But the birthing had been such an assault on the senses that a few of the nearby inmates couldn't resist giving in to a curiosity about what they believed had to be an unnatural act.

To his credit, Aloysius had tried to hold back the relentless tide of nature, in hopes of a reprieve; but when Lilly had refused to rescue him immediately, he had been obliged to acknowledge that the forces of gravity (and peristalsis) couldn't be held at bay *ad infinitum*.

Now locked in the cell with the dirty deed done, he knew he had to make up his mind quickly. The offending waste was not getting any less stinky, and the necessary wiping with—and dropping of—paper would obscure the view. Aloysius was truly conflicted…tormented even. All of his social upbringing obliged an avoidance, a disavowal of any behavior that implied an awareness of the function of the human excretory tract; but the prideful little boy in him insisted that this might be a once in a lifetime production. Wondering where he fell on the deviance scale, he comforted himself by adhering to the belief that his scatological interest was much more mainstream than, say, those who embraced coprophilia.

Taking one more look at his down-and-out colleagues, he decided it wasn't possible to descend any further. Besides, he rationalized, in a few years he would be dead and none of this would matter. It was at that moment that he recognized how little separated him from his predecessors in animal skins—or even the dog on the street.

It was very simple, he had made up his mind. It seems his bowl-bound creation was controlling him from the depths and demanding his immediate attention. He stared hard to make a nearby intrusive inmate avert his eyes and then quickly did the necessary contortions to take a peak behind (and beneath) him into the polished metallic bowl.

Holy shit!

Too preoccupied by the sight to recognize the spontaneous pun spun by his brain, the matching, chocolate Everests confirmed his suspicions, forcing him to marvel at the flexibility of the human body. The stupefyingly large volume of consumption at the Quaking Aspen, coupled with two days of anal retention due to his incarceration, had given rise to a massive stoppage that had finally broken free in the form of the dual, dark freight trains that had sequentially traversed the rubicon of his rectum and now lay, uncorralled—wallowing, even—in untethered freedom at the bottom of the bowl. Their length and girth made him wonder about the total gestation period inside his lower gastrointestinal tract. He couldn't recall his last bowel movement, but given the most recent visual evidence, he estimated the obstruction could have been building for four or even five days. Looking like two, large, brown bass staring up at him from a water-filled grave, the twins implied a significantly forgiving colon and, he was certain, if subject to the rigors of measurement, would reign as personal bests.

The visual memory now safely stored inside the grey matter of his brain, he returned to the chilly seat, used some of the rough paper to swipe at the area of separation, and finally, somewhat reluctantly, sent the torpedoes on their way with several flushes. He marveled at the capacity of modern plumbing to swallow such a monstrosity with nary a hiccup.

After reassembling his Elvis costume (during which process he recognized the irony, given the circumstances of the King's passing), he moved back towards the long, metal bench where he had been sitting before his sphincter released its captive. His cape had been lost much earlier. It was currently wrapped around a shivering drunk who had fallen asleep on the unswept floor. The momentous discharge left him feeling lean and light on his feet—body and soul purged of the burden of his sins and newly committed to a diet of virtue and restraint—like a hooker who had received back-to-back absolutions at the free clinic and the confessional.

During his internment, Aloysius' senses had adjusted to the smell of unhygienic men. What had initially been an overpowering aroma of urine, sweat, and tobacco had now become hardly noticeable. Not thinking it possible, he discovered that his recent, violent expurgation had made even this dyspeptic crew view him as an untouchable. As he approached his former seat, the men separated for him like the Red Sea parting for Moses, and he soon found himself reclined, with his back against a concrete wall, in the middle of a ten-foot half circle that apparently delineated the area of quarantine.

Whatever it was that possessed him, no one wanted to catch it.

After what seemed a long time but was probably only five minutes, a youngish, large black man came over and sat down beside him. Aloysius felt intimidated by his presence, his mind playing snippets of prison films involving homosexual dominance. After a minute or two of silence, Aloysius felt the man staring at him. His brain had settled down to alternating clips of *Shawshank Redemption* and *Midnight Express*. No one else approached. The cell was awkwardly silent. The suspenseful moment started the grandfather hyperventilating, until the African-American eventually broke the silence.

"Mr. Barton?"

Not expecting any acquaintances to be in a similar predicament, he was aghast that his recent toilet behavior might have been seen by someone he knew. Aloysius quickly ran through his mental library, filtering for black people who were alive and not his son. There were two who quickly came to mind. The first, Patrick Bowman, had been a friend and business associate of his son Keenan. Aloysius had met him briefly years ago. The second, a professional football player named Deion Sanders, had been a several-times client when Aloysius worked as a "whale watcher" at the casino. He searched the man's face, clothing, even body language for a clue. Lighter skinned...tight Afro...attractive facial symmetry...relatively kempt.... But the features failed to come up with a match. Aloysius had never shown much interest in statistics, but even he realized he had a fifty-fifty chance. He figured Trick would be less offended if he misremembered him, given the time between interactions and his lack of celebrity.

"Deion?"

The younger man's expression revealed a miss.

Immediately ashamed, Aloysius decided to shut up and let things play out. He assuaged his guilt by reminding himself that interracial facial recognition was more difficult for most than *intra*racial facial recognition.

"You don't remember me...or my mom, do you?"

Aloysius was now really scrambling to solve the mystery. The process was being made that much harder by a growing internal fear.

I know I've fucked up, he acknowledged, still staring timidly into the man's face, *but please, if there's a God...don't let this be another illegitimate kid of mine.*

He was also concerned with an alternate possibility. At some point in his past he may have offended this intimidating man, and now the payback was sitting right next to him.

"Eight years ago? You were going to law school. You were in CASA and got assigned to me? Cassius? Cassius Jones? I was only fifteen back then."

Relieved to not be in physical danger, he acknowledged his earlier negotiation with a happy exhalation.

Okay, Big Guy, he granted. *Pencil me in for the next four Sundays.*

Aloysius had forgotten about his volunteer stint as a Court

Appointed Special Advocate (CASA) during his first year in law school. Going back to academia had been hard enough, but Lilly had suggested he do some volunteer work. "Give back to the community" is what she had said. She thought it might help him get past some of the backsliding that usually happens with recovering addicts.

The year had been so challenging for him, with classes, CASA work, and limited sleep, that his recollection of that time was mostly a blur. He reached back and recovered the memory of Cassius, a young man, barely more than a boy, posturing and defiant.

"Cassius? Oh my goodness, you've grown! Yes, I remember you now."

The dad wasn't around and Mom had some felony drug convictions. Cassius had started to get into trouble too, most notably by stealing a car. The system didn't know what to do with him. The state was pushing for incarceration, in the name of protecting law-abiding citizens, and his overwhelmed public defender had struggled to find an alternative solution. It wasn't an unusual situation in Vegas—black family struggling with the judicial system—with the important exception that this family had Aloysius, and it was his first assignment. He engaged the bureaucracy with the enthusiasm of a man unencumbered by the lessons of Sisyphus and Kafka. The boulder came in the form of finding the mom, getting her cleaned up, and presenting her to the court as a capable caretaker for Cassius. After successfully planting that rock atop the hill, he went back down and started working on Cassius. By the end of his commitment, he had Cassius free on parole, had found the mother a job as a receptionist at his law school, and had arranged a subsidized, two-bedroom rental a mile from Aloysius' place, well away from their old neighborhood.

"Mr. Barton, man," Cassius now candidly lauded, "you saved my life. I never got to thank you. Now I know why I'm here today. God is giving me that chance."

Aloysius had shepherded Cassius and his mother to work and school nearly every morning, helping them to develop productive behavioral patterns that, in turn (he hoped) would lead to functional habits. Basic things like flossing and brushing their teeth, healthy eating, reading books, limiting television, and getting to bed early so as to get enough sleep.

The big black man started softly weeping as he repeated himself.

"Dude, you saved me…you saved my life, you saved my mom's life…thank you, thank you so much."

For the second time in fifteen minutes, Aloysius was the focal point of the holding tank. This time he was bursting with pride (and a few empathetic tears). He wrapped his arm around his neighbor's broad shoulders.

"Cassius, are you okay? Why are you in here?"

After drying his tears, the younger man quickly pulled himself together.

"No, Mr. Barton, it's not like that. I was just out for a run, getting some exercise like you taught me, and they rounded me up…the police, man. I wasn't carrying ID, so…." He shrugged with resignation. "Here I am."

Aloysius was indignant, started sputtering.

"But, but, that's preposterous…"

"You know that, and I know that, but it's just the way it is. I always do what you said, be respectful, don't make any threatening moves, but they still grab us brothers and haul us in…just to remind us who's boss."

Forgetting about his own predicament, Aloysius started playing the responsible adult, looking around for a lever to extract his mentee from the unjust predicament.

"This is crazy, they can't hold you. We're getting you out of here…"

"No, man," Cassius replied. "Relax, Mr. Barton. God put me here so I could show you my gratitude. It's all good. My fiancée will be down soon with my wallet, she'll straighten them out. It's just an inconvenience."

"Fiancée?" Al stared at the young man with undisguised admiration. "You're getting married? That's great!"

"Yeah, I'm doin' great. I met her in law school. I'm goin' just like you went. She's great. *We're* great. We're gonna help people by workin' inside the system."

Aloysius started smiling uncontrollably as he thought about his week. Finally, he had blundered into a happy story—a story that he helped to construct.

Cassius interrupted the mini-celebration.

"What about you, Mr. Barton? What are you doing in here?"

Aloysius frowned. He wasn't proud of his recent behavior, but he didn't exactly have a clear recollection of his evening at the Quaking Aspen. The warm night and his Elvis costume were still within reach… but after that most of the event faded into a smoky haze, with images intermittently reappearing with varying degrees of clarity. He remembered a competition with the diamond miner, Jake—it involved eating pickled eggs and drinking shots—but he couldn't recall who won. Then there was the fight, he remembered that too…but only the part that involved hitting another patron over the head with a beer bottle, then dodging a flying mug that ended up hitting Captain Ahabito.

He couldn't bring himself to unmask his mentee's hero as flawed.

"Young Cassius, I made a huge mistake. I…ummm…well, the short story is…I …I've been so busy lately with my legal practice that I forgot to pay a buncha parking tickets. Pretty straightforward. Unlike you, I pretty much deserve to be in here."

It was now Cassius's turn to wrap an arm around his neighbor, carefully collecting his thoughts before trying to console.

"Ahhh, man...Mr. Barton...we all make mistakes...don't be so hard on yourself."

He then paused for emphasis before squeezing the old man and continuing.

"Hey, look, you need to hear this. People like you...you don't deserve to be in here...no sir...you need to be back out on the streets, helping people like young me."

Aloysius felt some tears rising. Cassius was right, he did need to hear that. He wanted to ask the young man to repeat what he said, as if he hadn't fully understood, but a guard came in with some paperwork and interrupted with a bark.

"Cassius Jones! Front and center. You're free to go."

Cassius jumped to his feet.

"Right here, man!"

But the dark man hesitated, turning back to Aloysius.

"Hey, Mr. Barton, are you gonna be okay? I mean, you got friends coming to post bail, right?"

Aloysius didn't want to be a burden, and he definitely didn't want anyone to know how much of a derelict he was. So he lied.

"Me?" he said. "Of course, I'm fine. One of the partners from my law firm is on his way now. I'll be five minutes behind you."

He put on his bravest smile.

"I'm so happy to have been able to catch up."

Cassius was in a hurry, as he didn't want anyone in the county's hierarchy to change their mind. Experience had taught him not to grow comfortable lingering in the grasp of the Las Vegas judicial system.

"Me too, Mr. Barton," he said. "Me too."

Aloysius called to the receding man's back:

"Please greet your mother for me!"

The nearly departed didn't want to share the news about his deceased mom. He threw the last few words back over his shoulder with a slight turn of his head as he hustled off to freedom, already separating himself from the earlier emotion.

"Will do, Mr. Barton. Thanks, again."

Aloysius slumped back against the concrete wall like a castaway watching his only friend sail away. He wasn't sure he had ever felt so abandoned.

CHAPTER 20 —

Psycho Killer, Qu'est-ce Que C'est?

After the La Jolla Massacre (as the insiders in the murder-for-hire industry were calling it), Clay did what he always did after a job—he vanished. He couldn't totally disappear, as he needed to maintain enough contact to make sure he got paid. But with the exception of a few short bursts of wifi to check his bank accounts, he tried to move as far off the grid as possible while simultaneously smoking his brain into a stupor.

Despite the efforts to lose himself, he knew the beast would eventually find him, coming without warning, in the middle of the night, with no apparent catalyst. It always interrupted his sleep, usually between one and three A.M. His only lasting memory of the experience would be of an invisible apparition standing over him, probing his brain, its frosty, horrifying presence penetrating the air with a malevolent chill. It was more a feeling than something real or tangible, but he felt it deeply, all the way to the marrow in his bones. He once described it to a VA shrink as the grim reaper, but as soon as the syllables left his mouth he realized the clichéd nature of the appellation and wished he could take it back. What bothered him about the phrase *grim reaper* was its generic overuse. The words had become impotent, cartoonish even, like when a teenager wears out a favorite curse word such that it no longer has the ability to offend. The words—*grim reaper*—didn't adequately convey the deeply

2009 - Still Out West (Mostly)

personal, idiosyncratic nature of the demon that was terrifying Clay. The ghost haunting him had a thorough understanding of its subject. It had access to Clay's conscience, knew all of his vulnerable spots, and could see all of the snarling machinations inside of his target's thoughts, right down to the roots of his soul.

Over time Clay had come to expect the beast, as it came most often after he had murdered. Ever since San Diego he had been woken regularly, often by his own screaming; and despite doubling his cannabis dosage and regularly changing his location, he hadn't been able to avoid the petrifying episodes.

Tonight, somehow, the beast found Clay camping under the stars in Nevada—specifically, in the Black Rock Desert on the western edge of the Great Basin. It was part of the BLM's jurisdiction, a designation that allowed Clay to camp freely, wherever he wanted. This wasn't the first time he had vanished into the sparsely populated, arid region east of the Sierra Nevadas. He liked the way people in this part of the country kept to themselves, didn't ask a lot of questions. Most of them were suspicious of authority, which suited him fine.

He had settled his rig in the middle of a dusty lake bed that his GPS coordinates had told him served as the site for the Burning Man festival. It was late spring, and the annual countercultural gathering didn't happen until later in the year, so it made sense that there were no other people in sight. His muddled thesis was that the demon's tracking radar would be confused by the remnants of all the exaggerated auras from the Burning Man participants. Part of him knew the idea was silly, but he had not a clue how the apparition was trailing him. Given his decaying state of mind he was willing to try anything.

Pathologically afraid of snakes, Clay had been sleeping in the back of his decrepit pick-up. He had provisioned a down sleeping bag and foam pad to fight off the nightly desert cold. As a boy he had learned the names of the constellations, and ever since he had enjoyed falling asleep while identifying the stars.

He didn't know why, but when it did happen it was always the same. One moment found him sound asleep and the next brought him to full alert, with an unambiguous conviction that somebody was standing over him. This time, when his eyes popped open, the night was pitch black. The absence of stars meant a front must have moved in while he was sleeping, bringing with it an impermeable gauze of clouds. With limited visibility, his mind started playing tricks on him, and he frantically worked at retrieving the gun from under his pillow while his skin prickled with an approaching chill. Panicked, his heart started pounding in his ears while his brain told him to MOVE! but the synthetic cocoon of the sleeping bag restricted his motion. Realizing how vulnerable he was, he urgently tried to shimmy to a more defensible place without losing the grip on his Sig. Shaking, he felt the jaws of his predator closing in and knew it had again found him. This would have to be where he made his stand.

Fighting his way to a seated position, he imagined the invisible demons pressing all around him in the black night air. Before their claws could tear at his flesh, his limbs finally responded to the orders being issued by his brain, and he did what he always did when feeling threatened—what he had been trained to do—he went on the offensive. Suppressing his doubts and gathering his courage, he jumped to his feet and started spinning, pointing his gun skyward, aiming at the invisible demons. With his head thrust back he defiantly exposed his pulsing neck and yelled a stream of vitriol into the swirling blackness:

"I'M HERE! C'MON, YOU SON OF A BITCH! YOU CAN'T SCARE ME! COME AND GET ME, FUCKIN' PUSSY! I'LL KICK YOUR ASS! I'M RIGHT HERE! IF YOU EXIST, FUCKIN' DEVIL,

LUCIFER, MEPHISTOPHELES, OR WHATEVER THE FUCK YOU ARE, COME ON AND GET ME! I'M NOT AFRAID OF YOU, MOTHER-FUCKER!!!"

As his words faded into the madness, he stood like a statue, all of his senses twitching, waiting for a revealing. After two minutes of uninterrupted and unnatural stillness, he found himself dreading what he knew would come next.

It was the same every time—the beast approaching at its own pace, as though it took pleasure in making Clay wait; reminding the trembling soldier who was in charge. That was when he most clearly sensed it. The icy cold breath on his skin. Not a normal cold, like the nighttime desert air. Not even a terrible cold, like the arctic chill that had inhabited his body during his team's winter training in the North Sea. This chill was different, a feeling he had long ago identified as otherworldly. The frigid air that was strangling his body was at a temperature that left no room for hope.

As he agonized, forced to his knees in the bed of the truck, the silent, unforgiving presence constricted him from all sides like a frozen python wrapped around his torso, his arms, his legs. It brought with it an inevitable, empty feeling as it crept closer to his heart. Soon, he was flooded with an overwhelming sense that he was alone and would soon cease to exist. Terrified, he understood that this was death. Visions of his childhood, his family, his unborn children played kaleidoscopically in his head, and he openly wept at the shame and failure that was his life. Then the demon showed the faces of the people he had dismissed from this world, and he fell to his side in a pronounced stage of suffering. Just when Clay was certain his last breath would be sucked from him, the beast loosened its grip, retrieved the visions from the whimpering man's head—and was gone.

CHAPTER 21 —

Stones and Bones

Surprisingly for Lilly Stein, it was turning into quite an interesting evening for she and her guest, Ravi Throckmorton. The pair had dined *al fresco* in Lilly's backyard, nestled comfortably between the citrus trees and gardenias, caressed by the perfumed air. After dinner Lilly had gone inside to grab some extra candles before returning to the carved, outdoor dinner table. They were now engaged in a mostly friendly game of Scrabble, which was being used partially as subtext to the finishing of their second bottle of wine.

In the kitchen sat a small pile of dishes and the leftover grilled flank steak. Despite Ravi's repeated offers to help clean up, Lilly had insisted the mess could wait until the morning. She didn't want to disrupt the infatuation that seemed to be developing in lockstep with her intoxication. Overhead, the black desert sky provided backdrop for a luminous crescent moon and a supporting cast of twinkling stars.

Ravi had caught her eye several years earlier, when he first started visiting her wellness center with his wife, Amanda. Of course Lilly had been romantically occupied with Aloysius at the time, so there had been no effort to encourage the spark. On their initial trip, the Throckmortons visited for a week, but they soon decided the long journey from India necessitated a minimum two-week stay. This year Ravi had booked the whole month of May and, in the wake of a messy divorce from Amanda, he had come alone.

He was handsome enough, with distinctive features born from an Indian mother and British father; but what really captured Lilly's attention was his carriage. Despite being two years her senior and a few inches shorter, he comported himself in a lithe manner characteristic of a much younger person. He was gracious to a fault, not conferring more attention on those whom might be able to help him in some way, nor favoring those who were more attractive. Having been raised on the subcontinent, he was a practicing Hindu and yogi, yet he never shoved it in people's faces. He had politely picked around the charred cow until Lilly realized what was going on and changed out the beef for extra portions of capellini and grilled vegetables.

Ravi was the most recent in a long line of esteemed Throckmorton archaeologists. The preceding generations had spent much of their time excavating sites in and around the Indus River Valley, an area that the family felt offered as much to the study of ancient hominid cultures as Mesopotamia did in the Tigris and Euphrates Basin. He was a family deviant in several ways, with two aberrations that were particularly pronounced. One, he was the first Throckmorton to have Indian blood; and, two, he had committed the heresy of choosing to get his doctorate in geology rather than archaeology. He described his choice as a personal preference for stones over bones.

Perhaps what Lilly found most intriguing about Ravi Throckmorton was the courageous and trailblazing work he was undertaking in his chosen field. Dr. Throckmorton had dedicated his professional life to the study of stones upon which people stubbed their toes. He was convinced that there was something about certain rocks, outside of their obvious shape and placement, that attracted human feet. His focus was to figure out what that something was and how to measure it. He wasn't so stupid as to think the stones were consciously waylaying people; it was more of a belief in an energy that made the seemingly random physical interaction more likely. A heretofore undiscovered relationship or pattern might be a better way to think about it. He rationalized that history was strewn with all sorts of misunderstood natural phenomena, the explanation of which men had assumed was random luck (or the work of the gods) before recognizing an underlying pattern or relationship that allowed for greater transparency. It was this perspective that pushed his research forward despite the ridicule. He was convinced he was the Galileo of his time.

As she finished her third glass of wine, Lilly gazed at her tiles, trying to figure out an impressive opening play to start their new game. Not used to losing, after two games she found herself trailing Ravi by a significant margin. Her usual opponent was Aloysius, and by nine P.M. he would either be nodding off or defending his play of some archaic word he claimed was a Latin derivative for which he should be credited. She wondered if he would approve of a gentleman caller at this time of the night.

Probably not, she decided.

After refilling each of their glasses with a healthy pour, she got on with her first move, a strategic play that would optimize her options and limit his. Avoiding eye contact, her heart picked up a beat as she laid out her tiles horizontally in the center of the board.

D-I-S-C-R-E-T-E

The definition of nonchalant, Ravi added up and announced her score before writing it down on the score pad. Lilly had always done the accounting with Aloysius, but Dr. Throckmorton had insisted on manning the pencil tonight. For some unknown reason Lilly had comfortably acquiesced.

Now his turn, Ravi pushed over three tiles—A-R-T—then slid them slowly and deliberately into place, vertically, under the T in DISCRETE.

T-A-R-T

He looked up into Lilly's eyes while announcing his score, a nearly imperceptible smile curling at the edges of his mouth. Lilly's heart jumped as she considered the implications.

Oh you clever, naughty man.

The play continued aggressively, each defending their positions while trying to set themselves up for the big score. Back and forth across the dictionary they battled, with Lilly focused maniacally on recovering ground, as she generally felt uncomfortable ceding dominance, especially to a man. From experience she had learned it was important to put "the testicled ones" in their place early, or else things could get quickly out of hand. Meanwhile their conversation meandered innocently enough around the weather, Arizona rock formations, and the difficulties of running a small business.

Then, out of the blue, Ravi dug a little deeper.

"Lilly, what's the most embarrassing situation you've ever found yourself in?"

There was a pregnant pause as she wondered if he knew about her institutionalization, and the events that had preceded it—especially her fixation with baring her breasts publicly as a political statement.

Maybe he's just trying to distract me from the game? she thought, shuffling her tiles to try and uncover a high-scoring word.

She decided to avoid the obvious confessional, and offered something more recent and benign.

"Hmm, that's a tough one," she answered airily, and with a laugh. "There are so many."

His interest piqued, Ravi lowered the wine glass from his lips, eyes trying hard not to drop below Lilly's chin as he waited for her to continue.

"Let's see...you know Mrs. Artemenko, the full-figured woman, right?"

"Yes." Ravi nodded. "Lovely woman, brunette. Big boned."

"Exactly. Well, just last month, on the first of April, I saw her kibitzing with a bunch of ladies outside the Pilates studio. They were all dressed in tight workout clothes. I walked right up to her, interrupted the group conversation, and asked her how she had lost so much weight. I immediately followed the first question by asking her what she had been doing to get that 'healthy glow.' I ended by telling her she looked—and I quote—'amazing.' "

Dr. Throckmorton was now intrigued. He had no idea where Lilly might be going with this.

"And then what?"

"I waited a few seconds and then shouted, 'April Fools'!' "

Feeling the blood rise in her cheeks as she relived the situation, she looked at her guest hopefully, not realizing the recollection would hurt so much.

The crickets chirped in the doldrums as Ravi considered the likelihood that he had never met someone with her level of intelligence who was so lacking in social guile. He suspected a mild form of Asperger's. Not sure how to respond, he tried not to giggle, but a little chuckle slipped out.

"Yeah," Lilly said, "I thought it was funny too, but no one else even smiled."

"Hmm, well…yes, I can see how a lot of people would miss the humor hiding in that one. It's quite…uh…subtle."

Lilly smiled at him but quickly returned to her tiles. *At least he understood the joke.* It seemed so many people just didn't "get" her.

The recollection of her *faux pas* reminded Lilly of exactly how much she missed Aloysius. He helped manage the front end of their business, mostly the interactions with clients. She managed the back end, things like purchasing, human resources, scheduling, and accounting. They were a complementary team.

Aloysius would never have made the mistake with Mrs. Artemenko, she thought, draining her wine glass before turning the tables on her guest. "How about you, Doc, what's your most embarrassing moment?"

Ravi took a deep breath to prepare for a long, wistful sigh. This was a topic he considered frequently. His fingers played mindlessly with his tiles while he stared off into space.

"Well Lilly, I guess some would say my whole career has pretty much been one long embarrassment. As you know, it's not easy championing the theory that biped-rock interaction is non-random, especially with no measurable evidence to support the idea. Basically, I've spent my adult life chasing Bigfoot."

Lilly nodded with sympathy.

"But you haven't lost your conviction?"

"Oh, no…please don't confuse me with my wife…ex-wife… although I don't blame her for leaving, the ridicule can be quite isolating at times."

"The world can be a lonely place for people who are different."

They both idly studied the board, recognizing that some of the night's magic had been lost, and not sure how to regain it. Gradually the draw of competition brought them back to the moment, allowing them to temporarily put aside their regrets.

After ten minutes of solemn scrabbling, an impulse overcame Lilly. She had a weird interest in humor that many would find tasteless, especially wordplays, and with the last of her better judgment receding along with her fourth glass of wine, she broke the silence with a joke she hoped he might appreciate.

"What do you call a man with no arms and no legs in your hot tub?"

Without missing a beat, Ravi reverted.

"Stu."

Breathing a sigh of relief, the riddles kept coming like an out-of-control case of the hiccups. The alcohol had obliterated her already abnormally weak impulse control.

"With a shovel in his back?"

He grinned.

"Doug?"

A smile erupted from her lips. *Oh, this could be good*, she thought. She knew she should stop but was so delighted to find a playmate she decided to just ride it into the ground and deal with the consequences then.

"On the edge of an embankment?"

"Cliff."

Like a young child in a petting zoo, she ran from kid to lamb, hugging each of her riddles with glee.

"In a bank vault?"

He had to think about that one for a moment.

"Rich?"

Simultaneously ecstatic that he knew the game but frustrated that she couldn't stump him, she had to dig deep. She wasn't using the basic names like Art, Bob, Matt, and Skip. No, these were second- and third derivative word plays, most of which she had invented—or so she thought.

"In a prophylactic?"

"Too easy."

"What then?"

"Dick. Rod. Johnson. You pick."

Pausing for a second, Lilly reached deep for an obscure favorite.

"What do you call a man with no arms and no legs who's rudely brief?"

Now it was Throckmorton's turn to hesitate. The pause gave Lilly hope that she had confounded him. Unfortunately for her, a moment later the doctor's eyes lit up with glee.

"Curt!"

"You're really good."

"I have a weird fascination with these…and of course, dead baby jokes."

"Me too!"

She stared at him like he was something she had been missing for a long time. He returned the compliment.

"I believe it's your move, Doctor."

As they refocused on the letters, she realized she needed an exquisite play to catch up in one fell swoop. A word that used the board and all the lousy tiles she had been accumulating. After another twenty minutes of competition, the bone pile was empty; they were each down to their last ten tiles. As her brain rifled through the permutations inherent in her letters, she decided she couldn't hold off peeing any longer. She excused herself and headed inside to the loo.

She called over her shoulder.

"No cheating!"

"I'm offended you feel I would be capable."

His reply brought a silent laugh and a smile to her lips. *Oh, I'm learning quickly not to underestimate your capabilities, Herr Doctor.*

After completing her business, she found herself looking in the mirror as she washed her hands. Her face…even in the subdued light of her bathroom….she just never got used to the aging. *Oh my God!* She shook her head, drying her hands quickly on a towel. *Who is that depressing person?* The alcohol helped her down the well-flogged path. *Let's face it, I'm a hag. What am I even doing here, playing the young schoolgirl?* Fighting off the negative comments, she finished with the towel then recited her mirror-hating mantra, trying hard to execute the U-turn: *There is a strong relationship between skin damage and the frequency of memorable experiences. If I were a man nobody would even notice.*

She hated the world for putting her, and all aging women, in the default position of self-loathing. Setting the towel back straight, she decided on a strong course of action. She walked into the living room, pulled out her favorite album from 1972, and placed it on the old turntable. Her reflection had reminded her she was no longer a princess, and as she turned up the volume, a feeling of semi-defiance accompanied her walk back outside to the dinner table.

Sitting down across from Ravi, she reconsidered her tiles, more convinced than ever that she could beat him.

Ravi perked up as the lyrics made their way outside.

"Is this John and Yoko?"

Lilly was shocked.

"You know this album?"

Ravi nodded vigorously.

"I was addicted to the Beatles. My mom and I shared that passion. When Yoko stole John away, most fans hated her, but I loved her influence on him. I used to play this record all the time. In fact this was my mom's favorite song…so powerful and obvious…she was about thirty-five years ahead of her time."

Woman is the nigger of the world…

"No way! Wait, Yoko or your mom?"

"I guess both, but I meant my mom."

"She sounds like an amazing woman."

"She was…she passed away three years ago."

Lilly tried to hide her dismay. *Oh my god, did I just kill the moment again?* She looked up from her tiles. "I'm sorry."

She didn't know what else to say. The crickets serenaded with disinterest.

As if on cue, the braying of the telephone interrupted the awkward moment. Usually Lilly wouldn't take calls after nine, but at that moment the ringing was a welcome break. She excused herself and headed back inside the house, turning down the stereo's volume before answering the phone.

"Hello?"

"Lilly, it's me," Aloysius hurriedly threw the syllables at her through the telephone. "It's been three days, I'm rotting in here, please come and get me, I'm truly sorry…I've learned my lesson."

"Who is this?"

"Lilly, please don't do this, I'm begging you."

"I talked to your son, he should be there to get you tomorrow."

"Keenan? Keenan is coming tomorrow?"

"Aloysius, this isn't working for me."

Lilly could practically hear Aloysius' eyes widen. "*What?* I make one mistake in nine years and you want to bail?"

"Bad word choice."

"You are a miserable human being."

Lilly laughed. "What? *Me?*"

"I've had a lot of time to think…while you left me here to rot…forced to eat Soylent Green and drink treated sewage water…."

Aloysius was gaining momentum.

"I'll give you five good reasons why you are the biggest asshole…. One…"

Lilly interrupted forcefully.

"Careful Aloysius, we know you're not good with math…wouldn't want to hurt yourself."

And with that she hung up and headed back out to her date. As she sat down in her seat, fuming, Ravi looked at her with upraised eyebrows.

"Anything I can do to help?"

Pausing for a second to consider the question, Lilly wondered about Ravi's view on what for her was a lifelong fascination.

"Why are men always obsessing about boobs?"

Again, Ravi wasn't sure of her intent with the non sequitur but was finding her quirks more charming than off-putting, so he decided to roll with.

"I'm okay with your gerund but take issue with your gender."

"What?"

"It's not just men…everyone's obsessed with boobs. Especially babies."

"Not like men."

"Well, I don't know…the number one cosmetic procedure in the world, by far, is breast augmentation. It's not men getting those surgeries."

"Yes, but women do it to attract men."

"That's a whole different ball of worms."

"You mean can of wax."

"Do I?"

The candlelight danced off of their faces, making them both look much younger. The moment caught them gazing at each other, searching for something in the past, until eventually they became uncomfortable and simultaneously looked away. Above their heads, the arbor supported the slow entwinement of bougainvillea and scented jasmine.

Lilly's distracted mind went back to her tiles…

Oh my God! There it is, staring me right in the face!

X-Y-L-O-P-H-O-N-E

Her heart racing, she searched the board to try and find a place where it would fit.

"I believe it's your turn, Lilly."

"What? Oh, yeah, thanks. Give me a sec."

After spending two minutes studying the board, she couldn't find a way to position the musical instrument within the constraints of the board. She saw one dangling *S* with enough room around it, but there was no *S* in XYLOPHONE. There was a risky option, which involved legging into it over two moves, but she would need to use the spare *E* she had been hoarding. It would require spelling S-E-X off of the dangling *S* and hope he didn't use the ensuing exposed *X* with his turn. If he left the *X* open, she could then use it to spell XYLOPHONE *and* finish the game with no tiles. But if he blocked her by using the *X* then she was hosed—stuck with all of her useless letters. She counted up her theoretical points (assuming the plan worked) and concluded that if things went well it would put her slightly ahead of him—if, of course, she could lay down XYLOPHONE on top of SEX.

Lilly now turned her thoughts to the real dilemma.

Does a proper lady play such a suggestive word when in the presence of a proper man? A proper man, who is unchaperoned, in the lady's quarters, after ten P.M. and two bottles of wine?

It took only a second for her competitive instinct to make quick road kill of her primness. She added the *E* and *X* to the dangling *S*.

S-E-X

Now she clearly had his attention.

Not only am I going to beat him, she divined with rare satisfaction, *but I'm going to get there by distracting him with his own libido.*

Lilly was vibrating with anticipation. Whatever a body does when the brain comes up with a stroke of genius, her body was doing it. The seconds felt agonizingly long as she waited for his play, but she used the time to consider how one should celebrate in this situation. Would taunting be too offensive?

She decided she would play it cool, go all Vince Lombardi on him and act like she'd been there before.

Finally, after what seemed like forever, he pushed out eight of his ten tiles. He slowly advanced them in a cluster in the direction of the *X* she had laid down.

Lilly was stunned. **No! Not her X!**

Then, slowly, he built a word around the *X* she had left dangling off of SEX.

E-X-C-E-L-L-E-N-T

After laying down his tiles, he got up slowly, without a word, and humbly made his way to the kitchen. This was his version of a mic drop.

Stunned to have the rug so abruptly pulled out from under her, Lilly wasn't sure her body was prepared to move. The chemicals that had been accumulating in anticipation of victory were now redirecting themselves, as the words on the Scrabble board suggested something that her intuitive self seemed to be quite open to. His voice called out to her from the open kitchen window.

"Where can I find an apron? I'd like to get this place tidied up a bit before we move on to…s-s-something…else."

She wondered if he had a penis, and then decided that even if he didn't she could still love him.

Before she could get it together enough to help in the kitchen, Ravi had already found the apron and worked his way through most of the dishes. There were only two of them for dinner, so it wasn't a lot. As he wiped the countertops and started the dishwasher, she coaxed Al Green out of the speakers. Grabbing what was left of the wine, she turned out the lights, and started climbing the stairs to her bedroom. The moon shone through the skylight over the stairwell, giving everything a luminescent glow. Before she reached the top of the stairs, she turned to see him waiting in the shadows on the bottom landing, his teeth shining up through the darkness. She smiled at him, put the bottle seductively to her lips, and let the juice linger on her tongue before swallowing.

"One more riddle, clever man…"

"Okay."

"What do you call a man with no arms and no legs getting blown by a bagpiper?"

"What do I win if I get it right?"

"You're a smart boy, you'll figure it out."

He climbed the stairs, gently put his arms around her, and nestled his mouth against her neck. She could feel his moist breath against her sensitive skin, and he could feel her shiver.

"Reed."

CHAPTER 22 —

The Prodigal Son

All temptation, no soul.

That's what Clay thought as he hit the roaring lights on the outskirts of the Las Vegas strip. It was ironic, he noted, because most of the American West was the exact opposite. He had sequestered himself for over a year, mostly camping in the desert, during which time he had started journaling about his life experiences. He liked to think of his writing as sort of an autobiographical fiction. He thought he might some day turn it into a book, but he was at a loss for a title. But maybe that was it?

All Temptation, No Soul

He wondered whether it would do. The simple contemplation was quickly overwhelmed by the sensory overload of the "come hither" artifice glaring through his windshield.

Shit, he thought, watching acres of neon flash by. *It's not even noon. The power bill alone must be crazy.*

A vision of the Hoover Dam (and all the low-cost hydroelectric energy it generated) satisfactorily completed the equation in his head.

A near constant paranoia had kept him from interacting with more than a handful of people since finishing the job in La Jolla. As he rolled down Las Vegas Boulevard in his battered Ford pick-up, the imposition of modernity and the great unwashed had an unsettling effect on his previously disengaged mind. His recent writing efforts had forced him to ruminate on his origins, and those swirling wisps, interlaced with his retirement goals, had him romanticizing about a return to a life with his family—a return home, to a place where he would grow old with his parents and brothers—all of them sharing their lives and offspring.

A variant on his theoretical book title wandered into the internal conversation.

All Facade, No Soul

After considering both titles briefly, he decided he wasn't happy with either and moved on to the task at hand. Clay had an agenda and needed some help. It had been about twenty-five years since he had seen his dad, and he wondered if they would recognize each other.

"Al-Loy-Cyrus Barton! Front and center…you've made bail."

Hopping to his feet with the spryness of a forty-year old, Aloysius was so happy to be sprung that he didn't even correct the guard's mangling of his name. In an unappreciated nod to *Cool Hand Luke*, he did his best Paul Newman impersonation.

"Shaking the bush, boss!"

Ignoring the glaring artificial light of the small anteroom, Aloysius quickly signed the paperwork that was attached to the clipboard in front of him. He then gathered all of the possessions that had been pushed at him through the small aperture at the bottom of the bullet-proof glass. He could barely recall their confiscation four days previous. Peering at the bored, uniformed official seated on the other side of the transparent barrier, he asked if their business was completed.

"You're good," came the response through the electronic grill.

Puzzled by the statement, Aloysius offered a cheery response.

"I'd like to think so, but external confirmation is always welcome."

The two men stared at each other for a few confusing seconds. Finally, the younger one reached under his desk and buzzed open the door directly behind the older, all the while shaking his head and using his other hand to point the way. Bewildered by their interaction, Aloysius turned and moved into an outer space that served as both reception and waiting area. The windows of the room allowed a filtered advancement of the mid-morning desert glow, a natural phenomenon that he embraced with the attentiveness of a sunflower. He had never before been so aware of the deficiencies of fluorescent light. The chicken wire-impregnated glass offered a glimpse of arid landscape that exerted a gravitational pull on his soul, akin to what he imagined those nearing death must feel from heaven.

He scanned the room for Keenan, expecting his boy to be in a suit (or at least sport coat and slacks), given he probably had to rush away from his job when he heard his father needed him. Being a priority for his successful son, especially in a context where others could see them together, gave him a sense of pride that he hadn't expected to feel so strongly. After several sweeps of the room, the tendrils of trepidation started insinuating disappointment, as no one in the sparse crowd was dressed with even a slight nod to formality.

He started wondering who had arranged for his release, and considered his friends in Carefree. Visions of his voluntary ejection from

Skye's class flashed through his brain, and he yearned for a solid hour of yoga to get him back into balance. As he thought about Downward Dog, he remembered the lower back pain that had triggered his whole misadventure, and wondered about its absence.

His mind quickly returned to his current conundrum. The suspense that accompanied the continuing anonymity of his benefactor was building.

Maybe Lilly? he thought. *God, that would be so fantastic! We could just go back to the way it was…but the beating she would give me for being so stupid!*

He considered another option.

What if it's the diamond miner whom I cracked over the head with a long neck Bud? That would mean the potential for a different kind of beating.

His eyes searched furiously, trying to match faces to his mental lineup, but he couldn't remember what any of the patrons at the Quaking Aspen looked like, except, of course, for the opthalmologically disfigured barkeep.

Just as he was starting to panic, a voice sounded from his four o'clock.

"Hey Dad."

Surprised by the familiar timbre of the quiet greeting, Aloysius turned to the source. He was at a momentary loss. He thought he recognized the face of the man standing before him, but there was a hardness that didn't fit. The inability to self-diagnose dementia again crossed his mind. The shorter man's somewhat intimidating veneer was exaggerated by several scars and a salt-and-pepper, short-cropped beard that extended from his chin up the sides of his face where it then spread out and covered the crown of his head. The familiar stranger shyly held a dusty, felt cowboy hat in both gnarled hands but wasn't afraid to return his father's stare.

It took another moment before Aloysius was certain.

"Clay?"

The younger man was quiet for an awkward moment, as if his mind was taking a breath. He was comfortable with the silence.

"Yeah, Dad, it's me."

If anybody had been watching, they would've thought the scene sweet. The middle-aged cowboy helping the elderly man into the aging pick-up then carefully securing the lap belt before gently pushing the door shut. A tenderness was conveyed by the younger man's motions that belied the rough exterior of the wrangler and his truck. The elder man's Elvis jumpsuit and sandals were a curiosity, but more in an endearing than a creepy way, like a young boy out parading his Spider-Man costume the day before Halloween. Clay rounded the back of the truck and headed toward the driver's side, wondering what his father was thinking as he climbed behind the wheel. He turned the key in the ignition, maneuvered out of the parking lot, and started heading south, towards the freeway that would take them to Carefree.

Both men had no idea where to start. Neither felt apology nor gratitude seemed appropriate. Finally Aloysius held out what he thought was an olive branch.

"I really regret that the circumstances of our reunion aren't more flattering for me."

"It's okay, Dad, it's not that different from what I expected."

"No, Clay, I'm not like that anymore. I've changed…I'm…a better man…"

Clay waved him off.

"Happy to be able to help. No need for an explanation."

Still feeling the need to justify his behavior, Aloysius ignored Clay's indifference and continued with his case.

"I don't know what compelled me…it's like this demon…that I thought I had under control…just took over and…it's so hard to explain…I'm not sure I even understand."

Clay looked straight ahead with a brief, crooked, resigned smile.

"We're all just rats lookin' for a lever, Dad. Some of us are just better at hidin' it."

First Aloysius considered the veracity of the provocative statement and then the intent. He decided he should feel only mildly offended.

"Clay, how'd you know where I was?"

"It wasn't hard, Dad," Clay offered a curt smile. "Your name and picture are plastered all over the internet. I only had to make a few calls before I found your partner—Lilly, right?"

With upraised eyebrows, Clay paused here to glance at his father. Aloysius wasn't sure what to say.

"Anyway, nice lady. She told me she was coming to bail you out today. I told her not to bother, that I wanted to do it."

Keeping his eyes on the road, Clay then reached over and turned up the stereo, indicating the end of the conversation. He was used to being alone and wasn't looking forward to explaining the last twenty-five years. The distinctive rasp of Lucinda Williams carried them across the desert in an embrace of heartbroken loneliness.

After ten minutes without conversation, Aloysius could no longer stand the suspense.

"Clay, what is going on? Why are you here? Where have you been? Where are you taking me?"

Clay considered the questions independently but immediately saw they were stacked on top of each other like rocks in a fragile cairn: each one depending on the other for relevance. He was ready for the inquiry, knew it was coming, but would answer in his own time, for his own—and his father's—sake.

He reached back into a small Styrofoam cooler, pulled a soda out of the surrounding ice, and silently offered the chilled can to his dad. With a cursory shake of his head, Aloysius turned him down, his eyes still hoping for answers. Steering with his knees positioned at four and eight o'clock, Clay used both hands to pop the top of the bright red Coke; then he took a long pull of caffeine and sugar, his first of the day. The effervescence bubbled across his tongue—his taste buds exploded in an ecstasy of welcome. He could have had one earlier, but there were times when he liked to manufacture an artificial scarcity to amplify certain sensations. He knew from experience that each successive gulp would register less impressively, so he took his time savoring the pleasure, observing his biological response with interest.

Funny how quickly the taste buds adjust to a new indulgence, he mused to himself, even as the fireworks in his mouth reached their peak. *They always require more just to reach the previous level of satisfaction.*

This reminder of the temporary nature of things brought an audible sigh as he considered what came next. Returning both hands to the wheel, he let the can rest between his denim-clad thighs then started with his own interrogation.

"Dad, do you believe in karma?"

Aloysius considered the question briefly before answering. He understood intuitively that the man driving the car was not one to waste words.

"Sometimes. Mostly when I'm doing something good."

"What about when you're doing something bad?"

Aloysius started feeling a little defensive—paranoid, even—as he looked out at the expanse of barren wasteland lying just beyond the windshield. He wondered where this line of inquiry—and Clay's truck—were headed. Out of the corner of his eye the corded arms of his eldest son registered as extremely capable. *Is Clay asking about himself,* he wondered. *Or is he asking about me…or just about people in general?*

The paterfamilias chose his words carefully as he considered his past transgressions. He tried not to be too committal.

"When I'm doing something bad, I think karma and conscience serve the same purpose."

Clay quietly nodded, letting the words sink in as the father waited for what came next.

"Do you have a conscience?"

Though the truck was assembled decades before cars were loaded with electronic gadgets, Aloysius felt like someone had just turned his theoretical seat warmer to *high*. He realized he was trapped, but he also recognized he didn't yet have enough information to conclude he was in danger. He decided not to make a scene; instead, he would try to mollify.

"I'd like to think…much more so now…but, maybe, when you were younger, some might say I was lacking in that area."

Again the long pause. Clay digested the words one by one. Aloysius couldn't recall a time when he had more greatly desired air-conditioning. The sweat started pouring off of him.

"What about choice? Do you believe we choose how to behave?"

Feeling like he was walking in a minefield, Aloysius interpreted the question as an academic one to try and push the paranoid thoughts away.

"Sometimes…mostly, I guess. Our whole criminal justice system is built on that concept, so I suppose it better be true."

Clay took a deep breath. Then he removed his well-worn hat and tossed it up on the dashboard between them. Again, Aloysius noted the coiled strength, wrapped in sun-damaged skin, poised to burst forth at a moment's notice. The assassin turned down the radio, first shaking then lightly nodding his head. Finally, with his eyes locked on the road, he revealed why he had come.

"Dad, someone's trying to kill Keno."

CHAPTER 23 —

A Wolf at the Door

Loneliness was mostly what she felt. Her children were separating—no longer seeming to really need or want her help—never offering to confide in her with any details of their lives. Her attempts at physical contact, simple things like hugs (which she desperately needed from her babies) were rebuffed with an indifference that sometimes carried a tone of annoyance. She had been told to expect this stage, that when her boys reached adolescence (aka "assholescence" by their similarly plighted friends) it would be challenging. But nothing could have prepared her for the experience of having her offspring greet her attempts at intimacy with looks of revulsion.

Her other natural source of solace, her husband Keno, was getting more and more consumed by his role at work. During the diminishing times when he was with her physically, his mind was too distracted by the challenges of his position—challenges that were exaggerated by the constant presence of his Personal Digital Assistant. The invasions had gone beyond boorish, as Keno had recently started Blackberrying during meals. The first time he had whipped out the vibrating electronic gadget (over a plate of homemade lasagna), she had immediately protested, sensing a precedent-setting violation of sacred ground. He had overruled her by playing the "it's an emergency" card, and then used that beachhead to expand his use at the dinner table from "not at all" to "frequent." With their boys regularly eating at different times and venues, she often found herself preparing and eating complete meals at home without conversing with another human being. She seemed to be the only one bothered by this.

Not surprisingly, given their lack of intellectual sharing, the sex had become predictable and methodical. There were times when her need had accumulated to the point that he could suck an orgasm out of her, but she would more frequently fake it just so she could end the whole charade. Usually on those nights she would fall asleep resenting the fact that he couldn't tell the difference.

The silver lining of her husband's increasing obsession with work was that the money was getting easier and easier. This allowed her the means and time to pamper herself, and to some extent she did it with an eye on vengeance. *Ignore me at your own peril*, she seemed to be saying while enthusiastically buying a new German car or some artwork she knew Keno would find unnecessary and expensive. They both probably should've recognized her cry for help, but no one was really paying attention. The momentum of the Marin herd held them firmly in its grasp.

Like so many before them who had found themselves newly wealthy, they integrated (with a sense of self-congratulation) into the socioeconomic demographic residing immediately above them. With a sense of belonging (and without a second thought), they left behind their friends in the lower strata and bought a bigger house with more land and taller fences. Though not their intention, all of this upward mobility ended up isolating Lola from regular intercourse with the world. Her "to do" list now consisted mainly of sporadic, whimsical calendar entries like: *Junior League/SF Opera Charity Auction* or *Mud w/Rhonda@Sonoma Mission Inn.*

She did have a compact team of small brown persons (the managing of whom she found very tedious) who came and did all the menial tasks that had previously kept her days partially occupied. Most of these people were recent immigrants who struggled with English and couldn't relate to any of her problems.

She was adrift, with no purpose, and desperately needed to share her thoughts with someone. Being a psychology major, she started considering the destabilizing effect that an overwhelmingly abundant environment had on a human brain that was hardwired for scarcity.

Her closest friend and doubles partner, Elise Haversham, had just gotten a divorce from her venture capitalist husband, and so it made sense that Lola would start spending more time with her, as both their families were suffering through a centrifugal disruption.

After twenty-five years of marriage, and the departure of their last child to college, Elise had calculated that living as a single woman with half of her husband's assets would be a lot more invigorating than waiting at home for a man who showed less and less interest in her. She had been having an ongoing affair with their tennis professional before the divorce, and now, after gaining independence, Elise regularly shared (with Lola) lurid details about the continuing naughtiness. The elixir of frequent sex with a "younger man who was eager" was her oft-repeated enthusiasm. Recently, following an afternoon of fun tennis and an early G&T, Elise had testified to Lola and their two vanquished opponents about the health benefits of polyamory. The descriptions that Elise brought to her proselytizing were so convincing that she had all of the women's rapt attention. The opposing duo would return home that evening with a renewed intolerance for any marital behavior that could be interpreted as lacking focus. Elise's charisma was having a particularly strong influence on the younger Lola.

Despite all of these destabilizing crosscurrents, Lola was able to mostly stay monogamous. But there were times when her husband was particularly absent (especially during long business trips) when she felt abandoned and vulnerable to Wolfgang's advances. She never actually invited him, it was more that he sensed a slight weakening in her defenses and would then somehow materialize in a sort of intimate but clever way that always allowed her plausible deniability.

This tormented pattern had been going on for the last twelve months, but Lola couldn't possibly confide in any one. She always felt incredibly shameful following the sessions, swearing that each time would be the last. Her problem was that the moments when Wolfgang was fucking her were so intensely raw that the sensations of them coupling had become seared into her cerebral hard drive. She couldn't help but allow her thoughts to return and linger on those memories, especially when she was feeling particularly neglected.

Alone again, Lola turned the key that unlocked the front door, comforted by the sound of the dog on the other side. As her pumps clicked over the wooden parquet of the foyer, she wondered about her decision to hurry home to the echoes. She had been out for dinner and drinks with Elise, and had enjoyed the attention of the men who had approached them at the bar. Following a course of prudence, she had declined Elise's invitation for a later evening of possibilities, dragged herself out of the bar, and pointed the family's Mercedes wagon to her empty house.

With the boys away at soccer camp and Keno gone for a week to oversee the opening of the new Portland office, she wondered what *exactly* her men were doing at that moment. She suspected her kids were up to some form of shenanigans, but that was expected from teenagers, and she took comfort in knowing that at least they were in a safe environment. It was Keno she was most worried about; her mind couldn't help but recall that they had met so many years ago in a bar. They had been introduced by mutual friends at the time, so she had some idea that he wasn't a psychopath. Keno had been quite charming and had intrigued her from the outset, so much so that he had convinced her to come home with him that first night, although she hadn't allowed him to completely close the deal. Now, twenty-six years later, with Keno over five hundred miles away, her brain was focused on the fact that her missing husband was handsome, resourceful, and likely in an environment similar to the one in which they had first met. More specifically, she pictured him in the middle of an upscale vodka print ad (most likely a bar) featuring gorgeous people who were all laughing and positioned in ways that implied a forthcoming intimacy. The fact that he hadn't made the effort to contact her that evening only added to a frayed emotional state that had her vacillating between worry and irritation. As her neuroses allowed the narrative to move in a troubling direction, she poured herself a full glass of Pinot, kicked off her heels, and headed over to the couch and her laptop. Logging on to Facebook, she glanced through her notifications and found nothing of interest. Moving away from Facebook, the *photos* icon was calling to her, and she started sorting through the images, looking for a recent twilight shot Keno had taken of her during their vacation in Baja. Ten days of surfing and long walks on the beach had whipped her tanned body into bikini shape, and she liked the way the sunset had cast her skin in a honey glow. She felt the picture was actually quite flattering in a smoldering sort of way, with dark red lipstick and mascara having been applied right before the shot. When she found the photo, she used two fingers to enlarge and shift the perspective, taking a close-up look at all the strategic body parts. When satisfied that everything had passed muster, she uploaded the photo to her Facebook timeline and posted it with the caption "MISSING MY BOYS!" She then finished the wine, climbed up to her bedroom, and let the smoke signal waft.

Nearly three thousand miles away, Wolfgang sat in an upscale Miami bar, entertaining two young women while simultaneously contemplating his fifth boilermaker. As he took a big gulp from the beer, he pulled the vibrating phone out of his pocket. Reading Lola's post, he immediately knew what it meant. Nearly quivering with anticipation, he started getting ready to implement the next phase of his plan. A sense of urgency overcame him as he depth-charged the whiskey, quaffed the whole concoction, and excused himself. A half hour later Wolfgang was smiling to himself as he pulled into the hotel garage. He was happily working through his plan and had not given a second thought to the girls back at the bar (whom he had stuck with the bill).

CHAPTER 24 —

The Trap

Viewing the room through her eyes, he realized he was trying too hard.

*Too risky…way over the top…not my usual **modus operandi**.*

Wolfgang fretted that she would smell a trap and be scared away. Experience had taught him that his best strategy for capturing the opposite sex was a casual indifference, not overt pandering. He needed to get her to instinctually trust him, and to do that he had to play it cool.

Through the windows he could see the tendrils of fog reaching eastward, across San Francisco Bay, lazily trying to connect the Golden Gate and Bay Bridges. He looked longingly first at the water and then at the picturesque hills and buildings beyond the incoming ghosts. He imagined himself sailing through windblown spray under the watchful sentry of the Transamerica Pyramid. The mental image was so real that he could taste the brine rolling down his cheeks and sliding into his mouth. Catching himself in his daydream, he shook his head and returned his attention to the bed in front of him.

Yes, definitely too much….

He quickly relieved the pillow of the modest weight of the Tiffany box and slipped it into his coat pocket. At the end of the evening, if all went well, he would reward her with the contents hidden inside the robin's egg-blue packaging. The diamond bracelet was something she had coveted but hadn't felt right purchasing for herself. Keno had been predictably distracted during the times she had dropped hints. Wolfgang hoped she would be impressed that he had been paying attention.

Though she had agreed only to drinks, he was expecting more and hence had booked the honeymoon suite at the Casa Madrona Hotel in Sausalito. A recent remodel had the inn feeling vibrant, but not so much so that it diminished the romantic Old World feel of a rambling Italian villa. The multi-level architecture clung to the hills that thrust out of Richardson Bay, giving each room not only a view but also a feeling of privacy. The hotel was a short drive from her home…but still far enough away to allow Lola a degree of anonymity. Having stayed in the suite before, Wolfgang knew the bedroom had all the features necessary to stage his plan.

They were scheduled to meet at the hotel's award-winning restaurant, La Petite Mort, which he thought couldn't have been better named, given the nature of his plans. They had arranged to meet for drinks at six o'clock, nothing too scandalous if their rendezvous were ever scrutinized. Realizing that the names of the hotel and the restaurant were inconsistent linguistically, he scoffed at the American longing for aristocracy, using European references to try and imply a refinement that was undeserved.

Despite all their money, he thought, shaking his head, *the mutts still can't buy breeding and sophistication.*

Not wanting to be late, he also needed to make sure everything was in place, so he took one final visual tour. Thoughtfully positioned around the suite were several items he knew Lola loved or craved, and the smells alone were delicious. White lilies occupied two vases on each side of the four-poster bed. The sublime fragrance of the blossoms was engaged in an olfactory foreplay with three thick, cinnamon-scented rouge candles.

It had taken significant effort, but he had obtained a liter of Alto Cielo mezcal from Mexico City. During a recent vacation Lola had raved about the elixir on a social media site that he had been cyberstalking. The bottle of fermented agave was on display atop the credenza that supported the TV.

Perched two feet to the left of the mezcal, atop a small, Sterno flame, was a fondue pot filled with molten, dark chocolate. A silver tray protected the mahogany cabinet from the heat, and the whole set-up was accessorized not with skewers but rather with a one-inch wide paintbrush. Wolfgang had purchased the brush specifically for spreading the sticky chocolate on Lola's skin.

Sitting on the bedside table farthest from the door, and intended to be used in a blindfolded guessing game, was a glass bowl filled with differently textured and uniquely flavored mouth-sized morsels. A linen napkin lay over the top. A kiwi and banana peeked out from under the white cloth.

A silk, hand-painted kimono with two fluffy slippers in attendance (in case Lola's feet got cold) were waiting in the warmly paneled tile-and-cedar bathroom.

As a backup if Lola wasn't in the mood for mezcal, Wolfgang had a bottle of Dom Pérignon chilling in an ice bucket, which rested under the window nearest the bed. It was silly in its simplicity; but to a great extent his strategy depended on the time-tested goal of getting Lola drunk. Before he could spring his trap, she had to trust him enough to lose her inhibitions. He had to make her feel *safe*. If he could just nurse her along to that point, then by the time she realized that he had changed the rules of engagement it would be too late.

As he compulsively wandered the room making last-minute

adjustments, he passed the fondue bowl, dipped one finger into the chocolate, and then placed the gooey treat in his mouth. He needed to make sure it wasn't too hot for Lola's most-delicate areas.

Is it still too much? he thought, enjoying the chocolate. *Should I tone it down some more?*

He went over to each of the candles and blew them out before hiding them on the windowsill behind the curtains.

He decided to keep the flame under the chocolate burning, but made sure the whole concoction was positioned well away from anything flammable. The final tidying came when he moved the glass bowl filled with textured morsels under the bedside table.

Still accessible, he reasoned, *but not so obvious.*

A noticeable amount of blood started redirecting itself towards the contents of his trousers as he did a last inspection of the most important components of his plan. Strategically hidden in coils under the duvet were four braided, silk lengths of cord that were finished in slipknots and secured to each of the four bedposts. Under one of the pillows, standing at attention next to the extra-large velvet-and-flannel eye mask, was a delicately textured, impressively sized, battery operated vibrator. In three separate locations, including directly over the bed, he had hidden miniature, high-definition cameras equipped with infrared capabilities. These would be used to capture their romp electronically, regardless of the level of ambient light. As he thought through the different ways the seduction could play out, he hoped he would never have to publicly release the sex tape in which Lola would star, but he had also grown tired of being a passive player in what he viewed as a budding relationship. The cameras would allow him to accelerate the frequency of their meetings, which, he was certain, would open her eyes to the inevitability of their long-term union.

When he was sure he had the trap set just right, Wolfgang used his iPod to dial up a playlist of what he knew to be Lola's favorite songs, including a heavy dose of Roxy Music and Nora Jones. He checked his watch to keep from being too late; then, he went down to La Petite Mort to meet her for drinks.

"So, Wolfgang, what brings you to San Francisco?"

Even though his intentions were obvious, her conscience required a credible commitment to keeping up the pretenses of their charade, right up to the moment they began grinding like wild animals. Besides, she told herself, she had yet to decide how far she would allow their date to go, although her choice of undergarments and removal of all traces of below-the-waist hair indicated her serious bias. Feeling in control, she knew what he wanted; she would probably reward him if he played by her rules.

Wolfgang understood he needed to be respectful, and hence he accepted Lola's outward formality without hesitation. He was willing to provide whatever she required to get there. Picking up his oversized wine glass, he swirled the red intoxicant before lazily smelling, sipping, and then returning the goblet to the table. The goal was to convey a self-indulgent sense of nonchalance before answering her question.

"Well, we're considering loaning some of our Frida pieces to the SFMoMA, and during the negotiations they offered me a board seat. So...I thought I should at least come out and meet some of the board members before deciding."

It wasn't a complete lie. His family did control two pieces of Frida Kahlo's more obscure work, but he didn't intend to meet with anybody from the SFMoMA, and a board seat wasn't being offered. He chose the local museum (and Frida) because he hoped to impress, but he also wanted to introduce a context of passion and infidelity wrapped in the fabric of artistic tolerance. As a bonus, he thought the legend of Frida implied a unique cohabitation of sexual freedom and feminism.

Lola saw through her lover's attempts, but was still influenced by the suggestion.

"I don't think of Frida's work as being 'modern'? More Mexican folk-artsy?"

"It's a grey area. Maybe magical realist? It probably won't surprise you to hear that the SFMoMA has commercial motivations, and Frida is hot now, so…"

"Aha, sort of a corollary to the old adage that success has many parents, but failure is an orphan."

"Exactly."

"Do you think if Moe from the Three Stooges had done a cubist doodling modern museums would want to display it?"

"If they thought it would fill the seats."

They both laughed at the idea that the self-important, supposedly incorruptible world of art curators was not at all above money-grubbing.

"I suppose they would call it being 'pragmatic'…or…'open-minded.'"

"Yes, I think that rolls off the tongue better than 'mercenary,' don't you?"

She glanced down at her smooth legs pouring out of the dark blue fabric and admired their tone as if they belonged to someone else. Absentmindedly, she picked at a stray thread at the hemline of her skirt then looked past her ankles to see her feet disappearing into the navy pumps she had purchased just for their meeting.

The evening was unusual. The sun was keeping the fog from totally enveloping the waterfront. With each passing minute the late-day shadows pushed to erase the natural light that glistened across the bay. Lola took a big gulp from her drink. She was luxuriating in the setting, feeling like she belonged with the lively crowd. It had been a while since she had been in an upscale restaurant, enjoying the attention of an attractive male companion, with the evening's outcome undetermined.

"*Bonjour*. Perhaps I can share tonight's specials with you, and answer any questions you might have about the menu?"

Lola had noticed their young waiter the moment she entered the restaurant. He was dark and moved like a dancer, with a round, muscular rear that stretched the back of his tailored pants under his tapered waist. His teeth were almost glowing in contrast to his skin, and he had a knowing sparkle to his eyes. When he had seated them and taken their drink orders she noticed his gaze lingered for a moment too long on her cleavage before he caught himself and focused on her face. At first she thought he was too beautiful and too well put together to not be gay, but now she wasn't so sure. Her eyes flirted with his, before she smiled and crossed her naked legs under her short business skirt. She was feeling confident and in control, and offered a flirtatious greeting.

"*Bonjour, beau garcon...*"

She didn't want Wolfgang to think she would be staying long.

"...no need on menus, we're not eating...just enjoying a quick round of drinks."

Wolfgang was pretty sure that at that moment, in that light, she was the sexiest creature on the planet. With his poker face intact, he immediately agreed with her on the menus, not wanting to seem needy or disappointed.

"Yes, sorry, only drinks. Gotta be an early night."

Before their server could politely retreat, Wolfgang had a second thought.

"Wait…I believe Jean-Luc is your new executive chef? I'd love to hear what he's cooking up tonight…I loved his creations when he was at French Laundry, particularly his starters…Also, another round of the same."

His fingers pointed nonchalantly at their wine glasses. He thought he had caught Lola staring a bit too hungrily at the man-child who was poised at attention between them. He wasn't sure…it was just a glimpse.

"Very good, sir. Yes, Jean-Luc is worth changing your plans for… you won't be disappointed. It's the Malbec you're both enjoying?"

"Yes, please, the Malbec."

As the waiter started meandering through the specials with the appropriate degree of hyperbole, Wolfgang immediately interrupted him, trying to entice Lola with something that wouldn't imply too much of a commitment.

"Lola, do you still enjoy a fresh bruschetta?"

Lola casually drained her glass and decided to have some fun. The wine had her feeling flirtatious, and she couldn't recall the last time she had been ogled by a man nearly half her age. She shifted her positioning while sarcastically answering Wolfgang's question.

"Bruschetta? In a French restaurant headlining the famous Jean-Luc? It's a bit like asking Babe Ruth to bunt with the bases loaded, don't you think?"

The young man laughed but Wolfgang was confused.

"Who's Babe Ruth?"

"Really?"

Their waiter behaved as his title implied he should, while Wolfgang tried to regain his footing.

"Apparently, I've committed some sort of unintentional social blunder?"

"Let's leave our parents out of this."

Wolfgang was now completely lost, and Lola was thinking about how comfortable her time with Keno was.

With a smile on his face, the server took the ongoing pause to continue his menu debriefing. Wolfgang scrambled mentally to try and recapture their moment.

Pulling her hair up and behind her in a ponytail, Lola arched her back and removed the wool, pin-striped jacket that matched her skirt, carefully draping it over the back of her chair. Still glowing from her workout two hours earlier, the whole maneuver allowed her form-fitting, silk blouse to stretch tightly across her upper body, displaying not only the suppleness of her torso but also the assets that were being supported by her push-up *bandeau*. Despite his efforts at professionalism, the *garçon's* libido betrayed him, and he fumbled the rehearsed monologue several times during Lola's show. Lola made a mental note to undo at least one more blouse button. Thoughts of her husband quickly drifted out of sight.

Why not live a little, let the girls breathe? In a few more years no one will even give me a second look. At my age, I'm surprised I'm showing up on this boy's radar at all....

Wolfgang, taking it all in, was starting to feel better about the direction the evening was going. He considered her contentiousness to be just a brief speed bump. As he asked the young man if the oysters were fresh from Tomales Bay, he made some minor additions to his original plan and then, a few minutes later, followed the waiter towards the kitchen. When he returned with two more glasses of wine the sun had fully set, and the restaurant was buzzing with a bevy of young, available clientele. He placed the wine glasses on the table and then stepped behind Lola to turn up the space heater positioned well overhead. Making sure she was warm, he touched her shoulder in passing before returning to his seat across from her.

"Do you think you could help me if I ordered a dozen oysters?"

He smiled at her, and she returned the favor.

"You know I have a weakness for local oysters."

Embracing the silence, he took a deep breath and let the night and wine work their magic.

CHAPTER 25 —

Sprung

The suite was swimming with the scent of lilies and cinnamon intermingled with the fertile, intoxicating smells of carnally engaged adults. The pressed, white cotton sheets were deliciously bunched around a nearly naked Lola, who was partially secured by the silk cords that attached each of her wrists to the uppermost bedposts. The alcohol had done its job, making it easy to entice Lola to first stay for some food, then join Wolfgang in his room for a sip of mezcal.

So far, Wolfgang had brought her along masterfully, pressing when the opportunities presented themselves then retreating when he sensed resistance. He knew patience was required to gain confidence, and eventually, access. It seemed to him to be very similar to training an easily frightened mare.

She was in a semi-vulnerable, supine position, and soon Wolfgang had her sampling treats from behind a blindfold while he slowly appropriated her clothes. They had agreed on a safe word before she had allowed the first wrist to be tied, and with that agreement there had been a growing sense of trust. She had tested his fidelity several times by invoking the safe word (*PUMPKIN*), and each time he had promptly released her from the restraints. This degree of compliance had allowed her to comfortably submit to his game, and although not without reservations, she found herself starting to enjoy the passive role. The unpredictability inherent in her subservience put her in a state of exaggerated sensitivity; the current level of her arousal was far higher than what she had recently been able to achieve during her intimate moments with Keno. She was grateful that Wolfgang was creative enough to provide her with an interesting variety of tastes and textures and not just an unimaginative assortment of penis-shaped foods.

The game they were playing was simple. Wolfgang would feed her tasties out of the bowl he had prepared, and if she didn't describe the morsel with perfect accuracy and diction, he would take a piece of her clothing. Of course he was the arbiter. Thus Lola was rapidly becoming undressed. The indulgent eye mask was in place. It served to heighten her non-visual senses but kept Lola from appreciating the starlit sky pushing through the windows. Up until now the whole evening had been a fun escape for her, a well-deserved adventure to break up the monotony of her predictable suburban routine.

Wolfgang inserted an ornate teaspoon into a delicate ramekin filled with *foie gras*.

"Open sesame, beautiful."

Lola complied, wondering what he would next introduce to her palette as she opened her mouth and pushed her tongue over the top of her bottom lip. He lightly dropped a small portion of the puréed goose liver onto her taste buds, and she hungrily swished it around in her mouth.

"Mmmmm...you remembered...I love *pâté*."

Wolfgang responded with exaggerated concern.

"Oh... *mon amour*...are you sure? I'd hate to see you lose one of those two, remaining, lovely snippets of fabric."

He had been misdirecting her all night, trying to get her to change her mind on her correct answers and offering no counsel when she was wrong. She was pretty sure the food in her mouth was *pâté*. He had been patient with her, but not overly so given the game show framework.

"Final guess, Mrs. Barton?"

He liked calling her Mrs. Barton, as it highlighted the forbidden nature of the act they were engaged in. Lola seemed to get a little thrill out of it as well, as she had yet to protest. He noticed a slight change in her breathing when he used the moniker.

She wasn't sure how to answer his question. The image of her, Lola Barton (*Mrs.* Barton!), lying in bed, restrained and nearly naked as he, Wolfgang Dalman, removed one of her last remaining garments, flashed in front of her eyes. A light breeze skipped across her naked stomach. She simultaneously wiggled and shivered before giving her answer.

"I'm stickin' with *pâté*."

Wolfgang smiled triumphantly before offering some insincere consolation.

"Oh… my precious little bunny…I'm so sorry…seriously…really close…but French law requires I differentiate between *pâté* and what I fed you…*foie gras*.… In Paris, you know, your error would be considered by many to be a serious *foie gras faux pas*."

Not hearing him giggle, she was pretty sure he was as close to delighted as one could be without making any noise. She then wondered which piece of clothing he would take.

"I understand that was a tough one for your average, underexposed American. So, to show my sympathy for your geographic handicap, I'll let you choose which piece of garment to keep. No dillydallying—upstairs or downstairs, which stays?"

She considered her options. Protesting his rulings had been useless so far, as Wolfgang was both inquisitor and judge. Lola knew that the room wasn't pitch-black, and considered the strengths and weaknesses afforded by each of her two pieces. If she kept her top, he would see that she had recently (and embarrassingly) shaved her mons Venus. On the other hand, if he removed her top she wasn't sure how things would spill out from an aesthetic perspective, and, when considering stretch marks, scars, and her age, she didn't want to spoil their shared fantasy of her as the perfect female sex object.

She considered bailing on the whole game as the alcohol was starting to wear off and her right arm was showing early signs of falling asleep. Another chill draft left her covered in goose bumps; she wondered if he had left a window open. She let the first syllable of *pumpkin* roll around in her mouth.

Alarmed at her delayed response, Wolfgang sensed they were at a critical juncture. As a result, he decided to intervene and increase her dosage—but he had to be clever, he couldn't force-feed her.

"Again, in light of your cultural handicap, I am willing to offer a third alternative…but first, you'll have to pass an easy test."

She liked surprises.

"I'm listening."

"Open wide, Mrs. Barton."

Curious, she opened her mouth, although with less enthusiasm than before. Wolfgang used his fingers to put two vodka-infused Jell-O shots onto her tongue. Without hesitation she squished both of the sweet, wiggling cubes in her mouth then let them slide down her throat. The taste immediately put her on a Proustian journey back to one of her craziest nights with Wolfgang. They had been dancing and doing Jell-O shots at an NYU frat party in the East Village, and Lola had gotten really drunk. Cocaine had never been her deal, but that night she had shared a couple of lines with some friends and was feeling immortal. She ended up having sloppy, semi-public sex with Wolfgang in an indeterminate foreign student's loft. She vaguely remembered others in the room and wasn't sure if Wolfgang was the only one who had fucked her, given the tight quarters and the amount of intoxicants in her system. The whole recollection of how free and uninhibited she used to be elicited a strange mix of longing, remorse, and titillation.

"Jell-O shots."

"What color?"

"Asshole."

"Not a color, Miss Potty Mouth."

She mentally stumbled through the mist of decades and alcohol, trying to remember the color.

"Green."

"Very good."

"What's my third option?"

"Oh, Mrs. Barton…nothing too challenging… a simple trade… keep your two remaining articles of clothing, upstairs and downstairs, but agree to have one of your legs encumbered."

The suggestion set off chemical fireworks that quickly mixed with the sugar and vodka in her bloodstream. Her imagination was running rampant. *So far he's behaved himself…hasn't he? More than "behaved"—he's actually been quite thoughtful and entertaining.*

The concept that Wolfgang wanted to tie her up and perform sex acts on her was now front and center. The issue was, could she trust him? The uncertainty of it all was hugely intriguing, but also frightening. A huge wave of arousal started forming from the deep water of her psyche. As it lifted her up, she peered over the cresting swell, gathered her courage, and considered taking the drop.

She reviewed her options.

A) Go home to an empty house.

B) Stay and see what Wolfgang had planned.

It was already obvious he had given the evening a lot of thought, and she was flattered that he had gone to such an effort to please her. She took a quick inventory of her life, the gilded cage and all, and started leaning towards the adventure. A little voice started warning that it was too risky, but she blocked out the voice with an explanation.

We're in a hotel. There are people all around us. I can always scream for help if things get creepy-crazy.

Her verbal response showed an effort to simultaneously keep things light while letting him know she had her limits:

"I'll take what's behind door number three…but, Wolfgang, you have to promise not to go all Marquise de Sade on me."

He took a deep and silent breath as her words worked their way fully into his consciousness.

She was so close.

"I promise."

His shaking hands uncovered the third soft rope from the wrinkles of the duvet, and he carefully slipped the noose around her ankle. He worked slowly, making sure she couldn't feel his hands quiver as he removed most of the slack from the line.

"A fair trade, Mrs. Barton. Please, let me know if the knots are uncomfortable?"

Lola was struggling with letting go, despite the fact that the physical restraints explicitly demanded she do so. Total submission would have meant her brain was no longer considering escape routes, and she definitely hadn't reached that point.

"So far, so good," she barely whispered. She half-heartedly tested the ropes.

She kept the safe word within reach, like a falling sky diver keeping a hand on her rip cord. If things ever got out of control, she told herself, she had safe passage back to civilization and order.

What she hadn't been prepared for was the heightened state of arousal that accompanied her inner turmoil. Her body was tingling, with a focus on the sensitive areas from which she had removed the most hair. Experience had led her to believe that anxiety always killed her sexual hunger, but right now she noticed a hypersensitivity…especially given the blindfold. Whenever he subtly touched her with his mouth or hands, which he had been doing frequently all night, she responded as if a delicious electric current coursed from the point of contact throughout her body. Everything was amplified, the taste of the things he fed her, his scent, the sound of the fog horn across the bay—all leading to a crisp feeling of what it meant to be alive. Her sensory pleasures were increasingly superseding all of her mental spinning, and she liked it.

Wolfgang occupied the other side of the same coin. Total control now required only that he secure her last appendage, a relatively easy task if he chose to undertake it. He moved to the other side of the bed, where he had the chocolate fondue waiting. He inserted his finger into the pot then removed it and brought it up to his mouth, testing the temperature with his tongue.

"Yummy…just right, Mrs. Barton."

In the dark, Lola didn't know what he was talking about.

Wolfgang inserted his finger into the dark fondue again then carefully brought it over to Lola's closed lips. She reached hesitantly with the tip of her tongue. After ascertaining the nature of the sticky confection, she slowly sucked his whole digit into her mouth.

"We have a new game, Mrs. Barton," Wolfgang declared. His voice carried an authority it hadn't possessed before.

Wolfgang picked up the paintbrush again. He swirled the bristles in the chocolate while he continued:

"It's very simple. Your job is to be silent. Success at your assignment requires you be blind and mute. Do you understand?"

She nodded.

"Very good, Mrs. Barton. My job is equally simple."

He removed the warm paintbrush from the pot and painted a three-inch smear across her throat as he moved his mouth down next to her ear and whispered.

"My job is to make you feel good."

Before the chocolate could dry, he licked it off of her neck. He then reached perpendicularly across her body and grabbed the bottle of mezcal from the table on the other side of the bed, consciously aware that his torso grazed hers in the process.

"Remember, blind and mute…open wide, Mrs. Barton."

She opened her mouth and tilted her head back in response.

"Careful…liquid."

He accommodated her acquiescence to his request by pouring the liquor into her mouth—just enough for her to enjoy the flavor while a little of the mezcal dribbled down her chin and onto her chest. While she swallowed, he quickly lapped up the excess; then he filled her navel with another shot, which he also slurped up—but not before allowing some of the liquid to run downhill on her abdomen and be absorbed by her lingerie.

"Oh no, now look what I've done, Mrs. Barton. I've soiled your new underpants."

The earthy agave burned righteously in Lola's mouth, down her throat, and into her stomach.

"Oh my god, that's good."

"Mrs. Barton, you know the rules. Blind and mute."

Situating himself down by her one free limb, he set her lower leg in his lap and started massaging her foot.

"Hmm…what to do when one breaks the rules…"

He patiently worked his attention up from her foot to her inner thigh, delicately kneading her muscles in an experienced way.

"Mrs. Barton, I think we should remove the downstairs garment, don't you? We've already soiled the fabric with the mezcal, and we should probably start it soaking in the sink before it's ruined. The removal could also serve as payment for breaking the rules."

"Do I have a choice?"

"Oh, Mrs. Barton…again with the talking? You're being such a bad girl tonight."

Unhurriedly, Wolfgang crawled on his knees to a place straddling her legs, slid one finger of each hand under the elastic waistband on each side of her hips, and slowly started pulling the lingerie down, revealing her bareness below the fabric. With satisfaction he noticed that she lifted her hips ever so slightly to aid in the undressing. Soon her shaved pubic area was fully exposed. Lola shivered under what she could only guess was his gaze. His next words left no doubt.

"Mrs. Barton, you naughty, naughty girl. You've been thinking of me, haven't you?"

Lola tried to cover up the embarrassing evidence, even crossing her legs, but the ropes made her efforts look ridiculous. Wolfgang laughed at her wriggling shame. Then he reached over to the fondue pot, swirled the brush in the warm chocolate and proceeded to paint her hairless area a dark, sticky brown.

"There, that looks a bit more natural…"

Before he went down to clean things up, he decided she might need a bit more fortification. He grabbed the topless Cielo Azul bottle and took a swig.

"Open wide, Mrs. Barton…more delicious firewater."

Wolfgang's instincts were right. Lola was drowning in a haze of sensations and was struggling to regain the surface. She wasn't sure she should be drinking more, but she also really wanted Wolfgang's downtown attention. Wolfgang began pouring the tequila, but Lola was slow to open her mouth fully. A reasonable percentage of the liquor ran down her chin, sliding into her already wet top.

"Oh, Mrs. Barton, did you spill? And on your last piece of clothing! You really should be more careful, it's obvious you're a fully grown woman, not a giggling school girl. I suppose something will have to be done with that top, but first we've got to clean up that sticky party you're hosting downstairs."

Wolfgang slowly started following the mezcal trail from her neck, over her partially covered breasts, then down past her stomach, until his mouth eventually started lapping at the cocoa between her legs. Lola was vibrating with anticipation. She hoped Wolfgang would stop teasing her, but she did not voice her desire lest he decide to force another deprivation on her. Several times, in a final-ditch effort to assert some input, she used her free leg to try and control the positioning of his head. Finally, after her third unsuccessful attempt, he interrupted his oration and grabbed her rebellious foot.

"I can see this leg is feeling left out, Mrs. Barton? I think we can solve that, don't you?"

Kicking half-heartedly, she tried to free her foot from his grasp, but he easily looped the final slip knot around her ankle, incontrovertibly securing her to the bed.

"You seem conflicted, Mrs. Barton…are you sincerely trying to be chaste?"

After making sure her range of movement was limited, he pushed pillows under her bum and under each of her knees, leaving her totally accessible.

"Or perhaps you just like being chased?"

He chuckled at his wordplay even as he admired his handiwork. The room was dimly lit, but his eyes had adjusted: he could now clearly see all the suite's distinguishing features. He noted with satisfaction that Lola was absolutely under his control…and the cameras would prove it was all consensual. He started blowing gently on the wet areas of her skin just to watch her squirm.

"It appears you want something, Mrs. Barton? You have some noteworthy need?"

Before she could find out what might be coming next, a loud knocking from the suite's front door interrupted their fun. Lola instinctively reached for the sheets, wanting to cover her body from intrusive strangers. The ropes held her arms and legs firmly in place.

"Wolfgang…who is that?" she demanded in a frightened stage whisper.

She could see her lower half through the bottom of her mask, exposed and thrust invitingly upward by the pillows. Her legs were spread wide, suspended about two feet over the mattress by the bedpost tethers. Only her bra was still intact…and it was resting more *under* than over her breasts.

This was the moment Wolfgang had been waiting for. Everything else had just been a warm-up. He didn't answer her.

She whispered again, this time with greater urgency.

"Wolfgang—who's at the door? Don't let them in."

Wolfgang could only imagine what was going through Lola's head…the fear…the suspense. His imagination left him trembling with excitement.

"Wolfgang, I'm serious. I can't be seen like this. I'm married, I live here. *Pumpkin,* dammit."

"Shhhh, Mrs. Barton, you're safe with me…nothing bad is going to happen. Trust me."

"*Don't* let them in!"

Wolfgang stood up from the bed and headed to the door.

"*Pumpkin,* Wolfgang…Dammit, *PUMP-KIN!*"

Lola went silent as soon as she heard him open the door. Wolfgang's voice could be clearly heard.

"There you are, we've been waiting for you."

A moment of terror shook Lola's body. *Oh my God,* she thought, *this isn't an accident. He's planning to make me available to other people.*

Her body was on fire, her fears running rampant. She considered her options. The safe word had already been disrespected, so she considered screaming for help. *And then what?* she asked herself. *Have the whole hotel descend on our suite and see me tied up, spread-eagled with a shaved coochie, covered in tequila and chocolate?*

She reconsidered. *Maybe it's not a devious plan? Maybe it's just room service he ordered earlier?*

The justification gave her hope, and hence allowed her to relax a bit. *Let's not get ahead of ourselves here,* she told herself reassuringly. *This might all be an innocent misunderstanding. Just keep your mouth shut for now and let this play out.*

The voices were muffled, but she thought one of the people at the door sounded like their waiter from earlier that evening. She nearly cried out. *No! Not the boy!* She wondered if he could see her already, fully exposed. Her thoughts went to how she had teased him earlier that evening.

Earlier this evening. She almost laughed as she repeated the words in her head. *That seems like forever ago…Wolfgang is probably pointing me out right now, snickering while he offers up the nympho MILF who can't get enough!*

A moment later she heard the door shut. The dead bolt engaged… and then the sound of feet came into the bedroom. She couldn't tell for sure how many people had entered, as her judgment was blurred by the alcohol. Her imagination was spinning hard, totally out of control. Straining all of her senses for any clues as to what might be about to happen to her, she thought she felt a stirring in the air on her left. She focused all of her attention in that direction. When the first hand lightly caressed her throat she flinched—then she strained aggressively at the ropes. Panting hard, barely able to move, she realized Wolfgang had done a meticulous job.

"Who's there? Wolfgang, this isn't funny!"

She felt an arm graze her chest. Then strong hands pulled her bra completely under both breasts, offering them up in a dramatic fashion, as her arms stayed outstretched over her head. There was a brief pause, before a brushstroke of sticky chocolate…and then a mouth warmly engaged one of her nipples. Another presence moved at the foot of the bed. Again she wondered how many were in the room. Soon the big hand on her throat moved, and she felt an overly ripe strawberry, dripping with mezcal, being pushed gently between her lips. As the berry scraped across her teeth, a mixture of juice from the fruit and agave ran down the sides of her face and across her neck. Eventually the liquid formed a sultry pink stain under her disheveled hair on the cotton sheets.

She tried to relax, but the sound of a small motor, like an electric hummingbird, hovered over her body. Her sightless mind started spinning stories about what might come next. The buzzing then moved up, past her face, towards the headboard where her hands were secured. Pressed into her palm, her fingers could only partially close around the firm, vibrating phallus, and after allowing her to briefly get a sense for the texture and earnestness of the device, it was slowly removed from her hand, tracing the warm flesh on her wrist, passing gently down her arm and her armpit, where it took a lazy U-turn and began teasing the sensitive skin at the front of her throat. After lingering for a few seconds, the vibrator headed south, slowly massaging her breasts along the way, before deciding to pause at her navel. After playfully pressing and retreating, it haltingly started working its way down to her mons, where it rotated in a large circle around her upwardly thrust vulva. As the concentric circles started narrowing, the intended bull's-eye became obvious.

Without urgency the attention continued. A few minutes later Lola felt a ferocity growing between her legs that would soon need to be released. As the intensity of the phallic explorations grew, hands continued massaging her breasts, pinching her nipples and firmly gripping her throat. Fingers explored her open, gasping mouth, and her wild, captive body increased its undignified response in time to the physical stimulus. She heard a soft moan escape her lips as the tempo between her legs became more insistent and her hips began to involuntarily twitch. A warm breath intimately visited her ear, half coaxing and half taunting.

"That's right, Mrs. Barton…good girl…let it all go. It's gonna be a long night, but you'll do just fine. You're built for this."

CHAPTER 26 —

Across the Border

"What the *fuck*!"

Keno struck at the sea in frustration. He had just missed the latest of many curling walls. Despite an hour of trying, he had yet to catch his first wave, and his irritation had increased with every unsuccessful attempt. There was a significant gap between how well he thought he could surf and how poorly he was performing that morning, and the cognitive dissonance was dredging up some complicated feelings. In fact, the struggle was triggering such a multi-layered emotional response that he didn't have a clue as to how to control the thoughts that seemed intent on torturing him. For some irrational reason all of his past surfing accomplishments provided no relief from his current insecurity. It was as if his brain had a "happiness" dispenser that required daily payment in the currency of *achievement*. No proficiency, no peace.

Further complicating the situation were the witnesses to his incompetence. Three other surfers were sharing the waves with Keno, and like the effect a strong magnet has on sensitive electronic gear, the other nearby humans were messing with Keno's brain. They were all undergoing a sort of out-of-the-lab Heisenberg experience: Each of the wave-riders thought they were being intensely observed by the others, when in reality they were each so self-absorbed that they barely noticed what their colleagues were doing.

Keno didn't even recognize that his egocentric thoughts fed nicely into the paranoid comparisons often found in herd animals. He had long ago grown tired of Lola's harping on the dominance hierarchy; but if he were paying attention he would have recognized that the presence of others caused a subconscious parsing in his mind of his appropriate place in the group, and a competitive, reflexive consideration of how he could move up. He unconsciously suspected he occupied a superior position relative to the others within the castes determined by age, career, and wealth; but the current most important trait was surfing capability—and it was killing Keno that he was the *untouchable*. Of course, all of this swirling existed solely in his mind, but it seemed to him that the other surfers were actually starting to avoid him. It was as if his stumbling was contagious and no one wanted to be infected.

In some ways his expletive-laced water-thrashing was performance art, a spontaneous effort to influence the opinions of the other three. When faced with evidence of his deficiencies, the little man in him threw a calculated temper tantrum intended to convince the strangers that he was better than his recent flailings implied. By violently and publicly protesting his situation—he threw in a heavy dose of feigned disbelief for good measure—he hoped to convey that his bumbling over the last hour was an anomaly.

Things hadn't been this bad earlier in the week, when it was just Keno and Trick in the water. But now they were sharing their central Baja "secret spot" with two young adults from Huntington Beach, a man and woman who seemed to be romantically involved. The girl went by Dani, and her boyfriend was Harley. About twelve hours earlier, their ancient rig had rolled (uninvited) into Keno and Trick's remote coast camp in a cloud of dust and red-eyed confusion. Their rusted-out Suburban was a gift from Harley's parents, and he had been doing the driving. Dani was the navigator and did most of the talking. Both of them seemed to be quite baked when they first arrived. Shockingly, given the Mexican drug laws, they had no qualms about bringing weed across the border. There was enough olfactory evidence to eliminate reasonable doubt, but from Keno's perspective the real clincher came during their initial interaction. Pulling up at sunset, Dani stumbled out of the car, gazed into the disappearing sun, and with open mouth and glazed eyes inquired of their hosts, "Do you partake?" Trick, looking at them with amusement, subtly shook his head, "No thanks, amigos." They were understandably confused by the contradiction of Trick's dreadlocks on the one hand, and his lack of interest in their cannabis "sacrament" on the other. Trick didn't subscribe to the Rasta social movement; he just liked not having to manage his hair.

Like wandering gypsies, Dani and Harley had been looking for a spot about twenty miles up the coast but had made a wrong turn at one of the many unsigned Baja road forks. Now, they needed direction. They had never before ventured out of California and had come south of the border only that morning, on a whim, using years of surfer campfire stories to provide guidance. Trick and Keno were concerned about the disoriented guests driving at night on isolated Baja roads, so the grown-ups insisted the kids stay, at least until sunrise, when the *banditos* and livestock would usually return home. Informed travelers knew this stretch of Baja was particularly lawless, with limited transportation and communication infrastructure. To not get in trouble, one needed a reasonable amount of preparation, usually in the form of prior knowledge and supplies. The newcomers seemed to be lacking both.

The two older *gringos* knew this rough section of the *Sierra Gigantes* had been worked for generations by fishermen and ranchers. The former worked the coastline with their modest, open-air *pangas*, and the latter ran their livestock up in the mountains, where water and forage could be had. These were hard people, mostly untainted by modern indulgence and used to living in isolated communities. The rough environment had required a clan-type social structure: extended families who made their own rules and depended on each other to survive. Over the previous two decades, the aquifers and fisheries had started to dry up, and the indigenous population had to either change or leave. This only added to the attractiveness of the area as a prime transit zone for drug traffickers and other criminal activity, as the dwindling insular communities needed a new way to earn a living and there was no law enforcement to speak of.

Unaware of the risks to unwelcome travelers, Dani and Harley decided to stay for a more primal reason—Trick was frying up some biscuits and bacon, and the smell was supercharging their post-toke munchies. After they all sat down and packed away a good-sized dinner, the youngsters climbed into the back of their rig, where they used rolled-up beach towels as pillows and ratty wool *serapes* as blankets. They both passed out before Keno could suggest they stash their surfboards under their car rather than share their sleeping quarters with the bony, wax-coated companions.

The next morning, the powerful elixirs of sleep and youth revealed themselves in the vibrating forms of the kids. Not only did the two beach rats easily refuse the coffee Trick offered (they didn't believe in "unhealthy coping mechanisms"), but they had woken and climbed into their wetsuits at first light, waiting for Trick and Keno like children waiting for their parents on Christmas morning. Between the board waxing and the frothing over the beautiful waves forming out front, Keno was surprised the blond twins had been able to restrain themselves. He took their patient behavior as evidence that regular cannabis use didn't always lead to failing the marshmallow test.

With the adolescents bouncing in place at the water's edge, Keno and Trick rubbed the sand out of their eyes, gathered their boards, and wandered down to join them. After briefly explaining some of the local hazards, they started the several hundred yard paddle to the peak. Trick and Keno were on "step up" boards that were shaped with a little more foam than the tiny sticks used by the pros. The intention of these hybrid boards was to help intermediate or aging surfers more easily paddle into waves, while simultaneously maintaining a degree of the maneuverability that surfers have with shorter boards. Keno noticed both of the youngsters were on performance short boards. He wondered if they could walk the walk. After duck diving under a few rolling lines of white water, it was obvious the hemp couple knew what they were doing. Despite the advantage Keno enjoyed in the buoyancy department (because of his board), he was soon wallowing in their wake…and so began his feelings of inadequacy.

After lagging a minute behind, the elder surfers soon aggregated with their younger colleagues just above the underwater reef. They moved from prone to sitting on their boards. After taking a brief moment to assess the conditions, the kids and Trick each immediately caught consecutive chest-high rollers. Wanting to keep up with the group, Keno started to feel the pressure to catch a wave. It wasn't unusual for him to need a few attempts to warm up, and he didn't freak out when he bungled his first wave; but after twenty minutes it became painfully clear that he was the anchorman. The other three were catching waves effortlessly and bubbling with enthusiasm from their shared experience. It was as if everyone in the foursome was shooting par except for Keno, who kept slicing his shots badly into the woods. With each failure he felt his social status plunging.

It was at this point that the tangled emotions started to take control; rising up like raging monsters from a dark, internal abyss, forcing the violent and verbal karate chop of the water, and blindsiding him with sudden, venomous mental interpretations. The twisted demons' first plan was to blame someone (or something) else for the humiliating inadequacies:

These SoCal kids are so inconsiderate! Hogging all the waves…getting in my way and distracting me!

He begrudged the newcomers their effortless joy, catching wave after wave as he struggled so hard and reaped nothing. It was unjust that they could smoke weed all day and catch so many waves, while he, who took pride in his athletic skills and industrious ways, was being shut out. He silently filed a formal protest with the universe.

As he played this narrative a few times in his head, he maintained enough of a grasp on reality to recognize that there were clear inconsistencies, the most obvious being the generous way the youngsters had been treating him. Throughout the morning the kids had been deferring to their elders when it came to wave selection, patiently waiting in a polite queue. Being confronted with the evidence, the voices in Keno's head reluctantly retreated from the first battle, but they continued to plan for the war.

After missing another wave and being compelled by surf etiquette to move to the back of the line, the demons performed a flanking move to protect his crumbling ego, starting with the second of the ongoing barrage of excuses.

My board is too short, I need more volume.

As soon as this new rationalization coalesced in his head, the universe provided contrary evidence: Trick, ten pounds heavier and on a smaller board, took off on a head-high beauty. Chastened by the evidence, Keno's ego wasn't yet ready to give up the siege; his next excuse came easily.

These waves are too mushy for me.

Again, seemingly incapable of egregiously lying to himself, his conscience reminded him that Dani was riding a potato chip, and *she* was catching everything.

His next alibi for his aquatic inability brought forth a whiny internal voice primed with an old standby—self-pity.

I'm too old. I'm losing my strength-to-weight ratio and my flexibility. I can't compete with these kids. Maybe I'm not good enough to do this anymore?

As soon as he accepted that thought there came a physical and mental deflation, a loss of the confidence necessary to feel at one with the ocean. Over the next sixty minutes he missed at least half a dozen more waves and suffered through an intense and growing self-flagellation. His mojo was totally gone. After Mother Nature once again allowed him to prove his inadequacy, he floated alone at the peak for five minutes, waiting for the others to paddle back from their successful rides.

Keno's calm veneer was in stark contrast to his screaming, internal mess. Try as he could, it was a serious struggle to deal with all of the emotions competing for a soapbox in his brain. Soon the other surfers would rejoin him at the take-off spot, tired from the long return paddle, but invigorated (no doubt) from the many waves they had been riding all morning. It was as if Keno could clearly see his companions partying in the VIP lounge, gesturing for him to join, but Neptune was managing the velvet rope, denying access to the inept. He stewed in his self-imposed humiliation.

As the group clustered back at the top of the peak they deferred to Keno, who was sitting in "priority" position. *Priority* meant he got the pick of the litter when the next set rolled in. With a weird sort of masochism, he reminded himself that he had gained the pole position solely because of his incompetence. On the previous group of waves, he was (once again) the only one of the four who had failed to get to his feet and allow one of the pulses of energy to carry him the several hundred yards along the edge of the reef, towards the shore. As a result, he didn't need to make the paddle back to the take-off area. He had gained his current spot at the head of the queue by failure and default.

Not aware of how tormented Keno was, the other three were now verbally celebrating their shared good fortune with gushing congratulations.

"Great wave, Dani!"

"Thanks, Trick! Your cutbacks are *sick!*"

"Sicker than sick…Diseased!"

"Hospitalized!"

"ICU!"

Dani and Harley clearly had a schtick when it came to sharing surf slang. They both laughed at the exchange.

Irrationally but predictably, Keno perceived the joyful comments as indignations. He seethed with resentment at the new friendships that were being formed. Dani wasn't making things any easier.

"Can you believe how perfect these conditions are!"

Keno ignored the rhetorical question, but Trick was quick to respond.

"Oh, you like perfectly shaped, slightly overhead, right points with a mild offshore breeze?"

Everyone but Keno laughed at the sarcasm. Despite being aware of how silly his resentments were, he continued to silently boil as the capable shared in the glories of their accomplishments. Their enthusiasms just made him feel that much more the outcast, highlighting, in his mind, his ineptitude. Not realizing the salt he was pouring into Keno's wounds, Trick spread the love to Dani's boyfriend.

"Harley, I think your last wave was the biggest of the day!"

Harley nodded. "Thanks, man! I was sooo late I almost missed it…barely kept from pearling on the drop!"

"Sweet! Nice recovery! Throwing buckets, *amigo!*"

"Ah, dude, so much fun!"

Bobbing quietly on his board, Keno caught himself asphyxiating on tiny sips of air and reminded himself to take deep breaths.

God, I am so fucked up! he thought. *What's with this crazy sport?*

Before he had started surfing, he used to think surfers were so zen—chilling out at the beach, or floating in the water, serenely watching wave after wave pass and eventually break on the shore. But now, as a participant, he knew what was really going on: they weren't chillaxin' at all. In fact it was quite the opposite. Serious surfers were all addicts, jonesin' for their next wave like junkies fixated on the syringe. The habit was so bad for the hard core that nothing else mattered. Money, relationships, personal hygiene…all inconsequential to the daily wave rider. All they cared about were waves. They respected only those who could ride them well, which required a constant judgment, and usually dismissal, of others' abilities. Their problem received no attention from the mental health profession due to a misunderstanding that begot acceptance. Everyone incorrectly assumed that the surfers' toned, sun-streaked, physical exteriors implied a similar level of mental fitness. Unfortunately for Keno, being aware of the problem didn't mean he had a remedy, and he was currently struggling through some major withdrawal and self-image issues. Everyone around him was flying high, but he couldn't access the palliative.

Working through the voices as best he could, Keno focused on the path to redemption—his fix. If he could catch just one, good wave, he knew his whole emotional state would flip…he would become one with the enraptured tribe. Then he could make his timely payment, and the dispenser would provide his daily dose of happiness—or at least that was how it had always worked previously.

Keno looked skyward for strength. It was still early in the morning, and he decided to run through his usual coping mechanisms. First, he focused on gaining a new perspective by acknowledging his insignificance—a tiny dot floating in the immense, dark blue Pacific. He took a long breath and let himself be absorbed by the magnificent display of nature that surrounded them.

A notable gust whistled over the gritty bones of the Baja desert, bringing a powdery dust to their camp that infiltrated every crevice. Coffee pots, car windows, tent flaps…all had to be buttoned up tight or there would be a thin layer of reddish brown dirt covering everything inside. The breeze pushed into the oncoming walls of seawater, forcing the waves to stack up taller and steeper. The wind had been building since first light, grooming the symmetrical lines of energy that had been birthed from a distant Asian typhoon. Joining the gusts from the east, the sun was now fully exposed above the bleached escarpment that provided modest protection to their camp. Keno welcomed the radiant heat as it bathed the back of his thick wetsuit.

He didn't want to lose the sublime nature of the moment; to fully capture it, he knew he had to figure out the source of his angst. He started running through the possible triggers. Fear of his bodily decline and eventual death. Unmet expectations. Simple chemical addiction. The need to belong to a community. Insecurity rooted in a dysfunctional childhood….He wanted to believe that his issues were somehow unique to him, that he was a special case; but the more he unraveled his feelings, the more the evidence started piling up that his problems were similar to everyone else's. These suspicions had an unsettling effect on him—the human condition and all—and he decided to try and get comfortable with keeping the question alive. Finally running out of gas with his soul-searching, he hoped he could find a modicum of relief later, whenever his head stopped bothering him.

He stared off to the west, out towards Japan. *Damn,* he thought, *this surfing stuff is becoming way too complicated.* A pod of dolphins breached, frolicking in their marine cafeteria. Just north of the pod, a squadron of pelicans, searching for schools of fish, glided in formation just above the ocean's oily surface.

Nothing and everything changed. Far out at sea, a set of waves appeared as a slight shadow, rolling towards the surfers like a galloping herd of oversized bison. Spotting the telltale signs, Keno's pulse rate accelerated. All of his previous ruminations were shoved aside. He recognized an opportunity to put points on the board, and so he gathered data to try and better prepare. After nearly thirty seconds of scrutinizing the ocean, he felt he had the beginnings of a grasp on the intentions of the inrushing rolls of corduroy. He decided the second of the group was the best. He casually put his companions on red alert.

"Hey guys, outside…I think I'm takin' the second one."

As the words left his lips, everyone stopped talking. They looked seaward and started paddling to where they thought the freight trains would start to break. Twenty seconds later, the berms of overhead water bore down on the foursome at over twenty miles per hour. Their adrenaline levels and heart rates skyrocketed; their last-minute jockeying became critical. With Keno having already reserved the second wave, Trick now had first option on all the others. Harley and Dani gave him a little room to catch the initial wave as it approached, but they also stayed focused on the incoming bombs in case the big man decided to pass at the last moment. As the seconds ticked by, they could tell from Trick's body language that he was likely taking the first of the set, a ballsy move, given the mountains of water that he would take on the head if he blew the takeoff. Trick, who was feeling confident with his skills and judgment, paddled hard to get under the peak, took one final look over both shoulders, and then dug his hands deeply into the water. As the energy from the wave started grabbing at the shallow reef, the wave jacked up and lifted his polyester sled. With his board accelerating, Trick anticipated the slide down the wave face by pressing hard on the board with both hands. He arched his back and simultaneously used his knees and thighs to lightly push down on the rear of the board, allowing him to imperceptibly stall his forward momentum. As the front half of his board defied gravity, jutting for a split second at a perpendicular angle to the near vertical wave face, he undulated to his feet, simultaneously releasing the stalling pressure exerted by his lower body. This acrobatic move—the "pop up"—was the true barrier to entry for performance surfing; it had to be done with a timing and agility that required years of practice. As Trick pulled his feet up and under him, he simultaneously altered the direction of his board, pointing the nose down and to the right, parallel to the wave face, and weighting his front foot so he could "make the drop"—pushing his stick down the growing and steepening green wall. With gravity and momentum urging him forward, his fins and right rail dug into the water as he carved down the sucking bronco, speeding forward in a tuck to avoid the exploding froth as it chased him down the line. From behind, Dani could only see the intermittent, spraying arcs of water and the top of Trick's head as he climbed and descended the glassy wave face, gouging out liquid divots from the pitching lip as he raced ahead of the thundering surge.

 Trick's efforts only partially registered with Keno, as he was committed to catching the next wave. He had about sixteen seconds after

Trick popped up to make his own last-minute adjustments. The biggest of the set, Keno's chosen wave required him to paddle out wide to avoid getting consumed by the sucking monster. As he scratched hard at the water, his eyes were searching for the right entry point, a small access zone on the wave face that was not too steep and yet not too benign. This frantic exploration was made that much more difficult by the constantly changing nature of his galloping mount, so he had to make an educated guess about where to position himself, turn, and then paddle for his life. Harley and Dani were both scratching hard to get into position for the following waves, but they couldn't help but admire Keno's chosen stallion.

"That's a beauty Keno—you got it brother!"

"Perfect spot! Paddle hard!"

With the sound of crashing waves roaring in his ears, Keno continued to paddle. He took one last glance over his shoulder to confirm his position then felt his board start to elevate from behind. He knew he was deep in the jaws of the cresting leviathan, and so he started his pop up early, to make his escape down the shoulder. As he rotated his board to the right, his back foot landed just short on the right rail and slipped off of the unwaxed edge. He pitched, headfirst, down the face of the snarling beast, his board and fins oscillating in close proximity, searching for exposed flesh. To protect his face, he covered his head with both arms. To keep seawater from entering his nose, he exhaled out of his nostrils as the wave pushed him under. The force of the water tumbled him forward, and his body screamed for oxygen. He bounced, twice, off of the reef. After what seemed like an eternity—but was only ten seconds—he was able to climb his leash and fill his lungs with air. Then five more waves repeated the punishment. He was finally spat out just yards from the shore, like a neoprene-clad Jonah.

Slowly unfolding himself from his jumbled position, he checked his body for blood and broken bones. His initial fear and dejection were soon overwhelmed by a new combination of self-loathing and rage. Like a teenager denied the family car on Saturday night, he refused to accept his overseer's verdict, and the beginnings of a temper tantrum started brewing from deep within his chest. It was as if the aquatic mugging had triggered a violent response that had erased all of his earlier meditation on the subject. *I do not suck this bad!* he assured himself as he gathered his board and continued to assess the damage. He became single-minded in his desire to leave fresh proof that he was a legitimate surfer. Not that his internal fire needed any fuel, but watching Dani (a girl!) ride the last, stupendous wave of the set all the way down to the beach only added to his conviction.

As he rearranged his hood and leash, a second review revealed some minor gouges to his wetsuit, damage that he dismissed as repairable before starting the long paddle back through the white water. An unbiased observer might have been reminded of a high schooler taking the SAT again and again, hoping for the one good score that would wipe out all of the earlier, contrary testimony, and hence prove his worthiness to the desired colleges. Everything else became insignificant to Keno—the cold water, his aching upper body, the bruises where he had hit the reef: these were all just signs of a disrespect thrown his way by a dismissive universe.

By the time he made it back to the lineup a new set of waves was approaching, and the other three surfers were scrambling for position. Watching his fellow campers all catch waves yet again, he was inspired to turn on one of the last of the grouping and make an attempt to paddle into the arching crescent. Without the benefit of a few minutes of rest, his arm strength was deficient, and despite his mental ferocity, he was again pitched over the falls and into the waiting cruelty of the reef. After repeating the previous spin cycle, he collected himself in the shallows and seriously considered Einstein's definition of insanity and how it might apply to him. A moment later he shook the quit out of his head, hopped the front of his torso onto his board, and paddled back out to the lineup.

It would take another ninety minutes, long after his sunscreen and the other three had called it quits, before things finally fell into place. With the sun floating lazily overhead, a wave called his name. Keno responded by straining to pull himself into position. In retrospect, it seemed the hands of God had lifted his tired assemblage, placed his feet correctly on the board, and, in a divine act of mercy, allowed him to slide into an overhead beauty and ride it all the way to the beach. When his board finally stopped in the knee-high white water in front of the camp, the other three were already napping in the late morning heat. Keno quietly picked up his Rusty, undid his ankle leash and wrapped it around his fins, and then walked up the sand like nothing noticeable had just happened. But deep inside, he was doing the most incredible dance of joy, like Snoopy with his nose pointed directly to the sky. He marveled at the recuperative power of catching a single wave. A state of deep contentment imbued him as he stumbled the final forty meters to his tent. Before reaching the canvas flap that served as a door, the offshore winds shifted to strong side/onshore, destroying the glassy surface that had made that morning's session so perfect, and giving Keno one more reason to feel special. Physically exhausted, he didn't even take the time to fully remove his wetsuit. As he entered his sand-filled tent, he smiled at the small lizard guarding his lightweight sleeping bag, and gratefully laid his sunburned cheek onto his dirty white pillow. He fell asleep to the memory of crystal clear water beckoning him into a curling room of glistening green, while underfoot the reef raced gloriously by. No matter how many times he conjured it, the movie took him to a place he felt must be very close to heaven.

CHAPTER 27 —

Calexico

Lisa Drehmel was savoring the hint of possibility. It was waltzing delicately across the motel room with the filtered early morning light. She didn't usually have sex on the first date, but this time was different. He didn't talk a lot, but she had grown to learn that most of them didn't, and at least this cowboy had been kind and gentle during their lovemaking. It was rare to find a man who put her needs first, but he seemed to be the exception, helping her to reach her destination a moment prior to his arrival. There was something else about the person currently sleeping with his back to hers—something missing in his motel room, but in a good way. Casting about for clues, she surveyed the tidiness of the stark room. She noted his few clothes folded or hung in the exposed closet, the boots resting side by side, and the bathroom essentials lined up in descending order underneath the mirror. In contrast, her clothes lay in hurried heaps on the floor, undergarments buried under the covers at the bottom of the bed. Her purse lay unmolested, where she had left it, next to the TV. Search as she would, she couldn't quite put her finger on it, the nagging thing that was missing. Then she realized it was more of a feeling as opposed to a tangible item…but that recognition still didn't get her to a complete understanding.

She reached over to reassure herself that he existed, that he hadn't fled in the middle of the night or been some sort of hopeful conjuring. After lightly touching his muscled shoulder, she returned her hand to rest under her pillow, her eyes gazing out towards the future. Although she had happily gained freedom from her ex-husband years before, lying next to a sleeping man made her feel good—less vulnerable and more optimistic. It was what she imagined things would be like if she had a bodyguard—a bodyguard with money, one who was also handy around the house and *always* available. More optimistic than naive, she had firsthand experience with all the risks embedded in intimate relationships, but she felt she had learned from her mistakes. She recited the simple philosophy that she had developed through trial and error, a strategy that she reviewed during those moments when life provided a glimmer of promise in the form of companionship:

Men are simple. They need to be cared for appropriately—stroke their egos and let them know you appreciate them on a regular basis. And, most importantly, keep them happily fed and happily bed—before the hunger gets so great as to cause resentment or restless wandering.

As Lisa enjoyed the lingering of fresh sheets on her naked body, she reflected back on her marriage, which ended nearly a decade ago. They had both been selfish, young, and unpracticed in the art of compromise. In the first few months after the divorce she had celebrated her freedom. After all, she had been in her early thirties and could still turn heads. But after eight years her life had turned into a series of solitary, Saturday nights, usually with just her daughter. Every now and then she would reluctantly agree to a blind date; or worse, in an effort to accommodate the demands of her biology, get drunk enough for a one-night stand. She always regretted both the next morning.

With each passing year, the fear of growing old in solitude became more palpable, and the options in the romance department, for a middle-aged woman in a small town like Calexico, became more limited. There were times when she wanted to leave, move back up the Central Valley to Modesto, where she had grown up, but in her heart she knew there was nothing there for her either.

Years ago she had been promised a fast-track future with Bank of America. The oral commitment required that she be patient and work her way up through the farm system. For the first few years she made a sincere effort; but at some point her career and work ethic had both stalled, and she became a nine-to-five white collar drone. She was clearly competent at her job but no longer displayed any real ambition. Most of the time, when she wasn't preoccupied with the bank or being a single parent, she just felt abandoned, irrelevantly adrift in the relentless tide of life.

Her secular review was abruptly interrupted by a wave of guilt. Her daughter, Samantha, was only twelve, but there were times when she seemed closer to twenty. The night before, when things were going particularly well with her date, Lisa had called home and said she needed to stay over with a "sick friend." Lisa didn't feel too guilty about the untruth, especially when Sam had reassured her, saying that she could "take care of everything just fine" in their apartment for one night. It was easy for Lisa to rationalize that the white lie was intended to protect her daughter from a reality she wasn't ready for. As to which of the two Drehmels weren't yet ready was open for debate. She wondered about the person next to her and how he would get along with Sam. Was he patient with children? Would he be willing to send Sam to a good college if the opportunity presented itself? Could he persevere if things got tough? Experience had left her with a half-empty view of most men when it came to their ability to shoulder responsibility.

After a few minutes of hopeful what-ifs, Lisa's mind identified how this particular encounter was different from her previous promiscuities. She started listing all the things that *weren't* present. Front and center was the overwhelming feeling of regret, or disappointment, which, when accompanied by the usual visual and olfactory stench, would leave her head vibrating with a frequency akin to that of fingernails on a chalkboard. Second in the list of missing things was the strong feeling of repulsion that she could usually relieve only by putting immediate, significant, and solitary distance between herself and the scene of the crime. Third on the list was the usual post-coital shame of allowing another loser to infiltrate her cockpit and make a mess. Fourth, and most happily *not* there, was the crushing weight of hopelessness, as if she were being suffocated by the smallness of her life, and so, in a frantic attempt to claw her way out, had made yet another bad choice. The fifth, sixth, and seventh items AWOL that morning were the dead bodies of *optimism, aspiration,* and *grace* that would usually start the evening as vibrant souls only to be extinguished, one by one, during a fumbling intercourse over the length of the evening's encounter. The last thing that was missing from the cowboy's hotel room were the jumbled clutter of empty alcohol containers and piles of smoking ash that provided the physical evidence of a shared dysfunction and inability to reach even a brief moment of intimacy and self-acceptance without chemical assistance. Taking the place of all these usual totems of regret was a sort of relative peace; maybe even the early sowing of what she could consider to be the seeds of love—or at least a glimpse of hope for a relationship in which two adults would support and care for each other with trust, fidelity, and respect.

She looked over at the man beside her. *Could he be the Prince? Finally, after all the frogs? Right here in bed with me?*

Another sharp pang of anxiety interrupted the romantic fantasy: she realized she had turned off her phone the night before. Hence, she had been unavailable for several hours. With her mind racing to the intersection of potential crisis and parental inaccessibility, she decided she had to call her child. However, she didn't want the cowboy, Tommie, to be able to eavesdrop, as that would oblige too much transparency for so early in the relationship. She didn't want him to learn about her daughter until she had a better handle on how he felt about kids. It was also important she manage her appearance as soon as possible. Knowing how visually oriented men were, she preferred that he not see her in the harsh morning light, before she could do some cosmetic damage control in front of a mirror. As she looked at him, she heard the reassuring sound of deep breathing and decided to try and slip out and check on her daughter from the lobby of the Days Inn. She could then quickly visit the powder room before returning with two coffees and some Danish from the complimentary breakfast buffet. If she was lucky Tommie would never even know she was gone. Then, when he woke up, she would brainstorm with him to try and come up with some Sunday activity that would appeal so they could spend the day together.

Who knows, she thought as she slipped out of bed (and shimmied into her dress), *maybe he wants to go to church? Not likely, but stranger things could happen!*

She rifled through their conversation from the day before, trying to remember if he had revealed anything about what he liked to do. There weren't a lot of options in Calexico, but she was creative, and maybe she could figure something out? They had first met only the previous morning, when he had come in to her branch, trying unsuccessfully to withdraw money from a poorly mannered automated teller. Being the assistant manager, she was usually locked away behind her desk reviewing paperwork, but it was a Saturday morning, and a confluence of events had conspired to push her to the front lines, interacting with the customers when traffic required. The two had engaged in some awkward small talk while Lisa coached him through the withdrawal process, and he had seemed pleasant enough. But, she had to admit, his felt hat and boots became much more appealing when she noticed that he had a balance of $687,591.47 in his checking account. When he shyly mumbled something about her plans for dinner, decorum required that she briefly play coy before enthusiastically accepting the invitation.

As she quickly replayed their dialogue, she realized he had been remarkably good at redirecting the conversation back to her. She really didn't know much about him except that he was from out of town and visiting his mom. In hindsight, his introverted behavior seemed odd, since most of the people she ran into couldn't wait to share all the boring minutiae from their lives.

Carrying her sandals in her hand, she almost made it to the door before tripping over a small bundle and making some noise. She looked down at the backpack she had inadvertently kicked, and in the faint light she thought she saw the barrel of a pistol poking through the partially closed top aperture…although she couldn't be sure.

A groggy Clay Barton opened one eye and oriented himself. He hadn't been with a woman since Tory in La Jolla, but his evening with Lisa had reminded him of what an enjoyable experience it could be.

"Hey, Lisa…where are you going?"

Putting the backpack out of her mind, she tried not to act disappointed that he had woken up before she could implement her plan. She put a smile into her voice and acted nonchalant.

"Oh, hi, Tommie…sorry, I didn't mean to wake you."

"Is everything okay?"

"Me?...oh yeah…I was just going to grab some coffee for us in the lobby."

"I'm not really a coffee person, but you go ahead."

Grateful for the chance to get her things done, she picked up her purse and blew him a kiss before heading out the door.

"See you in a few!"

When Clay heard the door latch after the pneumatic hiss, he slowly got out of bed and started for the bathroom. The warm water in the shower tempted him, but he knew the foreseeable future would require he function in a hellishly hot environment, so he ended his quick shower by spending the last two minutes under a stream of cold water. This was a strategy he had developed in the Middle East whenever he wanted to lower his core temperature. By the time Lisa got back he was already dressed and packed, sitting on the bed and watching ESPN. His smaller pack was slung over his shoulder. The larger duffle waited by the door.

Lisa let herself in with the room key, quietly pushing through the door with her hip. A cardboard cup holder laden with bagels and drinks was balanced on her palm as she backed into the room. The "bed" part of her core philosophy was taken care of, and now she was working on the "fed" part. It took a moment for her pupils to dilate after their exposure to the bright morning light, but it soon became apparent where things stood. As their eyes locked he could see the disappointment in hers, like those of a wounded animal begging for mercy. She broke the silence.

"You're going?"

Clay realized he had made a mistake. In the beginning there had been a fleeting glimpse of *maybe* with this girl; but now it was obvious he never should have asked her to dinner. He could see she would need too much from him to be happy…more than he had historically been able to give. She had seemed so capable at the bank—confident and independent. And then, of course, there was the job—the only reason he was even in Calexico—which required he cross the border and head south…*today*. He had given very specific handwritten instructions (including maps and

GPS coordinates) to Aloysius to pass on. Like a highly choreographed play, everyone had a role to play, including him.

"I have to go back to Canada," he lied. "I start a job in the oil fields in two days."

Lisa bent down and placed the tray on the folding luggage stand next to the door. She didn't move from her blocking position. Distrust crept into her voice.

"I thought you were visiting your sick mom?"

"Yes, but now I have to go back to work."

"I'll go with you."

The words lay naked, vulnerable and deeply needy, on the ground between them. Neither of them had had any idea how desperate she was; how little she valued her current existence.

"Lisa, you…I…have a life…you have a life…"

"We could at least try…?"

"Don't do this…"

"Do what? Be kind and considerate? Care about someone?"

"No…it's not that…you're not a child."

He stared at his lap, hands folded, searching for the words.

"You know how this works. You show me your best. I show you my best. And we have a great time. But we aren't really that good, or at least I'm not. Sooner or later, the ugly comes out…we get inattentive…or fat…or bored…and then one of us feels deceived and we start to lose trust, or try to change the other, and the whole thing collapses into a yelling mess…a big pile of disappointment and frustration."

She was struck by how dramatically different his narrative was from hers. Onto his silence she had projected a lifetime of empathy.

"I thought you were different."

"I'm sorry…I…just don't think I can give you what you deserve…I'm not capable."

As she realized she was being rejected, her defense mechanisms ignited involuntarily.

"That's such a crock of bullshit. The whole pile of it. You don't have any idea what I need…let alone deserve…it's just a long-winded way of hiding the fact that you're selfish."

Clay took a deep breath. *Here it comes,* he thought. *God, I hate this.* He left the TV on and got to his feet.

"So quick to cast the first stone," he mumbled.

"What!" She glared at him. "What the fuck is *that* supposed to mean?"

Clay kept his head down and mouth shut. He suspected there would be more and hoped she would quickly wear herself out.

"You are so full of shit."

He readjusted his pack and prepared to make his exit.

"Maybe so." He sighed.

On the way to the door he slipped by her, eyes on the ground as he reached for the duffle. He opened the door and turned back as he moved halfway across the threshold. He could smell her perfume.

"I had a great—"

She interrupted him while choking back the tears.

"Don't…don't pity me…just go, asshole."

Resigned to his plight, Clay turned away and prepared to move out of her life.

"By the way, I saw your gun."

He stopped in his tracks. The duffle kept the door from closing.

This might change everything, he thought.

He recalled the proverb from the play *The Mourning Bride* by William Congreve: *"Hell hath no fury like a woman scorned."*

He took a deep breath and gathered his thoughts. *Don't get yourself into trouble, Lisa.*

He looked back at her with hard, unapologetic eyes.

"What gun?"

His look chilled her, took some of the bite out of her bark.

"In your backpack. What are you? A cop? A drug dealer?"

"I have a license for that."

"Whatever."

He decided to try and defuse.

"I'll be back…my mom…can I see you again?"

"Probably not, but it's a free world…you know where I am."

His nervous system stood down. He didn't have to decide now.

"I've gotta go. I'll hunt you down when I'm back in town."

Neither wanted to look at the other. She had opened up completely to him and now felt foolish, betrayed. She pulled her shawl tighter around her slumping shoulders and tried not to act hysterical. Her brain was having major problems adjusting from the hopeful reality it had already begun to inhabit. In an effort to gain control, her hand lightly shoved Tommie's departing shoulder then pushed the door shut behind him. As she listened to his boots click away across the concrete, she lay down on the bed, shivering.

Then, she started to cry.

CHAPTER 28 —

Día de los Muertos

Like a splotch of blood hovering beside the road, the tattered piece of red cloth was right where Clay had said it would be. It hung flaccidly off the arm of a cactus as if it had long ago given up hope. Three buzzards had positioned themselves on the spiny cardon, wings partially spread as they perched like sentries above the crimson fabric, guarding the mountain pass while absorbing the desert heat. Keno checked his GPS coordinates one more time, just to be sure, then lifted his gaze to inspect his surroundings. The arid landscape was still, without a drop of sound or wind to disturb the sweat pouring out of his skin. He interpreted the whole setting as ominous. The beady stare of the birds was doing nothing to alleviate his concerns.

He and the Isuzu had been climbing the winding grade most of the day, away from Trick and the ocean and up into the Sierra Gigantes. There were several times when he was sure he was going to get stuck, when the sand was so deep, the road so steep and narrow, or the rocks so challenging that even with his partially deflated off-road tires and four-wheel drive the Trooper was struggling. It had been hours since he'd seen any evidence of humans, and, as the afternoon started to wane, he had begun to worry that he had made a wrong turn and was lost.

Reexamining the red piece of cotton from his place behind the wheel, he realized it was an old T-shirt. He worried that its location might be just a coincidence, the result of a New World scirocco that had lifted and deposited it at its current spot, as opposed to being intentionally placed by Clay. He climbed out of the truck and wandered to the edge of the road, bringing his eyes to within inches of the dirty fabric. Some barely decipherable lettering revealed itself as he got closer…he was able to make out the insignia of the San Francisco 49ers football team. He knew he was in the right place when he carefully removed the shirt from the plant's barbs and saw his name, "BARTON," in faded block print on the back. Both he and Clay had been given matching jerseys as Christmas presents long ago, and somehow his brother had either kept one or had a replica made.

Keno took off his ball cap and spread the weathered cloth over his hair, allowing the tailpiece to hang down and protect his neck before returning the hat to his head. To his right, an abyss beckoned treacherously; he edged his way over for a better look. The dirt road offered no guardrail before it abruptly disappeared into a steep, rocky ravine more than three hundred feet below. At the bottom was a dry creek bed, with a few stunted shrubs growing out of the sand. Starting to feel a bit vertiginous, he moved slowly away from the cliff and began scouring the embankment on the other side of the road. He was looking for his brother—but he wasn't even sure he would be able to identify him after so many years.

He shook his head disparagingly as he laughed to himself. *Luckily, I won't have to pick him out of a crowd.*

Clay's instructions were to find the flag and wait. So he walked back to the car, found some shade cast by the vehicle, and positioned himself in a third-world squat, haunches settling in on his calves while his sandaled feet spread flat on the ground.

After about fifteen minutes, he heard some scree sliding down from the steep slope above the road. He had sporadically changed his position from squat to lean, so with minimal effort he got up and looked over the hood. From up above he saw a man working his way down the hill, jumping from rock to rock with reasonable agility, belying any infirmity that otherwise would have been suggested by his clipped, grey beard. On his back was a full pack, and as the man drew closer, Keno realized that this was indeed his older brother.

In a few minutes Clay had made it to the road, tall hiking boots protecting his feet and legs from the danger of snake bites, desert camouflage covering the rest of his skin. He quickly approached Keno, who was watching in silence, wondering what would happen next. The soldier strode with a sense of urgency towards the truck.

"Brother, is that you?"

"Clay?"

Clay reached out his hand, took his brother's complementary offering, then pulled him in for a hug.

"Been a long time, Keno."

"No kiddin', man…long time."

The older pushed the younger back to arm's length then removed his brother's headgear.

"Let me take a look at you."

Keno did the same with Clay's military-style bucket hat.

"Dude, what happened to your hair? It's all white!"

"Ahhh, little brother, happens to the best of us…you'll see."

Keno smiled back, waiting for the elder's lead as they both baked in the late afternoon sun. Unusually, Clay started with the pleasantries.

"How's Mom?…Paul? I understand he's got a serious girlfriend."

"You haven't heard? Oh man, Mom's back was really bad, so to avoid surgery she started doing yoga, and, no shit, it got better! She's crazy fit now, a fanatic—body like a forty-year old. Sits only on a big rubber ball, no chairs."

Clay started laughing.

"No way…I guess our whole family…we're all a little strange."

"Dude, that's not all. When she retired from the ball bearing company…"

Keno paused, realizing he was gushing while Clay was putting off impatient body language.

"Sorry man, I'm going on, we've got stuff to do."

"Yeah, we do…but I asked…I'm interested."

"Well…it's just so crazy…Mom…she went back to some online computer school and learned how to program…you know, write software code and stuff."

"You shittin' me? *Our* Mom?"

Keno started laughing.

"One and the same. She's supposedly a whiz, works for some anti-virus company as an independent contractor. She's PRINTING it!"

"No fuckin' way! That's great…really great. And Paul? Your boys? Lola?"

"All healthy. Paul has a great girl, Roshan. They adopted a baby, she's almost two. They run an art business. Mom built their website. Lola and I have our ups and downs, but nothing we can't work through. Kids are a pain, going through assholescence, just like we all did, I guess."

Clay started laughing again. He hadn't realized how much he missed his brother and his family.

"Yeah, I'm sure we were more than a handful at that age…"

They both became quiet as their thoughts drifted to the night Paul got hurt.

After a few seconds, Clay checked his watch. He had a schedule.

"You sure about Lola? It's nothing serious?"

Keno resented the implication about his wife.

"Clay, where have you been? What's going on?"

"Dad didn't fill you in?"

"Only briefly. When he sent me your packet."

Clay knew what Keno wanted, but he wasn't ready to talk about it.

"Well, basically I've been camped out just below that ridge line, trying to keep the snakes out of my sleeping bag at night, while I make sure nothing gets in the way of us pulling this thing off."

Keno didn't fall for the diversion.

"No, not the last few days…I mean the last few *decades*?"

Clay dodged the question with his own.

"Who else knows about this?"

Keno let out a long, soft exhale. Even after all these years he knew his brother well enough not to pry where he wasn't welcome.

"Only Trick, Dad, you, and me."

"Not Lola?"

"No…why?"

"It's just usually the spouse."

"I can't believe that. Not Lola."

Clay looked up at the sun as it worked its way towards the western horizon.

"C'mon brother…no time now…we're burning daylight."

Clay unshouldered his pack and started pulling out some of the contents.

"Take off your clothes, all of them, including your shoes, and put these on."

"Everything, right now, right here?"

Clay stopped and looked solemnly at Keno.

"Keenan, this isn't a game. There are other people, people like me, who may be coming soon if they figure out who we are."

Clay had a way of conveying urgency that was captivating. Keno started paying rapt attention as he continued.

"Right now they don't know you're my brother. Whoever hired me thinks I'm Tommie Smith. If we pull this off it gives me time, it gives you time, so maybe I can figure this thing out. I don't have any better ideas. They won't stop coming unless they think your dead, or else the people who are paying call it off."

The assassin paused as he looked for a sign of understanding from Keno.

"Dad told me about this…it's just hard to believe anyone would want to kill me. I don't have any enemies."

"Everyone has enemies, Keno."

Keno started taking off his clothes. Clay used them to fill the knapsack.

"Did you bring the gas and the beer?"

Keno nodded as he pulled his shirt over his head.

"Five-gallon can and a case in the way back."

"Perfecto."

"How exactly are we gonna do this?"

"Sorry, brother-man, but you're about to get drunk and have a really bad accident in that old Trooper."

Keno took a deep breath. He and the Isuzu had been through a lot.

"I was afraid you were gonna say that."

"Don't worry, it'll be painless." He set his hand firmly on Keno's shoulder and nodded once. *"Listo, amigo."*

CHAPTER 29 —

The Devil You Know

❝ 'Everybody loves Augustus, Mrs. Barton. Girls, boys, most of his teachers…but he's just not putting in the effort he needs to stay up with the workload of an academically focused college preparatory curriculum like we provide here at Brinson Academy.' ❞

"That's what he said? About Gus?"

"Pretty much word for word."

Lola and Elise were in the women's locker room at the Mountain Club. It was slow, like most weekday mornings, and they had just shared a bucket of balls at the driving range. Although it had taken great effort, they didn't let the golf spoil the perfect spring day, or their opportunity to share gossip. Elise had dominated most of the morning conversation with a soup-to-nuts description of her most recent dalliance with the golf pro from another club. After enthusiastically reliving each salacious detail, she had at least been thoughtful enough to inquire about her friend's travails. Elise knew Lola's youngest was struggling academically, so she started there. Lola was grateful to be able to share the conversation she had had with Gus' headmaster the previous day. The interaction had been painfully bouncing around in her head ever since, and she had nearly perfect recall of the most alarming details. Before the meeting she had resigned herself to the reality that Gus was an average to indifferent student, but she had had no idea that his current semester's grades were in the middle of such a dramatic, slow-motion belly flop towards the bottom decile. Vacillating between outrage (for what she perceived was the unfair singling out of her son) and panic, she started worrying that both her offspring were shiftless, hormone-saturated mediocrities. She desperately needed a second opinion, and her tennis partner was pretty much always good at putting her parenting crises into perspective.

Elise went to work trying to assuage Lola's concerns.

"Four years ago, he said almost the exact same thing to Lois MacAdams about her oldest…and he still got into Stanford."

Getting in to Stanford was the ultimate achievement for Bay Area parents clamoring to thrust their children up the trophy school ladder. The couples whose kids reached the Palo Alto summit received lifetime tenure to the "excellent parent" club, regardless of their other shortcomings, and could casually drop the Stanford name in any local context where they felt they weren't being sufficiently respected.

"Yeah, but wasn't he some all-world lacrosse player? And, didn't Joe MacAdams go there? I heard they donated something like fifteen million to get him in."

"It was just thirteen million."

"It doesn't matter. We don't have those kind of connections, or that kind of money…and Gus barely made the swim team at Brinson."

"Don't worry, he'll get in somewhere. There's nothing magical about the curriculum or the professors at any of these places. You're just paying for the peer group and brand."

Lola's concerns went beyond the Brinson classroom. Lately it seemed as if both her boys were enrolled in a self-directed, online course in masturbation that was taking up an inordinate amount of their time and energy. The evidence of spewed DNA was so overwhelming that their Guatemalan maid, Elosia, had felt it necessary to bring the boys' stained sheets to Lola's attention. Being a staunch Roman Catholic, Elosia was concerned for the boys' souls, as she had been taught that unrepentant solitary sex was a mortal sin. Embarrassed as she was when confronted with the secretions, Lola was concerned less about her boys' damnation and more about their ambition, or lack thereof. Either way she was alarmed by the frequency of the self-occupations. She felt like she was surrounded by a posse of spraying tomcats…which resulted in her thoughts being more frequently invaded by sterilization fantasies. Wanting to consult with Elise on the topic, she hadn't yet worked up the nerve to do so, due to her concerns that her friend would think her children deviant. But then she recalled the details of Elise's earlier sexual testimony involving the golf pro, and she quickly got over her fears of embarrassment.

"I know this is a weird question, but how much do boys usually masturbate? I mean, I know it's supposedly a lot, but—"

Elise interrupted with a look of concern.

"Your boys masturbate?"

Caught off guard, Lola realized she had expected something different from her irreverent friend.

"Um, well…yeah, I think so…I mean I've never caught them in the act or anything…"

"You know that's a mortal sin, right?"

"What?"

"You have to put an end to that shit right away…even if you have to pleasure them personally…the Bible makes it clear that sex is between a man and a woman and is *not* to be done alone. Yes, Lola, as shocking as it may sound, the Bible would prefer you relieve your sons manually rather than have them beat off and hence go to hell."

Lola searched Elise's face for some sort of clue.

"For a minute there you had me."

They both started laughing.

"Can you believe some of those nutcases actually believe that crazy shit?"

"I thought maybe you had this weird religious side I had never seen before."

"I definitely have some weird sides I haven't shared with you, but when it comes to teenage boys and masturbation, the only thing abnormal is if your kid *isn't* doing it."

"I mean, when I was a teenager, I liked to rub a few out. But I think my boys are gonna die from dehydration."

"Yeah, mine too. And with the internet now, everything's available for free, all just a mouse click away. I'm amazed these kids ever go on dates anymore…let alone get married."

"Right? How do real girls even compete with guys' expectations of perfect, airbrushed models?"

Lola became silent as a blue-haired tennis player walked into the locker room. Both of the younger women were acutely aware that their conversation had been inappropriate. The reptilian club matron walked to a locker opposite Elise's. Lola watched her spin the combination, open the door, and pull a feminine napkin from a box labeled "KOTEX" that was sitting on the top shelf. Without even acknowledging the two younger women, the sun-wizened, sharp-elbowed senior grabbed her oversized racquet and headed back to the green Har-Tru courts, leaving

Elise and Lola alone in her wake.

Lola had trouble believing that the fossil who had just passed them was still fertile.

"What was that?"

"You mean the Kotex?"

"Exactly."

"They put them inside the front of their visors…great at absorbing sweat."

"*Really?* That's ingenious."

Elise laughed.

"Right? I've even tried it. It actually works."

She then lowered her voice to a conspiratorial whisper:

"What's going on with the Wolf?"

Having found herself seriously upset from the night with Wolfgang at the Casa Madrona, Lola had revealed a lot of the details to Elise, again soliciting her advice. She sometimes wished she hadn't.

"I still think I should go to the police."

"It's never too late."

"Except all the physical evidence is gone now, so it's just a 'he said, she said' thing."

"That's true. You know what I would do…"

Lola rolled her eyes, having a good idea from their previous conversations what was coming next.

"I'd take his calls and play him like a Stradivarius."

"Yeah, thanks for the support."

"Lola, what's not to like? A rich, handsome man plans an extensive, extravagant evening; feeds you your favorite mezcal and *foie gras;* pays rabid attention to you all night; gives you multiple orgasms; and you go home in the morning with a Tiffany bracelet. What girl wouldn't die for a date like that?"

"He basically orchestrated a gang rape."

"I know, I get hot every time I think about it…. Why don't you give him my number?"

Before Lola could warn her away from Wolfgang's sociopathic tendencies, her cell phone started vibrating in her locker. She plucked it from the shelf over her head and checked the caller ID.

"Speak of the devil…"

"That's him calling now?"

"Yep."

"Well…answer it. Or I will."

Lola pushed a button and held the phone to her ear.

"Hello…?"

"It's me, Wolfgang."

"Yes, I know it's Wolfgang."

"When can I see you again? I need to see you."

"Never."

Elise let out a choking, gasping sound. She shook her head in violent disapproval.

"Lola, don't do this to me, I'm a desperate man."

"I don't care."

"Why? Why…are you doing this? We had a great time in Sausalito."

"You had a great time, I was gang raped."

"Gang raped! Wha—?"

"That's what they call it when multiple people have sex with you against your will."

"Lola…that was just me. I made it appear that more than one man was involved in seducing you, because I recalled that that was one of your college fantasies…and it worked, I've never seen you so hot."

"Bullshit."

"God's truth."

Lola started reorienting some of her convictions.

"I can't talk now, I'm with someone."

"I'll call back tomorrow."

"Please don't."

Then she hung up the phone and looked hard at Elise, challenging her to make some snide comment while her brain worked through the new information.

"Is the Wolf still hungry?"

"He's *always* hungry."

"I've got something he can eat…"

"Elise Haversham! Behave yourself! You're a mother!"

"And…?"

Lola was wondering what exactly playing someone like a Stradivarius implied. Keno had gone on yet another boys' trip, this time surfing for a week in the Baja, and she was getting fed up with his inattention. Feeling lonely and underappreciated, she started thinking about all the men in her life—her sons, Keno, Wolfgang—and how much all of them were driven by testosterone and their overwhelming need to procreate. Before she could share this thought with Elise, her phone started vibrating again. She picked it up and answered with an annoyed tone.

"What part of 'never' don't you understand, Wolfgang?"

"Hi Lola, this is Aloysius."

Lola was silent for a moment. She didn't know any other Aloysiuses, but she hadn't seen or spoken to her father-in-law for years, and she had no idea why he would call. She was worried he might mention Wolfgang to Keno. Aloysius took the silence as a sign of confusion.

"Aloysius Barton? Your father-in-law? Who's Wolfgang?"

"Sorry. Hi Aloysius…of course I know who you are. Wolfgang is just a…pesky local realtor."

There was a pause. Aloysius tried to figure out how to reboot.

"Lola, I have some bad news. Are you sitting down?"

CHAPTER 30 —

The Blank Canvas

Dr. Concepcion Blanco sat in a nonjudgmental slump. Her demeanor revealed little about her degree of interest in the patient reclining in her office. The bottom half of the doctor's tailored, woolen pantsuit covered toned legs that benefitted from a brisk, daily, two-mile walk between home and office. The legs were now crossed at the knee, right over left. Dangling from her top foot was one of a pair of Christian Louboutin, red-soled pumps. She had agonized over their purchase a year ago but now harbored no remorse. On the contrary, one of her great daily pleasures came when she arrived at her office thirty minutes before her first appointment, slid the ridiculously expensive shoes out from their hiding place under the mahogany desk, and transferred her feet out of her comfy but frumpy New Balance trainers and into the conspicuously sultry heels. Being a doctor she was well aware of the placebo effect, but that didn't stop the notable invigoration that the footwear always brought. She hypothesized that if Ponce de Leon could have found a pair of Louboutins he would have ended his search.

The designer shoes were a gift to herself for terminating a relationship with a local engineering professor whose approach to lovemaking she found too mechanical. She had been wishing their intimate sharing would evolve beyond civil interaction towards something more electric, with better chemistry; but after three years she had given up hope. Despite having no interest in him as a long-term partner, she had nonetheless continued to invite him into her bed when her libido—and her optimism—were simultaneously peaking. Unfortunately the engineer had fallen head over heels. He regularly pushed her for a greater commitment. Eventually the incongruence of their feelings became so obvious that she decided it was poor form for someone in her position to string along another human being solely for the sake of sexual convenience. He was devastated.

The third of eight siblings raised by Nicaraguan immigrants, Blanco had grown up in the working class suburbs of the San Gabriel Valley—an area called El Monte. She was easily the most academically gifted, and despite never wanting to live anywhere other than Southern California, she had left for an East Coast college at the age of seventeen. Four years later, when she was accepted to medical school at UCLA, she leapfrogged left, back towards the Pacific Ocean, to join the upper crust on the Westside of Los Angeles.

After medical school but before the beginning of her residency, Blanco moved out of campus housing and signed a one-year lease for a cozy, one-bedroom pied-à-terre in Westwood. Much later, about twenty years into her tenancy, her long-standing landlord died abruptly from a brain aneurysm. Dr. Blanco was able to purchase the whole Southwestern-style apartment building from the owner's children (and heirs) in an effortless transaction that added landlord and real estate investor to her resume. The price negotiation took one day. During her decades as a tenant, a sort of trust had developed between the landlord's family and the quiet lady psychiatrist. There had evolved the type of familiarity and respect that often builds between people who live in close quarters and watch each other go through their daily routines without faltering or allowing the burdens of existence to break their stride. She had been able to purchase the adobe abode in an "all cash" deal, using nearly every penny she had saved during her first twenty years of professional practice. Growing up in an environment of scarcity, she had learned how to do without at a young age, and hence she had an all-consuming predilection for saving that some might have considered to be a compulsion. She had continued living in the same apartment after purchasing the building—a total of more than thirty years, counting her time as a tenant.

Upon completing her medical residency, she had taken the leap of faith required of most young entrepreneurs and rented some office space a couple of miles from her home. Her expertise in anxiety disorders and depression, her focus on children and young adults, and her gentle bedside manner allowed her to grow her practice through referrals. By the end of her first year she had a run rate that provided enough revenue to hire an office administrator (who doubled as a bookkeeper) and still pay the rent. As her practice grew, she persisted in her settled ways, keeping the same office in which she had started. For nearly three decades her daily commute had her following a path through the same, leafy, Westwood neighborhood, almost always on foot, and rarely with deviation.

Though she had had suitors over the years, she had never married nor conceived a child. She periodically worried about her fertility, and when she was lonely she would sometimes contemplate the DNA cul-de-sac on which she lived. These sorts of thoughts, especially when she was tired, brought about an empty sort of melancholy that made her feel as though she was the last person on earth.

An obvious creature of habit, Dr. Blanco used routine to effectively overcome her own mental health issues, most of which revolved around anxiety. Personal experience had taught her that there was a fine line separating the functional from the incapacitated, and she used this self-awareness and a unique inner discipline to her advantage. Sizing up a situation, she would decide on a goal, develop a time-motion strategy to most efficiently achieve that goal, and then go about rigidly implementing the plan. Most days were scheduled with a specific nuance and creativity. She would carve out fifteen-minute slots to practice a Salsa dance step, review French verb conjugation, or mulch a rose bush. She rarely left any time in her calendar unoccupied; hence there was little space for the predations of paranoia to filter in. So committed was she to this methodology that she even scheduled regular sexual interludes, although as she approached sixty years of age, the frequency was decreasing. Regardless of the quality of her partner, she would complete the sessions when a one-hour timer went off. Many of her lovers had developed capable biological clocks and a nearly Pavlovian softening as the sixtieth minute approached. Every morning, without fail, Dr. Blanco got up and made her bed.

After pushing back the sleeves on her jacket for the umpteenth time, Blanco casually worked her pencil across the top of her notebook. She had already let ten minutes pass since her patient had reclined on the tufted chocolate chaise lounge. Neither had said much more than a cursory greeting, but the older woman wasn't worried. After practicing for nearly thirty years, "Dr. Connie" (as the kids called her) had an approach that always prioritized patience. With a bird's-eye view towards the top back quarter of Scout Stein's head she noticed a tuffet of blue and red intermingled with her natural brunette hair color. Scout had been visiting twice a week for about two months, and though Blanco thought they were making progress, it was slow. When the time was right she hoped Scout's thoughts would prioritize themselves and percolate to the surface in a spasm of emotional release.

While Scout lay quietly, the doctor continued a lazy scrawl in her notebook. She had taken up sketching with a graphite pencil, and many of her sessions were spent drawing one of the objects in her office or re-creating a vision in her mind's eye. Right now she was sketching the back of Scout's multicolored head. She made a note to herself to explore colored pencils as a medium to more fully capture moments like this.

As inconsiderate as this may have appeared to patients (if they had ever discovered the nature of Dr. Blanco's scrawls), her method actually served dual purposes. One, it allowed her to be patient, therefore not leading her charges (or implying judgment) until a critical point; two, it sent the message that she was working hard for her clients, documenting and analyzing, even during the quiet moments. At first she had felt somewhat unprofessional and even duplicitous with the hobby. She worried that her doodling might be interpreted as shortchanging her customers. But she soon realized that she had a strong intuition for when a patient reached a crucial point and needed shepherding. She had come to believe that her job was similar to that of a cop on the beat—hours of boredom spent patrolling and listening, with infrequent punctuations of short, dramatic events that required the intervention of a well-trained professional. During the slow times, the artwork allowed her to survive the repetition, minutiae, and frustration embedded in thirty years of listening to people who often were incapable or unwilling to make simple, healthy changes to their behavioral patterns.

As Blanco worked to keep her palm from smudging the pencil scratches, Scout came alive.

"I almost didn't come today."

Excited to start working, Blanco knew not to pounce. She gave the notepad a break from the stabbing of graphite.

"Is it the agoraphobia, or did something else happen?"

"It's my brother, he's missing."

"Paul, your half brother?"

"No, I have two other half brothers, Keno and Clay."

This was news to Blanco. It added to the complexity of her patient's treatment. She decided she would use the family web to establish a benign dialogue of fact-checking that would hopefully get Scout talking and eventually allow her to share more of her emotions.

"I don't recall you ever mentioning them? Are they Paul's brothers as well?"

"Half brothers. We all share the same father, but Paul and I have different mothers than Clay and Keno."

Scratching furiously to make sure she documented all the players and relationships correctly, Blanco asked for clarification.

"And Clay and Keno share the same mother *and* father?"

"As far as we know, but I don't think anyone's ever done a DNA test."

"And you grew up without knowledge of any of these siblings?"

"Not until my senior year at Pomona."

"Yes, I remember that fantastically strange coincidence."

"Unbelievable, right?" Scout challenged with sarcasm.

Blanco recognized the fragile nature of trust.

"Almost, but I believe you. Stranger things have happened."

The conversation stopped. The doctor wanted to continue, but still treaded lightly. After about a minute, Blanco softly pried.

"So what exactly happened, and to which brother?"

Scout sighed. She then started shaking and choking back her tears. In a well-practiced move, Dr. Blanco leaned forward, handed her a box of tissues, and put a reassuring hand on her shoulder. Scout's words came out as mumbling.

"It's very hard for me to talk about."

"I'm sure it is, but I'm interested…if you feel like sharing…"

Scout made an effort at composure, dabbed at her eyes and nose, and then started talking in a halting rhythm.

"It's Keno…he's the normal one, the strong one…out of all of us…never a burden…good husband and Dad…successful businessman…all the rest of us are total weirdos…damaged goods."

Feeling invigorated now that Scout was talking, revealing how she felt about herself and the others close to her, Dr. Blanco fell into a mental groove. She knew these were the moments when her patients were the most receptive to considering alternative paths, either consciously or subconsciously, and she was excited about her moment to try and effect a healthy change. She wanted to explore more deeply the psychological treasure trove inherent in Scout's characterizations of her family members as "weirdos" and "damaged goods." She took a breath to slow herself, knowing she had to allow the catharsis to come on its own time. She kept silent during Scout's ensuing pause, leaving room for her patient to gather herself and continue without interruption. Her restraint was rewarded less than a minute later.

"It's just…what's the point, ya know? If someone as capable as that can just disappear? He's got two boys and a wife who need him…so much can go wrong to anybody at any time."

"What do you mean 'just disappear'?"

"All they know is he was on a surf trip with a friend in some remote part of Baja. He drove out of their camp one morning to get some supplies and no one has seen him since. His friend had to hike out twenty miles to get cell coverage and call for help after he didn't show up."

"Oh my god, Scout." Blanco kept her tone level as she needed to validate without escalating. "That's a terrible situation, I'm so sorry. All of your family must be devastated."

"It's really terrible."

"Were you close to Keno?"

"We…used to…I've thought about him a lot…but…we…we haven't really talked in a few years…he's really busy."

Hesitating for a second, Scout decided to add some more information that made her appear closer to the victim's family, and hence more encumbered by the loss.

"I just talked to his wife, Lola, last month. I feel much closer to her. She's a strong woman, no nonsense…and beautiful…inside and out. She understands how hard it can be for a woman out there…she's always made time to talk to me, and I lived with their family for a couple of months after…"

Scout let her sentence trail off…she didn't want to think about Tate Chalk and the assault. Dr. Blanco understood and tried to move them away from the memory of that experience. If time allowed, they could revisit the sensitive area later.

"How long has he been missing?"

"It's been nearly three days."

Blanco wasn't sure how to respond, so she stuck to something with no sharp edges.

"That's very unusual. I hope they find him soon."

As she went back to her sketching, she knew the next step would take some finesse—she had to be extremely careful not to appear to be pushing anything that implied too much judgment.

While graphite carefully replicated Scout's hair, the older woman embraced the discomfort of the silence. She was again rewarded for allowing Scout to make the first move when the patient started on what initially appeared to be a verbal non sequitur.

"All this arm waving…this running around and keeping busy. It's just stupid to me…filling the void until we die. It's like we're all pigs and everyone is putting on lipstick and tutus and building these supposedly *meaningful* lives, but it doesn't change the fact that we're all headed to the same slaughterhouse and we don't know when—or even who gets the bacon."

Again the pause. Blanco gave Scout's eruption the respect it deserved and then blew gently on what she thought was a smoldering cinder.

"This event has clearly brought forth some deep feelings. You've mentioned these feelings of despair and hopelessness before. Have they become more consuming?"

"I can barely get out of bed."

A lot of Dr. Blanco's patients weren't self-aware enough to consider the source of their symptoms, but she knew Scout was exceptional in this area, so she pressed for more information.

"Are you having symptoms that you would describe as depression or are you experiencing panic attacks?"

"Both. First I feel bad, and then I feel guilty for feeling bad…for not…I don't know…*willing* myself to feel good…like all the normal, productive people out there."

"Hmm…that sounds challenging. Are you self-medicating? Are you using any of the coping mechanisms we discussed?"

*You mean **you** discussed*, thought Scout.

She was skeptical when it came to her brain and simple solutions. Some would say she preferred more drama.

"I'm trying."

Blanco recognized the non–answer. She knew about Scout's resistance to discussing her unhealthy habits and decided now wasn't the time to push. Instead, she wanted to explore her patient's symptoms.

"Can you tell me more about your daily struggles?"

"Well…yeah…I mean…. It's like when I wake up if I have something on my calendar that requires…I don't know…human interaction…I immediately start to worry about what they'll think of me. I worry about whether or not I can get up, get my shit together, and make the meeting on time. It often grows into a full-on panic attack. I'll start making up excuses not to go…and I'll totally resent the fact that the event has even been scheduled. I'll even fantasize about how great it would be to have no commitments and just lie in bed all day."

"And the depression?"

"I know it sounds crazy, but the opposite. When I wake up with nothing on my calendar I get totally depressed about being a social outcast with no friends and no interests…and I can't imagine anybody or anything ever being interesting…or taking an interest in me."

Searching for a way to keep Scout talking, Blanco decided on a sincere compliment.

"Scout, it's really good that you are doing and sharing this degree of self-examination. I believe it's necessary to get you to a healthier place."

Blanco paused to let the words sink in before continuing.

"Are you ever able to see the irony in your dilemma and use that to get more comfortable and functioning?"

"I realize it's absurd, but the whole thing is absurd."

For the last two months, during their biweekly sessions, Blanco had noticed Scout repeatedly use the term "absurd" to describe the human experience. Concerned her patient might be using this conclusion to hide from a world replete with responsibilities, Dr. Blanco had an idea she wanted to try out in order to get her client to consider other perspectives.

The problem was that the implementation of her plan would require some direct verbal medicine, and she felt it was crucial to administer the right dosage in a non-adversarial way. Deciding now was the time to enact her agenda, she hoped she wouldn't push Scout back into her cave.

"Do you think this recent event triggered the trauma you carry from your sexual assault?"

"Duh."

Blanco decided she had to try and draw attention to Scout's consistent sarcasm.

"How about anger management? Are you still having periodic, sudden onsets of rage?"

Noticeably flinching, Scout felt the question carried an implied criticism, and she barely kept from retaliating aggressively before realizing how obviously unthinking that would have been. Instead she tried to shift the blame.

"Doc, aren't you being a bit sensitive? Jeez, I was just kidding…does everything always have to be so serious?"

"No offense taken, Scout."

Blanco took a moment to let the smoke settle from the near miss before reinitiating.

"So, no anger issues since our last session?"

Scout struggled between resistance and collaboration. Finally, realizing that it was her dime, and the project was her mental health, she decided to go with the latter.

"I'm sorry, Dr. Blanco…I…ummm…sometimes it's really hard for me to…I don't know… disarm? Lately it's been a real struggle, it feels like I'm always under siege…ya know what I mean? The slightest thing seems to set me off. Someone smoking a cigarette that I barely smell…or the tone of someone's voice…or a song that's not even intended for me to hear…. Sometimes I feel like a bull and the whole world is waving a red cape at me. I don't know how to turn it off."

Blanco was feeling a bit outgunned. In less than ten minutes her patient had revealed that she suffered from anxiety, depression, and rage, all incapacitating to varying degrees. Since the beginning of their sessions together, the doctor had been focused on a combination of talk therapy and medication; but the conversations seemed to be growing more contentious rather than less, and none of the prescribed compounds seemed to be working. Even more worrisome was Scout's hinting at suicidal thoughts. Blanco was concerned that she was running out of time and was already at the bottom of a very limited toolbox. Working through the options, she decided to take a chance and be more direct. Her plantar fascia started throbbing.

Before asking the next question, Blanco slowly counted to ten then inquired in as gentle and nurturing a way as she could.

"Do you think you're the first one to struggle with the meaning of life…existential angst?"

"What do you mean?"

"Let me ask this another way. Are you happy with the state of your life?"

"Of course not, that's why I'm here."

The doctor decided to keep pushing.

"Scout, I think there are some questions we need to consider before we can make any meaningful progress together. You may not like them, but I think you are strong enough to hear what I have to say."

Feeling threatened, Scout immediately felt her defenses go up, ready to dismiss anything her shrink was about to offer. Dr. Blanco expected this to be difficult, but after two relatively uneventful months, Blanco hoped she had built up enough trust with her patient to plant the seed. Putting down the pencil, the doctor picked up her psychiatric scalpel.

"Do you think you're the first one to suffer an injustice, to be violated, to lose a loved one, to hurt?"

"Of course not."

"Then why are you here? Lots of people suffer, but most of them don't allow their negative experiences to define them in a dysfunctional way."

Scout sat up higher, rigid, revealing a couple of more inches of the back of her head to the therapist. Old habits die hard.

"Well, I'm certainly not here to be insulted…called dysfunctional. I know I'm dysfunctional…I thought I was here so you could help me get better?"

Blanco picked her words carefully.

"My point isn't that you're dysfunctional. My point is that a lot of people are traumatized in terrible ways, yet they figure out how to move on and live healthy lives. My point is that you're here not because you have been damaged in some way; you're here because you aren't sure how, or don't want, to move on."

Taking the words as critical, Scout started moving from defensive to angry and decided to up the ante, as if she could hurt the doctor by implying her treatment was ineffective.

"I'm not sure any of this is even worth the effort…or expense…the ridiculousness of it all."

Dr. Blanco had been waiting for this opening. She watched Scout carefully, with empathy and admiration.

Now we're getting somewhere, she thought.

"So you're telling me you're searching for meaning? A reason to live?"

Scout hadn't been prepared for the detour.

"Maybe…if it exists."

"And, continuing with your metaphor, you'd rather neglect the lipstick and tutus and instead scramble around naked digging for truffles as nature intended?"

Still seeing red, Scout sensed a trap, so she groped her way forward carefully.

"I'm skeptical that your metaphor holds, but…maybe…something like that."

"So why aren't you doing it?"

"Doing what?"

"Digging for truffles? Getting on with living…building your life? Giving yourself a purpose, a reason to move on and stop focusing on your pain?"

Scout was in full fight-or-flight mode now. She felt like she was being attacked. Taking a defiant stance, she chose the former, going on the offensive.

"What makes you the expert in all this? You don't know any more than me or anyone else about what behavior is rational. You all describe life as this amazing thing, something we should all cherish…like we can just pick being happy as easy as we pick our breakfast cereal. Well for me it's not like that at all. It's hell. Every day a nightmare, just trying to make it through, and then comes the night…the fuckin' misery of night… highlighting how alone and empty the whole mess is. Of course I do stupid, dysfunctional things…drugs…casual sex…all these 'unhealthy coping mechanisms,' as you people say…anything to escape the pain… to feel good for just a moment."

It wasn't unusual for one of Dr. Blanco's patients to swing rapidly from a crying, vulnerable mess to a vehement antagonist, but the speed at which Scout just effected the transition was particularly intense. After all the years of being a psychiatrist, these were the moments that Dr. Blanco most cherished. An authentic conversation wrought from pain and suppressed emotional struggle. Like a swollen infection that finally bursts forth its contents, Scout's inner turmoil had now emerged, and Blanco suspected there was more discharge lingering beneath the surface; patiently returning to her sketching, she was curious to see if she would need to apply more pressure for its release. She didn't have to wait long, as it took only a moment for Scout to gather her breath and her thoughts. The ideas that had been swirling in her head for years now burst forth in a second, irreverent liberation.

"You doctors go through all this schooling and claim superior knowledge but it's superior only because we all know so little. You don't even know what life is…what causes it. One moment a conscious being and the next a corpse. Why? Why can't all you experts reanimate all the dead tissue like Doctor Frankenstein? Everything is still there, all the organs and cells. Where did the living organism go?"

Scout briefly came up for air and then dove back in.

"You tell me I should cling to life as if suicide is something a crazy, immoral person considers. But you don't know! You don't know that life is much better for me than death. You don't know where we come from before conception, where we go after death; you just know that we no longer communicate in a way living people can comprehend. Maybe I'm the sane one and all you *life clingers* are idiots? Maybe all the dead people have moved on to a much better place…where there is no pain and suffering…and they are all begging us to join them as soon as possible, to leave this hell we call life, but only those who commit suicide are actually listening? Maybe Earth is a way station between two heavens…a brief, horrific transition zone that God needed as he perfected Nirvana A and Utopia B. Maybe life as we know it is the absolute worst period we will ever go through…yet we ignorantly grasp for every second."

Scout had been gesticulating wildly with her hands, and as her final sentence left her lips, her arms and the words slowly floated downward in relief. Sweat had formed on her brow…the intensity of her discourse had increased her metabolic rate. In a rare display of discomfort and confusion, Dr. Blanco put down her pad and pencil, then took off her jacket. Needing time to think, she recrossed her legs and paused to briefly remove the Louboutin and massage the arch on the bottom of her left foot. She had been feeling some minor pain in her plantar fascia, and Scout's monologue had sharpened the tenderness and increased her worry that the inflammation would prevent her from enjoying her daily commute. After it appeared Scout was done (at least for a while), Blanco tried to address some of her issues.

"Thank you for trusting me enough to share your thoughts. You obviously feel strongly about these things…and you're right, I don't know what comes next."

Pausing to let that sink in, Blanco returned to massaging her plantar fascia.

Feeling a little post-partum depression, Scout tried to walk back some of the vitriol.

"You probably think I'm terrible."

"Not at all. In my experience your feelings fall well within the normal range, especially for the millions who suffer from depression or anxiety disorders."

"I'm just so offended by all these people that tell me they have all the answers. They're everywhere."

Not sure where Scout's comments were leading, Dr. Blanco recognized she had a decision to make. She had been hoping for the extemporaneous explosion that Scout had just released, but now wanted to dig through some of the expurgation, and to do so she needed to regain control of the dialogue. Having to choose between allowing Scout to continue with her unrehearsed discourse or trying to contain and shepherd the conversation, she decided to let Scout run free for a few more minutes.

"I'm not sure I'm following you?"

"It's the uncertainty, the complexity and constant changing of it all…all the endless choices and possibilities with no guarantee as to outcome…it's paralyzing. I wake up every day afraid I'll make a mistake, offend someone, waste a lot of effort on a career that's going away or that I don't like…put myself in a dangerous position, like my brother, and just disappear. Fuck, I can't even decide which cable channel to watch…I end up flipping through them all, one by one, searching for *something* that makes me want to commit…something that I can't even describe."

By now Blanco had totally given up on the sketching and was writing furiously to try and keep up with the stream of consciousness.

"Let's go back a step. Which people are everywhere and claim to have the answers?"

"Everybody on the TV…the internet…preachers, politicians, Wall Street gurus…all the marketing people…doctors…you."

"I've tried hard not to…"

"None of you *know*…not in any prescient sense, what really comes next…or have any power to shape the future. You all have your theories…and promises…oh, the *promises!*…the sheer hubris of your *conviction* makes me jealous. And the most charismatic of you use a…a…polysyllabic hyperbole to express a confidence…and ask for our allegiance, our votes, or our money…to supposedly make our lives better…but none of you really *KNOWS* what comes next…not any better than me or anyone else."

Continuing with the scribbling, trying to document Scout's words as best she could, the doctor decided to verbally establish some common ground.

"Just to be clear, I've never implied any superior insight about why you're on this planet. In fact, I have no idea why any of us are here, and I don't believe anybody does. As we talked about during our early sessions, first you need to know who you are, and then you need to forge your own path. No one can do this for you. I can give you tips, help guide you, but this is your journey. And my first suggestion is that you accept the uncertainty that accompanies all of our lives."

As Blanco finished her sentence, she realized something was bothering her, professionally, and she wanted to address it before their hour ran out.

"There's a lot going on here, and I'm not sure we can cover it all in our remaining time. With your permission, I'd really like to focus on an earlier comment…"—Blanco turned back a few pages in her notebook to find the phrase—"…where you talked about not being sure it was worth the effort, the ridiculousness of it all…I think you were talking about the possibility that the experience we think of as life may represent the peak of our suffering…and suicide may be the appropriate answer?"

Scout took a rare pause to set a filter onto her thoughts before answering.

"It's just…everybody talks about happiness as if it's a choice. To me the real choice that no one talks about is whether or not we should continue with the daily struggle until nature or an accident kills us…or should we have some ovaries? Take control, and end it on our own terms?"

"So you're contemplating suicide?"

"Aren't you?"

The doctor paused before she understood the question.

"Yes, but not my own."

"Isn't that called murder?"

Dr. Blanco barely suppressed a laugh.

"See, now that…that ability of yours to rise above the moment, and see something funny…that's not the trait of someone who is hopelessly trapped in darkness…it implies to me that you can have fun with life despite the apparent absurdity of it all."

Scout briefly turned her head like an owl, looking the doctor right in the eye.

"I'm not sure that's enough to make me want to stay around."

Not letting her dismay become noticeable, Dr. Blanco made space for Scout to continue to air her grievances. "Okay, let's go back to the suicidal thoughts. How often are they occurring?"

Returning the back of her head to its more comfortable position, Scout resumed her role.

"Not all the time, but sometimes…"

"Let's talk more about those."

"I think I have been."

"Fair enough. Specifically, let's talk more about uncertainty."

"It's terrifying sometimes…overwhelming to me, all the ways I can fail."

"But if we agree that nobody knows why we're here, that our presence in and of itself is absurd, why do you care about the uncertain nature of outcomes? If it's all just a pointless game, a blank canvas, aren't you free to make the rules, choose the colors? We could call it your own personal morality. If you get to choose, why choose fear? Why only paint with black? Splash some color in there. Why choose suffering? Have some fun. Instead of thinking about all the ways you can fail, why not focus on all the ways you can succeed?"

The doctor hoped they were making some progress, but Scout wasn't willing to be moved from her well-worn, comfy spot. At least not right away.

"Easier said than done."

"Scout, living a healthy life isn't easy, it takes work, intentional effort and thought…but I firmly believe that for most people it is a choice."

Scout didn't respond. Already exhausted, she was tired of being told she needed to try harder. Blanco took advantage of the silence.

"Look, you're not alone in any of this. Although brains are incredibly complicated and misunderstood organs, your affliction is relatively common. Let's call it fear of change, the future, or the unknown, whatever you want, but I think it's really a fear that something in the future will hurt you…because you were badly hurt in the past…and so you lose trust in the world, in people…become obsessed with what danger may be lurking around the corner…all the ways you can get hurt, all the potential negative outcomes…you want to be prepared, to protect yourself…because you feel that in the past no one else has…and you build this narrative that the world is this hugely terrible place, that you have to always be on guard, there's no room for joy or trust or openness in your story…you build walls to try and protect your feelings…which necessitates becoming inwardly focused…closed off from the love of other humans…and slowly, little pieces inside of you die."

Scout's twisted expression didn't reveal whether she was agonizing over what Dr. Blanco was saying or just trying to better understand it.

The doctor paused to make sure she hadn't lost the only patient in her psychiatric operating room.

"You with me?"

Scout nodded the back of her head in a noncommittal affirmation.

"Okay, so my theory for you is that fear of trauma is at the root of a lot of these problems. By 'trauma' I mean big and small, death of a loved one, or the simple random challenges that confront us daily, like worrying that others won't accept us or running out of TP."

Blanco paused again as she prepared to finish the cutting and hopefully start the suturing.

"Still with me?"

"I think so."

"Okay, so hopefully you're noticing some of your situation already. People that suffer acutely from these symptoms are diagnosed as 'anxious'…but…and it's a big but…there's no indication that the world is going to stop changing any time soon or that uncertainty will no longer exist, which means that living an open, trusting life will likely bring random trauma or suffering as well as moments of wonder and grace. You can't have one without the other."

Dr. Blanco waited a beat before dropping her punch line.

"So don't you think we should learn how to live with it?"

Scout recognized it was her turn to participate.

"Okay, and how do I do that?"

"Well, we've already established that uncertainty, change and the accompanying random trauma aren't going away, so what's left?"

"Mmmm…the…fear?"

"Exactly! People waste all of their time trying to insulate or control their lives in an effort to eliminate change and the accompanying uncertainty, when the thing they need to get rid of is their fear. And since you already believe life is a pointless absurdity, then any emotion exists only in your head—so why choose to be so fearful and morose?"

"So you think my laying in bed all day is my way of trying to control my environment, to keep change from happening, insulate me from the daily shit that accompanies the daily grace?"

"I think it could be. It's pointless, obviously, but the brain will justify a lot of irrational behavior when it's afraid. We need to be able to embrace change, be open to it."

"So, I'm sorry, I must've missed that part...what's to like about change and uncertainty again?"

"Well, first of all it's unavoidable. But if you need a reason to like it, maybe trying to understand that change is what leads to growth. Moving out of our comfort zone is definitionally uncomfortable. I believe we desperately need growth—and spiritual growth qualifies—to be healthy."

Trying hard to come up with a refutation, Scout was struggling, so she asked for more clarification, partially as a challenge but mostly out of a growing curiosity.

"So the ones who try to close themselves off from daily interaction with the world, because they have become afraid, or even distrustful, of the random shit that accompanies living in a normal, changing environment...they end up being stagnate and dysfunctional?"

"That's a theory that some believe is appropriate for some patients. The theory is that these patients try to filter their experiences to exclude trauma and only include pleasure, and this leads to a variety of unhealthy coping mechanisms. You can't live an open, healthy life without having periodic rough patches, or, as you say, *shit*, and therefore we need to learn how to deal with it in a nonjudgmental way."

"You're using trauma synonymously with pain and suffering? And we should embrace these things as good?"

"We should embrace them not as good or bad, but as necessary for growth."

"That's a tough one to wrap my head around."

"Let's go back to our first session, when I asked what you wanted to get out of therapy. Do you remember?"

"Vaguely."

"I remember, because I ask the same thing of all my patients when they start with me."

"Okay."

"No matter how dark and hopeless life appears to them when they're in my office, I ask them to trust me enough to be open to the idea that there might be a path to a better place."

"Okay, I remember that now."

"My question to you is, are you going to capitulate to your fears of the unknown, surrender to unhealthy coping mechanisms, including the ultimate unhealthy coping mechanism—suicide—or do you embrace the challenge of life?"

"The 'challenge' of life?"

"At the risk of offending you, your issues are not unique, or even new. You were baptized with a good liberal arts education. I'm sure you've been exposed to the works of Shakespeare? Hamlet? 'To be or not to be'? The existentialists, Sartre and Camus? The question as to whether or not life is worth living has been pondered forever. I think it is, and I think you want me to try and convince you that I'm right, otherwise you wouldn't be here."

"You make me sound like such a stereotype."

"I think we all have our unique challenges, yet at the same time most of us share similarities. For most people, making life worth living takes work, just like any good relationship. It has its ups and downs. Did we have the conversation yet about Harry Potter and the Myth of Quidditch?"

"I'm not sure."

"You've read the Harry Potter series?"

"Yes, all of them…I loved them."

"In the books, the first time Harry tries Quidditch he is a phenom. This is a common theme in fairy tales, even those as intricately woven as the Harry Potter series…the idea that we have a predefined path that is 'right' for us and all we need to do is find and follow. I believe that this idea, and the related idea that we are inherently great at something, without having to work at it, are not always productive. 'Follow your passion' can be terrible advice to young people. To become competent at something takes diligent effort. This includes the challenge of living a healthy, productive, loving life."

"Wait, you're saying, '*don't* follow your passion'?"

"I'm saying that initially most people don't even understand what their passion is. Committed digging often reveals that what initially captured our naive imaginations is actually disinteresting, and what we originally thought was boring may turn out to be captivating. There is rarely one path that reveals itself immediately when we take our first few steps. Our passions reveal themselves over time and are often entwined with expertise developed from long periods of hard work and years of sifting. Exploration of different paths is required. Perseverance is what we need for competence, and competence is what we need for passion. We become passionate about something when we become good at it, not the other way around."

"Maybe, but there's gotta be exceptions to that. I mean, sounds a little chicken-or-egg to me."

"Yes, with seven-point-three billion people on the planet there are always exceptions, the rare savants…but as children, most of us thought we were passionate about many things, only to try them, and then discard them, one by one, sometimes with breathtaking speed. This is normal and healthy, but at some point, as we become adults, we need to pick something and spend a little more time with it. Careers and relationships take work before we get good at them…most of us grow up with a false presumption about life. We think happiness is the default state, and if we don't wake up feeling good we are disappointed and go into a funk. We think somehow we got gypped, and we ruminate on the injustice, or make up narratives about why we're unhappy. Often these stories revolve around past traumas, or injustices, and the dwelling can continue until the funk becomes a deep, inescapable morass."

Scout felt a little uncomfortable with that characterization, as it seemed to hit a little too close to home, but she held her tongue. After a brief silence, Blanco continued planting the seed.

"I look at life as something that is full of challenges, like playing tennis or chess, or learning ballroom dancing…you have to work at it to improve, just like most acquired skills."

"And then just when you start mastering it, your faculties deteriorate, you shit your pants, and you die."

Frustrated, Blanco put down her pencil and reverted to a technique she rarely used—sarcasm.

"Scout, you're such the optimist!"

"But it's true!"

"You've been reading too much Cormac McCarthy, or Proulx, haven't you?"

"Mostly Eddie Poe."

"There, you did it again!"

Not giving the courtesy of a response, Scout wondered how many bricks it would take to seal her into her apartment bathroom.

Deep breath, Blanco self-prescribed.

"Yes, no matter how successful you are at mastering life, the ending often isn't pretty, but why focus on the negative? Focusing on the positive is so much more healthy, don't you think?"

" 'Focus on the positive'? That's the best I get for four hundred dollars an hour?"

It was rare to realize instant success with a patient. Blanco knew it might take years, or she might never have the pleasure of seeing progress with Scout, but her job required that she keep trying.

"Look, I know it's much cooler to wear black and wander around with a grim look on your pale, somber face. In fact, there are studies that show people ascribe greater intellect to those who appear solemn than they do to those who appear jolly. But being dour is not healthy. There's a ton of good research that supports the idea that a positive attitude leads to a healthier life, a better social network, more opportunities for personal growth…"

"I'm really struggling with this. Most mornings I don't feel like I have anything to be positive about."

"I understand, and that also isn't uncommon. I can't presume to understand your degree of pain, but I can say that my patients who successfully navigate the journey to mental wellness, who build a life they feel is worth keeping, usually focus on things outside of themselves. They commit a part of their lives to helping others. Even something as simple as caring for a pet. I think this sort of selfless act could be called *love*, and it is very healing. With someone as capable as you, I think coming up with healthy coping mechanisms that bring a degree of peace and periodic joy would be quite possible. I can help you develop little daily rituals, tricks that help you gain a feeling of control, like making your bed, going for a brisk walk, and smiling at strangers. You just have to decide, every day, to try."

"Look…I know…I'm…I'm… not stupid…I've, um…read a lot of this stuff…it's just…it's so hard… seems so hokey…and even when I go to bed with the best intentions, I usually wake up paralyzed."

Dr. Blanco glanced at her watch. They were already three minutes late, and her next patient was usually an emotional handful.

"I think we made a lot of progress today. Let's try and continue from here when our next session starts. Remember, your emotions are temporary and only live inside your head. Fear is the opposite of love. You need to have a trusting and open heart for love to grow. Our brains are hardwired for scarcity, not abundance, so try to artificially limit your choices so you're not overwhelmed. Try to keep things simple, one foot in front of the other, small successes that allow you to start to trust that the world isn't a scary place. Embrace the challenge of life."

The next morning, Scout made it out of her bed and as far as the bathroom. After a serious contemplative struggle, she decided that leaving a note would be too hypocritical—more of a narcisside. Not having the stomach for a crimson tub, she remembered the bottle of barbiturates that she had been hoarding for just such an occasion, and she swallowed all the Seconal pills therein.

Dr. Blanco's assistant slipped a message to her boss between the ten and eleven o'clock appointments: Scout's roommate had found her lying unconscious on the floor of her bedroom. The ambulance had handed her off to the hospital with a pulse, but her condition was listed as critical. As Blanco worked her way through her assistant's scribble, the doctor felt a wave of disappointment wash over her and knew from experience that there would be accompanying feelings of inadequacy and self-doubt. She wondered whether her decades of professional effort had made any difference to her many clients. Over the years she had had two patients kill themselves and at least a dozen more try. It was an *occupational hazard*, she reminded herself. If she took each suicide attempt as a personal failure she would have had to shutter her practice long ago.

It's unfortunate, she thought, *that there isn't the same dramatic evidence for the patients whom my professional training has helped.*

Her assistant, Gabriella, guessed correctly at what was passing through Dr. Blanco's brain. She offered some sympathy.

"This too shall pass."

Blanco remembered sharing the exact same words with a patient the day before. A wisp of wisdom that she used during those moments when life was closing in, snarling with bared fangs and there seemed no escape.

"Thanks, Gabby."

She paused, thinking back to something she had recently read.

"Did you know that's a medieval Sufi phrase?"

Gabriella had thought it biblical in origin.

"Really?" she replied. "No, I always thought it was religious or something. My grandmother used to always say it…she called it her 'ruby red slippers,' because it allowed her to go to her safe place whenever things got bad."

"Her ruby red slippers?"

"Yeah, you know, click your heels three times and go home…like

Dorothy in *The Wizard of Oz?*"

The doctor thought about how sometimes the most basic and simple statement could provide the most elegant and miraculous enlightenment—in this instance a reminder of the intangible and temporary nature of all emotions.

"Un huh…'ruby red slippers'…cute… kinda like a 'get-out-of-jail-free card'."

"Exactly. It's just a simple way to remind us that our emotions are generated by our brains…you know, they're not real."

Blanco stared at her assistant for a few seconds longer than usual, making the subordinate a little uncomfortable. Checking her watch, Gabby realized only two minutes remained before the scheduled eleven o'clock.

"Doctor, your eleven o'clock is already here, you've really got to get moving."

Blanco smiled back at her associate.

"Gabby, you're my best student. If only my other patients were as open to my proselytizing as you are."

Gabriella smiled at the compliment, and then, as if they had practiced it, both ladies performed a synchronized about-face and headed back to their workstations. Walking towards the private entrance that led through the washroom and into her office, Blanco paused with her hand on the doorknob and called back down the hall.

"Gabby, can you please let the hospital know I'll be visiting Scout Stein this evening? And add it to my calendar? Thanks!"

Without waiting for a response, she walked over the threshold, carefully turned and locked the door behind her, and then hustled through the palatial bathroom. Glancing at her profile in the full-length mirror, she scolded herself for the small FUPA that caught her eye. She knew it was birthed more from poor posture than a weight problem and recommitted to a straighter spine. Before she stepped away from the mirror, the red soles of the Louboutins grabbed her attention, bringing her to a halt. She pivoted ninety degrees and spent a minute admiring the magnificent shoes that enveloped her tiny feet. Not aware of what was happening until a moment after it occurred, a half smile broke out across her face. After a few seconds she decided she had to try. Closing her eyes, she brought herself to full attention, clicked her heels together three times, and said the magic words. After a brief wait, she opened her eyes, and, as a woman of science, chided herself for the wasted time and feelings of disappointment. Not giving it another thought, she made a quarter turn right with military precision and headed into her office to face the next challenge.

CHAPTER 31 —

Piercing the Veil

Clay was getting frustrated. His cramped Panama City apartment was hot, as the area was suffering through a heat wave that had brought on rolling brown-outs and limited air-conditioning. Fanning himself with a newspaper, he forced his attention back on his current dilemma. Identifying who had hired him to kill Keno, without alerting the intermediaries, just seemed to be an impossibly delicate task. He had spent nearly two months trying to reverse engineer the communications channel that provided him instruction (and payment) regarding his jobs, but he was having limited success. Working with just a single email address and an emergency phone number (which changed with each job) he had no idea how to track his handlers without notifying them. If information or documents were needed for an assignment, they would be delivered to a preordained P.O. Box (near his Panama City apartment) with no return address.

Almost at the end of his rope, he went back to the locked drawer where he kept all the original documents. Like any struggling independent contractor, he wanted to review the "work order." Digging through the graveyard of job parameters for long-dead targets, the cryptic instructions brought back vivid memories of past jobs. After thoroughly sifting through the paperwork, his paranoia started to grow when he couldn't find the documents for Keno. He wondered whether his apartment office had been infiltrated, and the degree to which he was being watched.

Where the fuck did I put that file? he thought, rifling through another stack of papers. *Are they that good? How could they possibly know about my place in Panama City? Fuckin' computers...*

When it came to the ancient knowledge of weaponry and assassination—of slashing steel and smashing bullets—he was an expert. But he found his competence in the new world of computers and technology lacking; things were simply moving too quickly and he couldn't (or wouldn't) keep up. He was openly disdainful of social media sites, so he didn't really understand the power of whole sectors of the internet and hadn't taken the time to move up the learning curves. It was almost as if he didn't expect any of this web stuff to stick, and hence felt it would be a waste of time to try and do the necessary heavy lifting.

In exasperation he finally resorted to an educated guess—actually, more of a grasping than a calculation—that involved an old work colleague. Starting at the beginning, he recalled that the soldier who had introduced him to his original post-government employer (Hightower Incorporated) was Recek "Ray" Ibrahim. Ray was a smooth-talking country boy, whose Turkish ancestry didn't align cleanly with his redneck, Alabama upbringing. Ray and Clay had gone through Airborne school together and were teammates on Clay's last tour in the Middle East. In a stroke of unvarnished luck, Clay recalled the Tuscaloosa native's nonstop reminiscing of his carnal time in a Costa Rican hotel. At the war-induced confluence of testosterone, boredom, and random bursts of violence, Ray shared intimate stories with the other team members in a repetitious soliloquy that verged on annoying. Like it was yesterday, Clay could hear Ray's southern drawl rolling over his brown-stained teeth. A tobacco-plugged cheek leaned on the stock of his rifle while his eye scanned for the enemy through his scope. Ray wasn't the type to let professional responsibilities interrupt the endless testimony to his *Tico* love nest.

"…ya know boys, it's…uh…mostly a brothel, with just the riiiight amount of hotel sprinkled in…ya know?...to allow your conscience and the local constable to turn a blind eye?"

His buddy's characterization of the place reminded Clay of his high school English teacher—aka Dr. Jekyll and Ms. Jezebel: buttoned-up and off limits during the day but salaciously active at night.

With no other leads and increasing pressure from Aloysius and Trick, Clay flew north in search of Recek and a way to unravel the mystery of who wanted his brother removed. Ray had spent so much verbal energy imagining an early retirement at his beloved hotel that Clay thought rhetorical commitment alone might've allowed the good ole boy to pull it off. Landing in the navel of the continental isthmus, Clay was armed with only the name of the hotel: *Casa de Sueños Secretos.* Within a few hours of navigating Costa Rican customs, he found the House of Secret Dreams situated in a grimy neighborhood that either time hadn't treated well or his expectations had treated too kindly.

Maintaining his discipline, he started the reconnaissance from a rental room across the street. The squat, sweating quarters gave him an upstairs view of his target. After days of watching in the unfiltered heat, Clay had gathered little evidence that gave him hope. By noon on his fourth day he had already burned through his bag of weed, and with his sedentary intestines bulging with rice, beans, and tortillas, he knew he had to start shaking some trees. His brother's life was disintegrating with each passing day. Compelled by the growing anxiety that can accompany dependence on a soon-to-be-discovered lie, Clay put down his binoculars and headed down the stairs. Nodding at the manager in passing, he headed out into, and then across, the exhaust- and people-choked street.

A dozen strides later, he slid as unobtrusively as possible into the *Casa de Suenõs Secretos*.

After taking a quick tour of the depressing lobby, he was pretty sure that his Alabama buddy wouldn't have chosen to spend his last few decades in the sad place. Although the building had pretty good bones, it was worn beyond her years, like a sixty-year-old Cinderella whose fairy godmother had never shown up. After making one final tour of the dilapidated perimeter, he decided his trip to San Jose had been a waste. In a disappointed funk he started planning his next move.

Just to be thorough, he headed back to the front desk and asked the clerk if he had ever heard of a gringo named Recek or Ray Ibrahim. Without hesitating, the young man pointed to a dark alcove positioned off to the side of the main lobby.

"*Señor Ray? Él está allí.*"

Peering into the darkness, Clay barely made out a La-Z-Boy recliner positioned in front of a flickering black-and-white TV. Incredulous, he looked back at the clerk for reassurance.

"Ray Ibrahim…*allí?*"

The clerk nodded.

"*Sí.*"

Out of habit, Clay's brain checked for the reassuring impression of his gun. He felt the L-shaped metal squeezed by his belt against the small of his back and hidden by his untucked *guayabera*. His senses heightened, he sauntered towards the partially reclined chair. Experience had taught him that things often weren't as they seemed. He wasn't sure what to expect from the scene in front of him, but he sensed a strong odor of…capitulation. As he came closer, Clay could see that someone was reclining in the chair—he made out gray wisps of hair hovering in a sparse and random array over the man's pate. Standing next to the near side of the chair, a short metal pillar supported a shiny bowl overflowing with dozens of used up Pall-Malls. A nearly finished, unfiltered butt was pinched between the chrome-skinned knuckles that formed an arch over the top of the bowl. Grey tendrils of smoke wound out of its smoldering end; drifting up to the ceiling and joining the cloud of haze that was unbothered by the metallic tentacles of a slow-moving fan. The stub seemed to be waiting patiently to have the death sucked out of it.

As Clay continued approaching the chair, words screamed out of the small, front-mounted speaker as the unrepentant TV evangelist held up a bible and continued his stream of consciousness performance:

"You are NOT special! Say it with me, my brothers and sisters! I AM NOT SPECIAL!"

Two young, barely adolescent girls hung in attendance on the far side of the recliner. Clay heard a burst of whispered giggling come from their painted, swollen lips. In their tight clothing, they reminded Clay of remora, suckerfish, competing for whatever scraps might fall away from a flaccid corpus.

Not wanting to set off any alarm bells, Clay approached from the back and called out a benign greeting.

"Hello there."

The girls looked up curiously, but the back of the head didn't move. Slowing his approach, Clay kept wide of the chair, leaving plenty of room to move if necessary while he circled and took in the man's profile. Soon he was between the TV and the front of the chair. The slouching figure of what appeared to be a macabre caricature of his friend Ray greeted him with closed eyes.

The man's chin was cradled in his sunken chest, a yellow-under-the-arms T-shirt loosely hung from his scarecrow shoulders. The former Navy SEAL had unwittingly released a string of spittle from his lips that ended in a pool just over his sagging left breast. A pair of red-striped gauze pants provided a thin barrier separating the soldier's genitals from the nearly dead bottle resting beside them. His dress socks were elevated, a gold patch partially covering the toes of his shoeless feet. As Clay's imagination filled in the blanks, he understood why Hemingway had committed suicide.

After waiting for a few moments, Clay decided on a course of action. He mostly put aside his repugnance, but he still refrained from physical contact.

"Ray, Ray," he called softly, "wake up."

Clay didn't have time to dillydally. If this was going to be a dead end, which seemed likely, he wanted to find out promptly so he could purge today's experience as quickly as possible.

"Recek! Ibrahim! Attention on deck!"

Ray didn't respond.

Mentally holding his nose, Clay reached out with his left hand and gave the dozing man's left shoulder a push, making sure to avoid the drool. He kept his right hand near the gun.

"Ray! I need you to wake up."

The derelict in the chair stirred and started making snorting noises that implied an invasion of mucus into his breathing passageways.

"Whaaa...what the fuck?"

Clay stepped back, ready for anything, his weight on the balls of his feet. Ray partially opened his eyes and hoarsely let out a belching drawl that confirmed Clay's initial ID. In as nonthreatingly a way as possible, Clay continued.

"Sergeant Recek Ibrahim, it's me, Sergeant Clay Barton."

The man who had long ago abandoned pushing rocks up hills

squinted in confusion.

"No fuckin' way. Clay fuckin' Barton? Come here. Wait. Closer." He belched again then swiped the spittle from his mouth with the back of his hand. "Clay…. No fuckin' way!"

Clay took a cautious half step closer. Not knowing the terms of engagement he still kept a safe distance.

"It's me all right, you Crimson Tide asshole."

"Clay fuckin' Barton…well I'll be a coon-skinned sumbitch. Look at your magnificent, upright self. What the fuck are you doin' in this cesspool?"

"I need your help, Ray." Clay had to make his old buddy understand he was serious. "Is there a place we can talk?"

"Well 'how do' to you too, you perfunctory cocksucker. You never did have any manners…and you always were jealous of the Tide, you Ivy League wannabe pansy."

Recek coughed up some phlegm and spit it into a soiled handkerchief he kept in the waistband of his skivvies.

"Of course you need somethin'," Ray continued. "Why else would you be here? In case you didn't notice, I do most of my work right here in this chair. So if you want my help, you'll best get it here."

"What about *las niñas?*"

Clay had chosen the noun to show his disapproval.

Ray laughed sarcastically, putting his pointer finger up in a perpendicular fashion to his lips while speaking in a stage whisper.

"My princesses? Don't worry, Sergeant, they got fuckin' top secret security clearance…all hush, hush ya know."

"It's about Hightower."

Ray's mood changed immediately from cavalier to somber.

"Ahhh, shit. Let's go to my room."

Five minutes later, the two old mercenaries rested alone in a small, drearily furnished box whose interior offended Clay's senses just slightly less than the downstairs alcove. Worn drapes let in a filtered midday light that speckled the room like a sluggish, aging disco ball. A gasping, geriatric, wall unit worked hard to keep the room from sweltering. Ray immediately reclined into what was apparently his default position on the queen-sized bed: feet and head propped up with pillows, and in the middle a round belly swollen up like a massive, unharvested carbuncle. Clay pulled out a rickety plastic chair from under an equally impoverished desk. Turning the piece of furniture backwards, he cautiously sat down in it with his face towards his friend and access to his gun unimpeded.

Ray held out a plastic liter of Sprite from which he had just taken a swig.

"You want, *amigo*?"

Clay shook his head while still trying to understand how his old friend had poured the drink past the cigarette without dousing or displacing it. Eventually he chalked the inventive maneuver up to being the offspring of necessity.

"You drink that shit? You know that'll kill ya, man."

Ray did something that fell between a giggle and a scoff.

"The bubbles, man, they soothe my stomach…but I can't handle that caffeinated shit."

Shaking his head, Clay looked down at the floor with a half smile. He wasn't sure where to start.

"Right."

Then, examining his hands, Clay couldn't help himself.

"Ray, what are you doing here?"

The question set the unshaven, supine man off on a riotous convulsion of laughter. But the guffawing devolved quickly into a fit of coughing that lasted for nearly a minute before Ray regained control of his diaphragm.

"What am I doin' here? Ha! That's a fuckin' good one. Isn't it obvious? I'm fuckin' killin' myself, *hermano*. The more interesting question is what the fuck are *you* doin' here?"

Not sure how much to reveal, Clay started off delicately.

"Are you still involved with them?"

"With whommm?" Ray drew out the *m* with grammatical delight.

"C'mon, man. Hightower?"

Ray slowed down for a beat, enough to allow him to gather his thoughts and develop a strategy. But, despite his best efforts, his glee upon seeing the famous assassin in person overwhelmed his good sense. He grabbed his buddy's eyes and smiled as he prepared to reveal their shared secret. Starting off lethargically, the tempo and pitch of his testament built rapidly.

"Hightower Incorporated? Not much anymore…but, ya know, *amigo*, I'm ahhh…still in touch enough to know that…SOME DUDE NAMED TOMMIE FUCKIN' SMITH IS ONE CRAZY, BAD-ASS, MOTHER FUCKER WHO WILL LIKELY GO DOWN AS PULLING OFF THE BALLSIEST TWENTY-FOUR-HOUR, SOLO, MULTI-TARGET KILL EVER!"

Clay felt the ground under his feet become unsteady. He wasn't sure how Ray knew about the hits in La Jolla, why he was revealing this intel, or whether or not the strange behavior should be considered a threat.

After gathering a quick breath, Ray continued with the same elevated tone filled with enthusiasm and awe:

"AND NOT IN SOME THIRD-WORLD SHITHOLE, BUT WITHIN THE CONFINES OF THE LAW-AND-ORDER-ENCUMBERED U-S OF A....SHIT, HOMES, THEY'RE PROBABLY PRINTING UP SOME GAME CARDS AS WE SPEAK...FUCKIN' FUCKETY FUCK, CLAY...AND PEOPLE SAY *I* HAVE A FUCKIN' DEATH WISH!"

Reacting the way he always did when he sensed things were starting to go sideways, Clay was on his feet before Ray finished, gun pointed at the center of his old friend's abused chest. Though alarmed at what he perceived as an inappropriate reaction, the limp form feigned unconcern.

"Stand down, soldier, no one knows but me."

Clay's posture remained at full alert.

"Good, that'll make this loose end much easier to tidy."

Feeling like shit but not wanting to die, Ray pushed his fogged brain to consider a safe harbor. The air conditioner stumbled back into operation while he took another nearly simultaneous suck of smoke and Sprite. It appeared his adversary was unstable, he just didn't know to what degree. After sending the sugar and nicotine on their internal course, he decided on some hopefully disarming transparency. Looking humbly towards his feet, his first and second words were interrupted by a noxious belch.

"You...idiot, I've been your handler this whole fuckin' time...or at least for the last ten years...when no one else would take a chance on your old ass. You're my only asset...just two old killers trying to make a livin'. Hightower doesn't know who you are, except as Tommie Smith, and you don't know them. I figger it's been a purdy good arrangement for all."

Clay's eyes narrowed as he considered the deceit, but he didn't respond. Trying to make a connection, Ray decided to try some comedic gratitude.

"Thanks, by the fuckin' way…my commissions on your fuckin' jobs has done kept me livin' the highlife. I'm sure you can understand….you know…with inflation and such, my pension was gettin' pretty fuckin' stretched."

Ray squinted up at the assassin, not sure whether he was making any headway. They were at a standoff, both working through the permutations like two professionals engaged in a game of speed chess. With a perspiring nonchalance, the man on the bed pushed the bluff a step further.

"Go ahead…as those movie assholes like to say, you'd be doing me a favor."

Clay relaxed his trigger finger. He knew Ray was his only connection to the information he needed. Still keeping his gun raised, he slowly moved to a place where he could see both Ray and the passageway to the exterior hallway.

"You're being paranoid, Sergeant, ain't nobody listenin'…it's just you and me."

"So you say."

Pulling the chair with him, Clay sat back down while keeping his eye and gun on his old pal.

"You say you've been my go-between all these years?"

"Yep."

"Then who was my last target, and where did it happen?"

"After the La Jolla Massacre?"

"I hate that name."

"You testin' me?"

"No shit."

"No dice, *amigo*. There ain't been no jobs, brother. Your career is done. Toast."

"Wrong, Ray. Either you lied about being my only handler, or you're too fuckin' pickled to even remember your mommy's privates."

Ray's posture changed from accommodating to threatening.

"Don't you be talkin' about my momma."

A split-second smile revealed itself as Clay thought about the hard and fast rules in certain cultures.

"Sorry, man…didn't mean to step over the line."

For a bit both men eyed the other with curious suspicion. Then Ray spoke up.

"Anyway, in answer to your question, there ain't been no new targets…it's crazy, Clay…after word got out about the risks you took with the last job, nobody wants to touch Tommie Smith with my ten-foot dick. The business has changed, *amigo*. All corporate and buttoned-down…no room for mavericks…you know…no tolerance for the independent, creative sort. Too risky."

"That's bullshit, and you know it. I want my money for the last job."

"I done told you already, we got paid for La Jolla, and ain't been nothin' since."

This is interesting, thought Clay. *For all his smugness he hasn't even put together the possible connection that Keno and I share the same last name. He still has no idea why I'm here.*

"Who was on the other side?"

The chemicals were doing their job…Ray was starting to drift. His fear concerning his immediate predicament was becoming less intense.

"Look, if someone sent you here to off me, just do it…I'm sure I deserve it, and who better than you? The irony and all."

Clay chose his next words carefully, not wanting to reveal any part of his charade.

"Who hired me to kill Keenan?"

Something in Clay's eyes twisted Ray's stomach into a spasm of remembrance. Years ago, after their last mission together, rumor had it that Clay had ended up in a VA mental hospital. The docs had diagnosed paranoid schizophrenia. They said he was hearing voices—real multiple personality shit. The scuttlebutt among their friends was that Clay had "gone off the deep end." A few years later, Ray had bumped into one of their teammates who said the docs finally figured out the right pills to prescribe and Clay was back to normal. Ray searched Clay's face for any signs of instability.

"Clay, man, you still takin' your medication?"

Clay's face contorted into a mask of rage as he jumped to his feet.

"What the fuck! Do I fuckin' look like I need fuckin' medication? Don't change the subject!"

Ray flinched. Clay stepped forward and pushed the gun closer to Ray's torso.

"The question to the prisoner is who was on the other side for the last job."

Taking a deep breath, Ray considered the possibility that his opponent might be dealing with mental health issues that were making him massively paranoid.

"I told you, man, there weren't no job. But even if there was, what do you care?"

"Need to know."

Ray had to be careful. Not being sure of Clay's mental state, he also had to respect the possibility that his old friend was playing him. That

Clay might be in Costa Rica working for someone else.

"C'mon Clay, you know Hightower doesn't reveal that shit to me."

"But you could pull some strings, ask for a favor, get some intel."

"Do I look like a guy who has any outstanding favors? Besides, out of all your kills, why grow a conscience about this one?"

"We could do this the hard way."

Through the poorly lit, smoky room, Clay looked down into bloodshot eyes that revealed a taunting skepticism.

"What? You'd carve up a fellow SEAL? I don't think you have the stomach."

Slowly, a smile spread across Clay's face as his next move became obvious.

"Shit, Ray, no carving necessary. I'd just secure you where you lay…with some phone cord and a gag…watch you dry out. I figure in twenty-four hours you'd be willing to blow Mr. Ed for a cigarette and a sip of beer."

Shivers ran up Ray's spine.

"That's fuckin' cold, man. I told you, there ain't been no new assignments come through me since San Diego. Why would I lie to you?"

Keeping the barrel pointed at Ray, Clay took two steps towards the phone and pulled the long extension cord out of the wall.

"Up to you, Recek. I got plenty of time. In fact, you coon-skinned sumbitch, I figger sobering you up would be a purdy good arrangement for both of us. Might even catch me up with some of my indebted conscience….what with inflation and such."

Keeping the gun mostly pointed at his target, Keno looped the cord into a loosely consolidated handful. Terrified, Ray scooted backwards on the bed, but his dilapidated circumstances didn't allow much room for his retreat.

"I swear, man, I told ya all I know. Don't do this. Please."

But Clay had already decided to start by wrapping him in the bedding, and then winding up the package with the cord. He didn't look forward to the interrogation, but he felt like it was his only option.

CHAPTER 32 —

Squeezed

Every night she would snap awake at three A.M.—eyes wide open, heart racing, sweat-soaked hair plastered to the side of her face. For a few minutes her brain would swirl wildly before she would pull the soles of her feet up to her groin and press them together in a lying butterfly position. With her left hand over heart and right below her bellybutton, she would start her daily meditation. *You have to hold it together*, she told herself. *Keep the demons at bay, for the sake of the boys, our way of life.* If she was lucky, she would fall back to sleep within thirty minutes, happily submerging into one of her few trustworthy escapes. On the bad days, when she was still wide awake an hour later, she would get up and start journaling, hoping she could catch a nap at some later point so she wouldn't have to push through the day on just five hours of sleep.

Her husband, Keno, had been missing for over five months, and the problems had been piling up for a while. Not only was her personal life falling apart, but California real estate, in particular, was absolutely cratering. They were calling it the Great Financial Crisis, the Great Recession, the Bursting of the Housing Bubble, and every other name in the book; but to Lola it seemed like the end of life as she knew it. She had no idea her and Keno's finances had been so complicated…and the timing of Keno's absence couldn't have been worse. It wasn't that he had left them without assets, it was just that most of their wealth was tied up in illiquid real estate partnerships that were already over-levered. Half of her days were spent mourning the loss of her closest friend and lover, and the other half were spent cursing Keno for his insensitivity to the mess he had left behind. The insurance company was still investigating the death, specifically the inexplicable absence of an identifiable body, and hence had not yet been willing to pay out on Keno's universal term life policy. Basically Lola was suffering through a liquidity squeeze.

On the other side of the ledger, the expenses were relentless. A monstrous mortgage on an overpriced Marin house that now clearly felt like a reach…private school tuition…the Tahoe and Baja vacation homes…membership dues for the golf and tennis clubs…payments for Gus' psychiatrist and Sam's braces…charitable commitments…organic groceries for a family that included two ravenous teenagers. It was all too overwhelming—a series of daily challenges that constantly knocked Lola off-balance and tore at her sense of well-being.

It seemed that her family was trying to help, but most of them were dealing with their own problems. No matter how much she scrimped, every month she still came up short. On the East Coast, her father was suffering from Alzheimer's and needed round-the-clock, in-home care… the cost of which her arthritic mom worried was eating up all of their nest egg. Aloysius, her father-in-law, was helping to cover their monthly shortfalls, but she knew there was a limit to what he could do now that he was retired and fighting with Lilly for control of the Health and Wellness Center. Of course, Al had his own health problems that demanded medical attention, including colitis and early symptoms of dementia. Lilly and Aloysius' only child, Scout, had recently attempted suicide. Although she seemed to be doing better it was still a fragile situation that required significant financial and emotional resources.

In reality, most of their friends and family didn't have a lot of sympathy for Lola's plight. Partly because their own problems were the main focus of their attention, but also because of the envy that in some instances had morphed into resentment as they had watched the Bartons ascend out of the morass and towards the sun. It was the nature of some humans to inwardly rejoice at others' suffering, and the Bartons' troubles were epic. It was easy for the neighbors to wallow in the *schadenfreude* that accompanied watching Lola descend to Earth, tunic covered in hot wax. The Bartons' fall from grace was a reminder that their own shortcomings weren't nearly as significant.

Not surprisingly, Keno's best friend, Trick, had been a rock for Lola to lean on. In an effort to keep Bowman, Barton & Jones from foundering, he had resumed his role as CEO, with a focus on San Francisco operations. Competitors were spreading rumors about fraud and embezzlement, given the abrupt and strange disappearance of the firm's co-founder, and every perceived vulnerability was being attacked. Trick was fighting hard to keep the firm's clients and best producers from jumping ship, but the industry gossip and simmering infighting wasn't making his job any easier. Trick didn't have a clue about the new Portland office, which was rudderless and losing money without Keno's oversight, and so he was blindly considering whether or not the firm should cut their losses and shutter the outpost. The LA office was still making money, but just barely, and Pee Wee felt like all of his time was spent battling with lenders over loan covenants and valuations. This situation left him with little time to compete for new business or train his team, leaving the big man worried that his operation was turning into a melting ice cube. Trick had the unenviable task of trying to balance the conflicting liquidity needs of both Lola and a faltering Bowman, Barton & Jones. It didn't help that more than fifty percent of his net worth was tied up in a business that was teetering, and the physical stress of sitting all day (including the weekly commutes between the Gorge and SF) was exasperating all of his old football injuries.

As the only ones who knew about Clay's plan outside of Keno, Trick and Aloysius were working together to simultaneously support Lola, keep the hopes alive that Keno would return, and let Clay know that they couldn't carry on in this fashion indefinitely. Clay was rarely responding to their inquiries; when he did he never had any good news. The whole charade was hanging by a tautly stretched thread. Everyone was feeling the pressure.

Most of Lola's Marin friends had abandoned her, but to her credit Elise Haversham had hung in there. They had a regularly scheduled, Thursday morning hike up the south side of Mount Tamalpais, and despite Lola's frequent efforts to cancel, Elise always insisted. After the boys got themselves squared away and off to school, Elise would come by and physically haul Lola out of bed, lace her feet into her hiking shoes, and push her body out the front door and into Elise's Lexus. She would then drive them up to the Mountain Home Inn, where their climb would start halfway up the mountain.

This morning was particularly glorious, and as they worked their way up Hog's Back Ridge, Lola's cares receded further with each ascending step. The trail had been recently closed for erosion control, but the two women had been hiking up the challenging path for years. Their sense of local entitlement overrode their environmental concerns. Both women were pushing the pace, and Lola's heart rate was balancing delicately at her anaerobic threshold. Early that morning she had been certain she lacked the energy to even dress for the climb, but now she felt strong and free, like the hawks that regularly appeared in her peripheral vision, gliding on the thermals.

As they negotiated one of the steep, narrow portions of the trail, Elise took the lead, using her hands to scramble around a huge, horizontally jutting rock formation. All around them, the flora soaked up the heat of the midmorning sun. Behind them, and to their left, the Pacific Ocean supported a thin blanket of fog that pushed up against the coastline as far as the eye could see. To the south, Ocean Beach and San Francisco's Sunset District were just starting to reveal themselves under the dissipating layer; while to the north, just below the small village of Bolinas, Stinson Beach basked in an eddy of sunshine. A few ambitious, grey wisps wandered up the Marin valleys, with one chilly tentacle reaching out to caress the cluster of sequoias directly below them: Muir Woods.

When Elise reached the natural tabletop at the apex of the rock formation, she stretched a hand down to help a panting Lola. After hoisting her friend up the last few feet, they both sat down to let their senses absorb the moment. The ground was still moist from the drip of the overnight fog, and the earthy smell of manzanita and conifers joined the waft of the sea in a clean and welcome drowning.

From their position on the promontory, the panorama seemed so magnificently large and devoid of blemishes that Lola felt connected to everything. Believing she could feel Keno's heart beating along with hers, she was sure he was still out there, somewhere. She pictured all the times they had been together in this exact same spot, shoulder to shoulder, inhaling the world. A cool breeze carried a tuft of hair across her face, and she imagined his hand gently pushing the strands back behind her ear. Closing her eyes, she felt him smiling at her while his fingers lingered on her cheek, eyes filled with love and admiration. She used to make fun of his unabashed enthusiasm, his earnest encouragements to push herself, as if effort alone was a virtue. Taunting him, she would laugh at the implied moral convictions, relishing the role reversal from their early years. Their time together had allowed her to grow comfortable as a naughty layabout, happily relinquishing responsibility to her dutiful Sisyphus. The recollections made her feel simultaneously loved and alone, achingly terrified that the chapter of her life that involved Keno was over. A small tear formed at the corner of her eye; she was too slow in turning away, and Elise, seeing the symptoms, used a whispering voice to try and soothe.

"Oh Lolie…I know…I know…. You'll get through this, I know you will. You're strong."

"I know…I just feel…I don't know…. Empty? Alone?"

Elise reached out and grabbed her hand.

"God, Lola, I can only imagine. I mean, jeez, the abruptness of it all. When I separated from Phil it came after years of planning and contemplation, and there are still times I'm a mess."

There was a dark feeling that had been nagging at Lola, growing with each passing week.

"Each day that goes by I'm losing my faith…in Keno…in life…in a world that's worth hanging around for."

Elise was shocked, not realizing it had gotten this bad.

"God no, Lola…you have to fight that. It'll get better…I know it must hurt terribly, but your boys need you."

Suddenly, Lola was overwhelmed with emotion, and the tears were uncontrollable. Scooching over until the sides of their hips were touching, Elise put her arm around her friend's shoulders and hugged her close. After a long moment of quiet sobbing, Elise continued with her comforting.

"Oh, baby…you're safe with me, you can let it all out. I know…it's okay to cry…it's all right. I know it doesn't feel this way now, but…this too shall pass."

After a few minutes, Lola's crying lost most of its conviction and was soon just a stream of sniffles and reassessments. She started assembling herself with deliberation, and after a few minutes her body language let Elise know she was ready to resume their hike.

"I suppose none of my subjects are gonna come up here with my litter and carry me to the summit?"

Elise laughed sympathetically.

"I been waitin' for that train a long time, sister. I think the burden for your emancipation falls squarely on your shoulders."

"Amen, to that sister."

Lola turned and with a "let's do this!" challenge took off ahead of Elise at an enthusiastic pace. Ten minutes later she crested the empty summit slightly ahead of her exhausted friend. The vision of the bay area invigorated Lola's sense of purpose. With a decrepit, wooden lookout hut at their backs, both women sucked in large gulps of air as they stood with their hands interlaced at the back of their heads. The two had their elbows splayed out like wings, as Elise had been told that this position maximized lung capacity.

After regaining her breath, Lola turned to her friend and dropped the bombshell that had been bouncing around in her head for months.

"You know, Wolfgang has proposed."

Elise turned to her friend. "What? Proposed? Marriage? When? What did you tell him?"

"It was kinda creepy. He asked almost immediately after Keno disappeared. I just hung up on him…it was disgusting, the timing and all, but lately I'm having second thoughts."

"Do you think he's still interested?"

"He calls nearly every week, asking…almost *demanding* that we meet. He's maniacal about his theory that we were meant for each other."

"Lola, I don't want to sound mercenary, but that would solve all your problems. He has money, right?"

"Yes, but it's not his…it's the family business…his dad keeps him on a pretty short leash…supposedly a real Santini."

"Okay, it's not perfect, but it's better than what you're going through now, right?"

"Well, it would let me keep the house, and the boys could stay at Brinson."

"Sometimes you have to put your family's well-being first."

"I know, but…"

"Oh God, Lola, don't ignore this opportunity. I can't tell you what to do, but for women our age, well…let's just say there aren't as many options as you may think."

"I get it, thanks, but that's not how I think."

"No, seriously. *I know what it's like out there*. Plenty of guys will sleep with you, but long-term options that you would want to be with are scarce."

Elise grabbed both of Lola's hands and looked in her eyes.

"Listen, the first time you marry for love, and after that you're not so naive. Please, tell me you'll at least consider it."

"Okay…okay. I'll consider it."

As Lola looked south, she could see the brick red towers of the Golden Gate Bridge piercing through the fog. She tried hard to envision a life with a different man, specifically Wolfgang. Elise interrupted her imaginings.

"When did you last see him?"

"Not since the night in Sausalito."

"Do you love him?"

"I did, once, long ago, but…I don't know."

"Do you have any feelings for him at all?"

Lola shrugged.

"I don't know…after that night…trust is such a fragile thing."

Elise had her detective's hat on and wouldn't be deterred.

"What's going on with the three million?"

"You mean the life insurance?"

Elise nodded affirmatively.

"They're still dragging their feet."

"Really? What, almost six months now? Effin' bloodsuckers…. What does your lawyer say?"

Lola starting breaking down again, and Elise realized it was too early to push so hard.

"I'm sorry…it's none of my business. Try and forget I brought it up."

"No, it's not that…I can do this…I appreciate the help…to…to try and sort my thoughts." She wiped her nose on her sleeve. "Trick says they need a proper identification of the body. Unfortunately, by the time the police found the accident site, the scavengers had picked apart his remains so there were no clear identifiable features."

"No skull? Jawbone with teeth? Fingerprints? What about DNA testing?"

"Who are you? Agatha Christie?"

"I watch a lot of *Murder, She Wrote*."

"Apparently. Remember, it's Mexico, not the States. Trick says they're backwards and slow…he says they're treating it like a potential crime, so they aren't very cooperative with him about where things stand."

"Who's Trick?"

"Keno's business partner and best friend. He was surfing with him down in Mexico."

A gust of wind wrapped around the peak. An involuntary shiver possessed Lola for a long second.

"I'm getting cold."

Nodding, Elise pointed to the lee side of the fire lookout.

"Yeah, let's move over there and get out of this wind."

After getting settled in the sun, Elise kept digging.

"Does the insurance company suspect foul play? I mean, you mentioned the Mexicans think it might have been a crime?"

Lola's skin was still chilly, but at least the cooling effect of wind evaporating her sweat was addressed.

"I don't think so. I think they're just being thorough."

Elise looked skeptical, compelling Lola to defend herself.

"What? Who could possibly want to kill Keno?"

Elise was uncertain if she should go there. But she was worried her friend was being too trusting. She overruled her discretion and decided to at least introduce the possibility.

"I don't want to sound paranoid, but these 'accidents' are usually done by family members who have something to gain."

"Sorry, but you do sound paranoid."

In an effort to show she was uncomfortable with the conversation, Lola turned away from her friend and looked out at the Tiburon Peninsula.

To Elise, Lola was a little sister who needed guidance, and after a minute of silence she couldn't help herself. She pried as gently as she could.

"Does his estate planning leave anything to people other than you and the kids?"

Lola wasn't sure she wanted to continue being interrogated, but the question did invigorate some repressed concerns.

"Well, he's always wanted to make sure his siblings were taken care of, given how rocky their upbringing was, so they each get a decent chunk if he dies."

Elise raised her eyebrows in surprise.

"And you don't think that's strange?"

"Maybe, but in a good way. I like that he's compassionate…and grateful for his relative success. We have plenty…I just can't get at it right now with the crisis."

"Hmm…brothers killing brothers…yeah, that never happens."

"No way, Paul would never…"

"Not wheelchair boy…the other one. The crazy soldier dude you told me about."

"Clay? I've never even met him…I can't imagine. He might not even be alive."

Again, Elise scrunched up her face in a frowning way that implied if it were her, she would give the issue a lot more thought. She waited a minute and then continued the inquiry.

"And what about this Trick guy…wasn't he the last one to see him alive? And now he's handling the communications with Mexico? Does he gain anything if Keno dies?"

"No way! You're being crazy! Trick was happily retired before this mess. He's had to come out of retirement and start managing the partnership again to keep it from falling apart."

"Hmm…so he says. But how many competitive men in their late forties stay happily retired? Maybe he wanted to come back to work, but Keno rebuffed him?"

"I'm telling you, no way! Keno and Trick are like bro…thers…"

Lola let the last syllable drift off as she realized what she was saying. Elise's paranoia had started to infiltrate her brain. The older woman couldn't resist driving her point home further.

"You mean like Cain and Abel?"

CHAPTER 33 —

Casting

There was something about the rhythmic, orderly nature of the activity he found soothing. Perhaps the metamorphosis from an awkward clump of lead-weighted nylon into a flying, near-perfect circle. Pausing for a second, Keno took a chug from a friend's beer before once again sifting the weighted circumference through his adolescent hands. He quickly arranged the net into neat, folded layers over his arm, using his mouth like a third set of fingers to prepare for the cast. The salty taste of the net mixed with his saliva. The metallic, oval weights pressed against his tongue, unforgiving and harsh. As he simultaneously rotated his torso and sucked in a last breath through his teeth, an insulting layer of cigarette smoke coated his nostrils. Pausing his toss to find the source, he eyed the older fishermen who staked their claims twenty feet away at the end of the dock. These self-quarantined loners passed their hot, Florida evenings skewering earthworms with their tobacco-stained fingers. They would then submerge the blind, limbless creatures into the brine, agonizing their open, bleeding wounds while slowly, mercilessly leaving them to drown, or worse, be eaten alive by an unlucky fish who had mistaken the barbed hook for a meal.

As Keno watched without staring, one of the abandoned, wizened fishermen took one last pull of smoke deep into his lungs before flicking the butt in an arc high through the air and towards the water. He turned to Keno, pulled a beer out of his cooler, and gestured with the wet can—an invitation for Keno to come join the older men. Before Keno could reply, the man broke into a staccato, hacking cough, slumping to the ground on one knee. Keno froze, staring at the convulsing man but unable to will his feet to help. Riding the currents of the struggling man's bloodstream, concentrations of alcohol and nicotine raced past the clot of blood, a piece of which had already lost its grip on the arterial wall in his neck. The offered beer can dropped from the wrinkled hand, and Keno watched it slowly roll down the dock, towards him, until it finally came to rest against his bare foot. From his position on the floating wooden dock, Keno felt a mixture of sweat and seawater pool on his nose then watched as it dripped down onto the waiting beer can. Letting the net drop to his side, he picked up the aluminum invitation, considered the label carefully, and then placed it atop a nearby, creosote-asphyxiated wooden piling. Out on the bay, the cigarette ember had long stopped burning and now floated lifeless on the water's surface.

Returning his attention to his net, Keno forgot about the crumpled man who was now receding into the fog. He had to focus as he scanned for evidence of mullet fins breaking the placid surface. He knew the fish would periodically school in small groups under the pontoons after feeding on the bottom seagrass. They always seemed to be moving, but not so quickly that a well-aimed throw couldn't capture a few within its spinning, circular grasp.

Out of the corner of his eye he saw a girl, shining like an angel on the beach, also hunting for mullet. As he worked his dock, he noticed with admiration the practiced nonchalance of her spinning casts. Magically, without any conscious intention, he found himself floating over the water, touching down within a few feet of her on the sand. With neither looking at the other, they worked like independent discus throwers, side by side. On their first toss together they both caught a fish, and when he turned to share the moment with a smile, he saw it was Lola. She laughed back at him, and he *could smell and feel her breath, full of possibility and devoid of decay. When he reached out to touch her his hand met no resistance, although he could see her clear as a red chameleon on a green leaf. She turned back to the sea, and he watched her cast in a graceful arc, memorizing the arch in her back and her extended arm, hoping to mimic her refined technique. Before their next shared toss, he found himself working in thigh-deep water, while she remained on the beach. His efforts were rewarded with twice as many fish as she, and he walked back to her place on the beach to share his catch. He saw larger schools of fish farther out in the water, but he knew the bottom was notoriously mucky in that area, similar to quicksand. Before he could head farther out, she put aside her net and tied a rope around his waist, securing him by holding on to the end of the rope from her place onshore. While she watched and supported, he moved away from her. With each cast into deeper water he caught more fish, and she would pull him in so he could safely share his catch.*

Soon they had more than enough, and Lola asked him to stop and rest with her, but Keno was caught up in his task. It wasn't long before he found himself up to his neck in the water, unable to pull his feet from the sucking ooze. Despite her efforts, Lola was not strong enough to pull him to shore. Out of nowhere, a storm blew in, and small, wind-driven waves were suddenly lapping at his chin. From above, rivulets of rain started pouring down his face, making it hard for Keno to breath. He tried to call out for Lola, but the words got lost in the wind. Aching to reach her, he started thrashing more violently, but his limbs felt heavy, like they were covered in cement. While he tried unsuccessfully to extract his feet, he frantically screamed to get Lola's attention, but now he was surrounded by fog and could no longer see Lola or the shore. He felt the weighted net covering him and pulling him down. Just before he had fully sunk beneath the surface, he felt something pulling on him, shouting at him through the storm.

"*Señor* Keno, *Señor* Keno. *Levantarse!* Wake up!"

2009 - Still Out West (Mostly)

His heart raced as he gasped for air and pushed a sopping length of fabric from his face. The nightmare receded, and Keno realized he was still in Baja. The wooden gunwales of a fishing panga surrounded him. He looked up into a weathered face anchored by clear, kind eyes. Beyond the face a squid-ink sky spit large drops of water that bounced off the tarp that only partly covered the boat he was lying in. The woman above him displayed the concern of a mother who had put her child in harm's way in an effort to avoid a worse catastrophe.

"*Hijo*, are you okay? You are shaking."

His mind flashed back to when he had first met the old woman. She was a package of contradictions contained within an outer layer of dark brown skin and a *sarape* of tightly woven cotton and wool. She was short, with almond eyes and a flat, sloping forehead that suggested her family descended from indigenous ancestors, perhaps Mayan. The irony started below her chin. A lithe, delicate neck sat atop square-rigger shoulders. The whole sinewy construction was assembled around the old woman's upright posture, which implied Castilian nobility, or training at the barre. Keno wondered how Clay had managed to find such a person in such an out of the way place.

Señora Irma lived alone, in an unrefined setting, about a kilometer outside of a remote fishing village. A few years ago, she had retired from teaching the children in the village and moved into a small but tight house on the beach. The nearest school was now over three hours away on a dusty, washboard road that became impassable with even the smallest hint of rain. She was perhaps one of the most thoughtful, educated people Keno had ever met, despite (or perhaps because of) the isolation. Her greatest flaw, in Keno's view, was her nonstop coaching. He guessed that she had a continued need to teach, and that since her retirement the absence of that opportunity left her suffering like a lover separated from her mate. There were times when she conveyed such a sense of urgency that he wondered about her health.

"Yes, Irma, I'm fine. *Gracias.*"

She had stowed him in the boat earlier that evening so she wouldn't have to explain the *gringo*'s presence to the local men who were coming to visit her. Since Clay had deposited Keno at her beachfront *palapa* home, she had kept visitors away with a variety of excuses; but she couldn't keep them away forever without eventually arousing concern or suspicion. Earlier in the evening, when Irma was hiding him in the *panga*, Keno had wondered out loud if he should move closer to the house, in case there was trouble. She had insisted the visitors were harmless local men who had been her students over the years. The *hombres* were concerned about her isolation, and so the visits were routine but infrequent.

As the evening wore on, Keno stayed awake under the tarp for as long as possible, alert to the sounds of laughing and music, and the possibility that he might have to move again. Late into the darkness he had finally passed out from exhaustion. In the early morning a storm blew in, and both he and Irma were now getting soaked by the rain.

"It is safe, you can come back to the *casita*, the men are gone."

It seemed like forever since Keno and Clay had pushed the loyal Trooper into the ravine. One hundred and seventy days of hiding in remote, rustic, central Baja, with no external contact except the one time his brother had come to check on him. It was as if he had been exiled to a crude Elba without his Josephine. Clay's reassurances had been less and less convincing, and Keno's emotional state was deteriorating. He was harboring serious doubts about Clay's covert operations. At this point in his life he was no longer comfortable ceding control to another human being—certainly not one who was living in a clandestine world of smoke-and-mirrors conspiracy theories. Waking up from the drowning dream in the wet boat under the tarp was the final straw. He decided at that moment, on the hard seat of the *panga*, that it was time to go home.

"Thank you, *Señora*. Can you please contact my brother and tell him I need to talk to him?"

Concern clouded the widow's face.

"*Todo está bien, Señor?*"

"*Sí*, Irma, everything is fine. But *es muy importante* that I talk to him. It's time for me to go home."

"*Claro*…next time I go to town I try, *Señor* Keno."

"*Gracias.*"

Nodding with resignation, Irma turned and started working her way back up the steps from the beach. Experience had taught her that being alone was frightening at first; but over time one could make peace with the solitude.

CHAPTER 34 —

Leather Face

"I feel like one of those useless, shrieking girls in a slasher movie."

Trick looked up quizzically from his pork ribs. His mouth was too full to verbalize his lack of understanding, and he was unaware of the dab of mashed potatoes squatting at the left corner of his lower lip. Challenges from work occupied all of his bandwidth, so he wasn't really capable of sorting through whether Lola was being literal or speaking metaphorically. Lola's teenage boys, Sam and Gus, had already eaten and excused themselves; they were now sequestered in their rooms for an evening of homework, video games, and fapping.

"You know the type? Hyperventilating. Tight, ripped clothes. Stumbling around at night on one broken high heel?"

Feeling there was a point to Lola's description, Trick's face betrayed his lack of recognition. He had jettisoned his dreads in exchange for close-shorn business precision. Now he was listening attentively as Lola kept trying to explain herself.

"Running like a retard or a...I don't know...a...a chicken with its head chopped off? Right into the effin' arms of the chainsaw guy?"

Trick glanced at the clock in Lola's kitchen. He had twenty minutes to get to bed if he wanted any chance at six hours of sleep. He had been averaging five ever since he had moved down to San Francisco to cover for Keno, and he knew his efforts to catch up on the weekends were just Band-Aids. He was exhausted, and his calendar ruled his life. His return to the workforce had accelerated all his daily routines. It was simple math: he needed to cram more things into a finite time period. Now, even his meals elicited a sense of urgency. But tonight, with Lola's animated non sequitur, he sensed a need to slow down for a second. It was apparent, even to his preoccupied self, that the wife of his missing best friend (and business partner) seemed to be really worked up about something. Before he could put down the rib and offer a nod affirming his hostesses' assertion, Lola continued.

"God, I hated those women....so pathetic."

Trick swallowed the mouthful then swiped at the barbecue sauce with his napkin. *Treacherous territory,* he thought. *How to negotiate this without extending the conversation or seeming insensitive?*

"So not the *final girl*?" he asked, trying to clarify.

Now it was Lola's turn to be confused.

"What's the *final girl*?"

At Florida State, Trick had taken a film class, and one of the assigned books was *Men, Women, and Chainsaws: Gender in the Modern Horror Film*. It was meant to be a fluff course for jocks, but Trick had really gotten into it and actually read the material.

"It's a trope for the last person standing in horror flicks...usually a so-called 'good' girl...the only one of the group who doesn't sleep around or do drugs.... In the end, she perseveres and survives the slasher...or the monster."

"That's a thing?"

"The *final girl*? Definitely. It's received a lot of academic attention. Carol Clover..."

Trick caught himself before heading off on a long lecture about the topic. Reflecting on their conversation, he realized that he had come really close to hijacking the exchange without any consideration of Lola's needs. He hadn't lived with anyone else since he'd left college decades ago, and he was finding himself unaccustomed to the burdens of female community. Skills like having to carry on polite conversation about topics in which he had little interest, or supporting someone emotionally when they clearly needed help just weren't areas in which he was well practiced. He thought of himself as more of a problem solver—a Mr. Fix It type. Get in, make a correction, and get out. Sometimes he wondered if living with Lola had brought out in him a long-repressed streak of introversion, given their regular crossed signals. Putting the miscommunications aside, his biggest problem currently was a lack of time. He was trying to save a faltering business while simultaneously covering all of Lola's expenses. After some intense and stressful months, the Bowman & Barton real estate partnership was finally showing signs of righting itself…but the money was still tight. He looked down with embarrassment at the nearly twenty pounds he had gained since moving in to Keno's guest room. He then wondered if maybe his presence over the last few months had offended Lola in some way.

"Um…did I do something wrong?"

Lola was quick to correct the faulty assumption.

"God no, Trick! Without you I'm not sure where we'd be. I can't think of a better partner to help me through this mess. If anything I could use more of you."

It had been six months since either of them had had sex. Misreading her intention, Trick felt it necessary to be clear.

"You know I think you're attractive, Lola, but I'm not sure…"

Lola understood his interpretative shortcomings and quickly headed him off at the pass.

"Trick, stop....What I'm trying to say is I'm frustrated because I'm so dependent on you, and I don't know how I got here. I used to be able to take care of myself."

Grateful for the compliment, Trick was particularly relieved there wasn't another complication he'd have to deal with. Things were already tough enough. He was burning through his nest egg and wondering how much longer he could hold out before poverty forced a hard conversation. He had broached the topic several times over the last few weeks with Clay and Aloysius, but never definitively with Lola. Despite the obfuscation, Lola's instincts understood that her support team was nearing the end of their financial rope.

As he looked over at the frightened mother, Trick finally understood that Lola was trying to apologize.

"Lola, being a mom and wife doesn't make you any less legit than going to work and collecting a paycheck. By the way, you've really outdone yourself with these ribs…just spectacular."

Barely repressing a smile, Lola tried to brush off the compliment.

"Anyone can cook a dinner…"

Now it was Trick's turn to interrupt.

"No, listen…you shouldn't beat yourself up, none of this is your fault."

Lola couldn't help herself. She had been thinking a lot about karma lately.

"But what if it is?" she blurted out.

Trick looked at her closely, the narrowing of his eyes barely perceptible.

"What do you mean?"

Lola took a deep breath. She realized she wasn't ready to tell the whole truth. So she carefully backed away from the confessional booth. Over the last few weeks her brain had been overwhelmed with whirling demons. She was worried that her indiscretion with Wolfgang was somehow tied to Keno's untimely disappearance…which meant the financial burden her needs were placing on Trick and Aloysius might be her fault. Elise's comments about marrying for security also kept playing in her head as she fretted about making her boys' Brinson tuition payments. Having made up her mind during one of her recent panic attacks, she began gathering the courage to inform Trick.

Besides, she thought, *he should be happy. He'll get to go home.*

As she formulated the next difficult sentence in her mind, the words began to twist in her diaphragm before she forced them up her throat and quietly spat them from her lips like shards of glass. She pushed visions of her supposedly dead husband out of her head.

"Trick…I've…um…god this is hard to say…I feel like such a traitor…please don't judge me…"

A curious look came over Trick's face. He had no idea what was coming next, but Lola had his rapt attention.

"I've decided to remarry."

The statement hit Trick like the lip of a doubled-up, overhead wave. He was totally stunned, incapacitated, barely able to keep his dinner from levitating and his bowels from evacuating. After taking a few moments to reassemble his mental yard sale, he fired off the obvious questions in machine gun succession.

"What? Why? To whom? What about Keno? Lola, no! You can't!"

Expecting the questions, Lola channeled Elise for parts of her response.

2009 - Still Out West (Mostly)

"Think about it Trick, it makes total sense. I get to keep my house, my boys get to stay at Brinson, you and Aloysius don't have to worry about supporting me anymore, and I even get to go back to school and try and get my Physician's Assistant credential…so I can get a job, and not be so effin' dependent."

Incredulous, Trick wondered why she had neglected the most important detail. The part about love.

A selfish part of him saw the benefit in her decision. Remarrying provided the necessary catalyst to bring the current unsustainable situation to a head. With each passing week it had become clearer that Clay wasn't up to the task. It took a while before his head stopped spinning and he was able to calm down enough to ask the next question.

"Lola I don't know what to say. I mean I guess I should be happy for you, but this just seems so sudden. Who's the guy?"

"You don't know him. His name is Wolfgang Dalman. We dated back when I was at NYU."

"Wolfman Dahmer? What type of name is that?"

"No, Dalman. Wolfgang, like Mozart, and Dalman, like D-A-L-M-A-N. He's Argentinian, but his family left Germany during World War II."

File that away, thought Trick, before continuing with the questions.

"But what about Keno? Please, tell me this isn't happening soon."

"He asked me before, and I told him no, but a few nights ago…I just…I just felt so helpless and scared…you don't know how hard it is every night…how hard it is for a middle-aged woman with no career, no money, and two teenage boys…the thought of my future without Keno, alone, is…I don't know…*terrifying*. I called Wolfgang in the middle of the night and accepted. He wants to elope tomorrow, but I told him I needed more time. I don't want a big event, just something simple."

"You've stayed in touch all these years?"

"Not really, I know it sounds crazy, but we became friends on Facebook about a year ago."

"And Keno?"

Fighting back an uncomfortable combination of guilt and tears, Lola recited the words she had been practicing all day.

"Trick, believe me, this isn't how I wanted things to end up…and I know this seems like I'm abandoning him, but…he's only a memory now. I have other responsibilities I have to think about. I'll always love him with all my heart, but we have to let him go…It's been six months, where could he possibly be?"

"But the police…the insurance…do you actually love this guy?"

Captive to her circumstances, Lola quietly started crying.

"I think I could learn to love him…. He supports my decision to go back to school and start a career…. He wants to live here and be part of the family…I know it sounds like a contradiction, but I'm tired of being financially dependent on someone…. Remarrying gives me the opportunity to make that transition to a working career…I need to do this for so many reasons."

"Lola, you can go back to school *now*, you don't have to marry some rich guy to do that. We'll make that happen if you want."

Lola shook her head. "I'm so so so so grateful," she replied, "but you can't carry me for three more years, and it's not fair of me to ask."

Trick nodded silently, indicating he understood Lola's argument. His facial expression fell somewhere between offended and defeated. It was his job to take care of Lola and the boys until Clay gave the "all clear," and he was failing. His desire to support Keno's family was being diffused by his dwindling bank account. He tried a new front.

"Do the boys know?"

"Not yet."

"When are you going to tell them?"

"Tonight."

"How do you think they'll take it?"

"Not well," Lola acknowledged, "but they'll get used to it."

Trick knew he was running out of ammunition. He had to try and stall Lola, but he wasn't sure how. As he searched for a new strategy there was an awkward silence.

With watery eyes begging for understanding, Lola tried to offer a positive thought.

"You'd like him. His family owns a lot of real estate."

Trick briefly frowned at the implication that he was so unidimensional, then quickly moved on.

"Lola, I know you're a grown-up and it's not my business, but could you give me at least a few weeks to get some legal stuff squared away at work?"

Relieved that he wasn't fighting harder, Lola tried to find a middle ground.

"We tentatively set a date a week from now, but I'll do my best to hold Wolfgang off for the next ten days…I just hope he doesn't change his mind and back out."

That seemed a response tinged with desperation, but Trick let it slide.

"I'm worried that getting married may affect some issues with the trusts in Keno's estate…and our partnerships." It was a fib, but Trick thought it was excusable, given the circumstances. "I just want our counsel to check some documents."

"I understand." This, too, was a lie; but Lola, too, thought it was excusable. "I'll tell Wolfgang ix-nay on the edding-way for at least ten days and see what he says."

"Perfect." Trick nodded. "I'll get them started on this tomorrow, and maybe they'll get done sooner. I look forward to meeting…" Trick feigned forgetfulness.

"Wolfgang. Dalman."

"Yes, that's right. Wolfgang Dalman. Lucky man."

They finished their dinner in relative silence, with only snippets of small talk filling the few moments when Trick's mouth wasn't full. Working twice as hard as his jaw, his brain furiously planned his next steps. He was shocked that he had been living in the same house with Lola and had no clue that she was building a relationship with another man. Aloysius and he had discussed this as a possible risk with Clay's plan, but he had been caught totally unaware by her announcement. He knew it wasn't unusual for someone to think about their future responsibilities, but he had thought he and Keno would have more time before Lola started searching. He worried that she was making a hasty decision born from a stressful financial and emotional state, but he didn't know how to stop her. Also, there was a gnawing suspicion at the back of his mind… something strange about Lola's sense of urgency that he felt wasn't fully explained by her financial insecurity. He wanted to think Lola's motives were pure, but the whole situation was just so weird that it had injected a degree of paranoia into his thinking. His most urgent priority was getting all the details to Aloysius, so he could in turn update Clay, and then, hopefully, Clay would look into Dalman and come up with a plan.

After finishing dinner, Trick cleared his dishes to the sink then started scraping bones into the dog bowl. Lola interrupted him while loading the dishwasher.

"Trick, I can do that, just leave it."

Trick shook his head. "It's the least I can do after such an amazing dinner."

She noted the cake on the table. It hadn't been touched since Sam and Gus had mauled it an hour earlier.

"Didn't you see the dessert? I made your favorite, chocolate cake."

"Thanks, but I can't, my buttons are popping."

Pouting silently, Lola knew Trick was struggling with his weight so didn't push. Trick headed for the door with his mobile phone in his pocket.

"I think I'll take a little after-dinner stroll…enjoy the Marin air."

In a good mood as a result of getting the Wolfgang news off of her chest, Lola laughed playfully back at the big *jamanese*.

"Be careful, I'm told the Marin deer can be quite dangerous."

He smiled.

"I know you're kidding, but Lyme disease is no joke."

"Like I said, give the deer a wide berth."

They both grinned as Trick spun through the kitchen door, thinking about how easy Lola's laugh was. He lumbered across the patio then took the ten stone steps two at a time to get up to Manor Road. When he reached the top of the stairs he was already working hard to pull oxygen into his lungs.

God, he thought, pausing to catch his breath, *I can't believe how out of shape I am.*

After a few minutes his breathing calmed down from the short climb, and he looked back, making sure he was alone and out of earshot. He pulled out his cell and punched in Aloysius's number while continuing his slow walk from the Barton home.

Like a youngster struggling to rub his belly while simultaneously patting his head, Aloysius was losing his battle to coordinate the plastic bag and the hand lotion. Carefully sliding the large Ziploc over his head while gently coaxing the underside of his penis required a kinesthetic ability that he simply seemed to lack. He had already switched hands several times, hoping at some point a rhythm would overtake him, but all he had achieved was a very slippery bag, the surface of which had attracted a squadron of squirming pubic hairs. Taking a break, he placed the soiled bag over the plastic hula-girl lamp beside his bed, illuminating with great clarity the deviance of his undertaking. Removing the other hand from his penis, he opened his fifth Mike's Hard Lemonade and stared through the hairy bag that was suffocating the grass-skirted girl. He considered encasing the whole setup in a Lucite block and trying to peddle it as a lost collaboration between Damian Hirst and Robert Mapplethorpe. Just the thought of the insulated art world's response brought forth a quick giggle. He briefly started working through a plan before he realized he lacked the ambition and *cojones* to pull it off.

Ever since Lilly had forsaken him for the geologist (the recognition of which had sent his libido into a tailspin), Aloysius had decided he needed to experiment more. While scouring the internet he discovered he had a thing for Korean women…but he was also intrigued by the concept of autoerotic asphyxiation. From a distance he viewed the choking as a kind of Russian roulette with fringe benefits. Given how difficult it was to get to Asia, he decided to forgo the Koreans and focus on the asphyxiation. For some strange reason he was fixated on achieving a gasper orgasm, and he reminded himself that perseverance was the key to success. His first go involved a leather belt around his neck, but he couldn't get the hang of simultaneously hoisting himself with the belt while tugging on his uncommitted manhood. Plus he hated the way the silver Louis Vuitton buckle dug into his trachea. The plastic bag had been easier to manage, but so far neither technique had brought him to arousal. He made a mental note: *Next time try a thinner type of plastic. Perhaps a bag from the dry cleaners...?*

Aloysius had been living in relative isolation ever since Clay had bailed him out of jail. There was a professional distance between he and Lilly that she wouldn't allow him to cross, and her unwillingness to come to his aid left him feeling immensely awkward at best and abandoned at worst. Around the wellness center, the unwilling celibate was still allowed to act as concierge to the guests, but he was no longer allowed access to Lilly's cockpit. This coolness had turned icy after their daughter, Scout, had tried to take her own life. When Aloysius came around, Lilly was about as welcoming as a pair of brass knuckles. It was as if Lilly blamed their child's struggles on Aloysius's side of the gene pool. To Aloysius, it seemed like everything he cared about was crumbling, and he strongly yearned for the physical comfort of another human being.

Making things even more difficult from Aloysius's perspective was the public insinuation of the crazy rock doctor. In an act of retaliation that Aloysius felt was significant in its disproportion, the interloper and Lilly were now shamelessly mounting each other with a frequency that Aloysius felt lacked in discretion.

Now, as he viewed his current situation with a pair of fresh eyes, he realized the plastic-and-pubic-hair covered Hawaiian table lamp imbued feelings of embarrassment and resignation. He cursed his age and general deficiencies, and in an unthinking fit of rage his left arm shot out and swept the hula girl and sexual paraphernalia onto the floor. Initially, the absence of the sound of breaking glass brought some relief, but then his self-abhorrence caused an emotional reversal. He cursed himself for not even having the conviction to mount an effective display of destructive frustration.

I'm so pathetic I can't even throw a proper temper tantrum, he thought angrily.

With his head resting on the guest bedroom pillow, he examined the watermark on one of the ceiling tiles and thought about the occupants on the other side of the wall. A small tear formed in the well of his right eye. He wondered if he would once again be subject to the indignation of the sounds of heaving copulation coming from the owner of the vagina he used to share. In an act of plaintive rebellion, he decided he would give masturbation one more try, this time without the complications. He refused to admit the cuckolding was hurting him deeply, and like a man who doth protest too much, he was committed to spraying his sticky confetti all over the sheets in a celebratory act of defiance that implied indifference to the shenanigans next door.

After another five minutes of concerted effort Al realized it wasn't going to be his night. He discontinued the dismal assault on his beleaguered genitals. He fell asleep wondering about the variability of human tolerance for acts of indiscretion performed by their mates. As he approached the comfort of unconsciousness, a headboard bouncing off the other side of the wall brought him to a groggy consciousness. Jealous visions of a naked Lilly harvesting Dr. Ravi Throckmorton in the contiguous room tortured him with the precision of a jackhammer.

Fuckin' little half-breed Indian bastard, he silently but thoroughly disparaged. *Must be hung like a horse to get Lilly to make those sounds!*

But as he became more lucid he realized his mind had been playing tricks on him. The frenetic sounds were closer, and not indicative of fornication. He quickly triangulated the rhythmic pounding as originating inside his room; finally, he remembered that his mobile phone was set on *stun*. Already upset about his ineptitude, his anger grew with the intrusion of the rhythmic, electronic vibrations. In an effort to shake his head of the sexual images, he partially sat up and started rubbing his eyes. He was dressed in his pajamas and couldn't imagine who would be calling him at such a late hour.

All of my friends are either dead or dead asleep, he Eeyored, and so strongly considered not answering.

The vibrating seemed to be coming from a pair of trousers he had draped over a chair that evening; he wasn't sure, after all the hard lemonade. Given the rumpled slacks's location on the other side of the room, and his melancholy state, the distance seemed impossibly far away.

Probably a telemarketer, he pessimistically rationalized, reminding himself he needed to be careful when shifting from supine to upright, given his arthritic back.

He was grateful when the phone stopped pestering. But less than thirty seconds later it again started buzzing, this time with such ferocity he was concerned his draped trousers might ignite. Forcing the dyspeptic fantasies from his head, he pushed himself out of bed and stumbled across the room. From his perspective the act took extreme courage and discipline.

Fishing the old phone out of its sartorial resting place, he flipped it open without looking at the number. Distrust dominated his greeting.

"Hello!"

A familiar voice broke through the ether.

"Aloysius, it's me. Trick."

Aloysius had spent more time talking to Patrick in the last six months than he had over the previous forty years. A calming sort of competence came through during their conversations. Aloysius always felt better after they spoke. As he pulled up his sagging pajama bottoms, his mood picked up a bit.

"Trick, is everything okay?"

Pause.

Trick tried to choose his words without being alarmist.

"Um…I would say…abso-fucking-lutely not."

Aloysius' slight uptick in mood quickly reversed itself.

"Oh, no. What's going on?"

"Totally out of left field. Lola just told me she got engaged. The wedding is in a week, maybe ten days."

Aloysius tried to assimilate the news. "Whaaa? That's crazy! She can't!"

"I know, I tried. It's insane, but she's feeling cornered and extremely vulnerable…and this guy has some money and that gives her a way out."

Clay's paranoia had infected Aloysius over the last six months. His eyes narrowed in suspicion.

"Or so she says."

"I hate to think that about Lola…"

Aloysius' brain was spinning out of control. He hated how things had failed to sort themselves out, and the six-pack of Mike's was only adding to the centrifugal effect.

"Fucking, fuck, fuckety fuck…this is all so sudden…" He shut his eyes tightly, all the better to think. "I've gotta tell Clay." But the next moment a new thought occurred to him, and he opened his eyes. "Wait…who's the guy?"

Trick was surprised by the cursing, Aloysius was usually more refined. It was a trait he admired, being able to communicate effectively without the usual crude accoutrements of the younger generation. He wondered if the old guy had been drinking.

"I never heard of him…someone she dated in college…Wolfgang Dalman…D-A-L-M-A-N."

Aloysius repeated the name with a German accent. Trick wondered about his comedic timing.

"Wolfgang Dalman. That's a name you don't hear every day. I'll have Clay check him out. This might be the break we've been searching for."

"I dunno…maybe. Either way something's gotta change, we can't keep going on like this."

"No shit. Is there anything else I should tell Clay?"

Again with the language? thought Trick. It grated so much more harshly, coming from a grandfather.

Trick replayed the conversation he had just had with Lola over dinner.

"Um, let's see…reconnected a year ago on Facebook…went to NYU together…his family is from Argentina but they emigrated from Germany because of World War Two. Probably an industrial family."

"Fuckin' Nazis, I bet. Hey, wait…what's Fakebook?"

Trick was starting to get desensitized to Al's cursing. The intensity of the language started to make sense when he realized that one of the old man's children was being threatened. Despite that, immediately invoking the Nazi label made Trick a little uncomfortable. He decided to let it slide and moved on to answer the question about Facebook. Not sure how to describe the omnipresent social media platform to an aging technophobe, Trick tried simplicity.

"It's like a computer-based scrapbook that you can share with your friends."

There was a pregnant pause as Al tried to understand what Patrick might be talking about.

"Oh, Aloysius, one more thing," Trick said, breaking off Al's attempt. "Lola says the family owns a lot of real estate."

Aloysius summed up the available data. "Wolfgang Dalman. Argentina by way of Germany. NYU. Rich family. Fakebook." He nodded confidently. "Okay, I'll get to work. Fuck, this shit sucks."

"No kidding. Hey! Don't forget! Only seven days…ten max. Tell Clay no more of those disappearing acts. He needs to get on this and get Keno involved, *pronto!* And it's *Facebook*, not Fakebook."

"Got it, Facebook…I agree, I'll do my best…but Clay runs on his own schedule, you know."

"God, I hate this." The frustration in Trick's voice came through the ether loud and clear. "Shouldn't we tell Lola?"

"Not yet…we don't know what's going on here. Let me get this to Clay first."

"Okay, but again—we gotta move fast."

"Yep, roger that, Trick."

Trick was worried about the mental acuity of his coconspirator and so restated the need for a sense of urgency.

"Call me as soon as you hear anything."

Aloysius heard what he thought was for sure a banging on the wall from the master bedroom. His face blanched as if someone were scraping their fingers across a chalkboard in his heart.

"Shit, Trick, I gotta go."

The phone went dead before Trick could say good-bye. As he turned and headed back to Lola's house, he wondered if he and Aloysius were doing the right thing.

Ten minutes later, Trick had brushed and flossed his teeth and was slipping naked under the covers of his twin bed. The morning would come hard and fast and he needed to suck whatever recovery he could out of the next few hours before heading back into battle. He reminded his conscience he was already doing everything he could, and that he should leave the decision-making to Keno's father and older brother.

CHAPTER 35 —

Reginald Blundergusting

Hopping from foot to foot like a schoolboy needing to pee, Aloysius watched as Reginald Blundergusting held court. Reggie had just finished teaching a qigong class in Desert Lilly's yoga studio and was now surrounded, like virgins to a martyr, by a group of his devotees. Although practiced in China for over four thousand years, qigong was new to America. Despite (or perhaps because of) its newness, the activity had attracted a small but growing number of disciples. In the New World, Blundergusting was one of the martial art's most flamboyant proselytizers.

Lilly was among those buzzing around Reggie's hive, but her presence was more a statement on the amount of revenue the qigong master was drawing rather than a conviction regarding the efficacy of qigong. All six of Blundergusting's five-day retreats at the Wellness Center had been sold out for months, and Lilly's take was allowing her to plan some much needed updates to the facilities. She also was swimming in medical bills from Scout's battle with the demons; if she didn't start squeezing more money out of her business she would have to start tapping working capital lines. While she appeared to be listening rapturously to her old friend drone on shamelessly about his myriad experiences, she was actually calculating how many more Blundergusting qigong retreats she would need to host before being able to start paying off the bills and perhaps start construction on the renovations. If the flow of campers stayed consistent, she figured three more retreats would get her pretty close to debt free.

Not only had the supply of qigong attendees been steady, but the quirky guests were particularly attractive from an expense perspective. Lilly's food and beverage manager had confided that he was basically pulling weeds from the garden, sautéing them with a little olive oil, garlic and salt, and then serving the soggy greens on a bed of brown rice. With a high degree of incredulity in his voice, he reported that the qigong guests couldn't get enough. He figured he was feeding and watering ten of the teetotalers for the price of one normal guest. His biggest concern was that his weed supply was running out, and he was having to have a series of awkward conversations with the neighbors while trying to locate other sources of purslane.

As Lilly began to get comfortable with the idea that Blundergusting's celebrity was sustainable, she was also strongly considering adding a supersized, bamboo, multi-purpose qigong temple in an effort to keep him retained. She had been ignoring Aloysius' comparisons of Blundergusting to Jim Jones—and qigong to a cult—for a variety of reasons. The most pronounced was that Blundergusting's pattern of opportunistic profiteering was now strongly benefitting Lilly's bottom line. As her brain worked through the construction costs, Aloysius' efforts to capture her attention were lost in the numbers and the adoring hubbub of the Blundergusting crowd.

After the previous night's call with Trick, Aloysius had unilaterally decided that he needed to talk to Lilly about Lola. He was worried that the plan to fake Keno's death had run badly off the rails. Being that Lilly was the smartest person he knew, he hoped for her guidance. As he waited impatiently in the shadows of the reception area, he could hear

Blundergusting entertaining his followers with a booming articulation that filled the corners of the room.

"I figure I had my head buried as far up the camel's ass as anybody, and I still couldn't tell you which direction the beast was headed. Hell, I couldn't even tell you what he'd had for lunch."

As usual, most everybody but Aloysius laughed at Blundergusting's homespun description of his final year on Wall Street. The old whale watcher was not fond of the charismatic newcomer. Like a reporter following a candidate on the campaign trail, he had witnessed the unconventional guru's act too many times to not be jaded. In addition, with Lilly freezing him out, Aloysius was feeling more vulnerable than ever, subconsciously comparing himself to every other man in a way that left his assemblage wanting. If he could be honest with himself, he would recognize that it wasn't his doubts about Blundergusting's sincerity that drove his disdain. It was more that he perceived the Ivy grad as a legitimate male threat—a richer, younger, more credentialed version of himself, with an impeccable CV and an ability to spin stories like Huck Finn.

From a certain perspective, one could view Blundergusting as a more refined version of Forrest Gump. He seemed to have a front row seat to many of the most significant cultural phenomena of his generation. As a young Harvard linguist (with a specialty in Slavic dialects), he had been recruited into the CIA to fight the Cold War. It was there that he and Lilly had met while sharing the same training rotations. There was an obvious attraction upon which they had acted, but more out of curiosity than neediness. Although their couplings served to satiate the hormonal drive, they soon concluded independently that they were too career-oriented for a long-term, romantic relationship. Over the ensuing years they stayed in touch, achieving that rare balance of enjoying each other's company without one developing a resentment about the other's lack of commitment.

About a year after Reggie completed his introductory training, the CIA shipped him off to the Moscow station, where he was a deep-cover operator doing dead drops for such espionage superstars as Adolf Tolkachev. After twenty-plus years as a spook—a period during which many later credited his work as helping to accelerate the implosion of the Soviet Union—he retired from his government job and started a hedge fund that focused on Russian stocks. In two years he had doubled his friends' and his family's money, after which he opened the fund to outside investors.

After four years the smart money was beating a path to his door. By mid-2005 he was managing five billion dollars in global assets and paying himself over one hundred and fifty million dollars a year in deferred compensation. In April of 2006 he was diagnosed with early stage glaucoma, carpal tunnel syndrome, obesity, hypertension, severe lumbar stenosis, and radiculopathy in his cervical spine. Sitting in a chair and staring at screens all day was taking a severe toll. Following his doctor's advice, he shut down his fund and returned all of his clients' money (less than one year before the collapse of Bear Stearns and Lehman Brothers, as it happened). He put his six-hundred-and-eighty-million-dollar, ostrich-sized nest egg into the Vanguard Prime Money Market Fund and decided to orient his resources towards improving his health.

The third phase of his charmed life started with extensive travel through China and India, the parts of the world with which he was the least familiar. When he returned home a few years later he was glaucoma-, hypertension-, and pain-free—a qigong practitioner who was passionate about sharing his resurrection with the domesticated sheeple of the western world. It was at this point that he and Lilly reconnected, both recognizing the parallels in their lives despite independent, circuitous journeys. Acknowledging there was still some chemistry, neither was willing to act on it given the complexity of their current arrangements. Despite this resistance to consummation, they spent a few hours catching up over kombucha and avocado toast before she invited his traveling band of apostles to retreat periodically at her Wellness Center for five thousand dollars a head. The match had a celestial imprimatur, and Lilly and Reginald had been thick as thieves ever since. Lilly would provide the venue and handle logistics, and Blundergusting would bring the crowds and teach. They split the profits fifty-fifty.

The current group was halfway through the last scheduled retreat at Desert Lilly's. Lilly was lobbying hard to lock in the money train for another twelve months of workshops, but Reggie understood excess demand and was now playing coy.

After answering a few more questions from his admirers, Blundergusting made his way through the small crowd. Eventually, he sidled up next to Lilly.

"Do you still have time for lunch today?"

Lilly glanced at the bobble heads around Reggie and made a subtle sweeping motion with her eyes.

"*I* definitely have time. The real question is can *you* get away before you have to pull a fishes-and-loaves stunt out of your sarong?"

His eyes twinkled in response.

"Give me twenty minutes and I'll meet you at that dive Mexican place around the corner. That'll give me enough time to first raise a few of the dead."

Lilly's eyes showed disbelief.

"*Las Tres Hijas*? Really? That's Aloysius's favorite place."

Blundergusting leaned in and whispered in her ear.

"God, I'm dying for some good *carnitas*. I swear, it seems like I've been eating boiled weeds all week."

Grinning in response, Lilly let the secret remain hidden, going on the offensive for good measure.

"Reginald Blundergusting! How ungrateful of you! And here my chef has been bending over backwards to meet your group's strict dietary requirements. No gluten, no animal products, no peanuts, no nightshades, no alcohol, no caffeine, no sugar, no salt…should I continue?"

Blundergusting replied with a sly, knowing smile.

"Yeah, well, I guess appearances have to be managed…don't they, Lilly?"

Not sure exactly what he was getting at, Lilly parried with what she hoped would be interpreted as clever.

"The road to enlightenment is fraught with dietary boredom."

"And rocks that live to stub your toes!" Reggie responded with glee.

Seeing her boyfriend heading towards them a split second after Reggie's comment, Lilly smiled weakly then asked if Ravi could join them for lunch. Still a step ahead of her, Reggie looked around before answering. His eyes locked on to something that brought a mischievous grin to his face.

"Dr. Throckmorton? Of course, he's always good company. Hey… isn't that Aloysius over there trying to get your attention? Why don't you bring him too…it's his favorite place, right?"

All the playfulness left Lilly's face as she turned and saw Aloysius motioning for her to come over. She made a quick, muted *Stop* sign with her upraised palm and then held up a single finger while lifting her eyebrows. Her message was clear: *Wait there, I'll be over in a moment.*

After securing Aloysius, Lilly turned back to Blundergusting.

"Reggie, I don't think that's such a good idea, especially with Ravi coming. Al's going through some issues…"

The old spy turned hedge fund manager turned qigong master interrupted with an amused yet firm tone.

"C'mon, Lilly…I insist…it will be fun! You bring Ravi and I'll invite Aloysius on the way out. He can be my date. See y'all soon!"

Before Lilly could sputter further protest, Reginald Blundergusting gave her a good-bye peck on the cheek, turned on his heels, and led his congregation towards the door. After a perfunctory chat with Aloysius a moment later, Reggie shepherded his flock through the other guests like Moses leading the Israelites through the Red Sea. The last thing she heard was his deep timbre, resonating like a bell, clearing a path for his charges as if headed to the promised land:

"Make way for ducklings!"

CHAPTER 36 —

Las Tres Hijas Restaurante

Predictably, everyone showed up on time except for Blundergusting. Occupying the catbird seat was a position to which he had grown accustomed. In his defense, he had the greatest disentanglement challenges of all the parties attending the meal and arrived only a few minutes after Aloysius. As he joined the other three at the four top, he noted a brittle tension that he tried to dispel with a jovial, comedic greeting.

"Hi everyone! Sorry I'm late, the traffic was terrible and I got lost."

No one laughed. Not even a titter. The waitperson came by and distributed the usual ordering and eating tools. Blundergusting looked around and noticed the place was only a quarter full…and most of the patrons were *gringos*. His three tablemates were all hiding behind their menus, so he again tried to break the ice with some cheerful questions.

"Where is everybody? Isn't this place usually packed with locals for lunch? I hope the food is still good?"

Aloysius, certain that he had been invited solely so Blundergusting could watch him squirm, was already squirming. Being sandwiched between the upgraded version of himself on his left and the interloper on his right highlighted his shortcomings so obviously that his mind was seething with resentment at the mockery. Across the table, Lilly was oblivious to his suffering. In general Aloysius felt off-balance when not leading the conversation…and his vertigo was even more pronounced when Blundergusting was around. Despite his best efforts, he had been incapable of wresting the alpha position from the former spook; therefore, he always felt his conversational timing to be a half beat off. Since the group had room for only one charming savant, and Blundergusting already occupied that position, Aloysius was left to assume a different persona. Not having much experience in a supporting role, he usually defaulted into a grumpy, saltier version of himself—like an arthritic Popeye who had been abandoned by Olive Oyl the day after being diagnosed as spinach intolerant. Despite his debilitating gloom, Aloysius recognized that Blundergusting's attendance question was an opportunity to show his expertise—to put a few early points on the board in his never-ending effort to advance higher in the pecking order. He was wary of a Blundergusting trap, so he chose his words with caution. But his years of *pro bono* immigration work soon had him traveling down a well-worn and passionate path.

"It's the usual police-state racist bullshit. ICE has been raiding a lot of the local businesses, so a lot of the Hispanic population is cowering at home, afraid to go outside unless absolutely necessary. That's why everyone in here is white. Hoover did the same thing in the thirties… deporting one-point-eight million dark-skinned people to Mexico… sixty percent of whom were US citizens. He called it 'repatriation,' as if he were doing them a favor. He would send armed law enforcement to Sunday afternoon community picnics in Los Angeles, block all the park exits, detain everybody with brown skin, and then immediately load them onto trains headed deep inside Mexico without even a shred of explanation or due process. It was part of his 'American jobs for *real* Americans' federal program."

Lilly wanted to tuck herself into a ball and roll out the door. Aloysius and Ravi were on opposite sides of the immigration issue, and so bringing up the sensitive topic was about as welcome as condoms at a convent. Recalling that Reggie's nickname had been "the Spoon"—because he liked to stir things up—she wondered if he was intentionally orchestrating a train wreck. She started to lose her appetite. Trying to defuse, she reached over and put her hand on Ravi's leg then squeezed reassuringly, hoping he wouldn't rise to the bait. *Let it be*, she implored, trying to telepathically communicate to Ravi. *No need to escalate.*

Ravi, not realizing the possibility of manipulation by Blundergusting, resented the obvious effort Lilly was making to control him. He had spent a good chunk of his recent free time working with a victims' rights group in the US border city of Nogales, and the statistics made it pretty obvious that a disproportionate amount of the violent crime in Southern Arizona was being committed by illegal Hispanic immigrants. Brushing aside Lilly's hand, he surprised himself with the mild tone of indignation that permeated his comments, which were directed to his left, at Aloysius.

"Surely you don't believe a nation should give up its sovereignty by allowing free movement across its borders? Shouldn't we require minimal adherence to our laws for all those residing under our jurisdiction?"

In a flash Lilly's anxiety turned into fixation on a single turn of phrase. Before she could stop herself her mouth blurted out:

"Don't call me Shirley!"

The three men at the table were all well aware of Lilly's quirks, but none was as delighted as Blundergusting that she still hadn't fully domesticated them. He clapped his hands once and then rubbed them together, grinning all the while as if warming himself by the fire. The meal was turning out even better than he had hoped, and they hadn't even ordered yet.

Aloysius, forgetting that Blundergusting had invited him partially as entertainment, couldn't let his rival's words stand unchallenged. He ignored Lilly's outburst and launched into a well-rehearsed rhetoric.

"No, Ravi," he returned icily, "I am fully aware of the need to enforce the law when it comes to our borders. My issue is more about prioritization. We already spend billions of dollars on immigration control and enforcement, and we deport hundreds of thousands every year. There is already a nearly seven-hundred-mile wall between Mexico and the United States. We are throwing a huge amount of resources at a problem that isn't really a problem…why should we spend even more? Mexico and the United States share a population of nearly five hundred million that are culturally more similar than different. However, there is a significant difference between the two countries in terms of economic opportunity and standard of living. These factors create a staggering incentive for people to cross the border, and to imply that we can completely stop that flow is a ridiculous waste of time and resources that I believe is seated in xenophobia. The relationship between Mexico and the United States isn't parasitic, it's symbiotic. If we really wanted to save lives and improve our standard of living there are other areas we should prioritize in terms of resources that cause much more harm. Did you know we lose more American lives each year to automobile accidents, by far, than we do to illegal immigrants murdering people? Why not focus on better enforcement of our driving-while-texting laws? Or outfit every car with a Breathalyzer device attached to the ignition? Or spend more dollars educating people about the sugar-and-soft-drink epidemic that's causing our obesity problem? Require regular exercise from those who want free health care? Or stop sending our young warriors to the Middle East so they won't come home and commit suicide every twenty-two seconds? Do you know pollution kills thousands of our citizens every year? You want to save American jobs? Why not outlaw robots instead of brown people? All of these issues are much greater challenges and cause much more damage to our social fabric, but the villains are faceless corporations, or government, or white people who look like me, not little brown people whom our politicians can vilify as 'them.'"

As he looked at Ravi the irony of his words started sinking in, so he decided to try and distinguish between the man sitting next to him and the ethnic group that was the subject of his diatribe.

"By the way, aren't you a British citizen?"

Before Ravi could clarify the fact that he had dual citizenship, their server arrived to take the group's orders. The staff person's name tag read *Chris,* and their gender and ethnicity were indeterminate. They had long green hair and a pierced eyebrow. On both arms tattoos snaked up, under their shirt sleeves, and finally reappeared above the collar on their shirt.

"Any questions about the menu?"

After a polite pause, the diners all looked at Lilly.

"The *carnitas* platter special, please."

Without missing a beat, Blundergusting chimed in with delight.

"The same, please."

"Make that three."

Ravi hesitated.

"The blue marlin in your tacos? Do you know if it's sustainably harvested?"

The waitperson was too young and provincial to be thoughtfully sarcastic, although they affected a world-weariness that was likely contagious within their local peer group. Too self-involved to craft a compelling narrative, they offered Ravi the truth as best recalled, free of the guile and varnish of agenda.

"No, I'm sorry…I think the owner caught it last month, like, on vacation in Cabo and brought it, kinda, home frozen in an igloo?" A moment later they had another thought: "Wait, maybe some was smoked too…I'm not sure, but I think they got tired of it, ya know, because there was so much…and that's when he decided to, like, run the special…if that helps?"

Ravi didn't know if he should start another row, but he decided a point had to be made. Usually a modest sort, he had been a bit of a misfit growing up in India, where he had been bullied sporadically as a boy. His commitment to the field of stone-biped interaction had brought a fair degree of ridicule to his adult life as well. As a result, over the years he had developed a soft spot for those unable to defend themselves. Using his most gracious voice, he started lightly, but his indignation built with each syllable, along with his momentum.

"Hmm…well, it seems you personally have nothing to do with it…and I'm sorry to burden you with this when I should probably be talking to your manager…it's just that blue marlin are currently considered a threatened species by the IUCN due to overfishing, and, as usual, the most pernicious and obese species on the planet…us…humans…all seven billion of us…are still acting like we are part of the food chain, murdering spectacularly large and magnificent animals for sport, when, in fact, we should be stewards of the planet given our technological advantages…safeguarding the regeneration of those species which are being threatened by our misguided and selfish ways."

Ravi paused for an inhalation and to check the audience's temperature. The only meaningful feedback he was receiving was Lilly's hand under the table squeezing his quadriceps like it was the *off* switch for a mechanical bull that was running out of control. Everyone else was paying rapt attention, but Ravi couldn't tell if they were sympathetic or not. He decided to continue to ignore Lilly's squeezings and drive his point home. Using the indeterminate waitperson as the target of his rhetoric, he periodically made eye contact with his tablemates.

"I mean, how would you like it if a superior form of intelligence came to our planet and started behaving like we do, hunting and eating any species over which they have dominion...any knowledge or technology advantage, no matter how slight? We deceive ourselves into thinking we're special, made in God's image, whatever that is, but heaven forbid a smarter, alien species shows up on our planet and treats us with the same disregard we treat subordinate species. How would you feel if some species tortured, murdered, and ate you or members of your family, just for sport? Used your brother for lab experiments, or hunted your whole species to extinction, like we did to the dodo bird, just for fun? Or how about herding your whole village into a warehouse with cattle prods, keeping you there, cheek to jowl, to be harvested for protein, at which time they grab you and hang you from your heels while an assembly line robot slits your throat? Or maybe they shove a funnel down your throat daily and force-feed you grain so they can eat your fatty liver because they thought it a delicacy? Or how about they just harvest your eyes, ears, and left arm and boil them in a stew because they think it confers aphrodisiac qualities? How would any thinking, compassionate being feel?"

Their server stood still, pencil poised, along with the other diners at the table, unsure if the question was meant to be answered. Finally, after a silent moment, the waitperson hesitantly shrugged and answered the question with a question.

"So that's a 'no' on the blue marlin?"

Ravi realized he may have a gone a bit too far and tried to walk back some of the vitriol...rejoin the group.

"I guess, like everybody else, I'll take the *carnitas* special with *maize* tortillas. I'm pretty gluten intolerant."

Aloysius couldn't believe his ears.

"I thought you were a vegetarian?"

Ravi didn't want to admit he had succumbed to peer pressure rather than order something that he could eat.

"I'm broadening my horizons."

Blundergusting had to get involved.

"That's quite a leap...although if you're gonna take the bait, it might as well be for bacon."

Still incredulous, Al had to dig deeper.

"I'll say...a Hindu who eats pork? What's next, a Quaker who practices cannibalism?"

Ravi shrugged, and Lilly hoped they would just move on. She was okay with her boyfriend's passive tendencies; in fact she found them to be mannerly.

The server stopped writing furiously and looked up at the group. The tension had been growing during the diatribe but Ravi's efforts to defuse had been effective. The revelation that they all shared an appreciation for a delicious plate of shredded pork ratcheted down the edginess a notch.

"Four *carnitas* specials...corn tortillas for all...that's easy. Drinks?"

"*Horchata.*"

"*Horchata.*"

"*Jamaica.*"

Aloysius hesitated when it was his turn to order a drink. Blundergusting took the pause as an opportunity to interrupt. He had been dancing in his seat for much of their lunchtime interaction, barely able to contain his merriment. To him, anything was better than the inane small talk humans had contrived to pass the time socially. Not sure what was coming next, he was hoping it would be good. He could see Ravi was feeling he may have overdone it; so before the doctor could retreat too far into his shell, he decided to send him a little support…just to keep him engaged.

"Wow, Dr. Throckmorton…your thesis on evolution and human's place on the food chain…that was quite a mouthful. But I agree with you wholeheartedly, every single syllable. Most of our species is struggling with the changes effected by the rapid change in our technology…only a few STEM whizzes are keeping up…I'm afraid the rest are doomed to inhabit the plug-in incubators at *The Matrix* zombie farm."

Aloysius kept his nose in the menu, not wanting to make eye contact and keeping his voice casual. Already occupying the depths of the smoldering crater that was once his life, with shards of broken glass strewn all about his feet, he decided he could freely throw rocks at his tormentors without fear of reprisal.

"Ahem, excuse me…if it's not too late, I'd like to switch my order to the Blue Marlin Taco Special with flour tortillas? That sounded really good. Extra gluten, please."

The server started scratching on their pad.

"No problem." Still not making eye contact, he was struggling with something internally. "And to drink, sir?"

Fuck it, Aloysius told himself self-righteously. He put down his menu and looked the server directly in the mouth.

"A double *Patron* margarita, rocks and salt, and a *Dos Equis verde* chaser."

The server looked down at Aloysius and tried to clarify in a nonjudgmental way.

"Um, you want a single margarita but with *two* shots of *Patron*, not just one?"

On the outside, Al looked defiant. On the inside, a feeling between self-doubt and self-loathing pulsed through his brain. He hated the fact he was again failing the marshmallow test so publicly, but he could already taste the margarita.

"Yes…not blended, and with salt decorating the rim of a frosty glass…and… a crispy, cold *cerveza* at the same time…in case you get busy."

The server looked around at the nearly empty room and shrugged.

"Okay."

After collecting the menus, the genderless waitperson headed back to the kitchen to get the drinks and place the food order. Reggie turned back to the group.

"So why is the ICE turning up the heat? Didn't we just elect a liberal government?"

Aloysius and Ravi looked at each other. The forsaken reluctantly nodded at the chosen, inviting the smallish brown man to speak.

"It's just Obama paying back organized labor. They think unchecked immigration leads to lower wages."

"Hmm, strange bedfellows," observed Blundergusting.

"On that we agree," chimed Aloysius.

Lilly saw an opportunity in the group *detente* to nudge the conversation towards something less inflammatory while simultaneously gathering intel to help her better keep Blundergusting and his highly profitable qigong tribe captive at the wellness center for the foreseeable future.

"Reggie, where do you go next?"

Blundergusting smiled at Lilly, understanding her redirection but being okay with it for now.

"I've been scheduled in Scottsdale for a workshop. It's my first time teaching at a Four Seasons, so it should be interesting."

Lilly frowned. She didn't know how to hide her disappointment that her new meal ticket was being seduced by an upscale Goliath. Sensing her obvious discomfort, Ravi tried to be good company and focus on the positive.

"Wow, Reggie, that sounds really interesting. It seems like you are at the forefront of something really big. That must be so exciting."

Aloysius sulked, his thoughts turning the kind comments into pablum while silently mimicking like a six-year-old on the playground.

Forefront of something really big…so exciting…blah, blah, blah… God, he thought, looking around for the waitperson, *where are those fuckin' drinks?*

Aloysius was jolted out of his moping by Blundergusting sucking in a lungful of air. A glimmer of an opportunity presented itself, and in a competitive fit of hope, he prepared to front run the Harvard man's efforts to answer Ravi's rhetorical question. Not caring that he was about to unload a non sequitur, Aloysius badly needed some respect and felt the tidbit of tasty trivia he had recently learned was just the right thing to impress. It would be another small step in his ongoing effort to elevate his status and reverse his fall from grace.

"Did you know that the Amazon Basin depends on dust from the Sahara Desert to provide nutrients for the health of both flora and fauna?"

Both Lilly and Ravi fell somewhere between skeptical and confused following the out of place comment. Ravi was too off balance and polite to question the statement, and Lilly figured Aloysius' comment was so far out of left field that it might be true. Just as Aloysius prepared for his touchdown dance, Blundergusting tackled him on the one-yard line.

"Yes, Al, that's right...the Sahara sandstorms gather thousands of tons of dust, and the prevailing winds carry the dirt across the ten thousand kilometers of Atlantic Ocean from Africa to South America."

And then, to the elder man's horror, came the patronizing question.

"And of course you know what's special about the dust that makes it so nutritious for the Amazon watershed?"

Aloysius realized he had been warming his hands over a campfire built on very thin ice. Wracking his brain for more information on the Sahara dust, he came up empty. He recalled seeing the provocative internet headline and reading the first paragraph about the desert storms, but after that he had likely grown bored and clicked through on an adjacent Victoria's Secret ad. As the silence grew unbearable, Ravi piled on.

"I had no idea that Saharan dust made it to South America...but if I may, *common sense* would suggest phosphorous is the magical ingredient?"

Blundergusting's eyes danced with pleasure at the doctor's response. He was in full conversational control, had easily quelled Aloysius' insurrection, and Ravi was now also kicking dirt on the senior upstart's fire.

"Well done, Ravi. Although the answer was quite obvious to even a casual observer of geology, wasn't it? An ancient lake bed in Chad, the *Bodélé Depression*, is chock full of phosphorus from long-dead microorganisms."

Feeling like his long fly ball had been plucked at the warning track, Aloysius' old coping mechanisms started agitating. *Jesus, who's a guy gotta blow around here to get a drink?* Trying to act like he hadn't just been one-upped, he scanned the room with a look of impatience as his brain focused on an exit strategy. *Could that confused waitress, or whatever the fuck it is, be any slower?*

2009 - Still Out West (Mostly)

As if by magic, the androgynous attendant appeared with their drinks. Before the others had even tasted their beverages, Aloysius had sucked down half of his margarita. Lilly delicately tried her *Jamaica*. Immediately, her mood improved. She politely shoved her glass in front of Ravi.

"The *Jamaica* here is so good, you have to try it."

Ravi took a cautious sip and raised his eyebrows.

"Brilliant! You can so clearly taste the hibiscus."

He then lovingly handed the tumbler back to Lilly.

"Thank you, my sweet."

Aloysius sucked down a gulp of beer to keep from gagging.

Blundergusting was getting bored; it was time to reintroduce his favorite topic.

"Yes, Ravi, it's quite exciting, the growing interest in qigong. I had no ambitions to end up this way, I just wanted to cure my own ailments. But I'm convinced qigong can help with so many of our problems, both mental and physical. I'm now on a crusade, and the results we're getting from people…"—*Not to mention the money,* thought Al—"…it's amazing."

The alcohol now beginning to enter his bloodstream, Aloysius was moving from chastened to bitter. One of his enduring strengths had been an ability to rapidly shake off humiliation. He had lost round one but hadn't given up the fight and was still resentful of all the Blundergusting adulation. His next question leaked out with an obviously harsh undertone.

"What exactly are the results that people are *raving* about?"

Recognizing the fight in Al's posturing, Reggie took the mild insult in stride. So far, from Blundergusting's perspective, the old man hadn't been anything more than a minor annoyance.

"Well, for starters, on a personal level my glaucoma and hypertension symptoms have gone away...and my energy levels are through the roof."

Aloysius was on the scent and wouldn't give up easily.

"Wouldn't you have gotten the same results by doing *any* exercise? Basically you went from a sedentary, high stress, poor nutrition situation to a much healthier context. Qigong, yoga, tennis, walking...couldn't you have gotten the same results with any recreation? Especially combined with better nutrition and stress management techniques like meditation or tapping?"

Not wanting to interrupt the obvious competition unfolding before him, Ravi subtly elbowed Lilly and whispered:

"What's tapping?"

She whispered back:

"I'll tell you later."

Not wanting any outside skepticism (no matter how logical) to slow down his money train, Blundergusting tried to keep his voice light and cheery; but inside, he was girding his loins.

"I could see how the *uninitiated* could feel that way, but qigong is so much more than just another form of exercise."

Reginald's pace had been too relaxed, leaving Aloysius room to interrupt.

"And you, in turn, I am guessing, are so much more than just another Richard Simmons?"

Caught off guard for only a second, Blundergusting picked up his authoritarian tone (and his pace) in an effort to regain dominance. He refused to acknowledge the glancing blow.

"Again, only the *ignorant* would call a thriving, four-millennia discipline a fad; but knowing the limitations of ignorance I will try to offer more evidence."

Starting to feel at home as the alcohol crossed the blood-brain barrier, Aloysius again interrupted. He was just now fully reaching his stride.

"Ahhh, the scientific method, a process I embrace. Like democracy, a terrible system…but the best we have for now."

Blundergusting understood that Aloysius was trying to establish himself at Reginald's expense. He also recognized that defending the crown demanded he not appear ruffled.

"Another Churchill fan? I approve. Anyway, as I was saying…"

Aloysius once again tried to interrupt, but Blundergusting met the insertion attempt with an increase in oratorical volume and pace. Lilly and Ravi sat on the sidelines hoping not to be stepped on by the circling elephants.

". . . AS I WAS SAYING, I have had the pleasure of helping many practitioners of other forms of exercise, including yoga, tai chi, swimming, cycling, etcetera, all of whom were very competent in their disciplines…and ALL OF THEM have received benefits from qigong that they felt weren't available to them when practicing their previous forms of movement."

Resting his case with definitives was a technique Blundergusting had learned on the trading desks of Wall Street. Aloysius was undeterred.

"I hate to keep playing the naysayer," he lied, "but couldn't that just be the result of muscle confusion?"

Lilly wasn't very excited about the fact that Aloysius now turned his attention in her direction.

"Lilly, didn't you teach me that by merely changing one's routine you can stimulate the body to higher results? That the body gets used to the same stimulus pattern, and if you move from, say, weightlifting to yoga, or any break in the pattern, it will seem difficult at first, but the body will redouble its efforts to solve the new task, leaving the practitioner feeling a renewed sense of accomplishment and enthusiasm?"

Now in a mild tug-of-war between her romantic past and her financial future, Lilly leaned towards the promise of economic opportunity.

"Yes, I have been a proponent of muscle confusion workouts for some…but I think what Reggie is offering through his qigong teachings promises a whole new degree of magnitude when it comes to quality-of-life improvements."

What? Aloysius thought. *Is nothing sacred? Is no person immune to the charms of lucre?* He had miscalculated Lilly's mercenary tendencies. *Effin' traitor!*

Aloysius stayed focused on Lilly while gathering his resources and trying to retreat with some dignity

"Well, well, another devotee to the financial lure of qigong. Thank you both for the education."

Blundergusting was quick to acknowledge the assist.

"Thanks for the affirmation, Lilly."

With both his personal testimony and his livelihood supported by an apparent quorum, Blundergusting made an effort to appear the gracious winner by turning his companions' focus in a less contentious, more entertaining direction. He liked drama, but only the non-threatening kind; and so after wiping his mouth with his napkin he leaned back in his chair and casually pointed his next question across the table.

"Dr. Throckmorton, please, anything new you can share with us about your research?"

Ravi was dying to share his nascent breakthrough with anyone who expressed an interest, but until now he hadn't found that person. The excitement of revealing his creative genius to a captive audience was overwhelming his natural reticence.

"Well…I don't know…"

Not sure if Blundergusting was just pranking her boyfriend, Lilly decided anything was better than Aloysius strafing her qigong gravy train for the rest of the meal.

"Yes, Ravi, please, tell them about your new discovery."

Everyone turned to Ravi with expectation. Aloysius starting sifting through his memory banks for some good-sized throwing rocks. Taking a deep breath, Ravi began sorting his thoughts so he could present a lecture that would fit his audience.

"Well, have any of you noticed the football field-sized grid I have staked off in the desert behind the kitchen?"

There was an awkward silence. Nobody wanted to admit they hadn't a clue what the geologist was talking about.

"Nobody…?" Ravi said with mild disappointment.

Looking around, he saw he still had their attention. That alone was a victory, given his past experiences. His words took off at a gallop while he still had the chance.

"That's okay, no problem. Well, you see, I have staked out a grid approximately fifty by one hundred yards. This area contains a relatively flat surface, with rocks of all kinds and sizes protruding at multitudinal directions. I have classified the rocks as either igneous, which as you know are volcanic in nature, metamorphic, or sedimentary. Using a drone, I photograph the whole area every eight hours with a high enough pixel count to allow me to examine with detail the exact location and texture of the rocks, down to the millimeter. After sunset I use a special infrared lens so I can still record any change."

So far, he had literally been talking over their heads so he could keep his train of thought by avoiding eye contact. As he paused to assess his pupils' attentiveness, he noticed a flagging of interest. Not surprisingly, Aloysius was in open rebellion, slouching and yawning in cartoonish fashion, like the high school class clown. Ravi decided to cut to the chase, hoping they would recognize the significance of his discovery.

"Well, I know this isn't as interesting to non-geologists, but here comes the good part! Every day, before breakfast at six A.M. and after dinner at six P.M., I walk very carefully, barefoot and blindfolded, for five minutes, in a random pattern, through the grid. I record the precise details of every rock that stubs my toe, including the type of rock, its location, and its particular angle of repose. I don't weigh the rocks, because that would require moving them, but I do estimate their general size and dimensions. I have been doing this for three months now—ninety-two days, twice a day—and on average the rocks hinder my bipedal movement about seven times a session…so, on average, using laymen's terms, rocks stub my toes about fourteen times a day. So, I have fourteen times ninety-two, or one thousand, two hundred and eighty-eight data points that I have been crunching, looking for patterns."

Ravi stopped triumphantly, looking at his audience, whom he was sure were just as knotted up with suspense as he was. In fact, he was so excited about delivering the punch line he didn't even notice their lack of fervor.

"It turns out that more than fifty percent of the observations came from igneous rocks, after dinner, that were over three inches in diameter, and these rocks have an angle of repose of thirty-seven degrees, plus or minus five percent!"

Ready to enjoy the adulation that a knowledgeable group like this was sure to bestow, he prepared prematurely for his victory lap. When no one leapt to their feet with appreciative applause, he concluded the audience might be a bit less astute than he had originally credited. He decided to prime the pump.

"Don't you see? Statistically these results imply an extremely high correlation. This is clearly not a random occurrence. Now all I have to do is figure out which of the factors is pushing the rock-biped interaction. My guess is that there is something about the food in my stomach after dinner that is attracting the volcanic rocks, but I want to maintain an open mind to the size and angle-of-repose possibilities."

The server had arrived with their food at the tail end of the lecture and was the first to offer an opinion (while serving the platters of *carnitas*).

"Wow, a thousand, two-hundred and eighty-eight observations? That's gotta hurt."

Lilly watched the green-haired one sling the plates with no regard for the etiquette of "serve from the left and clear from the right." Their irresponsible methodology was driving her crazy. She soothed her OCD by compulsively rearranging her utensils in minute increments while Ravi responded to the gender-indistinguishable waitperson.

"It's not that bad. As I mentioned, I walk very carefully, so the experiment probably ruptures the skin only a few times a week. I do have to admit that my toenails are a mess, but it's nothing compared to what Newton went through during his alchemy experiments."

Blundergusting had to weigh in.

"If I recall correctly, didn't Newton fail at his multi-year effort to convert lead to gold?"

Quick to defend his diligence, Ravi responded.

"Yes, but he persevered to the end."

Aloysius couldn't help himself.

"There appears to be a fine line between perseverance and insanity—at least when considering Einstein's definition. By the way, how do you know animals didn't come in and disturb the angle of repose or location of the rocks? How do you know more than fifty percent of all the rocks aren't volcanic?"

"Animals do come in, but I see their tracks, and so I return the rocks to their previous positions, as best I can, based on the most recent photograph."

Aloysius wasn't letting him off with an incomplete answer.

"And the types of rocks in your sample?"

"I identified all the rocks, and only about forty-one percent were igneous."

Aloysius was incredulous.

"You *counted* all the rocks in the desert?"

"No…only in my sample space."

"The football field-sized area?" He scoffed openly. "You ID'd all the rocks in that space?"

Not sure whether he should be sheepish or proud, Ravi answered simply and honestly.

"Yes."

Now getting a clear sense of the grandness of Ravi's project, Aloysius wondered if he were the only one at the table who found the whole thing crazy.

"You do all this barefoot? Aren't you worried about scorpions? Cactus spines? Snakes?"

"I feel it's important not to impede any possible communication between the rocks and my organic sensory antennae."

Not sure if he should dig any deeper, Aloysius' curiosity got the better of him.

"And how'd you record all this data if you're blindfolded?"

Lilly cringed at what she knew was coming next.

"Lilly is nice enough to follow me on my random walks and record the data."

Aloysius nearly spit out his mouthful of beer and *carnitas*.

Lilly left me for this bullshit? he thought, unsure which to lament first, the loss of his respect for Lilly…or the near loss of his beer and carnitas. *I had no idea she was such a nut. These two deserve each other!*

Reggie again started dancing in his seat, amused by the vision of Lilly following the blindfolded doctor, clipboard in hand, through the desert minefield. The qigong master barely stifled a grin before asking the next question.

"Were you *both* shoeless and wearing blindfolds?"

Lilly had been frantically (and silently) typing the conversation on her invisible under-the-table keyboard when she finally decided enough was enough.

"I think it's amazing that after all these years Dr. Throckmorton is still playing by the rules. He develops a hypothesis and then tests it rigorously before reaching a conclusion…adhering to the objective procedures required by the scientific method before publishing his results."

"And how many peer-reviewed articles of his have been published?" Aloysius knew the answer—he was merely enjoying his current role as demolition man.

Lilly turned to him, pissed off at his intent to humiliate.

"That's not the point…"

"I also think it's wonderful he's not compromising his research, unlike so many in the academy," Blundergusting rescued. "I've been reading about academic journals in the so-called *social* sciences publishing harebrained speculations with little in the way of objective peer review; especially in some of the new, so-called *disciplines* like *gender* studies."

Aloysius couldn't resist the obvious irony.

"Oh that's ripe, coming from a burlap-clad, mystic, *gringo* imposteletyzer."

Blundergusting wasn't sure what was motivating Aloysius' vitriol, but he was willing to let it go given how much fun he was having. Ravi, however, his hopes of being understood once again dashed, was crestfallen. Realizing he was now being ridiculed, he spoke up forcefully.

"Thank you, Lilly, and Reginald, for your support, but I don't need the denigration of others' work to elevate my own. I am convinced it will eventually stand on its own two feet. I am sorry to have opened such a can of worms. My research clearly needs to take the next step before being presented openly. Can we please change the subject and enjoy the rest of our lunch?"

Aloysius was finally enjoying everything about the meal, especially the embarrassment of his rivals through the lens of a beer and double margarita. Deciding he would let Ravi off the hook for now, he belched his approval between bites of pork.

"Works for me, doc."

"And me as well."

After a few minutes of taut silence, Blundergusting was nearly done wolfing down his carnitas before good manners required him to again engage his fellow diners. He cautiously turned to Aloysius.

"So, Aloysius, how have you been keeping yourself entertained lately?"

Ignoring the question, Aloysius caught the passing, genderless server's attention.

"I'd like another round, please."

He pointed at both of his glasses to remove any doubt as to his intentions and then looked at his colleagues.

"Anyone else?"

Like a drowning person calling for a life preserver, Lilly raised her hand. *Even the best laid plans,* she thought....

"Double margarita, *Patrón.*"

"Ditto."

The thought of throwing alcohol on the smoldering group's collective fire thoroughly reinvigorated Blundergusting.

"Me too."

The server wrote down the orders on their pad while Aloysius chewed his mouthful and then washed it down with the last of his beer. The warm feeling spreading outward from his gut reminded him that misery truly does love company. Knowing that he at least had everyone's attention, if not approval, he took a deep breath and answered Blundergusting's question about his doings.

"Well, Reginald, let's see." Al paused here with finger pressed against the cleft in his chin for dramatic effect. "Aside from grieving my second son who's gone missing in Baja...getting locked in jail and then abandoned by my girlfriend and business partner...I've been spending most of my recent free time trying to master the art of asphyxiophilia."

Lilly was a little reticent to ask, but she had to know.

"*Asphyxio*-what?"

Slowly, to maximize the shock, Aloysius turned to Lilly and explained.

"Every time you and your little brown stallion over there start showing up on the Richter scale...in other words, whenever your canoodling starts the headboard a'knockin'...I put a plastic bag over my head and start masturbating."

With an over-the-top look of joyful glee, he turned his attention to the table and finished a microsecond second later with an addendum.

"Hey, isn't the food here great?"

Realizing he had been misguided in his belief that things couldn't get worse, Ravi immediately excused himself and limped to the bathroom on his damaged feet. Right behind him was a mortified Lilly. Reggie stayed in his seat; he was thoroughly enjoying the poop-a-palooza, but was also, admittedly, a bit curious.

"Does that shit really work? I mean, to me it seems kinda...I don't know...precarious?"

Aloysius, not wanting to reveal his ineptitude, responded like a seasoned hand.

"I think that's the point."

As Blundergusting pondered the logistics, a thought hit an alcohol-assisted, unfiltered Aloysius.

"Hey, Reggie, what the fuck type of a name is Blundergusting, anyway?"

Although originally he had not been proud of his name, Reginald had grown to embrace it like a good luck charm. He felt it had somewhat of an Old English-sounding pedigree, so he left the etymology undefined, allowing people to speculate about his roots—favorably, he hoped. Most were too polite to inquire deeply. Obviously, in his current state, Aloysius didn't suffer from that inhibition. Reggie preferred not to share the whole story with him, but he also wanted to be polite.

"Just another Ellis Island bastardization."

"Really? Who's responsible for that royal screwup? There's gotta be a good story behind it?"

Not wanting to arm a drunken antagonist—but also not wanting to imply a discomfort with his family name—Blundergusting decided to tell his history and hope the margaritas would wash it all from Aloysius' memory.

"Are you sure? It's quite boring and borders on the ludicrous."

Aloysius exhaled a giggle-laced laugh.

"Reggie, I would expect nothing less from a Blundergusting."

Pausing at the only slightly veiled insult, Reggie again chose not to parry. Instead he looked forward to his time in the spotlight, especially under cover of his 'boring and ludicrous' disclosure.

"Well, you asked for it."

He cleared his throat and started to move his hands with the syllables.

"The story goes something like this: My ancestors came from a part of the world that we now call Poland. They were distant relatives of the ruling family. One of my male forebears, in an act of ambition, made the not unusual mistake of infuriating a higher-ranking member of the aristocracy. As retribution approached, he was forced to flee for his life, with his pregnant wife and a few precious things, and head to the New World. This all happened in the late-nineteenth Century."

As the server arrived, Blundergusting stopped, greeted the beverage bearer, and hoped the interruption would be enough to divert his audience's short attention span.

"Ah, our drinks. Thank you, kind…person."

At this point, Aloysius didn't feel the need to thank the help; he was more than ready for round two. He thirstily dug into his second margarita before looking up at Blundergusting.

"And then what?"

"It's really not that interesting. Quite silly actually."

"Bullshit…c'mon, I'm interested."

Hesitating for just a moment, Blundergusting took a long pull from his drink, swirled the concoction around in his mouth, and then swallowed. Before the alcohol was even close to his bloodstream, his brain started making adjustments in anticipation.

"Okay, but remember, you asked."

"Yep."

"So, my ancestors are on this misguided trip across the Atlantic, royal blood packed like rats in steerage with all the other immigrants, when the husband catches typhoid or some sort of disease, and dies before making New York Harbor."

"No fuckin' way! So now your pregnant great-great-great-grandmother is all alone with the great unwashed, heading to Manhattan to fight with Daniel Day-Lewis and the *Gangs of New York?*"

"Precisely! And, as was normal in those times, she was only sixteen."

"Holy shit!"

"Right?" Blundergusting shook his head, impressed by his family's fortitude but questioning his ancestors' common sense. "Now pay attention, here's the part you've been waiting for."

"Yessir," Aloysius slurred.

"So when my Polish, duchess ancestor reaches the immigration table at the port of entry, she speaks not a word of English. Remember, there are huge lines of non-English speakers trying to get their papers, and the choreography is less like the Rockettes and more like the pandemonium that occurs when they open the gates for a Who concert that only has festival seating."

Blundergusting paused to see if the reference registered. Aloysius nodded recognition.

"Got it. Tens of thousands…screaming mobs…people trampled underfoot."

Pleased he had a somewhat capable audience, Blundergusting continued at an accelerating cadence.

"Exactly. Somehow she finds someone who can translate, and they ask her what name she wants to use for the New World documents. All around her people are jettisoning their old labels and choosing new names to go with their ambitions—names like Hope and Divine, Gold and Cash—but our heroine feels nothing but empty. At this point she is so broken by her recent change of fate, so overwhelmed by the raw, terrible nature of her predicament, that she feels nauseous, unable to move. Within this dark, pessimistic mental setting, she asks in her native language what the English words are for *sickening mistake*. The polish interpreter, who himself is only barely competent, tells her *disgusting blunder*. Just as the interpreter is about to fill in the forms with *Disgustingblunder* as the last name, her baby kicks and she realizes the terrible burden a name like that would place on her descendants. In a hormonally charged and rare burst of optimistic maternal foresight, she decides to send the opposite message and asks the interpreter how one would do that. Working together in a moment of illogical collaboration, made even more difficult by her weak language skills and the pushing throng of impatient incoming, they agreed in Polish that reversing the word order and dropping the 'dis' prefix would likely do the trick. Under relentless pressure, the teen widow signed the papers where instructed, and thus started the tradition that I carry today."

At this, Reginald puffed out his chest with theatrical pride.

"We are the legion of *Blundergusting*, known forever forward as the people who came to the New World as a result of a *wonderful* and *delicious mistake*."

Aloysius had a dubious look on his face.

"So the Polaks thought the opposite of 'disgusting' was 'gusting'?"

"An understandable misunderstanding, yes? By the way, we don't use 'Polak' anymore; people of Polish descent are just called *Poles*."

"So a Polak dancing is called a 'Pole dancer'?"

"Probably 'Polish dancer' would be more appropriate."

"That's a little confusing…and quite a story."

"So I'm told."

Like a starving coyote picking at the bones of a three-day-old rabbit carcass, Aloysius started using his straw to suck the margarita remnants hiding between the chunks of ice at the bottom of his glass. In the near-silence, Blundergusting hoped the curiosity about his family etymology had run its course. As Reginald stared at his only current lunch companion, Aloysius looked up from his drink, removed his mouth from the straw, and appeared ready to ask another question. A silence billowed into the space between the two before Aloysius concluded that an attack with no audience would be wasted breath. He returned his mouth to the straw. Sensing an opportunity to escape without cross-examination, Reginald excused himself while pushing to his feet.

"Aloysius, I hate to be rude, but I need to make a quick run to the loo."

Without waiting for approval, Reggie ambled off in the same direction he had last seen Ravi and Lilly heading.

Aloysius responded loudly to Blundergusting's retreating back:

"Oh, don't mind me, I'll just stay here alone, by myself…"

With a sad mumble into his empty margarita tumbler, he added:

"…with all the people who love and care about me."

A few minutes later, Blundergusting returned with a reluctant Ravi and a modestly defiant Lilly.

"Look who I found trying to dine and dash," Reginald teased. "Lilly and Clyde! Or Bonnie and the Doctor. Whichever, they didn't want to come back…but I promised them you would behave."

The qigong master threw a *faux* disapproving look at Aloysius before realizing he might not be able to keep his promise to Ravi and Lilly. Though not falling down drunk, the old man had clearly descended further into his cups. There were now three beer bottles and three margarita glasses surrounding the perimeter of his *carnitas* platter, all nearly empty. With apprehension the three settled back into their chairs. They hoped their server would soon appear and clear away the dead soldiers so they could at least imagine they were enjoying a normal lunch. As if sitting on pins and needles, they all quietly sipped their margaritas and nibbled at the *carnitas*. Except for Aloysius, appetites seemed to have receded like the tides of Fundy.

After a few minutes, Lilly started getting antsy.

"Where's that girl? Can't we just get the check?"

Aloysius had had the longest opportunity to examine their waitperson.

"I think she's a boy…"

Looking for confirmation, he found the others noncommittal.

"Anyway, last time I tried to get its attention it was doing something with its phone that required it not break away."

Too much screen time was a pet peeve of Blundergusting's.

"I don't know if you've noticed, but that table over in the far corner? Back by the loo? It has a group of five, all of them with noses pressed against their phones. I don't think they've spoken a word to each other since they sat down."

Ravi whispered to Lilly.

"That's not always a bad thing!"

He then joined the others as they all turned their heads and stared casually at the corner table by the loo, or at least that was their intent.

"I'm sorry, Ravi, what did you say?" asked Blundergusting politely.

Ever well mannered, Ravi massaged his previous comment so as not to offend or lie.

"I was saying that it's difficult to set hard and fast rules for every situation, but in general I worry about what technology is doing to our brains. I'm not sure our physiology is ready for such rapid social change."

Blundergusting was excited to find someone who shared his concerns.

"Hear, hear Ravi. It's all happening way too quickly…too many are unable to keep up, and the social fabric is seriously fraying."

Aloysius looked up from his empties.

"Didn't our parents and grandparents have the same concerns about television? Too much idiot-box watching was going to brainwash us? Give corporate America and their advertising gurus direct access to our souls?"

Here we go again, thought Lily, praying it wouldn't get too bad.

She wasn't feeling particularly warm towards Aloysius just then, but she did feel he had an intelligent point to make.

Blundergusting fought back comfortably.

"I think the jury's still out on TV, consumerism, and what it's doing to our health. Because the technology invasion comes incrementally from within our society, we might not recognize how it's reshaping us."

Ravi spoke up emphatically, happy to have an ally.

"Or destroying us."

Lilly jumped in without being interrupted for one of the few times that evening.

"Ravi, I think that's a bit melodramatic. By most measures—infant mortality, life expectancy, poverty, education, war—the globe is in a much better place now than one hundred years ago."

Turning to face Lilly, Ravi calmly took the other side.

"You know I don't agree. We are burning the furniture to heat the house, destroying our future to indulge our present appetites. Look at the environment—especially the degradation of our oceans—obesity rates, suicide and medication rates—all indicators that something is seriously amuck with our species. Advertising executives are using technology—big data algorithms—to trick us into buying way more stuff than we need. It's not sustainable."

Tagging in, it was Blundergusting's turn. He launched right into what was for him familiar territory.

"I think it would all be so much more obvious if it were suddenly and externally imposed. Say, I don't know, some outer space phenomenon created an overnight change in the earth's environment where our muscles were less useful...maybe the force of gravity was increased significantly such that we couldn't carry out everyday tasks like getting out of bed and making breakfast without the assistance of machines. In that environment our physical strength would be less valuable, and our mental ability to solve our problems would be much more valuable. Everyone who used physical strength to do their job would be immediately unemployed, because those positions wouldn't exist anymore—our bodies simply wouldn't have enough strength to overcome the new gravitational forces. Construction workers, fishermen, lumberjacks, farm workers, professional athletes—all toast. Only the strongest of us would be able to move from sitting to standing, and even for them walking ten feet would be a Herculean task. Anyone who could solve the new problem of extreme gravity would have a huge increase in demand for their services, and their pay would skyrocket. Engineers, entrepreneurs, scientists, desk jockeys—all celebrated and elevated. We would see a massive disequilibrium in things like compensation and wealth, and all the things that money buys, like access to housing, education, and health care. The nerds would all be even richer and the physically strong would be destitute. The accompanying social resentment would be huge, and the pressure to constantly change, to improve your skill set so as not to fall into the camp of the unemployed would be overwhelmingly stressful for most because the consequences would be so great."

Blundergusting paused to take a sip of his margarita before continuing. Nobody interrupted. Less than five seconds later he was back building his case.

"If this increase in gravity were imposed overnight as a sudden, natural phenomenon, we would likely and rightfully treat it like a natural disaster. We would implement emergency policies and programs to help those displaced, just like we do with hurricanes or earthquakes."

Their server finally came around to start clearing, and Aloysius nonchalantly checked for evidence that the being standing beside him harbored breasts—or an Adam's apple. Blundergusting paused to see if the group had any more interest in his topic. Not unexpectedly, the feedback to his convoluted metaphor had thus far been mixed. Ravi had nodded along in passionate agreement. Lilly was respectful—but far from enthusiastic. Before checking out the he/she who was clearing the table, Aloysius had been his usual caricature of rejection, effecting his regular eye rolls. Blundergusting, reminding himself that no one likes to be lectured, decided to wrap it up.

"Well, that's what's happening to humans, only instead of overnight it's taking several hundred years, and instead of externally imposed, we're developing it from within and we call it *technology*. More and more of our repetitious, physical tasks are being done by machines, and we have to physically and voluntarily stimulate our bodies to keep them from atrophying and falling into disrepair."

Ravi interrupted with enthusiasm to clarify.

"Exactly! We call that stimulation 'exercise' or 'recreation.' Our bodies need to move, evolution has required it, so when that stops we get sick."

Blundergusting resented the interruption but appreciated the support.

"Exactly, Ravi. The difference between any change taking place overnight rather than over the course of several centuries is huge to a single generation of humans, but it is insignificant when it comes to human evolution. Both instances are too short for mutation and natural selection to help us, so as a society we are left to plod forward, our bodies unprepared for the rapid changes technology is forcing on us."

Lilly tried to jump in, but Aloysius caught everyone's attention with a few loud claps of his hands. He had had this conversation with his daughter-in-law, Lola, before.

"Bravo, Blundergusting, a true credit to your family name."

Lilly glared at him but didn't make too much of a scene. As the waitperson passed, Lilly redirected her focus, lightly snagging their elbow to grab their attention before whispering in their direction:

"Check, please."

Aloysius heard Lilly, but it didn't deter him at all.

"Yes…check, please, this will only take a minute."

Ravi cringed. He prepared for a quick exit, hand squeezing hard upon Lilly's thigh. Aloysius shifted into high gear.

"Please indulge me, but I have a little story too. Now, let's see…how does it start?"

Doing his best *Le Penseur* imitation (chin supported by fist), he paused for dramatic effect and to gather his thoughts. His first few words were slurred, but after that he developed a nice cadence supported by reasonably clear enunciation.

"Ah, yes…long ago, before the printing press but after we discovered fire, my ancestors lived in a little village on the Euphrates River…or maybe it was somewhere on the African savannah…I can't remember…. Anyway, the chief of the village was a physically strong, mountain of a man who also headed a commercial group that did all of the heavy lifting and carrying for all of the nearby villages. This was considered honorable work; a young man had to train hard and pass many tests to be accepted into this brotherhood, known as the Special Porters Guild, or the SPG. The guild members were revered in the villages, they wore unique animal skins and were paid handsomely for their labor, because, much like a union, by rule the number of practitioners was limited. One day, one of my ancestors who was not in the SPG invented the wheel. He brought this invention to the attention of the villagers, and its usefulness immediately won over many of the citizens. Soon the weaker villagers started using the wheel to carry things, and the union of lifters and carriers, the SPG, began losing some of their customers to the Do-It-Yourself wheel people. With necessity birthing invention, it wasn't long before the sister of the wheel inventor, also one of my relatives, discovered the fulcrum. Soon she could do the work of several men by using the family tools—the levers and wheels—to lift and carry heavy things."

At this point, Aloysius stopped talking and again starting fishing through his ice cubes with his straw. After a few moments it became obvious he had lost his train of thought. Ravi achieved a level of irritation that forced him to interrupt Al's straw-poking.

"So what happened to the inventors? The brother and sister?"

Aloysius acted surprised, as if it was obvious the important part of the story was over.

"I'm not sure, but I think the chief murdered them."

The other two men looked nervously at each other, wondering if the climax was intentionally bungled to make a point, or if Aloysius was just too drunk to adequately recite his parable. Just when they had concluded the latter was the case, Al offered clarification in a belittling tone.

"Not at first, of course. First, the SPG tried to convince everyone that the wheel was bad for them, that people needed to lift and carry stuff for their physical and moral well-being."

After a few silent seconds, Blundergusting finally spoke up.

"But the ideas of the brother and sister lived on?"

"Apparently so."

Ravi was certain Aloysius was more idiot than savant, but he needed to spell it out.

"So...is there some moral to your story, a point you are trying to make that is eluding us?"

Aloysius waved his hand dismissively, as if Ravi were an annoying insect that he hadn't the time to educate. The old man was apparently done with his narrative, leaving in his wake a rude silence that the table collectively found awkward.

Aside from all the contentious behavior, a completely different irritant had been annoying Lilly for most of the lunch. As a woman, she was used to being ignored by men in a conversational setting, but today's situation particularly bothered her. During the meal that Blundergusting had bullied her into attending, she had counted no less than six different times when she had something to say but had not been allowed the courtesy of the floor. The men had mostly just spoken right over her attempts to participate, steamrolling her into submission, while the non-speakers had failed to offer her their attention. This from people she had faithfully supported despite their various intellectual, social, and/or moral failings. It was a frustrating, but common, phenomenon, one for which she had finally lost patience. Clearing her throat, she made an announcement in a clear but strained voice.

"I have something I'd like to add about Reggie's contention that technology is changing our environment faster than our species' ability to adapt."

She paused to make sure everyone's attention was captured. Reggie and Ravi's eyes focused on her face, while Aloysius' attention wobbled over a somewhat square-shaped region that ran from Lilly's forehead to her barely discernible nipples. His mildly disguised ogling touched a long-sensitive nerve that had been triggered so many times in the past that Lilly's response was somewhat numbed.

Predictably Aloysius, she thought. *The old dog… doesn't even know how disrespectful his behavior is.*

Ever patronizing under the guise of graciousness, Blundergusting gave her the green light.

"Please, Lilly, I'm sorry…have we been ignoring you?"

Knowing it would be bad form (and unproductive) to berate the three men at this point, Lilly took the high road. In the back of her mind she still hoped to capture Blundergusting's qigong revenues, a task she knew might require a bit of sucking up—even accepting, without complaint, a few moments as a doormat.

"No, Reginald, you've been the perfect host. My question to you is how do you know we're not evolving as a species…humans that is…to meet the challenges of the upside-down technology pyramid?"

Taking a soothing tone, Blundergusting helped guide Lilly to a safe harbor.

"Ahhh, I'm sorry, Lilly. My point isn't that we aren't evolving, it's that we aren't evolving at a pace to keep up with the change in technology."

Ignoring his soothing, paternal tone, she pressed on, her cheeks gaining some color as her metabolic rate picked up. Ravi and Al were now both focused on the same part of her anatomy.

"But, Reggie, how do you *know*?"

Not stupid, Blundergusting now understood Lilly had an agenda. He replaced a degree of his patronizing conviction with some cautious humility.

"I guess I don't *know*…but I don't see any evidence of it…do you?"

"I don't know, maybe…we probably won't know for a few generations, but maybe certain of us are changing right now."

None of the men had any idea what Lilly was getting at, but she could tell they were at least somewhat interested.

"For example, what if certain characteristics that we thought of as defects were actually enhancements…our species' efforts to meet the current challenges in real time?"

The server quietly slipped the check in front of Blundergusting. No one but Aloysius even noticed. Always looking for a slight, the elder Barton was pissed off at the implication that to outsiders Blundergusting conveyed a seniority over the rest of the group, and hence deserved the check. On the other hand, however, he was happy he didn't have to pay. He had been counting his pennies ever since he and Trick had taken on the financial responsibility of carrying Keno's family.

Ravi was curious about the idea that Lilly was hinting at, and though he hadn't a clue what she was about to say, he was surprised she hadn't shared something about this new theory with him privately. He wondered if maybe he had been so caught up in his own data gathering that he hadn't been showing enough interest in her thoughts. Moving his eyes up, he left Aloysius as the only one making sure her cleavage was intact, and asked the obvious:

"What specifically are you getting at, Lilly?"

Moving ahead hesitantly, Lilly unfolded her developing thesis.

"I'm not sure…this isn't necessarily well thought out…but maybe…I don't know…a lot of things. How about autism, for one? If your theory is humans have to become more adept at the STEM areas—science, technology, engineering, and math—well, people that are diagnosed as falling on the autism scale often do better in math and have difficulty in social sciences or human interaction. Maybe the autism epidemic, Asperger's, Tourette's, OCD, ADHD, and other conditions have nothing to do with vaccines or whatever…maybe they're not afflictions at all, but gifts…maybe they're nature's way of evolving an über-subspecies that can bridge the gap between humans and machines…computers…software…artificial intelligence…whatever you want to call technology? Certain autistics have proven to be exceptional at solving some of the challenges of engineering code…people that can focus for long hours without taking a break…almost like a machine."

The other three didn't know how to respond. They recognized Lilly was talking her book, but they also recognized her theory had some interesting merits. Even Aloysius had moved his focus about a foot higher over the last few minutes. Blundergusting casually slipped the bill across to Lilly while asking for clarification.

"So your hypothesis is that certain symptoms we describe as flaws or diseases, like autism, may actually be skills that are superhero-like in the right context?"

Lilly was gaining confidence.

"Yeah, I think so. Maybe autism is a superpower we just haven't learned how to use correctly."

Looking around the table for support from the men, she found very little and found herself getting a little defensive.

"Why not?"

Not having anything clever to add, Blundergusting went with the benign compliment.

"Well, I have to admit, that's definitely some creative, outside-the-box thinking."

Aloysius was still in a rock-throwing mood, but he couldn't come up with a reasonable target. So he decided to use his straw to poke again at his ice.

Ravi, always the sucker for quirky ideas, was falling deeper in love.

"My god, Lilly, it's genius."

Lilly fought gamely but couldn't suppress the color rising in her cheeks. Now clearer than ever she saw what she prized in Ravi that was so lacking in Aloysius.

Having second thoughts, Blundergusting reached back across the table and grabbed the check from where it rested, untouched, in front of Lilly.

"Oh my god, I had no idea...Lilly, I don't mean to cut you short, but the time!"

There was a 1:30 P.M. *History of Qigong* class due to start in ten minutes, and Reggie was the instructor. Pulling his wallet out from under his sarong, he laid seven crisp twenties in the tray on top of the bill and prepared to push back from the table.

"I'll get this...Lilly, can you run back and let my qigongees know I'm running a few minutes late?"

"Of course, Reggie."

Through the fog of the margaritas and beer, Aloysius realized he had failed at his most important task. As they all got up, he somewhat skillfully (for a man with six drinks under his belt) maneuvered himself next to Lilly and away from Ravi.

"Lilly...I really need to talk to you."

Already tired of Al's antics, Lilly shrugged him off.

"Hustling back right now—can we do it tomorrow?"

"I'll walk with you."

She thought she could drop him easily.

"Okay, but you'll have to keep up."

Taking off at a double-time pace she headed for the exit. Aloysius fell in by her side. Not sure whether he should stay or go, Ravi politely remained at the table to keep Blundergusting company while he waited for change.

About two minutes later, halfway through their quarter-mile return trip to the Wellness Center, Aloysius was fading badly. He had wanted to lay the appropriate verbal groundwork with Lilly but was running out of breath. Recognizing his window of opportunity was closing, he decided to cut to the chase before a heart attack buried him. He gathered all his strength, made a last-gasp push to catch up, and then hurled the words directly at her right ear from a foot away.

"Keno is alive!"

Then he stumbled and dropped to one knee before collapsing onto his side. As he watched Lilly racewalk away from him, his heart descended into his shoes. He was barely able to restrain a tablespoon-sized portion of vomit that hiccuped into his mouth. About thirty yards out, just before turning the corner that led to the driveway entrance of the Wellness Center, the facility's namesake stopped and looked back quizzically. When her reversal brought her within five yards of the still-prone Aloysius, she stopped warily.

"What did you say?"

He looked up, pathetically pleading with his eyes and trying not drool the upchuck.

"Please, I need to talk to you. My son didn't die in Mexico."

Lilly moved closer but remained suspicious. It was important she keep the qigongees content, but this was big news.

"Go on, I'm listening."

Aloysius launched into a hurried version of the events that led up to Clay's reemergence and the plan to save Keno. Before he was finished, but after he had relayed the most important facts, Lilly interrupted him.

"His mother doesn't know he's alive?"

"No, only me and Trick and Clay. That's the way Clay wanted it."

Lilly's face contorted into a look of incredulity as she slowly rotated her head from side to side.

"Testicled idiots…what's wrong with you?"

She didn't wait for the answer she knew wasn't coming.

"She still lives in Florida, right?"

Aloysius thought Lilly might kick him, so he pulled his knees up into a half-fetal position before answering.

"Elizabeth? Yes…but why?"

"Get up and meet me in my office in ten. I've got a plane to catch—and *you* have to get it together enough to run the center."

"Wait, I can't!" He watched Lilly turn and start re-traversing the distance she had come. The next moment, the meaning of her words struck him full force. "What? Where are you going?"

Before he could pull himself into a seated position and clear his mouth of the bile, the speedwalker had retraversed the entire thirty yards and was gone. His final vision—and he knew his mind was likely playing tricks on him—was a vague glimpse of a cape, fluttering in Lilly's lee, as she turned the corner and flew out of sight.

CHAPTER 37 —

Runaway Boys

There was a boy...
...a very strange, enchanted boy...

Pushing a few strands of grey out of her field of vision, Elizabeth Barton examined the toothpick for any sign of batter. She was baking a chocolate cake while playing Nat King Cole on the living room stereo, both of which had been longtime "go-tos" whenever she felt stressed. In the six months since her second son, Keenan, had disappeared, she had probably baked more cakes and shed more tears than she'd done during all the previous years combined.

And then one day...
...a magic day...
...he passed my way...

Her mind had been whirling with conflicting thoughts ever since Aloysius had told her that Lilly was coming to see her. It hadn't been a request as much as a notification—an approach that she found pushy, especially when combined with the last-minute nature of the whole communication. Aloysius had been tight-lipped about the purpose of Lilly's visit, which also had her feeling uneasy. Glancing at the clock, Elizabeth saw that Lilly was already a few minutes late. Instead of being grateful for the extra time to finish the baking, she interpreted the tardiness as another sign of disrespect.

Just like those two, she thought, tossing the toothpick onto the countertop. *Thinking their time's more valuable than mine. I've got three separate projects I'm consulting on, and now I'm supposed to drop everything for who knows what? God, I hope Keenan is okay. But if something's wrong, why would Lilly be bringing me the news?*

Though they had never met, Lilly Stein had been a tough one for Elizabeth. When she first became aware of the extramarital sex, she had considered Lilly just another in a long line of hussies who had helped her then husband, Aloysius, betray her. But after Lilly had helped uncover a conspiracy of police brutality (which years earlier had relegated her son, Paul, to a wheelchair), Elizabeth felt conflicted. On one level, she admired Lilly for her confidence and smarts…was even grateful that the concubine had used those skills to help her family out of a pickle. But the aiding and abetting of infidelity…well, she felt strongly that women shouldn't do that to each other. Eventually Elizabeth had filed away her feelings as complicated and unresolved. During the rare, recent times when Elizabeth thought about Lilly it mostly just reminded her of the fragile nature of trust and the eclectic ways of people.

She had nearly finished beating the three sticks of butter into a lump-free partnership with the sugar, milk, and cocoa powder when the oven timer had gone off. With the clean toothpick indicating that the dessert's rich body was ready, she moved the two chocolate cake pans onto the cooling racks then resumed her attack on the frosting. Just a bit of vanilla extract and a teaspoon of her secret ingredient—espresso powder—and the sugary, buttercream paste would be ready. Despite the number of times she had repeated the instructions, Elizabeth never tired of this moment. A dual feeling of competence and anticipation warmly resonated, halo-like, from her taste buds. Once again checking the clock to confirm how late Lilly was, she prepared to smother the two layers of baked chocolate corpus with the sticky, sweet, brown contents of the frosting bowl.

This cake was a treat destined for Roshan's birthday party. She and Paul were coming over the next evening to celebrate. Elizabeth was proud of the fact that her family hadn't abandoned the multi-racial, Greenwood neighborhood where Paul had grown up, despite her recent financial success. All the money she had made from her new career writing code had gone towards helping the younger couple buy their own house just down the street.

The greatest thing you'll ever learn…

is just to love…

…and be loved in return…

As Elizabeth stuck a finger into the gooey, chocolate concoction in order to test its flavor, a pair of masculine hands surprised her from behind. Immediately recognizing the MO of the attacker, she felt Roberto press his hips against hers, gently lobbying for a merger. Prying his big, dark fingers from her breasts, she pivoted deftly away from him and plugged her buttercream digit, pacifier-like, between his full lips. She looked up into smiling brown eyes framed with wrinkles and age spots. Loving the novelty and attention that came with her lover's Latin brazenness, she feigned offense at his trespass.

"You are such a *bad* man!"

Five years her junior, the widower teased her in a chocolate-coated, Spanglish jumble.

"Ees time to be gone from la keetchina…when da heat ees so *mucho…sí?*"

Pushing both hands against his chest, Elizabeth struggled half heartedly to escape Roberto's light grasp on her waist. Laughing, he pulled at her insistently, narrowing the distance between them, all the while giving her a knowing look. Yielding to his physical strength, she continued with the scolding.

"It's, 'if you can't stand the heat, get out of the kitchen,' *stupee*…by the way, have I told you lately what a *muy malo hombre* you are?"

Roberto looked at her quizzically. Then he buried his nose in her hair and inhaled deeply. She paused to enjoy the moment before continuing her damsel-in-distress role, forgetting that she expected a visitor at any moment.

"What will happen to me if I *stay* in la keetchina, bad man?"

His Venezuelan brain was just now registering the buttercream frosting, which was mixing in with the lavender scent drifting from Elizabeth's hair. In a previous life, he had managed one of the line shifts at a Pepsi bottling plant in Caracas; but he had lost everything when the business had been nationalized during the Hugo Chávez years. After his wife died from a bacterial infection (which the Venezuelan hospital couldn't treat promptly because the facility lacked the necessary antibiotics), he started joining—and then leading—some small street protests. Soon, *small* became *big*, and he found himself marching with thousands in the street, protesting the lack of basic necessities such as toilet paper. His claim to fame was throwing a rock that almost hit the

American actor Sean Penn. When a fellow organizer was arrested (and then "accidentally hit his head," dying while in custody), Roberto pulled the ripcord. He felt lucky to get out of the country with his life and a few shrinking Bolivars. Landing in Miami, he wandered north, taking odd jobs to support himself while he tried to learn English. When he first started gardening for Elizabeth, he believed his life was essentially over, and that he was destined to die a mendicant. He had noticed something about her from the start, but it took her a few months before she stopped fighting the obvious chemistry. With open minds and young hearts, their romantic spark had grown to a conflagration that currently engulfed them like a raging, late summer California wildfire.

"*Mi chiquita*, this chocolate…everthin' you put in *mi boca*…so yummy…how you say this? 'Yummy'? Yes? I think I will now eat *YOU!*"

He raised both hands and started growling like a Maurice Sendak wild thing. Quickly turning away from him, Elizabeth started leading him in a slow chase around the kitchen island.

"No, bad man, please, please…don't *EAT* me!" She shrieked and giggled Brer Rabbit- style. "ANYTHING but EATING ME!"

In a sudden burst, her gardener-cum-boyfriend caught her from behind, lifting and spinning the grandmother before planting her, faceup on the kitchen table. He reached for the hem of her apron while continuing the game.

"Oh-h-h, *sí*…Elizabed, now I will nibble on da liddle papaya *para mi alimento*."

Just as he hungrily buried his mouth, wolflike, into her throat, the doorbell rang. Carried away by the sensual enveloping of chocolate and pheromones, they both shared the sentiment that Elizabeth expressed.

"Don't answer it!"

But the moment was lost. As they froze, hoping the visitor would depart, the bell rang again, this time followed by a more insistent knock. Roberto sighed as he stood up over Elizabeth and shrugged.

"*Lo siento, Señora.*"

Feeling like she was just waking from a sleep, Elizabeth sat upright, realizing it was likely Lilly knocking at the door.

"Yes, bad man…*lo siento*…and I have to finish the cake."

As she shooed him towards the back door, she gave him a quick swat on the bottom.

"Come back soon, bad man."

He turned his head, offering a coy smile with the words.

"Maybe, *Señorita*…maybe *muy* soon."

Quickly checking that her goodies were safely cooling, she smoothed her apron before heading down the bungalow hallway. She stopped to straighten a family portrait of her three boys before reaching the tiny foyer by the front door.

As she tried to segue from chocolate-infused foreplay to society matron, the eclectic grandmother twisted the doorknob with a healthy mix of trepidation and curiosity.

Lilly was a bundle of nerves as she waited outside the front door. Her simple pumps were digging into her bunions due to the unexpectedly long walk in the Tampa airport. The combination of apprehension and pain had driven her to ring the door bell and then impatiently knock, with little time between, a move she already regretted. Protecting her from a total meltdown was the awareness that she had maybe the greatest trump card ever. She was arriving as the "other woman" but would leave as the bearer of the best news a mom could receive.

When Elizabeth opened the door in her apron, Lilly was relieved that she had guessed right. Aloysius' ex-wife reminded her of a younger, thinner, more attractive Barbara Bush, and Lilly's wardrobe choice (a conservative pantsuit) wasn't likely to offend the WASPy matriarch. The only thing that didn't fit was the tiny house in the blue collar neighborhood. But the woman in the doorway greeted her with a warmth and confidence that came from years of practice.

"Hello, you must be Lilly."

Elizabeth extended her hand with poise and grace. Lilly firmly (but not in a competitive way) gripped her hand, trying to respond in kind.

"Yes…and you must be Elizabeth."

And then, in a blurt of nervous energy:

"I'm so sorry I'm late!"

Elizabeth smiled coolly.

"That's all right, that's how all my boys started."

Pausing for a second, Lilly wasn't sure she had heard correctly.

Did she just make a menstruation joke? she wondered.

The younger woman, not wanting to step on a land mine, looked hard for a clue amidst the wrinkles surrounded by grey curls. She saw the corners of Elizabeth's mouth start to twitch up.

"I'm sorry. Not funny? Inappropriate?"

Lilly immediately let her guard down and released a relieved laugh.

"No, no…I, um…wasn't sure what to expect…I think we're gonna get along great…my daughter started the same way!"

A pang of resentment flashed through Elizabeth's consciousness at the thought of Lilly's pregnancy. She was tempted to add, *Yes, I know… and also with my husband's sperm.* But she thought better of it. Instead she smiled pleasantly.

"Please come in. Can I offer you some coffee or tea?"

She turned sideways to make room and waved Lilly in. As they made their way to the kitchen, the retired spy asked what at first seemed an innocuous question.

"So I've heard you're really good with computers?"

Elizabeth brushed aside the compliment. "Well, I don't know about *really good*, but I seem to have a knack for it."

"That could come in handy."

Nat King Cole broke through the small talk.

…that's what you are…
Unforgettable…

Lilly paused with head cocked before sitting at the kitchen table.

…like a song of love that clings to me…

"Oh my god! Is that Nat King Cole?"

"The one and only."

"I haven't heard him for years. I grew up listening to him and Louis Armstrong." She sighed and smiled quietly. "This music really brings back memories."

"When did you grow up? There's no way you're as ancient as me."

"I like to think I'm still growing up, but I graduated from high school in sixty-one. My parents had all these records…my dad would play them all the time"—she looked around the kitchen as Elizabeth now sat down—"in a house that was a lot like this one."

"Three beds, one bath, tiny kitchen that opens to a den, and a rarely used dining and living area?" Elizabeth paused for a moment. "Am I close?"

"Exactly. Don't forget the shag carpet and asbestos ceiling…the post-war, GI special, complete with noisy plumbing and hollow-core doors that alert everyone in the house to your business."

The women exchanged thoughtful smiles. Slowly the fear of insurmountable differences was melting away as their commonalities bridged the mist of paranoia. After a few moments of silence, during which Elizabeth prepared two cups of Pu'er and placed one in front of Lilly, the visitor felt the need to explain herself.

"You're probably wondering why I came so abruptly."

"Quite puzzled actually." Elizabeth blew on her tea. "Oops, hopefully that wasn't rude?"

Taking a small sip from her cup, Lilly looked up at her hostess.

"No, not at all…what tea is this? Chinese? It's delicious."

"Pu'er. I have a connection in Taiwan who gets it from the mainland…I'm so pleased you're enjoying it."

Lilly couldn't wait any longer, the information she was carrying was burning a hole.

"I'm here because…"

She paused then started again.

"It's come to my attention that your boys have concocted a well-intended but insensitive scheme…and at the root of that scheme is the falsified death of Keenan."

Elizabeth eyes widened like dinner plates; she had been caught completely off guard. But her new career and all the hours coding logic structures had rewired her brain to a more even-keeled place. Leaning forward in her chair, she cut to the chase.

"What exactly do you mean by 'falsified death'?"

Knowing the power each word would have on the mother sitting across the table, Lilly carefully released each syllable of the revelation.

"Keenan. Is. Alive."

CHAPTER 38 —

The Deschutes Pivot

It was late in the evening, and Aloysius was feeling good. Like a resplendent phoenix, he had once again picked himself up, dusted off the ashes, and set his flight course on a winged path of probity. The way he saw things, Lilly had shown her faith in him by leaving the management of their greatest possession in his capable hands.

This means she still has feelings for me, he thought, hopefully.

He had rewarded her trust with sobriety and a steady grip on the helm of the Wellness Center. Not only was he managing the hotel with clocklike precision, but he had been checking in on Scout daily. She seemed to be making progress.

His rival, Ravi, had left in tandem with Lilly, but to a different continent. Blundergusting was still there, winding up his five-day commitment, but Aloysius could tolerate Reginald's presence because (unlike Ravi) the qigong entrepreneur hadn't been banging Al's girlfriend in Al's bed. He still hated Blundergusting's smug self-assurance, but at least when Reggie was around money was coming in. In contrast, in Aloysius' view, Dr. Throckmorton was a parasite, offering nothing and stealing everything that was valuable, all while disguising himself under the ridiculous guise of being an expert in rock-bipedal interaction.

Whatever the fuck that is! Aloysius silently disparaged.

The old man had to calm himself down. Every time he thought about Ravi, a cold hand squeezed at his heart (and his scrotum).

He's gone now, he reminded himself. *Lilly left me in charge…and I'm not gonna fuck it up again!*

This had become the mantra Aloysius invoked to soothe himself during the fragile moments when he worried about growing old alone. For the last forty-eight hours he had been working hard as concierge while also trying to get his mind right. He felt like he was moving things in the appropriate direction.

After a long day schmoozing guests, the recently cuckolded whale watcher was winding down in bed. He was good at unruffling feathers and also at patting himself on the back when he did a good job. As a reward for his exemplary capabilities, he was allowing himself some late-night internet surfing on his tablet. His fingers had dialed up a YouTube montage titled *Best Cyst Popping of 2008*, starring Sandra Lee, aka, Dr. Pimple Popper. In most other situations, he would have been ashamed of his rabid interest in such deviance. However in this instance, when he reminded himself that his current viewing fascination had replaced his asphyxiophilia experimentation, he felt relatively virtuous. He noted that Dr. Lee's lancing exploits had 4.6 million unique subscribers, allowing him to justify his preoccupation as really more *mainstream* than *deviant*.

He recognized the parallels between his former and current fetishes—both made up largely of squeezings and eruptions—and he justified both as being healthy forms of expurgation. *Catharsis* was the word that came to mind.

If it was good enough for the Greeks, he reasoned, *then it's good enough for me.*

He told himself this with an etymological awareness that gave him a feeling of intellectual superiority similar to the feeling an academic might have while traveling with a competitive group of art historians and being the first to correctly identify the defining features of an obscure and partially buried sculpture that the group had stumbled upon after winding around the corner of a dusty goat path through a grove of olive trees in a remote village in the Cyclades.

Just as Dr. Lee was reaching a particularly sordid portion of the videotaped exorcism, the phone lying beside Aloysius started vibrating.

Probably just a robocaller, he thought, dismissing it out of hand.

Then he realized Lilly had been gone for two days, and he hadn't heard from her. He started getting excited about the possibility of a late-night call between two lonely hearts. Picking up the phone, he hoped to see the familiar incoming number displayed on the small screen.

Aloysius' spirits lifted. *It's her!*

A quick check of his watch showed the time in Carefree. Eleven o'clock. He flipped open the Nokia.

"Lilly!" he exclaimed. "Is everything okay? You're up so late!"

A breathless voice answered on the other end:

"We're doing great! I love Liz! She's a-maaa-zing! Oh my god, the stories!"

No matter how he tried, Aloysius couldn't figure out how this new friendship was good for him. His fear of rejection inhibited his ability to initiate any expression of affection.

"Um…that's great?"

Aloysius lowered his voice to a whisper in spite of the fact he was alone in his room.

"How is Elizabeth taking the Keno news?"

"Oh my god, like you would expect…mostly ecstatic. In fact, she's been really helpful, working nonstop. She was pissed that she wasn't informed from the start, but I told her Clay's training would've required limited information distribution when it came to Special Ops. She kinda understands. By the way, did you know she's really good at hacking into stuff? That's why I'm calling, I can't get ahold of Blundergusting, is he still there?"

Aloysius' heart fell as he realized Lilly hadn't called to talk to him.

She doesn't seem to miss me at all, he lamented.

"Yes, but his group is doing their thirty-six hour final meditation, so he won't be monitoring his phone."

"Oh, that's right. I forgot about the end-of-the-retreat mindfulness stuff."

"Did you find Clay? Did he find the guy?"

"We're trying, but your oldest boy is a slippery one. No contact with him, yet. Wolfgang Dalman is easy, though, he's all over the web… Facebook posts alone work like a GPS tracker. I'm sure Clay is on him, if that's the plan."

There was a pause as Lilly weighed the timeliness of what she needed. Aloysius heard Elizabeth's voice in the background say something like *"life and death.…"*

"Honey, could you please interrupt and ask Reggie to call me? We need to pursue an alternative hypothesis I have, and we could really use his help. It could be life or death."

"Okay, baby." He had hear her right, hadn't he? She called him *honey!* "I'll get right on it."

Lilly cringed, as she didn't like men calling her *baby,* but she needed help so bit her tongue.

"Great, thanks."

"What's your alternative hypothesis?"

Not wanting to get into it with Aloysius, Lilly tried to limit his access to the information in her possession.

"Do you remember our conversations about Dr. Angus Nelson Deschutes's work on dysfunction, diversions, and interpersonal relationships? We talked about it in therapy years ago; specifically, our therapist called a particular behavioral pattern the *Deschutes Pivot*."

"Is that the one where some people don't negotiate in good faith? I mean, they keep pressing for all they can get in a relationship, with no objective view as to what's fair or enough? If I remember correctly, typically the beleaguered party doesn't like conflict, or they really need something their partner has, like sex…so the other person keeps demanding more and more concessions, knowing that if they make a stink, or withhold the sex, the suffering party will accommodate them? Over time, the aggressor just wears down the more passive counterpart. Our therapist said that if left unchecked, it leaves either one party or the whole relationship broken. Is that the one?"

"Good memory, but…no. That's the McKenna Judgment Deficiency Supply and Demand Imbalance Syndrome. The Deschutes Pivot is different."

Aloysius was puzzled. "Then what's the other one?"

"Listen," Lilly returned, "it's late here, and Elizabeth is exhausted. Please have Reggie call me first thing tomorrow, and we can talk more about this later."

With the specter of loneliness peering over his shoulder, Aloysius didn't want to hang up. He frantically searched his brain for a distraction to keep Lilly on the phone. Without thinking, he blurted out the first thing that came to mind.

"Scout called for you. She has a huge cyst on her neck that needs surgery."

As he spoke the words he knew they were idiotic. The earpiece barked at him.

"What? Scout has a *what*?"

Knowing that the longer he waited the deeper he would bury himself, he quickly tried to reverse himself.

"No, not *Scout…Scott*, Sylvester's black lab."

He heard Lilly scoff. "Are you watching those disgusting videos again?"

"What?" He wasn't ready to admit that she had guessed his new preoccupation so easily. "No! That's crazy."

"I think you just pulled a Deschutes Pivot."

"*What?* What's a 'Deschutes Pivot'?"

But Lilly had already hung up.

CHAPTER 39 —

A Face with a View (or, Good for the Gander)

The bounce nearly gone from his step, Keno was having second thoughts about his plan to return to the living.

None of this would be happening if Clay had just responded to Irma, he thought. *Where the fuck is he? I should be home by now!*

The heat, dust, and endless horizon conspired to quell Keno's morning optimism. Despite Irma's warnings, he had been confident he could catch a ride from a passing car—a fisherman or maybe a rancher who was making the periodic trip for supplies. He had rationalized to himself that if no one picked him up, he could still make the thirty-mile hike out. His destination was the strip of poorly maintained asphalt called Highway 1. It was this heavily trafficked, zigzagging arterial that allowed cars and trucks to navigate the seven-hundred-and-sixty-mile-long peninsula, from Tijuana in the north to Cabo San Lucas in the south. During his serious triathlon days, about fifteen years back, Keno had completed a marathon in Las Vegas that included stumbling through a sudden and unexpected sand storm. This ancient data point led him to conclude that (worst case) he could walk all day at a moderate pace and make the slightly-longer-than-marathon journey from Irma's to the highway. Once he reached Highway 1 he planned on hitchhiking north to the border. From there he would hustle across on foot into San Diego. After entering the States, he hoped to get in touch with Trick or Aloysius and figure out his next step, with the main priority being a reunion with his family. Even though he had no phone or identification, he figured he could talk his way through whatever barriers confronted him. He was now realizing, in the stifling heat of the desert, that his passionate need to be with his family may have skewed his judgment.

It was just the night before, after not hearing anything from Clay for nearly a month, that he had made the final decision to leave Irma and head north on his own. He had been feeling abandoned for weeks now, like the overly ambitious kid in a game of kick-the-can who finds such a great hiding spot that everyone forgets about him. At the core of his concern was the fear of losing his family—especially Lola. Ever since his vivid cast-net dream, he hadn't been able to stop thinking about her. Like scratch to itch, the growing need had finally compelled him to begin the long journey home, overwhelming any concerns he had about his personal safety.

He had seen no signs of people since leaving the coast. What he had earlier felt to be starkly beautiful and promising now struck him as desolate and foreboding. Despite the fact that he had frequently stopped for snacks, the light pack he had stuffed with three liters of drinking water and some freshly made corn tortillas was starting to dig into his shoulders. Scanning the horizon for any clues that could help, he worried that somewhere along the way he had made a wrong turn. Looking down at the dirt, he wondered if any of the S-shaped snake tracks his flip-flops had been crossing belonged to rattlers.

Am I gonna make this? he wondered. *Am I stupid to think this is still doable?*

What he hadn't counted on was the significant increase in temperature as he moved inland, away from the Pacific Ocean. Sweat was rushing out of his pores, leaving white salt stains on certain, distinct areas of his shirt. A fine layer of silt coated his assemblage and left a gritty taste on his lips and in his mouth. By early afternoon, despite having worked his way through the first bottle of water, he was constantly fighting cottonmouth. It wasn't just the heat, but also the disorienting terrain, the relentless crisscrossing of trails. The roads through the hills frequently overlapped then veered off in irrational directions, leading him to wonder about the remaining distance he needed to cover. Scant and prickly desert foliage provided little in the way of protection from the sun.

With the immediate threat of exposure pushing the fears of snakes out of his mind, he started realizing that the peak fitness level he had extrapolated from his younger years hadn't carried over to middle age. Each hour that passed was making it abundantly clear that his escape plan had very little margin for error. When he stopped, yet again, to examine his compass, he started looking around for shelter, wondering how low the desert temperature might drop as the earth spun the sun out of sight. The pain coming from his leg muscles, and the blisters on his flip-flopped feet, were driving home the point that he hadn't done much in the way of hiking for over a decade. The circling buzzards also seemed to comprehend the difference between surfing and hiking fitness levels. The aging, white collar surfer inside Keno was sure the birds were hungrily grinning at him. He inwardly smiled at the macabre thought that the crimson-helmeted foragers might have *"gringo"* penciled in on their dinner menu.

Nice to know my brain still has a sense of humor, he thought, commending himself.

With the sun nearly directly overhead, he paused to take a drink in the brief shadow of a Boojum tree. As he pondered his predicament, the initial hot breath of the afternoon wind stirred up a dust devil that ran north to south across the baking road in front of him. Keno knew the *Nortes* would accelerate the extraction of moisture from his sun-abused skin, and he cursed his older brother for putting him in this predicament. Tilting his head back to drink from the second water bottle, he watched the scavenger *zopilotes* continuing to eye him beadily as they circled on the thermal currents. The birds' implied vote of no confidence galvanized his conviction to complete the odyssey.

Not today, mother fuckers, he whispered under his breath.

At first, he didn't hear it as much as feel it: a subtle interruption in the oven-like, suffocating, desert torpor. A palpable vibration from a rolling mass that registered in his bones a split second before the sound of the chugging machinery reached his ears. Lowering the plastic bottle from his lips, he pivoted hopefully towards the rumbling. A sizable rig, closing from about a hundred meters away, was laboring on the sandy, ochre road. As he watched the vehicle come into focus out of the simmering horizon, his heart leapt with recognition. It looked like a faded, four-wheel drive Bronco towing a kayak-laden trailer…which meant a likely sympathetic *gringo* driver. His feet hoped the whole thing wasn't a mirage.

Stepping to the left side of the road as the truck approached, he lifted his right arm and palm just to make sure the driver knew he wanted to parley. Squinting into the smoked windows, he considered how best to present himself so he could maximize his chances of gaining a ride. He imagined he didn't seem a very compelling passenger, given the nearly six months's growth of sun-bleached, snarled thatch atop his head. Also not helping his cause was the lackadaisical effort he'd made the day before to hack at his beard. He nonchalantly tried to smell under his right armpit, knowing that the left was generally more civil.

Not too offensive, he thought, *given the circumstances.*

Some painted lettering on the side of the Ford announced NOLS, the nonprofit global wilderness school. More good news.

Dialing up a cheerful smile, he stepped towards the jacked-up rig's left window as the glass started to lower. On the other side, staring down at him, was the tanned driver's face. She struck Keno as ruggedly beautiful, functional in a capable kind of no-nonsense way. The cheekbones were finely chiseled, and the nose pushed forward with confidence, as if not afraid to lead the rest of the body on a new adventure. Her blue-grey eyes were framed with freckles and a few wrinkles from the sun. A small, white scar ran away from her left eyebrow, traveling up to the questioning wrinkle on her forehead. As Keno took another hopeful step, closing to within five feet, the window stopped descending, about halfway down, just below her strong chin. He noticed the driver's full lips were moving, providing periodic glimpses of brilliant white teeth. It had only been a few seconds, but Keno already felt something inside him begin to simmer. He was intrigued by the stories that he was sure accompanied the woman's face (and, he thought, the unseen figure occupying the clothes below). He wondered how long since her last excavation and if she had a hunger that was similar to his. It was another moment or two before his eyes saw the pistol that she had set alongside the moving mouth, both directing him to obey. When his brain finally registered the threat, the accompanying rush of adrenaline only added to his growing infatuation. Finally, through the haze of chemical attraction, his mind was able to lock onto her words.

"That's close enough for now. Let's see what's in the pack."

Slowly raising his left arm to join the right, Keno tried to explain himself.

"Hey, I'm not dangerous…I just need a ride."

The Bacall-like voice washed over him like a mellifluous waterfall. He detected a slight accent, but he couldn't quite identify it.

"The pack," she said. "Slowly…"

Working through his options, Keno realized he had only one. He complied, methodically taking out the water bottles and carefully turning inside out the empty nylon sack.

"You've surfed any of those places?"

Keno realized she was referring to the *Pegasus Surf Lodges* logo emblazoned on the back.

"I spent a month out at Tenggara Point before they officially opened. Sort of a shake down cruise. One of the best months of my life."

"Right or left?"

"The house wave is a right, but there's a beautiful, heavy left about thirty minutes away."

"That's in Indo, right?"

"Yeah."

"Which island?"

"Sorry…but I'd have to kill you." He smiled at the irony, hoping she had a sense of humor and understood surf tradition when it came to secret spots.

The woman who looked like a Patagonia model smiled knowingly but didn't lower her weapon. Keno couldn't help but be further entranced by her twinkling eyes, even though the gun indicated there were still more questions aimed his way.

"What are you doing out here?"

"It's a long story, but I was on a surf trip and had car trouble. Some local fishermen helped me out with some water and tortillas and sent me on my way."

As Keno had given his answer, the driver pointed the gun toward the ceiling of the truck, indicating her partial—but not complete—trust in the forsaken surfer. Then she had proceeded with the inquisition.

"Really? What's your favorite break in Baja?"

"On a good day? Prob'ly a big southwest swell at Fourth Point San Juanico…when it carries all the way through to First. Pretty special."

"I just came through Scorpion Bay…'pretty special' is right."

"Oh, yeah."

"Where are you from?"

"I live in San Francisco, but I spend as much time as possible in Baja and the Gorge."

Seeing that the weapon was still in the picture, Keno was trying hard to come up with the right answers—working diligently to find common ground. The driver seemed to be looking at him with less suspicion than earlier, but she continued with the questions, trying to determine whether he was friend or foe.

"The Gorge, huh? Kiter or sailer?"

"Started windsurfing in the eighties, but pretty much only kite now."

"Favorite spot in the Gorge?"

"That's easy, six meter Rufus."

"Right answer, that, Wilson. You must know Steve Gates at Windance?"

Keno was struggling to keep up.

"You mean Big Winds? Who's Wilson?"

"The volleyball, Mr. Cast Away. How do you know Steve?"

"A-ha...*Cast Away*...um, he used to be the mayor...and we played tennis together for years?"

"What's his son's name?"

"As far as I know, he only has daughters. I can't imagine Ginny's had a boy since I've been gone...she's gotta be over fifty now."

The driver revealed a full-on grin, and Keno fell in. An inexplicable connection was forming, at least in his brain, and he felt like a force was pulling at him, like iron to a magnet, or mass into a black hole. The woman lowered the gun and continued with the questions.

"Where you headed?"

"Highway One, and then the border."

"Name?"

Keno hesitated for a split second.

"Fred...Biletnikoff."

"Well, Fred Biletnikoff, today might be your lucky day...if you're not in a hurry...but if you want a ride, you'll have to lift up your shirt and turn a pirouette for me. A lot of good people out here, but every once in a while a bad apple spoils everything. Some *gringo* surfer went missing about six months ago right around here...all they found was his burned-out truck. A single traveler can't be too careful."

Before Keno had completed the three-sixty, he recognized the accent. In college he had had an Israeli exchange student as a roommate for a semester; the female driver pronounced certain syllables in a similar way. It sounded like a Russian accent with a sense of urgency.

A blonde Israeli...with freckles, Keno thought. *Interesting.... What's she doing working for NOLS in Baja? And what's with the serious handgun?*

After watching him spin, the Israeli driver became comfortable that

Keno's waistband was empty, and she stowed the Glock back under her seat. He picked the water bottles out of the sand and dunked them into his pack before hustling 'round the front of the truck. Not wanting to give his angel time to change her mind, he quickly but politely opened the passenger door and stepped up onto the running board. The cab had the unique smell of Baja—salt and seaweed, mesquite smoke and poblanos, corn tortillas and fish tacos, and open latrines—with just the faint hint and softness of a woman's deodorant. And there was something else that demanded his identification. Another wisp of a smell with strong and pleasant associations. What was it? Looking in the back, he noticed a couple of longboards nosing their way toward the front seat. The sight of the boards jogged his memory on the divine smell.

Zog's Sex Wax!

One of the boards was a McTavish Fireball, and Keno thought the other might be a Stewart Redline 11.

Not a bad quiver.

He looked at the girl with respect, enjoying the outpouring of familiar smells and shade while she cleared what was left of her rice and beans from the tattered passenger seat. When she was finished, he threw his pack on the floor and climbed in. As he got settled in the seat, she casually glanced at his left hand, noticing the absence of a wedding band.

Turning to face his host, Keno locked eyes for an awkward and intimate moment.

"I can't tell you how grateful I am."

Breaking their shared gaze with a laugh and coquettish toss of her head, she shifted the Bronco into first gear and deftly let out the clutch, freeing the beast to push forward through the rocks and sand.

"I think you just did."

As she focused on the road, he could now more freely examine the details of her face. The skin was streaked with dust and pores and sun. It was apparent the surface of her nose had suffered under the unrelenting gaze of the cloudless Baja days. Her unattended, sun-tinged hair seemed to have been styled by the wind, and it was partially pinned up under a deteriorating, straw cowboy hat. Just at the cleft of her chin another smaller, unashamed scar revealed itself. These few small signs he interpreted broadly, projecting a life of promise and risk, an insatiable thirst for experience, and a disdain for entrapment. To him, the driver's face represented freedom and the authenticity of imperfection…the fact that it belonged to a woman made it all the more interesting. Glancing at the hands resting on the steering wheel, he noted the absence of any jewelry.

The memory of her voice, a dulcet languish, returned his attention to her mouth. As if on cue, she glanced over and smiled at him. He noticed the small chip on one of her central incisors. He reached his open hand across his torso and in her general direction; a traditional gesture of peace and trust.

"Please," he said, "call me Freddy."

The woman took her right hand off the wheel and grabbed for his hand. She wore a white, sleeveless T-shirt that hung loosely over a pair of cutoff jeans, and as she stretched, the striations of her shoulder and forearm revealed themselves, furrowing her freckled brown skin.

"Hi, Freddy," she returned easily. "I'm Calypso."

Again the siren voice…

They merged palms and wrapped fingers. For a moment, each curiously studied the other's face. Calypso smiled back at him with a gravitational pull that reached deep inside him. Her eyes revealed an amused knowing, as if she understood the nonsensical nature of their existence, and took that awareness as an opportunity to dance unfettered rather than fold up tent and mail it in. In the air between them they each sensed an optimistic hope that fed the spreading intoxication of possibility. Keno felt something was happening, wanted to resist, but seemed to lack the will. Lola receded away into the foggy recesses….

They both thought the same thing.

This could be interesting.

CHAPTER 40 —

Back in the Rocking Chair

It was an early Sunday morning, and Wolfgang was ecstatic. It was as if he had rediscovered a favorite toy, only it was an improved version, and the revelation had him buzzing like a sailor on leave. The object of his affection was his center-mounted appendage...namely his dick. The longtime friend was once again responding to any opportunity, only now with an obscene level of engorgement and staying power. Initially unsure, he had tested the waters with an assortment of women, not just Lola look-alikes—and there had been no hiccups. Last night was the sixth evening in seven that his externally mounted reproductive equipment had functioned magnificently—in his view, a strong set of observations. The only night during the previous week that hadn't seen him release his DNA into a willing female was Thursday, and that repression had been voluntary. He had spent the evening dining at his parents' flat, discussing family business, and going over wedding plans.

It wasn't just that things were working...it was bigger than that. He had become a ferocious performer, like Tiger Woods with an oversized driver, and with each successful canoodle his confidence was leaping and bounding. The most recent beneficiary of his newly discovered 1-wood lay in his immediate wake, soundly asleep in room 232 on the second floor of the Delano Hotel. The extremely satisfied blonde was casually studying at nearby Indian River College. She thought of herself as an accomplished cowgirl, but Wolfgang had pushed her to new limits before finally allowing her to collapse in an exhausted heap.

Basking in the afterglow of the session, Wolfgang smiled while he pushed the *L* button on the elevator control panel. He deliciously reminded himself that the platinum coed was about as different from his fiancée as one could get, and yet, if her exhortations were to be believed, their encounter had been a smashing success. She had been the easiest one yet, as the Palm Beach party girl had invited *him* up to *her* room. The seduction had been so effortless that he worried he might be developing a reputation as a "must do" stop among the fast crowd of South Beach players. As this thought flashed through his brain he made a mental note to visit the urologist.

The art deco elevator disgorged him into the Ian Schrager-inspired, fabric-draped lobby. Like taking a trip through the clouds, the New World Don Juan floated amidst the white columns and pre-dawn lull in surreal solitude. His personal conceit, and the partial opaqueness of the diaphanous curtains, compelled him to imagine he was a celebrity, swaggering down the polished wood floor, paparazzi separating and adoring while he moved towards the doorway. In the fantasy, his lean frame hovered vertically over the walnut planks, his conquering presence filling the room. Past the whimsical Dalí furniture, he strode towards the groggy doorman with purpose. As his rapid-fire brain moved on from the red carpet delusion, he began to again relive the pleasures from a few hours earlier. Visions of sweaty breasts and pouting vulvas danced through his head, and he reached down to give his penis a reassuring and congratulatory squeeze. As he looked towards the floor, past his bulge, his pointed-toe, burgundy-colored, left shoe came into view. Extending, jester-like, a good ten inches from the cuff of his designer, skinny jeans, the display of his Zota boot left him feeling immensely agreeable. A split second later, the matching, right, rococo foot chariot appeared as he thrust his other leg forward in his no-nonsense ambulation. He thought of the new Zota slip ons as stylishly flamboyant, just the right combination of money and devil-may-care for the modern playboy image he was so trying to cultivate. With his brain still enjoying the chemicals of physical and emotional satisfaction, he wasn't sure things could get any better.

I forgot how much fun this is! he thought as he proceeded through the Delano's lobby. *Am I sure I want to get hitched?*

Ever since Lola had agreed to marry him, a switch had flipped in his head. He was back to his insatiable, unconscionable self. With the burden of impotence lifted, a whole new optimism permeated his assemblage; the outrageous shoes merely added an exclamation point to the rebirth. Approaching the front of the lobby, he grinned at the uniformed adolescent struggling through the graveyard shift. As the door boy snapped to attention, his arm flexed. The glass barrier, which separated the chilled, internal air from the external Florida swamp, gave way. Immediately, the humidity of early morning Miami swept in. Wolfgang plunged into the natural moisture with relish, peacocking his way into the pre-dawn while soaking up the velvet oxygen with lungs and skin. Pausing for a second on the sidewalk, his left hand gave one more paternal squeeze to his junk, before he turned right and headed down Collins Avenue. Within half a block he took another right on Seventeenth Street, towards the beach, and caught the first glimpses of the glorious sun pushing colors up and over the eastern horizon.

Limping behind Wolfgang, wrapped in worn camouflage, a homeless vet slid unnoticed through the early morning grime. Clay had been shadowing Wolfgang Dalman over the previous six days, gathering as much data as he could about the target. Paranoid by nature, the news that his sister-in-law was planning to elope with her college boyfriend had aroused a strong suspicion. It was his first and only substantive lead since the staged Baja accident, and he was clinging to it like marshmallow to a campfire stick. His plan needed Dalman to be guilty, or the whole contrivance would soon unravel under the weight of its own convolution and Lola's unpaid expenses. Despite his best efforts, the episode in Costa Rica had only yielded a mess. Recek gave up nothing, except some disgusting bodily fluids and a textbook display of early onset delirium tremens. Clay was so worried the old soldier would die under his watch that he prematurely and surreptitiously abandoned the hotel, leaving Ray tied to the bed. Then he alerted the front desk via cell phone on his way to the San Jose airport.

Undeterred by the lack of evidence and his own moral shortcomings, Clay had just yesterday come to a verdict on Dalman's crimes. He wasn't sure of the Casanova's guilt, but time constraints and personal biases had softened the traditional "beyond a reasonable doubt" guideline. In the assassin's mind, Wolfgang's satyromaniacal behavior implied a degree of amorality…especially in such close proximity to his nuptial commitments. Applying the associative property of behavior allowed Clay to make the necessary leap between hyperpromiscuity and murder. With his judicial duties now complete, all that was left were those of executioner. Clay decided he would finish the task soon, and that night, with only a sliver of a moon, seemed particularly promising. In an oft-repeated sequence, his right hand first patted the holstered Sig pressed against his chest and then headed southwest, past his navel, where he reassuringly tapped the sheathed hunting knife strapped just to the right of his appendix.

Over the last week, Clay had been developing a conscience-clearing narrative of Wolfgang as monster—a predator who lacked empathy and was threatening the life of his brother and the stability of his family. The more he focused on the perceived psychopathy, the easier would be the killing. In light of the fomentations Wolfgang's behavior was causing him, Clay had initially wanted to use the knife, to prolong the suffering—but his military training had allowed him to resist the sadistic urge. Whenever the anger frothed, he reminded himself that emotion had no place in the work of a professional; survival depended on avoiding detection—and that meant limiting his public exposure. Taking all this into consideration, Clay had decided on a pre-dawn hit, outdoors, to make it look like an armed robbery or drug deal gone awry. A single chest shot (maybe a second to the head, just to be sure), then grab the wallet and move quickly away from the body. The murder rate on Miami Beach was well above Florida's average, so a random act of violence wouldn't be considered unusual.

There were two nagging concerns. The first was the potential for witnesses in a non-controlled environment. People, including police, were coming and going all the time in the South Beach neighborhood—both foot and vehicle traffic—and Clay had no way to manage potential intrusions. The second concern was the unusually short reconnaissance period. Usually he would go into a job with much more data on target and location patterns. Unfortunately, in this situation there was a sense of urgency, given the immediate wedding plans and the dwindling patience of Aloysius, Trick, and Keno. He had gone radio silent a week ago and hence wasn't up to date on the current magnitude of elevated angst. However, over the previous few months he had been hearing an obvious increase in the stress levels during his dad's phone calls. Clay knew he was running out of time.

As these worries ran through his brain, he reminded himself of the favorable circumstances. The most significant was the pattern Wolfgang had established over the previous week…it was an assassin's dream. Dalman would leave his apartment and start wandering the South Beach clubs at around eleven P.M. With unshakeable consistency, he would depart a few hours later with an attractive, inebriated woman and head back to his apartment or a local hotel. About an hour before dawn his profane figure would appear and stroll, either solo or with the girl, for at least a block along the beach boardwalk. After the slight nod to chivalry was complete (if the girl were there) and the ingestion of some fresh, salty air, he would turn abruptly away from the sea and head (alone) to the local twenty-four-hour Dunkin' Donuts franchise on Alton and Sixteenth Street. It was a brisk, ten-minute walk, and Wolfgang would arrive at the dive flush from the exercise. For about twenty minutes he would slum it in the fluorescent glare with the local bums and night owls, nursing his coffee and gobbling a glazed. He would then head back to his apartment and sleep until a mid-afternoon tanning session by the pool.

As Clay followed Wolfgang to the bike path that ran along the beach, an idea suddenly struck him. He quietly reversed course and dragged his foot back up Seventeenth Street, heading toward Collins. He then lost his limp, Verbal Kint style, before hustling south down the long block to Sixteenth Street. Then he headed west, towards Biscayne Bay and the Dunkin' Donuts. He was thinking about an unkempt area with heavy foliage on Sixteenth Street, just past Meridian. Perhaps it had been happenstance, but he remembered that Wolfgang had walked past the area every night that week. It was a quiet, poorly lit residential block, with limited early morning traffic—a perfect place for Clay to assemble his weapon and prepare the ambush. If his hunch was right, he'd have about eight minutes before Wolfgang appeared, walking with a purpose across the skinny barrier island to get his morning fix of caffeine and sugar. As Clay crossed Meridian he slowed, whispered a prayer, and started looking for a good spot. The cylindrical impression of the suppresser reassured him. It was in his left front pants pocket.

About five minutes later the soldier was set. He had screwed the silencer into place and was leaning with his back against a large coconut palm that was planted in the grassy meridian that separated street and sidewalk. To his immediate right was a faded, cement-block bungalow built in the Old Florida style. It was poorly maintained, with solar film peeling from the opaque windows and no sign of residents. The branches of a series of jacaranda trees extended from the yard, reaching out over the sidewalk, blocking the splinter of light that hazarded the long journey from an ancient street lamp a hundred yards away. The whole area wallowed in indifferent darkness. The final touch was the uncollected, deciduous leaves covering the ground. Clay's frame was totally obscured by the shadows and the outline of the tree. Critically, with his back against the west side of the palm, he was invisible to pedestrians traveling east to west down Sixteenth Street. The sounds of the early morning were limited, and Clay used the quiet as an opportunity to focus on his breathing and try to slow his heart rate. He was in a perfect spot…*if* Dalman stuck to his last few nights's pattern.

One house to the west, in the early morning gloom, Clay could barely make out a stooped lady in her bathrobe, dragging a large, white, plastic garbage bag to the curb. He kept his hand inside his jacket, fingers wrapped tightly on the grip of the Sig Sauer as he tracked the bag's progress. His ears nervously searched for any sound of Dalman approaching from the east as he mentally urged the old woman to complete her task and move out of the impact zone. About twenty feet from the sidewalk, the widow's plastic bag snagged on a sharp tree root and tore open, leaving a trail of white plastic diapers that followed the incontinent octogenarian to the street. Depositing the torn receptacle at the curb, she turned to see the trail of disposable swaddling and swore out loud. Under his breath, Clay joined her imprecation. Unwilling to yield to the forces of entropy, the woman slowly began the process of bending over to pick up the embarrassing artifacts. Working with the persistence of an ant and the speed of a sloth, she labored through the tidying, a single soldier on a solitary front in the losing battle against chaos. As he watched the wrinkled, female Sisyphus, Clay became deeply depressed. He wanted to terminate his target this morning, and he had a good plan, but he didn't want to risk leaving potential witnesses. On a deeper level, the scene drove home what he intuitively understood. The whole futility of it all.

Fuck, he thought, *it just never ends, does it? The onslaught of indignation?*

As he pushed ineffectively at the first mosquito that buzzed his still head, he heard the sound of the hard-soled, pointy Zotas clicking down the sidewalk, heading towards him.

Dalman was coming.

Clay's heart rate shifted to double time, and the surge of stress hormones stiffened the soft tissue throughout his body. Disciplining himself to a relaxed stillness, he ignored the mosquito as she landed on his cheek. He tried to forget her, just under his right eye, releasing saliva down her proboscis and preparing to feed. While the spit served to anesthetize his skin, it also served as an anticoagulant as she harpooned her straw-like nose into one of his capillaries and started sucking blood. Keeping his limbs still, Clay contorted the right side of his face and silently blew air up from the corner of his mouth in an effort to dissuade the mosquito from her meal.

Click, click, click! Dalman's hard-soled Zotas were advancing down the street. Clay guessed Wolfgang was just a few seconds from reaching the tree. He listened for the crunch of leaves. His heart was running at full sprint, sweat ran from his pores. Feeling as if his lungs were being squeezed by ribs of iron tightening around his chest, he recognized the symptoms. An oncoming panic attack. He fought it and cursed against the beast.

No! No! No! he silently commanded. *Not now…I won't have it!*

In an effort to regain control, he mashed the parasite with the meat of his fist, leaving a bloody pancake flattened against his cheekbone. Then he recommitted to his task, pulling the long barrel out of his jacket. His brain started working through the calculations. He prayed the old woman suffered from vision and hearing inadequacies.

First the heart, he said, steadying himself, *then the head.*

The crunching footsteps came to an abrupt halt. Clay guessed Wolfgang was five yards from pulling even with the tree.

Clay held his breath. *Did he hear me smash the bug? Or unholster the Sig?*

The barrel of the pistol started to shake in his hand; his heart was exploding in his chest. Could Wolfgang see him? He reviewed his perimeter, moving only his eyes. He thought he heard the sound of Wolfgang's breathing…and then an approaching car. But no headlights materialized. The shaking grew worse. His vision started narrowing, and he thought he might pass out. In the silence he worried that Wolfgang could hear his teeth bouncing off each other as they shivered in his mouth. Then, just as suddenly as they had stopped, the shoes resumed their rhythmic clicking through the detritus. Clay realized he had been holding his breath. As Wolfgang passed obliviously on his right, the assassin struggled to regain his composure. He was fighting hard to breathe without revealing his position, hoping he could complete the messy part of the job. In the shadows, Clay silently pointed the gun at the back of the passing man's torso, but he couldn't stop his hand from shaking.

Do it! Fuckin' pull the trigger!

Fifty feet beyond Wolfgang, lined up perfectly in the sights of Clay's gun, the old lady picked up the few remaining diapers. Clay watched in fascination as his shaking hand first aimed the pistol at Dalman...then at the plaid bathrobe...then, with metronomic precision, back at Dalman. It wasn't clear which he wanted to first put out of his misery. Ten seconds later he still couldn't pull the trigger. Wolfgang was now nearly upon the struggling senior.

"Mademoiselle"—his voice broke sharply through the night—"it appears you need some help. May I?"

Clay looked on in amazement as his psychopathic target stooped to help retrieve the trail of soiled undergarments that had kept their owner occupied over the last few minutes. At first the woman tried to resist, but Wolfgang insisted, overwhelming her embarrassment with charm. A moment later they were all collected and deposited back in the torn white bag at the curb.

"Shall we do it again tomorrow? Make it a date?"

Wolfgang showed no signs of disgust as he bowed deeply to the lady before backpedaling with a smile. In a flash he was again bouncing west towards the Dunkin' Donuts. Clay cursed his hesitation. He waited until his target was far down the block and the elderly woman back inside before disassembling the Sig and putting away all the hardware. He then returned to character, hobbling after his eclectic Argentinian suspect while all around him the purples and grays of the early morning began awakening.

CHAPTER 41 —

Donuts Are Meant to be Eaten

Limping in, Clay grabbed an empty stool at the counter and waited for the proprietor to ask for his order. To his right, Wolfgang was engaged in an animated conversation with a disheveled patron.

"So, Doc, do all guys hate their fathers?"

The local guru used an unwashed hand to contemplatively scratch at a scraggly, gray beard that looked like it might be housing lice. Wolfgang had asked the question good-naturedly, pitching underhand to Doc in an obvious effort to initiate small talk. As is usually the case, the question was rooted in a wisp of truth, in this case a thesis that resonated with the inquirer (Wolfgang). On the Formica counter, a glazed donut and what appeared to be a cup of iced coffee sat within Wolfgang's grasp. The man he was talking to was working his way through a cinnamon-raisin bagel and a sweet tea.

Doc cleared his throat.

"Well, Wolfgang…it is *Wolfgang*, right?"

"All week long, Doc."

"That's quite a provocative question now, isn't it?"

"Doc" was a former associate professor of psychology at a prestigious New England University. A tragic case of early onset dementia and the absence of a supportive family had left him living on the streets of Miami Beach. His long-term memory was still good, but his short-term memory had noticeable gaps, like a block of Swiss cheese. A few days earlier, Wolfgang had observed him holding court with some vagrants at the Dunkin' Donuts breakfast counter, and curiosity had driven him to slide over a few stools and join the conversation. Every morning since, he had been an active participant.

Doc began to hold forth.

"I would say, that for most men, their degree of dislike for their fathers just about matches their level of disappointment with their current station in life."

Knowing that his response might be considered a tad too honest, Doc examined the well-groomed younger man next to him for any glimpse of self-recognition. Wolfgang hadn't expected such a revelatory answer and was left with some internal squirming that he was trying hard to disguise.

"Hmm, now that squarely relocates the burden, doesn't it?"

Pleased to converse with someone educated in the traditional canon, Doc thoughtfully moved his comments out of Wolfgang's kitchen.

"I suppose some could read it that way. Of course, this is more of a parent and child conversation than just a father and son conversation, isn't it?"

Still feeling uncomfortable with the personal nature of the subject he had introduced, Wolfgang decided to pivot to a new area.

"Maybe so. Hey, new topic…I was just reading that more than one in five Americans are on anti-anxiety or depression medication…and with woman it's one in four. What's up with that?"

Excepting Wolfgang, everyone in the restaurant had taken Valium or Xanax or some other anti-anxiety medication at some point during the last year, but none of them was ready to admit to it until getting a lay of the land. They were afraid of being publicly outed as lacking in character. Understanding the stats and guessing right about his audience, Doc took the awkward silence as a green light to proceed.

"No one knows for sure, but I would guess a little anxiety might have been good for our ancestors. You know, maybe help us to get out of the cave and complete our three prehistoric tasks?"

"Find lunch, don't become lunch, find mate?"

Like a lecturer who had been plagiarized, Doc looked offended.

"Careful there, Mr. Wolfgang, that's my punch line."

Wolfgang looked surprise.

"Sorry, Doc, I was just playing the attentive pupil."

There were two hobos seated on the other side of Doc, and one of them let out a spontaneous sneeze of an epithet.

"Fuckin' yuppies…no one cares…this shit…fuck…Doc!"

No one else in the place seemed to notice the comment. Part Two immediately followed.

"Goddamn, mutha-fuckin', titty-suckin', sperm-drinkin', fart-breathin', sonofabitch!"

Clay guessed Tourette's. The counter man, Mo Smith, who had been listening with interest to Doc's talk, had heard enough.

"Lenny! Enough with the language! Another outburst like that and you're out for the rest of the day. You're scaring customers away."

All the patrons noshing in the desolate warmth of the restaurant's six A.M. artificial light looked around, trying to identify customers whom they might be scaring away. Eventually they all locked their eyes on

Clay, the newcomer. Lenny, the trespasser, responded to the proprietor's demand.

"Sorry, Smitty, it won't happen a-a-a-a-gain."

Smitty nodded at him then moved down the counter, resting in front of Clay's homeless vet facade. The proprietor was a small, paunchy man, but one who gave meaning to the "size of the fight in the dog" aphorism. There was an intensity that accompanied his stare, a menace that came partly from caffeine, partly from speed, and partly from the way he was hardwired. He had managed the donut shop over a span of twenty years and two wives, and at this point it owned him as much as the other way around. The decades of serving the public had left him not liking people, so he mostly worked the graveyard shift. He placed both of his hands on the counter, on either side of Clay, and leaned in.

"Whadaya call a man who lives on the street in a cardboard box, never changes clothes, shuffles around muttering to himself, and has no money?"

Clay, whose confused expression showed he had been expecting a different greeting, remained silent. After a pause, Smitty continued.

"Unwelcome." Smitty barely took a breath. "Whadaya call a man who lives on the street in a cardboard box, never changes clothes, shuffles around muttering to himself, and has a million dollars in the bank?"

The other four customers were all paying rapt attention to Smitty's performance. They had obviously been here before and were enjoying the newcomer's befuddlement. Clay used his elbows to pat his torso, confirming the location of his weapons, just in case.

Smitty grew impatient.

"Eccentric!"

Everyone stared at Clay as the clock on the wall ticked off the seconds and perspiration started forming on his brow. He didn't know what to do, and he wasn't sure he got the joke. Wolfgang offered his intended executioner a helping hand.

"He wants to know if you have any money…before you order?"

Clay and Wolfgang held each other's gaze for an awkward second too long. Wolfgang broke away first, turning towards Smitty with a charitable expression.

"I'll cover him…up to five bucks."

With an ironic smile, Smitty looked from Wolfgang back to Clay.

"What will you have, sir?"

Finally understanding the rules of engagement, Clay reached into his pocket. He pulled out a crumpled twenty and laid it on the counter. Smitty laughed.

"Aha! An eccentric! Your kind is always welcome here."

Everyone laughed as the room collectively exhaled.

"A maple bar and a cup of coffee. Black."

Smitty turned to the rack and started assembling the order. The early morning excitement was over, and the small crowd resumed sipping their coffees.

Wolfgang turned back to Doc.

"So, what's with this mass anxiety? Everybody taking pills? If you're right, worrying helped our ancestors swing safely out of the trees and into today's skyscrapers, right?"

Doc considered Wolfgang's sixty-million-dollar question.

"I don't know…too many people disappointed with their current station in life, I guess."

Wolfgang was the only one who got the joke.

"C'mon, man."

Not through with the infinite loop, he continued teasing Wolfgang.

"Bad parenting?"

"All right, Doc, forget it."

"Ahhh, Wolfman, sorry…you just made it too easy. Let's see, now…why all the fear? Hmm…something in the water? Gluten? Industrial food? UV rays? An alien experiment? Too much sugar? Maybe we've always had this level of agita and it's only now we're finally able to diagnose and treat it; before, we might have excused the same level of dread with a quaint term like 'the vapors.' "

Doc shook his head in resignation.

"The bottom line is we don't really know."

Smitty had delivered the coffee and pastry to Clay and was now back to eavesdropping.

"But all the pills. That can't be good for us?"

Doc shrugged.

"For a lot of people, medication has been a miracle…the only treatment that works."

The pause offered Smitty a chance for a follow-up that was particularly significant for him. He tried to wrap it in a bit of subterfuge.

"I know all these questions are stupid…but…why do you think we're always searching for new stuff? You know, the grass is always greener…we're never happy…our kids, jobs, houses…even our wives?"

This question was common, and Doc shared his theory.

"Well, everybody that lives here, in America, or their ancestors, fled from someplace else. We are a country of nomads…we were either pushed out or left in search of better—"

Lenny couldn't help himself, the mention of wives had moved his hatred to the front burner. He had been using alcohol and weed since he was thirteen, and after he had lost his third job in the first few years of his marriage, his wife divorced him and took the kids. Left alone, his drinking and smoking had increased to the point where he couldn't function. He blamed it all on her.

"Hey Smitty," he interjected now. "Why did God give women vaginas?"

Clay didn't notice the collective eye roll; everyone had already heard Lenny's joke. Like an owner trying to stop his dog from soiling the carpet, Smitty ordered him to cease.

"Lenny! *NO!*"

Despite Smitty's prohibition, after a brief and awkward silence, Lenny dropped his deuce.

"So men would talk to them!"

Smitty glared down the bar.

"I warned you Lenny."

"What, I can't say 'vagina'?"

"It's misogynist."

"Ma-saw-ja...what?"

"Besides, Mr. Fancy Shoes over here is gettin' married in a few days. Don't start makin' him have second thoughts about women. Ain't that right, Wolfgang?"

Before Dalman could answer, Lenny burst out incredulously.

"*He's* getting married? To a *woman*?"

To Lenny's right, a mentally diminished hobo named Rusty leaned close to Lenny's ear and whispered in a loud drawl:

"But you said he was one of them fellers likes to poke other fellers in the bucket?"

Few people enjoy having their private prejudices aired publicly, especially when they've erred. Lenny immediately turned on Rusty.

"Shut the *fuck* up, Rusty!"

Smitty pulled a sawed-off baseball bat from under the counter, and placed it in front of him.

"*Leeeennny…*"

Lenny and Rusty looked chastened, like a couple of rambunctious schoolboys discovered by the principal.

"Exercise."

Everyone turned to Clay. He was quietly sipping his coffee.

"Movement…any kind of physical action…our bodies and minds need it…to stop the fuckin' anxiety."

"That, or a bullet to the head."

Wolfgang delivered his light-hearted comment with a laugh, but when none of the other patrons joined in he immediately wiped the smile off of his face and got in line with the solemnity.

Clay had been looking straight ahead at Smitty, but now he addressed all the other customers.

"Fuck. Not just anxiety…it cures everything. Heart disease, stroke, depression, diabetes, obesity, arthritis, snoring, myopia, limp dick…"

He would never admit it, but one of the reasons Smitty enjoyed the graveyard shift was the low caliber of customer who typically visited at that time. The assortment of homeless, Kaczynski-esque, societal misfits made Smitty feel relatively normal, even high functioning, in comparison. Not one of his irregulars had ever suggested simple exercise as a panacea for all of society's ills, and he thought the newcomer's comments offensive—

especially in light of the fact that Mo's every attempt at a regular exercise program had ended in failure. He leaned in threateningly towards Clay.

"And who the fuck are you? Jack LaLanne?"

With soulless eyes and a set chin, Clay looked at the hard face unflinchingly while answering the question—each word patiently revealing itself.

"Maybe. Except. He's. Still. Alive. And. I'm. Already. Dead."

An awkward silence ensued as the two men locked stares. Neither man blinked. Smitty's grip tightened around the wooden handle of the club.

From two seats away, the professor lifted his eyebrows and looked to his left, in front of a backwards leaning Wolfgang, to reassess Clay with new appreciation. He tried to verbally defuse the situation.

"Well…I don't know about myopia.…but he's pretty much spot-on on the other stuff. In most instances, exercise is the most efficacious treatment. Works across broad segments of the population…gender and race indifferent. Unfortunately, we can't get people to do it. We won't give up our Twinkies and go for a daily walk."

The stressful environment was bringing out the worst in Lenny.

"Daily fuckin' commie pills…right?…Walkin' shit Twinkies…homo…right?…Doc?"

Smitty was still pissed, but Lenny's outburst brought a small smile to the corner of his mouth. He looked down the counter at the two bums.

"Whoa, whoa, whoa, ladies, let's not harsh on the pastries. Let's not forget where we are. A donut…maybe even five or six…every now and then…ain't gonna kill nobody."

Ignoring Smitty while turning his gaze to Wolfgang, Clay responded to Doc's comment.

"Pretty miserable species. Hardwired to be either too stressed or too bored, with nothing in-between. We can't even do the most simple things to keep ourselves healthy. We're like a herd of overfed sheep, bouncing off each other while we graze the pasture grass to extinction."

Continuing to stare at a confused Wolfgang, Clay considered pulling his gun and offing the whole pathetic passel. And then maybe himself. Slowly, he put his hand into his coat and caressed the grip of his Sig. The whole room froze. Wolfgang, only two feet from his hunter's hypnotic glare, sat immobilized. The rough cross-hatching of the Sig's handle felt warm and comfortable to Clay's fingers. Smitty's hand started twitching as he considered using the bat. Seeing the minute movements of the proprietor, Clay immediately visualized a kill sequence that started with Smitty and then worked down the counter through Wolfgang and Lenny. His bloody masterpiece would end with Rusty three seats away, before he would then turn the barrel on the artist himself.

Turning his full attention back to their server, Clay targeted a mole under Smitty's right eye as the entry point for the first bullet. Just before he animated the gun, he spotted the security camera mounted high on the wall above Smitty's left shoulder. He considered that it was probably absorbing everyone's features and sending the information to a hard drive somewhere off-site. It gave him pause, the thought of being memorialized as a crazed shooter.

What the fuck do I care? he thought, laughing grimly to himself. *I'll be gone.*

He thought about his mom, his dad, his family, Keno hiding in remote Baja. Slowly, he pulled his hand back out of his coat. Shaking his head in disgust, he pushed the twenty across the counter. As if they had seen a ghost, they all stared at him as he got up, looked hard at the maple bar without touching it, and then walked out into the oppressive morning heat.

CHAPTER 42 —

Making Flippy Floppy (or, I Had a Flame but She Had a Fire)

It was the denouement. He was almost asleep. The full weight of her body was impressed upon him, legs entwined, nothing but silence encumbering them. It felt to him like they were in their most elemental, primal state—the way nature intended—stripped of all the layering of modernity. Her question shattered the peace and marked what he suspected would be the end of the forbearance.

"There's somebody else, isn't there?"

It was more statement than question, delivered with a vulnerability and innocent matter-of-factness that belied its ability to disrupt. They had been camping at a remote surf break for three days; he knew that sooner or later it would have to be addressed. But every time she wrapped her naked, sublime legs around his waist he would submerge himself deeper into her world—a place that was so comfortable and devoid of obligation that he never wanted to leave. He tried to deflect the question…to understand better whether she was resolute or just probing, and hence how soon the dream would have to end.

"What? Why do you say that?"

He reflected on the recent experience and how he had gotten himself so entangled. At first, the walk away from Irma, wandering aimlessly through the desert, passionately focused on returning to Lola and the life they had built together. Then, the threatening midday heat and his concern that the sharp longing for a reunion might take a posthumous turn. Finally, Calypso showing up, like a godsend—just before the buzzards started probing more aggressively—pulling a kayak-laden rig and pausing beside him on the barren, desert track. As he considered the unlikely sequence and his current repose, he marveled at the vagaries of the human brain and, specifically, the fickle nature of attraction between men and women.

About an hour after he had climbed into the Bronco, Calypso made a left turn back towards the coast. He noted the mischievous twinkle in her eye but never questioned the decision. She "knew a spot" (she said) and given all the twists and turns involved in getting there, Keno (or so she told him) would never be able to find it on his own. The last three miles were hellaciously unstable, a true barrier to entry. At the beginning of the difficult stretch, Calypso had unhooked the trailer and hidden the kayaks behind a sandy berm. Then she deflated the truck tires down to about 20 PSI so they would enjoy even greater traction through the deep, sandy stretches. The final mile was negotiated completely in 4-wheel low. Keno thought the area would be a perfect place to commit a crime. The body would never be found. But by then he was already too curious about what came next, too hungry for the girl, to let any concerns impede the adventure. When they bounced down the last *arroyo* at five miles an hour, the desert opened up to reveal a beautiful, peeling right-hand point break, protected from the north wind by a majestic headland. Keno thought they must have discovered the Garden of Eden: he sat still after they parked, absorbing the scene in awe. She called it *El Punta de Dios,* or God's Point. She told him, with a level of solemnity that made him uncomfortable, that if he revealed its location to anyone else she'd have to kill him. Now, barely seventy-two hours later, the perfection was all coming unraveled.

"You're too well-trained. Someone has put a lot of effort into you."

Evading with clever repartee, he dunked his surfacing, accountable self, hoping to keep the truth at bay for as long as possible.

"Is that a compliment?"

They would surf all day, and then, at night, like wild, starved carnivores, they feasted, one gorging on the other until there was nothing left. In between they restocked their stomachs, hydrated, and slept. It didn't hurt that she could prepare a mean campfire *chorizo* stew and had a great inventory of tequila and red wine. The spirits were a particularly useful stiff-arm for those moments when his feeble conscience tried to tackle the galloping eroticism. His jobs were to clean the dishes, make sure they always had firewood, and investigate any noises she found unsettling. Keno found the last task a little strange, given her high level of competence in the area of wilderness survival.

Calypso continued with the observations.

"It's the little things…remembering to start away from the most sensitive areas, and then slowly working your way in for the kill…always being patient…building up trust. It's a feel thing…I'm not even sure I know how to describe it…maybe…you understand the nuances of a woman? That insinuations can be just as stimulating as the actual act… and…I don't know, but…you bring a certain dignity…or respect…to the whole…seduction."

By then Keno knew he had likely been found out; but he was willing to ignore the signals if it meant wallowing in her verbal appreciation. It was the sort of praise he rarely received from Lola, although ironically she had been the source of his learning. Inside his head a combination of dread and satisfaction were battling for control. In the brief silence, his ego won the battle, although his shame would win the war.

"I'm not sure what you're getting at?"

"The way you...when the time is right...you sense it...just as I do...and sometimes just before...and you remember exactly where my spots are...and what positions best stimulate me...and you attack with confidence."

Not hearing a question to respond to, he continued to caress the small of her back while she looked down at him in the dark. The directness of her observations was more graphic than he was used to hearing from a woman, but he considered that that might just be a reflection of her seeming indifference to the typical female deferences.

"And...you stay with me...after...like you really care. Someone taught you how to do all that."

He saw the surface moving towards him as she continued to press, but he deluded himself into believing he could stay submerged. He was intoxicated by the smell of their sex mingling with the sea. He thought he could be happy if she never again asked him to speak.

"At first I wanted you so badly, I was surprised by the intensity...I didn't even want to ask...didn't want to know."

The truth was now front and center. And he wasn't going to deny it just so he could entertain the sublime mirage for a few more hours. In the end, after the tequila ran out, he knew he wouldn't abandon his family.

"Tell me...I need to know...before it's too late. Because if you're taken...that's a no-fly zone for me."

There it was, the surface, his life with all the commitment and responsibility staring him in the face. It was calling him...he could no longer ignore it; and the need for the fantasy, of his wanting and embracing the escape, hit him full force in the stomach. It wasn't so much that he had planned the deception. It was more that he had let it unfold in a way that allowed him plausible deniability, refusing to acknowledge the likely difficult outcome under the guise of living in the present. The delusion that she didn't care, that like him she was just in it for the pure pleasure of the experience, was now on full display. He wondered when the sensation of being together, in the moment, had become no longer enough for her…at what point had her interest in the physical waned to the degree where she needed more to stay intrigued. Acknowledging the variability inherent in human relationships, and that the nature of the game had changed, he scrambled to cover his tracks.

"I'm sorry, I…I never lied about anything."

The sound of his words drifting off into the night struck him as particularly pathetic. It would have been better to say nothing.

It was too dark to see her face, but he could hear the sad, cold disappointment in her words.

"I was afraid you were going to say that."

He wondered where she kept the gun.

CHAPTER 43 —

Grey Panthers

"I can't believe you just did it."

Lilly was hyperventilating over their discovery. Feeling uncomfortable with the lonely pronoun, Elizabeth was quick to share the glory *and* the culpability.

"*We* just did it. We would've never found those files without Blundergusting's help."

Lilly understood Elizabeth's message and reassured her.

"Shoulder to shoulder, sister."

Curious about whether or not Lilly's friend was operating under a pseudonym or his real name, Elizabeth finally had to ask.

"What type of name is *Blundergusting*, anyway? Some sort of spy code?"

"Not a spy code…I think it's Old English, or something…. Did we really just hack into the Department of Defense's personnel files?"

Liz Barton nodded her grey curls in affirmation. She was shaking with an incredulous appreciation for what she could do with a little inside help and her newly developed computer skills.

"Yeah, I think we did."

"And those were Clay's medical records we downloaded?"

"No, no, no…we didn't download anything. I'm not getting caught with any of that stuff on my hard drive."

"But you're his mom!"

"I'm not sure the Feds care much about that…and, by the way, I still don't know how you read so fast. I was barely through the first sentences before you were turning the page."

"Yeah, I know, I'm weird that way. My one superhero power."

"And you remember it all?"

"Mostly. What'd you do with the parts I asked you to download?"

"Screen shots."

Looking at the clock, Lilly realized it was six in the evening. The wedding was only twenty-four hours away, and it had been nearly twenty hours since she had slept or eaten any real food. She picked up a utensil and hacked off a huge bite of the double chocolate cake, mostly butter cream frosting. Her brain anticipated the jolt of sugar and caffeine before the molecules even hit her bloodstream.

"That was *so* amazing! Let's go back in, I have some people I want to look up!"

"Uh, no? And keep your voice down, the NSA is probably listening to us as we speak. I feel like any minute now some *Men in Black* guys are gonna airdrop into Clearwater, barge in here with a huge magnet and a special fountain pen, and wipe all the hard drives and brains within a one-mile radius."

Lilly started giggling at the image of the two mature women being confronted by Tommie Lee Jones and Will Smith.

"They can do that? Should we lock the door?"

Elizabeth's judgment was lacking, along with her sleep. She wasn't sure if Lilly was laughing at, or with, her. During their collaboration, there had been frequent moments where she felt they were dancing together but each to a slightly different beat. It was becoming annoying. She answered the patronizing questions with a bit of prickle in her tone.

"You're the spook, you tell me."

Lilly didn't understand why the tone had just changed. She tried to dial back the tension.

"Hey...*retired* spook. And during my time, VCRs and clock radios were cutting edge. I learned spreadsheets on Lotus 1-2-3."

The ladies had been working for nearly three days straight, only grabbing catnaps when absolutely necessary. With only a few exceptions, when Lilly's peculiarities would cause her to launch into disruptive conversation, they were able to keep plowing forward. Elizabeth had been manning the keyboard while her new partner looked over her shoulder and kept them fueled. The only significant interruption had been the first night: Paul and Roshan had come over to celebrate her birthday. Since then, they'd been living on leftover cake and a case of kombucha, trying to get more insight into Clay's mental state without getting caught. Nearly fifty hours into their efforts, the real breakthrough came when Blundergusting delivered some important direction. With his guidance they were able to find the files they were looking for. Now all that was left was the exhilaration that comes from surmounting an incredible challenge (and the instability that comes from nine straight meals of, mostly, chocolate). They were both experienced enough to know a hard crash was right around the corner. Elizabeth, in particular, didn't function well when sleep-deprived. She knew they had to get to a conclusion soon, before her body shut down.

"So, I'm a mess. Your theory on Clay, tell me again? The *dash and pivot* or something?"

"The *Deschutes* Pivot. It's when one party *pivots* away from an unflattering situation. It's basically a fraudulent diversionary tactic."

Elizabeth looked at Lilly with exhausted but curious eyes.

"So, like a bomb or something?"

"No, it's more psychological……."

Lilly was struggling to come up with an example they could both appreciate.

"Hmm…let me think…"

Her red-rimmed eyes lit up.

"Okay…Let's say there's a married couple, and the woman suspects the husband is cheating, but she doesn't have enough information to prove it. The man senses the wife is getting close to discovering his infidelity, and he doesn't look forward to answering a bunch of painful questions. So he creates a diversion, a distraction, to avoid the hard questions."

Elizabeth was feeling like the example was a little too familiar but also wasn't sure she had the whole picture.

"Like what?"

"Like…the man comes home from work and announces he has a life-threatening disease…or maybe he tells his wife that the boss called him in that day, and they're considering him for a promotion which would entail a move to San Francisco."

"San Francisco? Who *wouldn't* want to move to San Francisco!"

"Exactly."

"Except for the rents. More money?"

"Probably."

"Hey, wait a minute…how did the man get his company to offer him a promotion that includes a raise and a move to a great city?"

"He didn't. The husband made it up. He picked a story that made him look good, or evoked sympathy, something that he knew would excite his wife and distract her from his bad behavior."

"Oh my God, that's a thing? How devious! People do that?"

"All the time, according to my therapist."

"And this Deschutes guy, he's some Scotsman?"

"Yeah, Angus Nelson Deschutes. Really interesting guy. His dad was a plumber and his mom was a teenage prostitute who immigrated from Tunisia."

Elizabeth was struggling with TMI. There seemed to be a joke in there somewhere, and clearly some serious familial dysfunction, but she was far too tired to sift through all the possibilities. She decided to stick closer to home.

"So, I'm still missing something. What's this have to do with Clay?"

"There's evidence that Clay made a habit of this during his time in the service. In one of the medical reports I think they even mention it, but they use the initials D.P. I think you saved it with a screen shot."

"I don't remember…what was the situation?"

"Well, the attending doc mentioned that every time the shrinks showed concern about his drug and alcohol use, Clay started to make up excuses to avoid his appointments. The reports describe one instance where he agreed to enter a thirty-day rehab program, but he told the docs at the last minute that he had been called up for immediate deployment to the Middle East for a top secret operation, so he couldn't enter rehab as scheduled. But a coupla days later one of the psychiatry corpsman saw him in his civvies at the base exchange buying a case of beer. They were actually considering going to his CO with the evidence and shutting him down."

"What's a CO?"

"Commanding Officer."

"Why didn't they do it?"

"The counseling sessions seem to have been voluntary, under a pilot program. My guess is that the sponsors were afraid if they started pulling a lot of Special Ops guys from active duty, upper brass would shut *them* down."

"Was that the only time?"

Lilly shook her head. "Nope. The notes show another time, when a shrink was asking him why he was struggling to show up to work on time…"

Pausing, Lilly tried to assess if Elizabeth could handle what came next. Elizabeth stared back, wondering why her co-conspirator had stopped talking.

"Um, well, Clay said his mom had passed away. In the notes, Clay described his relationship with his mom as 'very close'…he said that he was 'struggling with the loss.' "

Lilly stopped talking.

Elizabeth stared straight ahead at the monitor. The screen saver displayed a picture of Paul and Roshan and the baby girl they had adopted two years earlier, Rosalita. In a choked up voice, she finally spoke up.

"God, part of me is angry, and part of me wants to cry."

Thinking about her own daughter, Lilly offered some sympathy in her most gentle voice.

"I think… I understand. Mental health issues can be really tough… especially when addiction is involved. It's a difficult chicken-or-egg."

Elizabeth was doing what she regularly did: reviewing her history as a mom and fighting the self-flagellation.

"But why do you think Clay is doing a…a Deschutes Pivot now?"

This was the part where Lilly was operating with little evidence, but the medical reports did provide data that could be interpreted as supporting her theory.

"This is a bit of a leap," Lilly said, "but here goes." She briefly paused to gather her thoughts. "You ever hear about those rats that live in a cage with two levers?"

"The cocaine rats?"

"Yeah. One lever releases food and one lever dishes out some drug… and the rats pushed the drug lever nonstop until they starved to death."

"Yeah, I vaguely remember that from college psychiatry."

"Well, it turns out that those rats were living in isolation…rats are actually very social animals."

"Okay…?"

"When you put that solitary rat in with a healthy community of rats and offer the same lever choices, the rats stop choosing the cocaine."

"No way!"

"Yep."

Elizabeth was starting to catch up with Lilly's theory.

"So, towards the end of his military career, the records show Clay doing more isolated work, often solo terminations in urban areas for the CIA."

"Exactly." Lilly nodded.

"And then he leaves the government all together…and works as a mercenary…with no attachment to any particular team or community."

Again, Lilly nodded. "Yep. Also, the psychiatric reports show that in talk therapy, Clay regularly spoke in glowing terms about his family and his childhood. It wasn't just you he said he was close to, but also his brothers and father."

Elizabeth started to cry.

"It was all such a mess…we were all so young…babies having babies…I'm sure he blamed himself for Aloysius leaving us…the family just imploded…collapsed under the weight of its own entropy…I was just trying to survive…then he got into trouble at school…he was only a boy, a freshman in college…and they sent him away to the Navy. We didn't think we could do anything about it…we didn't have any money, didn't know any lawyers…we didn't even say good-bye…. And then he came home on leave…and Paul had the terrible accident…he always blamed himself for letting that happen too."

Lilly placed a hand on the older woman's shoulder as she got up.

"I'll be right back. Can I get you anything?"

"A new life?"

Lilly smiled compassionately before walking into the kitchen and grabbing two bottles of kombucha from the fridge. On the way back she noted all the faded pictures hanging on the wall—Elizabeth with Clay, Paul, and Keenan, she assumed—smiling back at her as she headed through the narrow hallway. She wondered if everyone's "normal" family was really just a facade. Before reentering the converted bedroom-office she stopped just outside the door and grabbed a box of Kleenex from atop a doily-laden side table. With all the curtains drawn tightly in the darkened room, the blue computer light cast an eerie glow around the unmoving, hunched back and head of Elizabeth. For a moment Lilly considered the possibility that the older woman might have given up.

"Elizabeth…?"

Lilly walked into the room and placed the box of tissue and one of the bottles between Elizabeth and the computer screen.

"Are you okay?"

"Yeah…I…it's just all such a struggle."

"This isn't anybody's fault."

"God, I feel like such a failure." Elizabeth grimaced at the words. "As a mom. A wife. A…person."

Wanting to console her new friend, Lilly weighed whether or not she should share her personal travails. Her main concern was that the revelation might be taken as one-upmanship, or in this case, one-downer-womanship. She decided the potential benefits outweighed the conjectured costs, as it might help Elizabeth feel she wasn't alone. Lilly tried to make the words sound less matter-of-fact than she felt.

"Did you know my daughter just tried to kill herself?"

Blowing her nose into a tissue, Elizabeth realized she had been too self-absorbed.

"Oh God, Lilly, I heard about that. I'm so sorry. That must be a terrible thing to deal with."

Lilly further dropped her voice and her eyes, trying to convey a sense of suffering that she felt somewhat remiss for not feeling more strongly.

"It is."

Both of the mothers sat in silence, listening to the whirring of the computer fan.

After a few minutes, Elizabeth had a thought.

"Do you think all this constant competition hurts them when they're growing up? All the sports and grades and sibling rivalry stuff?"

Lilly thought it a funny question, directed as it was towards a mother with only one child.

"I don't know…I'm sure there are plenty of theories out there…It probably depends on whom you talk to."

The sound of the back door opening, followed by footsteps approaching the room, froze them both. After a few seconds, Elizabeth was the first to jump into action. She turned off the computer, turned on a lamp, and grabbed some knitting out of a basket in the corner. Lilly was left to fend for herself. Elizabeth hissed a whisper at her.

"Look busy…and *old*."

Lilly picked up an AARP magazine and started looking through the pictures. Trying hard to keep her hands steady, she hoped the *Men in Black* intrusion would at least be quick and painless. She couldn't imagine they would harm two old ladies for hacking into a website.

A few seconds later, the footsteps stopped in the doorway. Roberto's head poked around the corner.

"*Señora?*"

Elizabeth lowered her knitting in relief.

"Oh my God, Roberto… you scared me to death! Come in, come in."

Taking in the scene, the Venezuelan took a few hesitant steps into the room.

"Roberto," Elizabeth said, "this is my…friend, Lilly."

Lilly extended her hand pleasantly. The wrinkled man stepped forward and gently grasped it.

"*Mucho gusto, Señora* Lilly."

Lilly nodded back politely.

"Lilly, this is my…gardener, Roberto."

Lilly noted the proud posture on the wizened man with the kind eyes. The awkwardness in Elizabeth's voice led her to believe something was up between the two. A wry smile formed on her lips.

"Yes, Roberto and I have met."

"Of course."

Releasing Lilly's hand, Roberto took a couple of respectful steps backwards, towards the door.

"You're busy, *Señora*, I will come back later."

Lilly saw a glimpse of pleading in Elizabeth's eyes.

"Yes, please, thank you, Roberto. Old friends catching up. Maybe tomorrow?"

"Si, Señora, mañana."

In a flash the man was gone. The sound of the closing screen door confirmed his departure. Elizabeth unsuccessfully tried to appear unflustered as she looked at Lilly.

"God, just when I think things are finally coming together for me, then…WHAM!—something hits me from out of the blue. I mean, who makes this shit up? Does it ever stop?"

"I don't know, but I don't think so."

"You know what? I think we have a flaw in our coding."

Lilly was still considering the back-door visitor.

"Menopause?"

"Well, a lot of flaws I guess, but one really big one."

Lilly was getting dingy with fatigue.

"We all come with expiration dates?"

"Come on, I'm serious."

"I'm sorry, you're right, you listened to my crazy theories. What's our big flaw?"

"I think our big flaw is that we expect too much."

"No kidding."

"We just don't get how soul-numbingly hard it is…modern-day suffering isn't invigorating at all…we've squeezed all the risk and excitement out of everything…we're so domesticated…no fending off dragons, no sailing adventures to new lands, no passionate romances…the challenge is dealing with the boring monotony of it all…"

Lilly gazed at her with empathy. "You know, I've heard that even Mick Jagger gets tired of singing 'Satisfaction.' "

Elizabeth blinked. Then she nodded. "Right?"

Lilly's emotional burdens of late revolved around Scout. When she got overly fatigued her brain started to skip between grooves of empathy and disconnection. The stylus was now positioned on *empathy*, at least as it pertained to Elizabeth's state of mind.

"And what about our kids? Those perfect little bundles of joy? Talk about elevated expectations."

"Oh my god! The kids! I thought I was the only heretic! Did you know my grand-kids can't even be bothered to write a brief thank-you after I make the effort to send them a gift?"

Lilly was so enjoying what seemed like a connection, finally, with Elizabeth, that she was comfortable adding fuel to the fire (ignoring the fact that she had no biological grandchildren).

"Mine neither!"

Not minding the disconnect, Liz started gaining momentum, like a runaway semi on Lombard Street.

"Oh my god! Our kids! If we're lucky or cursed enough to have them…those little bundles of hope and potential, who in their youth give us our much-needed relevance…those little beings that allow us to still dream that some day, through the reflected glory of their accomplishments, our neighbors will think of us as *special*, maybe even *better*…but then those perfect little creatures grow up and their flaws become increasingly obvious…at some point the imperfections impossible for even the most committed parent to ignore…and, eventually, they become just as disappointingly faceless as us…or worse, they are killed or damaged in some way…an event that grinds even our most modest ambitions under fate's indifferent boot heel."

Midway through Liz's rant, like a ping-pong ball crossing back and forth over the net, Lilly's brain shifted from the sympathetic side back towards one of logic and contentious judgment. In her new mental mode, she found herself taken aback by the conflagration she had unintentionally contributed to, and so she smiled very weakly at her shawl-wearing partner-in-crime. The former spook's brain didn't have an appreciation for the latitude allowed in dramatic license. Immediately, Liz noticed the change and felt abandoned, as if she had had the carpet pulled out from under her. All of a sudden she was over-committed and under-supported, and she tried to dilute her previous vitriol with some self-deprecation and a laugh.

"Don't get me started! Oh, wait…too late!"

Lilly listened in silence, realizing that things had taken an unusually dark turn, but not sure why that was the case. *Maybe she just needs sleep?* she thought. With her blank face giving nothing away, she also considered the possibility that her generally optimistic host might benefit from therapy.

Now that Lilly's obviously uncomfortable body language was on full display, Elizabeth wondered what had happened to their bonding moment. Feeling off-balance, she didn't trust her judgment and worried that her outburst might have been particularly boorish for a matron of her breeding. She retreated into the safe cocoon of gracious good manners.

"I'm so sorry, Lilly, I'm…being a…a terribly thoughtless hostess."

Having no social instincts, Lilly didn't realize how she had just sucked all the intimacy out of the room. All she knew was that at one point the spoken words seemed reasonable, and then a moment later the conversation seemed irrational and she could no longer appear sympathetic. Rhetoric for the sake of embellishment and shared comedic relief was a lost nuance for her. She knew the current circumstance with Liz's sons was particularly trying, but she had only so much patience for nonstop self-pity and rumination. Having long ago ruled out suicide as a viable option, Lilly had concluded that the only path was to carry on, regardless of the challenges—one foot in front of the other, until the next life beckoned. It was such a logical conclusion that she didn't understand why so many others struggled with such a simple decision tree. *Why all the angst about past transgressions and yet-to-be-named trespasses?* she frequently asked herself. *To be or not to be...I mean how hard is it?*

Wanting to get back on track, Elizabeth assumed that her rant on offspring was the point of discomfort for her guest. She went back to her original thesis about heightened expectations. Lilly tried to put a sympathetic look on her face and fight the urge to yawn as her host tried to summarize in a more academic drone.

"So, as I was saying, our big flaw is that we think that some day everything will be easy, an effortless, comfortable life. Our brains tell us that if we work hard enough, do enough planning, strategize with enough detail, that we can get rid of it—the constant disappointment and fear of not getting what we think we deserve. We actually think we can control our destinies; so we make daring commitments, vow *'til death do us part,'* open savings accounts, attend church, buy insurance, elect politicians with bold promises, all to protect us from...I don't know what...relief from the struggle...the uncertainty of it all?"

Her final question was an effort to get Lilly to buy back into their conversation, but her collaborator had a confused look on her face.

"So you don't think we should save money and buy insurance?"

2009 - Still Out West (Mostly)

At this point, Elizabeth wasn't sure if her guest was even listening. Two days ago, she considered that maybe her dotage was the problem, but as she examined the body of evidence she had a growing conviction that there was something slightly *off* about Lilly's conversational pacing.

"That man that was just here, Roberto? He lost his house, his wife, his job, his savings, his *country*, but he's more happy than most of the people I know who haven't seen a fraction of the challenges he has. He knows things can happen, but he has learned how to cope with life's challenges. He expects it, so when it happens, it doesn't bother him. Somehow he figured out how to hack his own software and fix the cerebral bug."

"Or maybe he was just born that way?"

Realizing she wasn't going to get the connection she had hoped for, Elizabeth sighed with resignation.

"Maybe."

Lilly was finishing the last of her kombucha and contemplating her host's condition. From the backyard, the sound of Roberto firing up the lawn mower shook Elizabeth out of her company-less misery, and reminded her that there was a task at hand.

"So what do we do with all this information and my crazy sons?"

"Do you want to hear my crazy theory?"

"Why not? It seems to be crazy week."

Both ladies shrugged and grinned mildly at each other in a grudging show of mutual acceptance.

"Okay, bear with me…"

Lilly put down her empty bottle, gathered her thoughts into two neat little compartments tagged *Symptom* and *Solution*, and then started talking rapidly, buttressing her words with animated hands.

"Look, I don't know Clay from Adam, but I have a hunch about this.

I think your oldest boy is trying to come home, but he's not proud of the man he's become. I think he wants to reintroduce himself to his family after all these years, but in his mind the best way to do it is by making himself a hero—so he's built a false narrative, maybe even unconsciously, where he is essentially saving his brother's life…Keno, the sibling who by all traditional metrics is the most normal and successful. It's a distraction, a diversion, a pivot away from the terrible things he's been doing, about which he feels ashamed…so he can rejoin the family without having to answer all the questions about his past and all the killing. It gives him a way to reenter the civilian world, a way for him to feel relevant and morally acceptable….a rebirth, sort of. It may sound like a crock, but I think he's longing for a community, like the rats with the levers, a place where he feels he belongs."

Nodding her head mildly in contemplation, Elizabeth showed some support.

"God, aren't we all?"

"Probably…to varying degrees."

Not knowing what to do with all of the information Lilly had just handed her, Elizabeth sat quietly with her kombucha. Before Lilly had come to visit she had never even tried the fermented beverage. The bottle label said GT's Multi-Green, and she wondered about the ingredients that gave the vinegar brew its green color. While she filtered the fragments across her taste buds, she thought maybe spirulina or blue-green algae. Reviewing her many conversations with Lilly, she pondered the retired spy's ability to seem totally locked-in to their situation one moment and then appear to have wandered off into her own daydream the next moment. She found the pattern somewhat unsettling. It wasn't long before her contemplations were overwhelmed by a feeling of exhaustion. She guessed she wouldn't be able to stay awake for much longer.

2009 - Still Out West (Mostly)

"So, assuming you're right, what do we do?"

Lilly had a plan. As always.

"First, call your daughter-in-law…tell her her husband's alive."

"Oh god, I don't know. That's not what Clay wanted. I'm not sure we can trust her.... She's already planning on getting remarried…what if you're wrong about the Deschutes Pivot? What if Lola did hire someone to kill Keno?"

Lilly couldn't believe what she was hearing.

God, she thought, *it's everywhere!*

This was one of Lilly's biggest exasperations—women being overly critical of other women. It was hard enough to compete with the old boy network without having other women not giving you the benefit of the doubt.

"Listen, Elizabeth, I think you're wrong about Lola. A few years ago, she took care of my Scout, when she was really struggling…welcomed her into her home like a daughter when I couldn't make any headway with her. And Keno freely admits Lola saved his life before they got married."

Although defensive at first, Elizabeth was carefully considering the younger woman's words.

"That's true, I have heard him say that."

"I think we should trust her. I talked to Trick about this…he agrees with me."

Patrick Bowman occupied a special place in Elizabeth's heart. He had come through again and again for both Paul and Keno, and she had known him since he was in high school, playing football against her son. She trusted Trick's judgment and softened up at the mention of his name.

"You talked to Patrick about this?"

Lilly stared incredulously at Elizabeth. *Again with the over-weighting of men's opinions relative to women's. Maybe it's a generational thing?*

Rather than make it an issue, Lilly just nodded before answering.

"He's been living with Lola for six months, trying to parent the boys and keep the business afloat."

Elizabeth was about to pass out from exhaustion, but with the wedding only a day away, she knew she had to push through these last few yards. There needed to be a decision. She closed her eyes for a minute to clear her head, then reopened them and exhaled audibly.

"Okay," she said, "let's call Lola."

Lilly nodded her head vigorously.

"Great!"

"But first we call Patrick and let him know what we're doing, so he's not caught unawares. Agreed?"

"Agreed. Can I start making the calls now?"

"Yes, please…but I don't think I can participate. I hate to be a terrible hostess, but I think I'll be lucky if I make it to my own bed."

Lilly stood from her chair and gently helped Elizabeth down the hall to her room. Momentarily seeing the world through her new friend's eyes, she hoped someone would be there for her when her time came. After helping the slumping sexagenarian remove her shoes and climb into bed, Lilly spread a crocheted throw over the reclining woman's body. With Elizabeth's peaceful breathing inhabiting the moment, Lilly quietly closed the bedroom door and went back to work.

CHAPTER 44 —

Ithaca Bound

Just when he thought it couldn't get any colder, he did.

With the suddenness of a lunar eclipse, the warm light Calypso had been shining on Keno for three days turned into a red moon, frigid and full of foreboding. Not that he should have been surprised. But the abrupt nature of their decampment left him wondering if he would be riding in the back of the truck, with the kayaks. Or, worse yet, left on the beach to fend for himself, his corpse possibly burdened by the weight of several lead bullets. He considered the possibility that her plan all along was to kill him—that she might be a professional competitor of his brother's, with some sort of twisted, predatory, sexual deviance that she fulfilled by sleeping with her victims.

Not sure about Calypso's general mental state, during the twenty-hour drive north to the border he focused on making himself small—so small that he could hide in the glove box if necessary. He would speak only when spoken to—which was rarely. Even then, he minded his Ps and Qs. Above all else, as they crawled their way through the traffic-clogged towns of San Quintin, Ensenada, and finally, Tijuana, he tried hard not to offend.

As they approached the border, the non-violent nature of her intentions revealed itself. Knowing he didn't have any money or ID, she wasn't willing to try and smuggle him across the border in her rig; so, with only the few words that were necessary, she pulled over at Playas de Tijuana and simply dropped him off. Stepping out of the rig (and onto the curb), he was hit with a flood of emotion. Part of him was happy to be alive…but an equal part had no idea what came next. He tried to acknowledge his state of confliction.

"Calypso, I—"

"Save it, Freddy."

And then, just as suddenly as they had met, she chugged off, body, truck, and cargo headed to San Luis Obispo, where she would drop off the kayaks and then hope to catch some late-summer kitesurfing sessions at Jalama. Freddy Biletnikoff had already been erased from her memory banks.

Watching the desert-covered Bronco fade into the swarming traffic, Keno turned and looked at the packed, late-summer beach. Wisps of accordion music and burning mesquite charcoal wafted above the crowd while vendors plied the mash-up with *bebidas* and *churros*. Couples whispered intimate promises in the soft light of the mist-filtered afternoon sun. Families thronged beside coolers of soda and *taquitos*, mothers scolding children, fathers settling heavily into their Saturday afternoon *cervezas*. Young teenagers played soccer among themselves. A few hundred yards up the coast, at the northern edge of the churning, honey-colored mass, a twelve-foot high series of vertical metal rods and slats ran east-west along the border. It was the westernmost portion of the six-hundred-and-fifty-mile-long wall that started in the Texas desert and abruptly ended after wading about one hundred meters into the Pacific. On the other side of the graffiti-covered barrier slept a broad patch of nearly empty sand, the joyless air above it permeated with the type of fear that inhabits people who have things they want protected. The only noticeable movement on the side of the Free and the Brave came from the solemn, uniformed patrol that kept an eye on the sprawling, brown infestation to the south.

Keno walked the quarter mile north, through the masses, and peered longingly through the thin gaps between the metal slats. Finding the north-south contrast stark, Keno took in the scene with a sense of fascination and concern. After briefly considering his options, he headed back to the sidewalk where Calypso had dropped him off. Nighttime was bearing down, and he had no idea how to find safe harbor in the infamously lawless border town. He had to get into the United States, but he was at a loss as to how to do it. His ragged clothing provided little protection from the elements, and he was worried about the freezing desert nights and hypothermia. The tight, red 49ers T-shirt that Clay had left him was starting to come apart at the seams, and his board shorts were hanging from his hungry, bony hips like a pair of Twiggy-occupied unisex trousers. His swollen, dirty feet had begun overlapping the boundaries of his worn flip-flops in a comedic yet functional response to six months of ambulating with no protection.

While considering his bleak options, a wet nose, lacking in decorum, pressed against his buttocks. He turned away from the beach and towards the intrusion to find an oversized, free-range, pit bull, with nary a wag, interested in his waste-disposal chute.

"Truck!" a voice called. "Come!"

A man similar in size to Keno but a few years older hustled over and attached the end of his leash to the dog's collar then forcefully pulled the brindle away. Without looking too closely at Keno's disassemblage, the stranger spoke up in Spanish.

"*Disculpe, amigo…mi perro es muy joven.*"

Not understanding the *gringo*, Keno, with longish unkempt hair sprouting in all directions from his head, spoke up in English.

"That dog doesn't seem too friendly."

As if to confirm the point, Truck growled and lunged at a pair of passing, yipping Chihuahuas. The man held the striped beast firmly in check with the leash then said:

"That dog isn't even one friendly."

It took a second, but Keno finally smiled at the pun and thought of Lilly.

"A dog named *Truck*, that must get interesting."

"His father was named *Monkey*…that really confused people."

Keno laughed and realized it had been a long time since he had last done so.

Through the unchecked growth on Keno's face, the man recognized a set of healthy teeth and the accent of a fellow American.

"Man…are you okay?"

"Uhhh…not sure yet? I need to get back home to San Francisco, and, well…it's a long story, but I don't have an ID or any money."

The dog owner examined Keno's dirty *gringo* self with a practiced sort of caution. He faced a conundrum. There were battalions of miscreants sliding south from the States, expecting an easier life in Mexico, but who were now spiraling downward at varying speeds to the lower socioeconomic classes. They all had ways of soliciting strangers for money, and most sounded sincere. It was the rare traveler whose story actually warranted sympathy due to circumstances outside of their control. He decided he would keep his wallet in his zippered pocket and instead offer some matter-of-fact advice.

"Are you a strong swimmer?"

"I think so."

"Afraid of sharks?"

"Should I be?"

"Do you play the lottery?"

"Never."

"Why not?"

"I understand math…?"

"Then, no."

Considering the entire conversation a bit odd, Keno wasn't sure what might come next. The dog owner appraised the skinny but strong-looking, sun-blackened derelict, and wondered about the clear eyes peering back at him.

"The fog will roll in in about an hour and the tide will be at a low in two hours. You'll have about three hours of daylight left, and there's no swell to speak of. If you really want to get home, you can almost walk out to the end of that wall at low tide. I'd walk out into the fog from this beach right here, until I was in chest-deep water, swim straight towards Japan for about one hundred yards, past the shore rips, and then hang a right and swim north for an hour or so, along the coast. After that, you should be well inside the U-S-A. Then you hang another right and you'll end up on Imperial Beach."

"That sounds really cold."

"The water's at its warmest right now, about seventy-two degrees… but, yeah, it will be cold."

The man stared at Keno's ribs pushing through the worn cotton and wondered about meth.

"Especially for someone with no insulation." Looking over his shoulder towards the placid Pacific, Keno considered his options.

"What if someone grabs me and asks for ID?"

" 'Someone?' "

"Yeah, like Border Patrol or something."

"You're a US citizen, right?"

"Yeah."

"Tell them you're a triathlete and you were out for a long training swim. Then give them your name and social security number. They can't deport a US citizen on US soil for not having an ID."

Keno considered the plan carefully while eyeing the stranger. He put out his hand.

"I'm Keno…Barton."

The man looked at the dirty hand and extended his elbow like a chicken wing.

"Sorry, I'm contagious, working past a bad flu…Alex Cook."

Keno touched elbows with Alex.

"Thanks for the advice, Alex. Any great ideas on what to do after that?"

"Well, I would go to the closest gas station and beg for someone's cell phone so you can call a friend and get some help. Heck, I'd start doing that right now."

Interrupting the dog owner, Keno asked the obvious.

"Can I borrow your mobile phone?"

Alex laughed at his own setup.

"Ah, would if I could…not carrying…that's probably gonna be a tough ask, given your bedraggled condition, but maybe someone will be charitable. Then I'd find a scrap of cardboard from the station garbage, bum a Sharpie from the attendant, write 'SF' in big block letters, and hope to catch a ride north on the 5."

"Sounds like you've done this before."

"I'm a writer, I have a vivid imagination."

"True that, brother-man."

A Jack Russell paused in front of Truck and started barking courageously at the larger terrier. The pit bull, with the intent of dining on the smaller canine, stretched the leash to its max. Smiling while he struggled with his adopted rescue mutt, Alex started walking away.

"I better move on. Good luck, Keno!"

"Thanks, Alex…I'll look up your books!"

The author threw a thumbs-up over his shoulder while lunging forward and trying to keep Truck from assaulting anyone around him on the sidewalk. It made for a fun fiction, but Alex doubted the troubled drug addict would actually have the courage to try the long swim in the fog.

Gaining energy from a plan that would bring him much closer to Lola and his boys, Keno turned and walked out onto the beach. Hopefully, he started using his eyes to sift through the sand. Eventually he found what he was looking for, and he used the old piece of twine to tie his sandals around his waist, secure against the small of his back. Then he sat down near the waterline and watched as the tide and fog began to trade places.

CHAPTER 45 —

Church on Time (or, Break Their Hearts and Have No Mercy)

Lola was jumpier than an NBA player juiced on Flubber. She was getting married in a little more than twenty-four hours, and her just-retrieved wedding dress didn't fit correctly. Fortunately her friend had been available, and *she* happened to have been a trained seamstress in a previous life.

"Hold still or I'm gonna end up sticking you!"

Elise was trying to give instruction through a mouthful of pins but her subject kept shifting her weight.

"Elise, I'm trying, it's just these heels are killing me!"

"I hope I don't screw this up, it's been decades since I did this."

"I don't know how to thank you. Name your price. Anything. You're a lifesaver."

Elise was confused. She needed to take in the waist while letting out the bust.

"Didn't this dress fit pretty well when we picked it out at the store? What's going on with you? Your waist is a few inches smaller and your boobs are a cup size bigger?"

Lola answered in exasperation.

"It's these new birth control pills. My boobs are growing like I'm pregnant!"

Elise was incredulous.

"You still need birth control?"

"I stopped after Keno disappeared, but I had to…start again…with…things."

Gus and Sam were both in the bedroom, trying to close their ears. The eldest, Sam, was more antsy than his mom.

"Do we have to be here for this?"

Lola snapped back with an insistent tone.

"Yes, I need to talk to you both about tomorrow's ceremony."

Elise grabbed a handful of material at the small of Lola's back.

"Holy feces, Lola! When was the last time you ate anything? You're all ribs."

"I know, I know, I'm trying, but I can't keep anything down…I'm too nervous."

Lola's phone awoke with Billy Idol singing *White Wedding*. Sam had downloaded the ringtone to Lola's Blackberry as a joke, and Lola didn't know how to remove it.

"Gus, my phone, on my bedside table…please get it and tell me who it is."

"Jesus mom, Elise is right there, she can do it."

Elise was used to inert teenagers. She spat the pins into her palm.

"Lazy is as lazy doesn't. Don't trouble yourself, Mr. Big Shot, I'm not doing anything important…I'll get it."

She put down the pins, picked up the phone and looked at the incoming number.

"It's a SoCal number…6-1-9 area code. Your address book doesn't recognize it."

Lola was at her wit's end.

"Another effin' robocaller? I am *so* fed up! I must be getting two dozen calls a day from those scammers!"

Elise nodded in agreement.

"Right? Me too!"

"And the numbers keep changing!"

Sputtering with frustration, Lola needed to share.

"If I don't recognize the number, I don't even pick them up anymore. It just lets them know you're a real person. If they leave a message I immediately erase it before it infects my phone."

Gus and Sam looked at each other and rolled their eyes. Elise eyed the singing phone with suspicion.

"That can happen?"

The last thing Lola wanted at this juncture was more interruptions.

"I don't know, but why take any chances? *Don't* answer it!"

Impatient with the older luddites, the boys again made a bid to exit.

"Mom! Can we go? We've got stuff to do."

Realizing she was losing them, Lola reprioritized.

"Elise, can you give us just a few minutes?"

Elise had been spending so much time over at the Bartons's she felt like a family member.

"Lola, we need to get this done. I have a life too, and this will probably take a few hours to get right."

Grateful but forced to choose, Lola smiled knowingly at her friend and took the mile.

"C'mon, Elise, we all know you don't have a life."

The boys barely stifled a laugh. Elise realized she'd been publicly outed.

"Wow, you give someone an inch! Five minutes. I'll be next door in Gus's bedroom trying not to stick to anything."

After Elise closed the door, Lola turned to the two boys.

"I know this is all happening too fast, but I could really use some help here."

Both boys looked at their untied high-tops. After a few seconds pause, Gus got up the courage to start with the debate they'd been having ever since Lola announced the engagement.

"But Mom, we don't even know this guy!"

Sam piled on.

"Dude's a total poser! I can't believe you're already giving up on Dad."

Back to Gus:

"A total loser. Have you seen him play baseball? He literally throws like a girl!"

Not knowing how to defend against the ghost of Keno, Lola started with the easiest topic.

"C'mon guys, at least give him a chance. I told you, he grew up in Argentina. They don't play baseball and football there, he grew up playing soccer."

The young men continued to avoid their mother's gaze while slouching in a pool of recalcitrance. After a few more moments of pleading from their mom, Sam finally spoke up.

"I don't see why we have to go to this wedding thing anyway. This guy's never gonna be our dad. In another few months I'll be outta here."

The nuclear option had become a frequently used weapon by Sam, but its regular unveiling didn't make it any less unsettling to Lola.

"C'mon, Sam, I know this is hard, but I'll always be your mom and this will always be your home."

Gus looked at her defiantly.

"And I'll be right behind him."

Lola stared at Gus dejectedly. *Great! Now it's contagious…they're both leaving home.*

"I looked it up. I can leave high school when I'm sixteen, and I can be my own legal guardian."

Feeling cornered, Lola didn't know where to go. Elise's voice came from outside the door.

"Time's up, I'm comin' in!"

"Just a sec!"

Lola looked up at her two nearly grown babies.

"Please, boys, be at Old Saint Hilary's tomorrow by six P.M. Wear your nice clothes. Slacks, blazers, and a tie. Trick will be leaving from here at four-thirty, and he expects to give you a ride."

"Uncle Trick's going?"

"Yes…please don't make it hard on him. The traffic out to Tiburon on a Sunday afternoon will be horrendous."

Both obstinate boys continued their well-practiced looks of non-compliance.

In a flash, like the tongue of a tree frog, Lola flicked out her right hand to grab Samuel's left ear and her left hand to grab Augustus's right ear.

"Hey! Ouch! What the fu—?"

The anger in her eyes screamed her question.

"Promise me?"

"You're hurting us!" Gus complained.

"Promise…?"

"Okay, okay, we'll be there!"

Satisfied that she had their word, and not remorseful at all about having to resort to corporal coercion, she released their ears.

"Okay, you two are free to go." She turned to the closed door and yelled, "ELISE, YOU CAN COME IN NOW!"

But before Elise could come in, the boys rudely rushed out, bumping her on the way.

"Sorry, Ms. Haversham!" Gus apologized.

Sam confirmed his brother's attempt at contrition. "Yeah, excuse us!"

Looking at the overgrown boys with disapproval, Elise finally made her way back into the bedroom.

"I can't wait until life gives those two a swift kick in the fanny. What was that all about?"

"Really, Elise?" Lola stared at her friend intently. "You don't think losing their dad was enough of a kick?"

"Oh, jeez, Lola," Elise immediately replied, understanding her mistake, "you're right, I'm sorry…it's just, you know, life goes on, right? They may not realize it, but what you're doing tomorrow is a good thing for them. Some day they'll look back at the sacrifices you made for their education and be grateful."

Lola wasn't sure if she should even tell Elise about her kids' intention to abandon their education.

"Yeah, about all that…I'm struggling a little with…"

With an insistent rebel yell, Billy Idol once again interrupted the tranquility of Lola's bedroom. Elise was the closest, so she picked up and looked at the phone before reporting back to the bride.

"Lilly Stein?"

"Um…Really? Lilly Stein? I should take that."

With raised eyebrows, Elise handed over the rockin' Blackberry. Lola pressed the appropriate button then placed the device against her head.

"Hi Lilly, how are you?"

"Hi Lola. I'm…we're okay…I'm…with Elizabeth…she's asleep…I've been eating a lot of chocolate cake…um…I'm not really sure how to say this…"

Lola was familiar with Lilly's conversational peculiarities, but today she thought her voice carried an unusual mixture of burden and commitment, as if it were coming from a Gomorrah-based Bible salesman.

Lilly's voice forged ahead in Lola's ear.

" …so I'll just say it. Elizabeth and I just learned that—Keenan is still alive."

Already a mess, Lola's emotional dishevelment took a turn for the worse. *Could it be? Keenan…alive?* She provided the answer to her own question. *YES! Oh, God…please!*

Lilly's claim wasn't new, everyone from Keno's world insisted he was still alive, but the messenger somehow gave the thesis additional heft. It was a running joke in the family that Lilly was unfeelingly analytical. Because of her training, everyone assumed her proclamations were supported not by emotion, but by cold, hard facts. If Lilly Stein said the world was flat you considered selling your sextant. Temporarily losing her breath, Lola was flooded with a jumble of thoughts.

"*What? What'd you say?* Keno…*alive?*"

But there was a part of Lola that had already separated, already buried her husband, and that part was tired of being jerked around. She had her doubts, especially when it came to Keenan's family. She needed evidence.

"You know I'm getting married tomorrow, right?"

Letting go of the silk she was pinching, Elise's attention was captured. She tried to eavesdrop on the tiny, tinny voice coming out of the phone's speaker.

"I know, I know…we called as soon as we could."

Lola pressed her case. "Are you sure? Where *is* he?"

"We're pretty sure…but…Clay seems to have"—*how to explain it?*—"misplaced him."

The mention of Keno's mythical brother fueled suspicions that were amplified by the obvious understatement.

"*Clay?*" Lola exclaimed. "What are you talking about?"

Knowing this was going to be the hard part, Lilly chose her words delicately.

"Well…it seems Clay uncovered a plot to kill Keno, and in an effort to trick the murder-for-hire people, he staged a fake accident and death…in Baja."

There was a long silence as Lola tried to work through the words she was being fed.

Lilly became uncomfortable. At this point she just wanted to stop the wedding and get Keno safely reunited with his family. After that, if the opportunity presented itself, she could share her theory on the

Deschutes Pivot. She knew she needed to try and build some trust.

"Elizabeth and I didn't know anything about it, I promise, we're just getting involved…last minute…to try and help."

"Is this some sort of a sick joke? Did Aloysius put you up to this?"

"No! I know it sounds crazy…but Clay was trying to hide Keno to buy some time to find the killer."

Putting together all the pieces of the unlikely narrative—on the eve of her marriage to Wolfgang—required more focus than Lola could assemble at the moment. But there was one question that beat all the others to the surface.

"Did Clay run this supposed operation alone? Who else knew about this?"

Not good at lying, even in instances where she would likely be linked to a regrettable activity over which she had no control, Lilly reluctantly told the truth and prepared for the blowback.

"Well, it appears that Clay hatched the plan and then got the boys involved but swore them to secrecy."

"The boys? Samuel and Augustus?"

Lilly cringed in anticipation of the detonation.

"No. I'm sorry. Aloysius and Patrick."

Two thoughts hit Lola's mind simultaneously. One, the story was too crazy to be fiction; and two, she was going to have a very serious conversation with Trick…and her insane father-in-law, Aloysius. She was very close to having a nervous breakdown.

"And, why did this brain trust neglect to inform Keno's wife of this supposed lifesaving deception? You remember his WIFE? The person closest to the supposed VICTIM? The person who has been ripping her hair out by the roots trying to pick up the pieces and maintain a family in the aftermath of this TOTALLY UNNECESSARY, RIDICULOUSLY FUCKIN' IDIOTIC PLAN! WHY THE FUCK DID YOU IDIOTS THINK ANYONE WOULD EVER WANT TO KILL KEENAN BARTON!"

It was at this point, descended about halfway down the razor blade towards the pool of alcohol, that Lilly wondered why she was involved at all in this mess. *God, it's true*, she thought, *that old saying about good deeds and punishment…. First, I save the youngest Barton, but that effort ruins my only child; and now I'm trying to save the other two…and I'm getting reamed a new one. What the fuck?*

She supposed her figuratively spilt blood was her reward for being the only adult in the room; recognizing that something had to be done and that no one else seemed willing to do it. Holding the phone a foot away from her head, she decided she'd had enough.

"You know what, Lola? You're way out of line here. I'm just trying to help. You were kind to me when Scout and I needed you, and that's the only reason I'm even involved now…so I don't want to hear any more of your shit. As far as I'm concerned, I've done my job…I don't know why these idiots didn't trust you…infer what you may. Good luck, you're gonna need it."

The line went dead. Lola was fuming but didn't really know what to believe. Naturally, after hearing most of the conversation, Elise had strong views.

"So, I only heard some of it. What's happening?"

Slowly playing the words again in her head, the sentences were getting jumbled in a stew of anger and confusion.

"Oh god, Elise, I am such a mess! I don't know what to do or who to believe."

"What is going on?"

"They say Keno is alive…that they faked his death because somebody put a contract out on him. But they don't know where he is, except somewhere in Baja."

"WHAT?" Elise's disbelief was full-bore. "That's insane! Who would want to kill Keno? *What the eff!* What sort of family even comes up with stuff like this anyway?"

"They said his crazy Special Forces brother is involved. Clay. That he came up with the plan to protect him."

"And no one bothered to tell his wife or kids? For six months? Who does that?"

"Right?" Lola shook her head with anger and incredulity. "That's what I said."

A light bulb went off in Elise's head.

"Oh my God, Lola! I don't believe it! You know what this means?"

"I'm too wrecked to think. Just tell me?"

"Well, one of two things. First, the whole thing is a ridiculous story, which in and of itself is reprehensible, and implies a family-wide conspiracy to treat you like a child. The second option is that the story is true, and the only reason they didn't include you in the whole fake death thing is that they think *YOU* hired the killer! They don't trust *YOU!*"

As Lola wrapped her head around the logic, she realized it was true. She was stunned, speechless. Elise was quick to push her agenda.

"My God, Lola, this is a total effin' gift! Whatever doubts you had before about leaving that nutcase family should now be totally obliterated. I say you run! Run away as fast as you can! You're lucky to have such a viable option as Wolfgang. Most women don't."

"Oh God, I don't know…what if Keno really is alive? What if he's trying to get back to us right now? He's the father of my boys? I know he loves me…he loves *us,* he said the words…"

There was love in her heart but doubt in her sentences. The wavering allowed Elise Haversham to hone in on the latter.

"Lola, you have to take care of yourself and your boys first. The whole thing with these people is…preposterous. They didn't even have the decency to let you in on their little scheme… *if* there ever even was a scheme! For all you know this is just their last-ditch attempt to keep you from taking your babies and moving on from your dead husband. They keep insisting Keno is alive…but where is he? And, even if the whole story is true, they didn't trust you enough to tell you! They actually thought you tried to have your husband killed! And Keno went along with it!"

At this point, Lola's head was spinning, but Elise knew she had her attention. The older woman lowered her voice to a mercenary whisper.

"Lola, you owe them nothing. There is no love in war. Protect yourself…break their hearts and have no mercy."

CHAPTER 46 —

T and HGH

Aloysius stared at the hex bar with a passionate ambition that belied his predilection for sloth. At seventy-two years of age he knew the effort would be difficult, but he sallied forth just the same. Gathering the necessary energy, he stepped his cadaverous legs into position, gripped the steel bar with chalk-covered hands, and prepared to dead lift the plates of iron. Out past his sides, in bilateral symmetry, hung metal disks of forty-five pounds, which, in conjunction with the weight of the bar, totaled one hundred and thirty-five pounds. Inhaling and exhaling three times in rapid succession, he sucked in the fourth breath, locked his diaphragm firmly against his body cavity to gain stability, and started slowly pushing up through his heels until his long arms were fully extended and his legs began to straighten at the knees. With his foaming effort, the veins in his neck started bulging like those of an engorged penis. A rumble started percolating from deep within his pelvic area, and as he pressed to move the weight up and off the hard rubber floor, a sound that fell somewhere between a groan and a roar burst forth from his straining assemblage. His gaze was focused upward, to the heavens, for spinal integrity and divine invigoration. Standing to Aloysius' right was Sylvester Wright, the mentally fluctuating masseuse from Desert Lilly's.

"C'mon Ally-Baby, you got this!"

Almost a decade earlier, both men had found themselves of an age that dictated a dramatic slide in the level of confidence-boosting hormones. It wasn't that the Grim Reaper had them reeled in, it was more that the faint waft of his cologne was infrequently visiting their periphery. Aloysius recognized that this was a time in his life when a man had to choose to either, (1) keep raging with vigor against the dying of the light, or (2) succumb to the incoming tide of the good night's gentle going. Sylvester had chosen the former, pushing back at the encroaching inevitable with a variety of strategies that included powerlifting. It was this notable defiance that had initially caught Aloysius' attention; that and the masseuse's reputation as a capable woodsmen—a man who could bring the timber when the opportunity presented itself. Unfortunately, in Aloysius' case, when it came to the timely delivery of lumber, he had been underperforming. In a moment of exasperation and weakness, he had asked Sly for his trade secrets. Expecting a pharmaceutical tip, Sly surprised him by proselytizing about the benefits of the bench press, squat, and, especially, "the king of them all," the dead lift. The pitch had included a promise that the workouts would naturally boost Aloysius's levels of testosterone and human growth hormone, as well as strengthen the posterior chain. Until that moment Aloysius wasn't aware he *had* a posterior chain. Just the same, after listening to Sly's testimony, he was certain his was due for an upgrade. Thus was his venture into the world of the dead lift begun.

Gritting his teeth under the strain, Aloysius crawled the weight up the front of his shins inch by inch, while Sylvester urged him on with the traditional emasculations.

"C'mon, you fuckin' pussy…don't quit now…do it for Lilly."

During their initial collaboration, many years previous, Sylvester had started their workouts slowly, making sure Aloysius managed the lifts with good form. Several years before meeting Sylvester, and with Lilly's help, the then sexagenarian (Aloysius) had pulled himself from the pit of despair and into the indulgences of inherited wealth. This accomplishment allowed him to embrace any new physical endeavor with a momentum and fervor that often accompanies a previous success. As advertised, the powerlifting boosted Aloysius' masculinity in a variety of ways, and he stuck with Sly and the libido-enhancing strategy religiously during the first few years.

Over time, as is often the case, his commitment to prioritizing the little things that made him a better romantic partner became less pronounced, and he started missing some of his sessions with Sylvester. He rationalized that the workouts were difficult and time-consuming, and that he had too many other more important engagements. Simply put, like many before him, he weighed heavily the task and lightly the benefit. In didn't help that he believed his and Lilly's lives were already inseparably entwined, and so the daily requirement to win her affections was less intense. Eventually, the dead-lifting, along with several other regular, small considerations, fell by the wayside, and, likewise, his hard-fought timber enhancement slipped flaccidly from his (and her) grasp.

His now septuagenarian grip weakening under the burden, Aloysius had nearly reached a fully erect position. Only a few more inches and his legs, like his arms, would be fully extended, the weight wholly supported by the mass of muscles that extended dorsally from his neck down to his ankles. With the summit within reach, Sylvester was not going to let him stop.

"Do not fuckin' QUIT! I repeat, do not fuckin' QUIT, YOU FOSSILIZED PIECE OF SHIT!"

In the timeless pattern of flooding and ebbing, Lilly had eventually become dissatisfied with the slumping efforts of Aloysius and set off for greener pastures. In her wake she left a forsaken cuckold who was left to contemplate his shortcomings and try to resurrect the man that Lilly had originally found compelling. This was the preoccupation that had pushed Aloysius back to Sylvester, the weight room, and the fountain of youth he knew as the ironically named "dead lift."

Just when he was certain he couldn't squeeze another micron of elevation from his overly exerted body, he reached lock out—full extension—with the bar stretching perpendicular to his legs at midthigh. He ended with a slight arch in his back, his grimace of exultation still directed at the gods.

"Holy shit, Ally-Baby, you did it! One hundred and thirty-five pounds! Now careful, let it down under control…use your legs, not your back."

This was only his second session since the Blundergusting lunch, but Aloysius was already making progress. His brain was bursting with self-congratulation as he rested the barbell back on the floor with only a minimal bounce. He hadn't had a touch of alcohol since the beer and margaritas at Tres Hijas, and he was now on a steady lifting program. Sylvester continued with the embarrassing enthusiasms as Aloysius walked over to grab his water bottle. As he tilted the mouthpiece of the metal canteen back into his lips, he began thinking about all the ways he was going to impress Lilly upon her return. Before he had completed the list, a vibrating ring interrupted his mental rehearsal and informed him he had forgotten to silence his phone. Sylvester immediately turned off the compliments and channeled his solemn drill sergeant.

"Hey man, you know the rules. You turn that shit off before you work out with me."

Hoping he wouldn't draw more fire, Aloysius casually returned his canteen to inside his bag, glancing at his phone during the process in hopes that it was Lilly.

Unknown number! He swore inwardly. *Fuck, another telemarketer!*

Disgusted, he picked up the device, turned off the power, and then returned to Sylvester to complete the remainder of his work out. He wondered when Lilly would fly back to Carefree. He hoped she would call first, so he could bring in some fresh flowers and get their place spruced up.

Sylvester looked at him with impatience.

"*Listo?*"

Nodding in return, Aloysius inhaled a deep lungful of commitment while getting his mind right.

"*Listo!*"

CHAPTER 47 —

Castaway

Keno was so hungry he could hide behind a straw. His clothes were hanging from him, wet and limp like wash on the line. The two-mile swim had chilled his lips to a color somewhere between bruise and blueberry. Twilight had brought a cooling to the air and goose bumps to his skin. The elation that had accompanied his unmolested entry into the country had already faded. It was becoming apparent he wouldn't be welcomed as a native son without the appropriate trappings. He had had to beg nearly forty people for access to their phones before making four outgoing calls. In that handful of instances, the distrustful owners insisted on maintaining possession of their devices, guardedly placing their mobile phones on speaker mode while dialing the numbers that Keno dictated. The only numbers he could remember where those of Lola and Aloysius…and neither were picking up. Keno urgently shouted a few syllables into voice mail before the somewhat Good Samaritans would be scared away by the frenzied, crazy man shouting gibberish from the tight confines of his tattered, scarlet 49ers T-shirt. The two brown attendants at the Arco AM/PM would occasionally try to shoo him away, but the burden of simultaneously manning the pumps and the cash register inside the store kept the young men occupied. It was at these moments—times of maximum commercial distraction—that Keno would swoop in from his sunny, curbside perch, like a pestering seagull, and solicit the refueling motorists.

Eventually the golden orb of the sun moved below the horizon and the temperature started to drop. Keno's moist clothes in combination with the rapidly cooling air triggered an evaporative cooling effect, which in turn effected diuresis…which meant he had to pee. Waiting for a sufficiently busy moment, Keno flip-flopped inside the building and headed directly to the restrooms. The attentive Sikh manning the cash register spotted him as he was approaching the men's room door.

"Hey! Bathrooms are for customers only!"

Knowing his nemesis couldn't leave the cash register unmanned, Keno accelerated his pace while tossing some defiant words back over his shoulder.

"I am a customer!"

And under his breath:

"Just not right now."

Immediately after entering the restroom, Keno turned and locked the door. The vision of a hot air hand dryer sent his freezing brain into a state of jubilation. But he needed to pee now, so he waded the rubber sandals through a small puddle on his way to the urinal. The sound of his evicted urine blasting into the porcelain receptacle brought comfort as he positively assessed the health of his contracting bladder and urethra. He let a small groan slip from his warming lips. The smell of his steaming pee arrived at the same time as the sound of an eruptive release of intestinal gas from the single stall on his left. He realized he wasn't alone. Stopping in midstream, he wondered about the person seated next door. The loud sound of solid plopping into liquid briefly turned his stomach but also allowed him the moral high ground when it came to embarrassing public bathroom sounds. Recommencing the bladder squeezing, he soon had his liquid outflow waltzing off of the white puck of mothball material with a practiced rhythm. The dark yellow color of his piss reminded him that he needed to hydrate. When he finished, he gave his trusty unit a brief shake then tucked him back into his already moist board shorts. As a nod to his upbringing, he briefly ran his soiled hands under the sink faucet, and then he happily embraced the chrome-plated hand dryer attached to the wall on the right of the sink. He pulled his shirt up to his chin then turned the swivel mouth and pressed his chest close against the dryer. The hard, hot air blew across his soft, cold skin.

After three minutes, Keno's body stopped shivering. Concurrently, the bathroom stall door opened, and out walked an indrawn, bespectacled, Hispanic man of indeterminate age. Keno made eye contact and offered a greeting.

"Hola, amigo."

The mustachioed man was a local cardiovascular surgeon at UCSD whose family was waiting for him outside in their Lexus RX. Looking at Keno with concern, he wasn't sure if he could approach the sink.

"Hello…ummm, are you okay?"

Realizing the ridiculous sight he must be offering, Keno separated himself from the metal dryer.

"Yeah, man, I'm sorry," he said, quickly pulling down his shirt. "You must think I'm crazy."

"Not at all . . . was just hoping to wash my hands."

"Oh yeah, of course, let me get out of your way."

Keno looked at the hot blower fondly as he backed away from the sink. The surgeon nodded in passing and started pressing the release knob under the soap dispenser. Feeling the need to explain, Keno started mumbling.

"I was just out doing a big training swim, getting ready for an upcoming triathlon, and…well…I got really cold."

"I see."

From the other side of the door came a voice that was joined by a fist, pounding on the metal.

"Hey! What are you doing in there! Unlock this door!"

With upraised eyebrows, the surgeon looked questioningly into the pleading eyes of the skinny homeless man that was Keno.

"And I lost my wallet…I need to get to San Francisco."

"You swam from San Francisco without a wallet?"

"No…I…ummm…I'm just trying to get home to my family in Marin County."

The doctor didn't like to give money to the homeless. His residency rotations had taught him that most homeless were suffering from mental health and substance abuse problems; they needed to get off the streets and into public assistance programs. That said, his parents had entered the country illegally from Jalisco state when they were barely adolescents. Arriving in San Diego penniless and without any English language skills, they had depended extensively upon the kindness of strangers. The surgeon examined the intelligent face behind the beard before pulling out his wallet.

Who am I to judge? he thought.

"How much do you need?"

"Twenty bucks?"

He handed a twenty to Keno, along with a closed-lip smile, then put away his wallet. After taking the offered bill with a shaking hand, Keno tucked it into the wax comb pocket of his board shorts. He couldn't believe his sudden change in luck.

"Thank you, thank you...so much!"

He wanted to hug the man, but he also didn't want to leave any charity untapped.

"Any way I can get a ride to the freeway and use your phone?"

Considering his family waiting outside and the voice on the other side of the door, the doctor made a quick decision.

"Don't push your luck."

The door started booming again.

"Hey! I'm gonna call the cops! Open the door! Now!"

The surgeon turned to open the door but quickly pivoted back to Keno. He recalled something that might be able to further help the castaway.

"Hey, do you know about the Mexican Underground Railroad?"

"What?"

"Yeah, it's not a set thing, but...if you're really trying to get to the Bay Area...I've seen people getting picked up a half block away from here...between the Western Union and the church on Twelfth Street... right across Palm."

"What is it?"

"It's like Uber for immigrants. People who feel bad for illegals come and help transport them around the state after they make it across the border."

"And it's free? And legal? I can use it?"

The Mexican-American shrugged before turning and grabbing the doorknob.

"What've you got to lose?"

The four watchful eyes of the two station attendants were bearing down on Keno. Despite their intent to hurry him, he couldn't make up his mind. He searched down the mini-mart aisles trying to optimize three variables: calorie max, cost min, and something that wouldn't immediately fuck him up. He had already decided that the Big Gulp would likely provide his body with the lowest-priced energy, but he was worried about the roller-coaster effect he would receive from dumping all that sugar and caffeine into his unbesmirched bloodstream. He finally made up his mind, dragging himself away from the Reese's section and back to the refrigerators. He grabbed a quart of whole milk, a box of Ritz crackers, a big bag of trail mix, a bean-and-cheese burrito (that seemed to have been made locally), and then, after agonizing over the Red Vines, reluctantly added an apple to his haul. Triumphantly ponying up to the counter, he laid down his treasure and pulled out his money. Just as the suspicious attendant began tallying his purchase, Keno grabbed a strategically placed Snickers Peanut Butter bar and added it to the goodies. It was a reward he allowed himself for successfully swimming from Tijuana. The whole bundle, after tax, cost a little more than ten bucks, and he walked out of the gas station with some provisions and $9.13 in change. Not able to wait, he opened the milk carton and drank half of the contents before reaching Palm Avenue.

The VW Microbus pulled up, and an aging, bearded passenger looked at Keno's sign. He had inherited a piece of "SF"-emblazoned cardboard from a Honduran couple with a young boy. The impoverished family had been positioned in front of Keno and were headed up to the San Francisco Bay Area. A close relative had jobs for them in a downtown SF restaurant. In addition there were beds awaiting them in a crowded but safe house in Hunter's Point. Back home, in Central America, there was no work, and roving gangs of armed thugs made any sort of entrepreneurial small business activity impossible. The small, underdressed child had a cleft palate and had been crying in the cold. His dirty, blue Nike T-shirt hung down, like a dress, to his knees. It wasn't easy given his recent food insecurities, but Keno had shared some of his trail mix with him (the boy mostly liked the M&Ms). It was a Saturday night, and the exhausted immigrant family had traveled over two thousand miles, mostly on foot, to get to this spot in San Diego. When it was their turn, the young trio had been picked up by an earnest-looking La Jolla entertainment lawyer driving a Prius. The little boy waved good-bye to Keno from the back window.

About an hour earlier, as suggested by the doctor (and immediately following his gas station departure), Keno had arrived at the sidewalk in front of the Pentecostal church. He had been last in a long line of about two dozen respectful *mestizos*, but he had his dinner to keep him busy, and things were moving along briskly. Not able to speak Spanish outside of a few words, he couldn't ask the weary travelers how they knew about this place or what the rules of engagement were. Watching nervously for the first ten minutes, he presumed the whole arrangement was accomplished by word of mouth. Soon he was near the front of the self-governing queue, and after the Hondurans got picked up he was the next to go. He wondered what was going on with the occupants of the VW, as they seemed to be engaged in an animated conversation but hadn't spoken to him since rolling up to the curb. Most of their words made it out the window to Keno's ears, but there were a few gaps.

"But Bernie, man…not a Mexican…"

"Jerry…stupid…look at him… one of us."

"But…supposed to help…immigrants, man, not hippies… homeless."

"Dude...c'mon man...compassion...all colors."

Finally the passenger, Jerry, poked his huge, leonine head out of the window.

"Hey man," he called, "where ya headed?"

Looking down, Keno saw the lettering on his sign was facing his stomach. He turned the cardboard around while answering hopefully.

"San Fran?"

Jerry reached out the window and yanked on the handle of the sliding rear door. The portal opened with a *whoosh*, and the innards of the paisley-lined retro-van were revealed to the night.

"Climb in, man!"

Clutching the brown paper bag that housed his provisions, Keno hopped directly into the time machine and its enveloping smell of *patchouli* and weed. He made a quarter turn and pointed his rear end in the direction of the unrefurbished bench seat while pushing the door shut. Bernie, the driver, manually shifted the transmission into first. All four cylinders coughed into action, turning the internal gears and axles... which in turn compelled the vehicle to start humming like a well-oiled sewing machine as it pulled away from the curb.

Jerry turned from his seat and laughingly threw two bungee cords into Keno's lap just as the new passenger had started searching for his seat belt.

"Hey, man, safety first!"

The two old men, who reminded Keno of Cheech & Chong headed to a Grateful Dead concert, both started giggling at the apparently oft-repeated joke. A few minutes later, as Keno was still struggling with the bungee cords, his initial impressions were confirmed: Bernie hollered at the extensive electronics flashing from the dashboard.

"Play the Dead, *Make Believe Ballroom*, shuffle!"

In a flash, the voice recognition software had Jerry Garcia singing "Sugaree" from an epically well-hidden troop of speakers. Unharnessed, Keno leaned back into his vinyl seat and watched old merge seamlessly with new as the VW clambered up the on-ramp for northbound Interstate 5. In less than five minutes the retired triathlete was fast asleep.

CHAPTER 48 —

Cold Feet

Strapped into the indulgence of his first class window seat on the United connection from Houston to SFO, Wolfgang harbored a bundle of nervous energy that needed to be unmoored with a few cocktails. A soft *ding!* signaled the Boeing 737 had just passed through the ten-thousand-foot level. The flight attendants were now fair game.

"Excuse me…Debbie, is it?"

"Debbie" was a thirty-five-year-old native of Galveston, an experienced pro who brought her "A" game to each flight. A pile of platinum hair levitated above her scalp like a zero gravity Cousin Itt. She hadn't spent much time putting herself together that morning, but it was nearly eight P.M. and her makeup was now meticulous.

"Yes, Mr. Dalman…what can we do for y'all?"

"Is it too late for a Bloody Mary?"

"Not at all, sir. I'll get that to y'all in a jiff."

The Galvestonian turned to Wolfgang's seatmate, who had been trying to make eye contact.

"Yes, Dr. Mason, can we get y'all something too?"

"Can you make that two Bloody Marys?"

2009 - Still Out West (Mostly)

With the first two fingers on his right hand extended like a peace sign, the doctor then turned to Wolfgang on his left, and gave him a smile.

"That sounded good. Mind if I join you?"

Wolfgang, volleying the doctor's shot with a weak smile, wasn't sure he wanted to open the door for a potentially chatty neighbor from the "Space City"—especially on a four-hour-and-twenty-minute flight.

"Cheers."

Quickly breaking eye contact, he pulled out a device he regularly kept on his flying personage to ward off unwanted intrusions. The doctor spotted the book.

"*The Hunger Games*? My youngest daughter is reading that!"

Feeling that the comment called into question his masculinity, Wolfgang again forced the cool smile, allowing little eye contact.

"Splendid, I'm sure."

Not one to misread social cues, Dr. Mason made a mental note to ignore his standoffish neighbor for the remainder of the flight. As Debbie hustled to gather the drinks, the head doctor returned to his Sudoku app. He was having a particularly difficult time solving a box in which only two numbers had been provided as clues. He spent the next five minutes unsuccessfully working through the permutations while agonizing over whether or not he should burn his one free guess.

From the aisle, Debbie—drinks in hand—interrupted his train of thought as she leaned in over his chest.

"Excuse me, has anyone ever told y'all you look like Rafael Nadal?"

Looking up, the doctor realized the question was addressed to the impolite window seat on his left.

Like a ravenous dog focused on an incoming bone, Wolfgang needed to not disrupt the delivery of vodka to his unsoothed brain. Summoning a patronizing smile, he reached across the seat divider to relieve the server of her tomato-and-ice-infused burden.

"All the time."

Dr. Mason, a tennis *aficionado*, resented the intrusion and the flirting.

Yeah, he quipped to himself, *like an older, malnourished Rafa… and even then, it's still a stretch.*

He decided it was important that he register his disagreement.

"Really?" he said. "I don't see it."

Securing a landing pad for the second Bloody Mary, the flight attendant placed a napkin—and then the drink—on the tray in front of the doctor. She ignored his contentious comment.

"Thank you, Debbie."

"*De nada,* Dr. Mason."

It wasn't long before the alcohol started to do its thing, which allowed Wolfgang to feel more charitable towards the world in general and the well-fed man on his right in particular. As he leaned back and watched the clouds pass by their fragile, aluminum-skinned tube, a small smile formed at the corners of his mouth.

With the vessel gliding at thirty-five thousand feet, the internal cabin pressure had dropped significantly since the plane had been boarded. The internal gases in the passengers's bodies responded to this imbalance by racing towards escape valves. The middle ear and sinuses were the most immediate pathways, but soon the collective sphincters of the more considerate passengers were squeezing back against the forces of reduced gravity. Wolfgang, not one to be particularly thoughtful when it came to others, subtly shifted his weight to his right buttocks and let fly through his silk undies and beige linen trousers. He hoped that it wouldn't be too ripe, but if it was he figured the silent release would be too difficult to ascribe to any one passenger in such tight quarters.

"So you're a doctor?" he said.

Dr. Mason was having his own problems internally. But he had been too well raised to gas the whole plane, let alone ignore a polite question from another nearby human. Besides, Wolfgang's inquiry would give the MD a chance to brandish his credentials, thereby putting the arrogant prick in his place. He decided he would start by dallying the fly lightly on the water's surface.

"Yes, I am," he answered modestly.

Wolfgang leaned in attentively.

"Do you mind if I ask your specialty?"

Wanting to answer "no," which would be in strict compliance with the word choice of the question, Dr. Mason instead decided to move things along.

"I'm a psychiatrist."

"Interesting."

Wolfgang turned away from the doctor, towards the window, implying that it wasn't. Dr. Mason started worrying that he hadn't made the bait sweet enough and now wouldn't be able to reveal his professional superiority. His intestinal gas ramped up its case for early release... he considered it a secondary option if he couldn't soon unleash his curriculum vitae. Just before his malodorous inmate made bail, the doctor's non-Rafaesque seatmate turned away from the window with a comment.

"I'm getting married tomorrow."

Dr. Mason thought that a strange introduction, but responded with a benign pleasantry.

"Well, now, that's news. Congratulations."

"I was married once before, it didn't work out so well."

"Me too," the doctor said. "It happens."

"You're a shrink?"

"Head of the psychiatry department at Stanford University."

There, he got it out. He felt better already.

Wolfgang reached up and opened the air vent above his seat.

"That's impressive. Do you still see patients?"

"Only when I fly first class."

The doctor's smile showed he was kidding. Wolfgang swallowed the remainder of the contents of his plastic cup after a polite guffaw. An unpleasant odor drifted through the air, but he wasn't sure if it was coming from him or the galley.

"Do you mind me asking...? I'm a little unsure about the whole thing at this point..."

Taking the pause as a chance to display his wisdom, the doctor cut in.

"Well, I can tell you it's not unusual to have doubts right before you pledge yourself to another human being for the remainder of your life."

The provocative statement served its intended purpose.

"Well, when you say it like that..."

Feeling at home as the solicited source of knowledge, the doctor considered his liability and again interrupted with his best patronizing smile.

"Some doubts are normal, but if your concerns are incapacitating, you might need more time to think about your level of commitment. It might make sense for you to seek the help of a mental health professional... although it sounds like time is of the essence in your situation?"

Wondering if he should waste his breath further discussing his worries, the alcohol decided the matter for Wolfgang.

"This girl, er...woman...my fiancée...I would've killed to win her a month ago, but now...now that she's said 'yes,' well, the treasure has lost some of its luster."

Nodding his head in a knowing way, the doctor let his advisee know he wasn't alone. He delivered his next line with theatrical precision.

"Ah! It seems many of us only want that which is out of our grasp."

Knowing the explanation made him sound immature, Wolfgang decided to cut to the chase.

"You were married before, are you're married now?"

"Yes, a new wife, new kids, a new life."

"Is it better?"

"Men and women—"

Pausing to gather his thoughts, the psychiatrist wasn't sure where to go from there.

"—I think there's always going to be some polite tension... like positively and negatively charged ions...they attract *and* repel... depending on the context...That's what makes it electric...sexual even... the challenge is how one manages the differences. That's kind of the beauty of it all—it's constantly evolving."

"Okay, but is it better...are you glad you re-upped?"

Dr. Mason finished the last of his Bloody Mary and set down his cup. It was the exact question he had been pondering for much of the last year. He knew what the answer was for him and most of his patients, but he wasn't sure he wanted to share it with a complete stranger. The university's president had been applying a tremendous amount of pressure on the doctor's entire department to publish and attract more research dollars for the school. In response to these marching orders, Dr. Mason had been working longer hours, traveling more, eating and drinking like John Blutarsky. The whole situation had been taking a toll on his home life. His wife was constantly nagging him to be more attentive, and he would fire back with a demand for more understanding, given his professional responsibilities. In direct defiance of his dentist's orders, he crushed an ice cube between his molars and let his warm saliva melt the shards before swallowing.

"Honestly? Is one better than the other? I think, for most, you just exchange one set of problems for another."

Wolfgang felt his throat tighten.

"That's not what I wanted to hear."

Dr. Mason shrugged. It wasn't his job to make people happy. Debbie's blond coiffured mountain appeared in the aisle just over his shoulder.

"Another round, gentlemen?"

The doctor looked over and raised his open palm while shaking his head.

"Not for me, thanks."

Doctor and flight attendant then turned their gazes to Wolfgang.

"Oh, I definitely think I should have another…what about you Debbie, are you married?"

Holding up her empty ring finger, she shook her head.

"Not anymore. I was married for fifteen years, right out of high school, had three kids…been emancipated for five months, one week, two days, and…"—she checked her watch for dramatic effect while lowering her voice—"…six hours. I'm having way too much fun being single. Be back soon, y'all."

She smiled with a wink before heading back to the galley. Once there, she wrote her phone number on a napkin that she strategically placed on her tray (and under Wolfgang's drink), before heading back out to her passengers. Wolfgang received the napkin (and the number) then finished the drink in two gulps. It was good to have options. Replaying his pre-flight, strained conversation with Lola, he realized that rejecting her invitation to spend that night with her and the boys might have been a good call. He fell asleep wondering where Debbie might be laying over for the night.

CHAPTER 49 —

The Dead

Hearing some rustling in the back, Bernie cast a quick glance over his shoulder, towards their rescued stray. They had been driving north on Interstate 5 for hours, through the megalopolis of Southern California, up and over the Grapevine, and then on through the San Joaquin Valley. They were almost to the 580 interchange, where they would shoot left, west, towards Oakland. Reaching over to the wall of electronics on the dashboard, he turned down "Sugar Magnolia." To the right of the volume knob flashed a digital clock that notified the paisley palace occupants that it was two A.M.

"Hey man," Bernie said, "welcome to the world of the living! Dude, what's your name?"

Keno had crashed for nearly eight hours. He felt a wet spot of drool on his chest. Everything but the Snickers and burrito were gone, and he was now working through his last few bites of apple. The lights of the East Bay were aglow to the west, like the hint of a sunrise on a backwards-spinning earth. He waited to swallow his most recent bite of apple before answering.

"Hey, I'ma…I'm Keno." He suppressed a burp then nodded to his micro mates. "*Muchas gracias* for the ride!"

"*Keno*," Bernie repeated. "Great name, man. I'm Bernie, and the peace warrior to my right here, is Jerry. What's happening for you in San Fran, man?"

The whole time Bernie conversed, he nodded his entire upper body and head, in a sort of Romper Room bounce, as if needing to affirm every syllable of anyone involved in the conversation.

"I'm actually trying to get north of San Fran...to Marin County."

"No way, man, that's where we're going!"

Jerry, in the passenger seat, turned back to Keno with a wild-eyed sort of self-assurance.

"You're going to see Phil, man, aren't you? I knew it, man!"

"Um, Phil who?"

"Phil Lesh and Friends, man...we're in on it...the Acid Test, man, we're on the bus...I knew you were one of us!"

Bernie interrupted Jerry's self-congratulation.

"No. *I* knew he was one of us. *You* said you didn't wanna give him a ride because he didn't look like a Mexican."

"No, man, I would never do that...I knew right away...he's going to Muir Beach for the Electric Kool-Aid Reunion, man, that's what I said, Bern. I swear that's what I said, man."

Keno, realizing he had been rude, offered the only food he had left.

"Hey, do you guys want to split my bean-and-cheese burrito?"

The driver, Bernie, answered first.

"Ahhh, man, we can't. We're vegans."

"Yeah, man, no dairy."

Bernie had some concerns about what he perceived as Jerry's pilfering of their dwindling onboard inventory.

"Man, I've seen you in that cooler a lot, Jerr. How many of those Jell-O shots have you had, dude?"

"Not many, man, a few…not sure? Maybe six?"

"*Six*? What the fuck, man! Those are for the concert! Dude, did you even offer Keno one?"

Chastened, Jerry turned from Bernie then sheepishly looked back to Keno.

"Hey, Keno, you wanna do a Jell-O shot, man?"

"Thanks. Maybe. What's in 'em, Jerry?"

"Oh man, you know, not much, just a smidge of acid, man…a micro-dose…just enough to stay in touch with Owsley…"

"…but not so much that we can't drive," Bernie put in.

"All wrapped in some groovy, neon-lime Jell-O…."

Alarmed at the revelation, Keno considered his next words carefully. If he sounded like he was freaking out, it might be construed as looking a gift horse in the mouth—or, worse, he might lose his acceptance as a kindred spirit. But his fears overcame his diplomacy.

"Wait…*what?* You're takin' LSD and drivin'? On the 5?"

Bernie tried to soothe his passenger's concerns.

"It's only ten micrograms, man…totally safe…and anyway, we drive better on acid, man…we were trippin' when we took our drivin' test!"

Jerry turned and high-fived Bernie.

"Yeah, man, further than furthur."

"*Right*, man?"

Keno tested the bungees he had strapped around his waist and across his chest before deciding his options were limited. Taking a few deep breaths, he decided his current ride was no less dangerous than anything else he'd been doing for the last few days.

"So, you guys are headed to an Electric Kool-Aid Acid Test, tonight...er, this morning...at Muir Beach?"

"Yeah, man. Forty-four years ago, come December eleventh," Jerry said. "The first one ever, man, when the Grateful Dead were still the Warlocks."

"No, man, I keep telling you," corrected Bernie, "it was the third one, and the Dead were already the Dead."

"Don't be such a stickler, man."

Keno was confused.

"But it's October."

"Yeah, man, we know. But in December nobody could get time off from work."

"Or family commitments...Tonight's the only time it worked for everyone."

"Or at least most everyone."

Bernie led Jerry in a silent ritual that required crossing themselves and whispering a prayer for the soul of Jerry Garcia.

Keno looked at his travelmates like they were something out of a time machine.

"You know Muir Beach is all million-dollar homes now, right? It's all tech and finance bazillionaires? People'll call the sheriff if you start flashing strobe lights and playing amped-up music."

"Yeah, man, we heard."

"Bummer, man, no respect for history nowadays."

"Or the dead, man."

Both of the aging Deadheads again crossed themselves and whispered a prayer.

"Yeah, man, it's okay...it's all gonna be acoustic, with candles, this time."

"Yeah, man, most of us have fake knees or hips anyway...so won't be much dancing...the amplifiers would just be a waste."

"Yeah, man, except for those with hearing problems."

Bernie had a sudden thought. "Hey man, why don't we all just max out our hearing aids to eleven?"

"What?"

"What!"

Their synchronized response had the two ancients laughing and high-fiving all over again. Keno wondered if, back in the day, with the Merry Pranksters, this had passed as high-quality humor. He then remembered there was a time when playing charades and reading poetry were also considered scintillating. He decided to pass on the LSD.

"Hey guys...I think I'll hold off on the Jell-O."

Both of his hosts looked disappointed.

"Man, you sure?"

"It's green, man," Jerry offered. "That's the best."

"And this is top-notch chemistry, man."

Keno searched for a way to maintain community and not lose his hallucinogenic virginity.

"I didn't want to tell you, buuuut... gelatin uses collagen to stick together. It's made from animal bones."

"Really?" both exclaimed.

"Sorry, guys, but, yeah."

Both looked horrified at first. But then, like coordinated siblings, they started smiling when they realized that neither was going to browbeat the other into abstaining from their sacrament.

"The vegan thing, man, it's really more like a guideline."

"Yeah, man, you know...everything in moderation."

With the Lawrence Livermore National Laboratory passing on their left, Keno wondered if any of the scientists inside were working late on new weaponry. Then his thoughts drifted to his remaining calorie stockpile, and he considered how great his Snickers bar was gonna taste. He decided to hold off breaking it out for now, given the uncertainty of his future itinerary.

"So Phil Lesh of the Grateful Dead is playing tonight?"

"Yeah man, we think so."

"Supposed to start at two A.M., man, and play until whenever."

"The concert started at *two* this morning? I hate to ask, but isn't that a long day for you? I mean, how old are you guys?"

Bernie and Jerry looked at each other with some embarrassment. Bernie responded first.

"Pretty darn?"

"Old?"

"We don't really want to know."

"Yeah, man, time doesn't really exist, you know...it's just a contrivance."

"Which explains why last week you missed the flight to your grandson's Bar Mitzvah."

Bernie was still pissed at the recent inconvenience caused by Jerry's insistence on not wearing a watch.

"Hey, Bern...jeez, man, shit happens. I mean, like, whatever happened to commitment, man? Like, you know, not letting time rule you? You *know* the road less traveled can be uncomfortable…but, man, there's a lot to be learned from our suffering. And you used to believe that."

Bernie looked back at Keno and rolled his eyes. "Says the dude who reaches for his bong at every sign of discomfort."

"Ahhh, man, that's not fair. What's *happened* to you, man? You know hemp is an unjustly maligned plant. Dude, my use is purely medicinal…a supplement, like vitamin C."

Keno found himself wishing Bernie spent more time watching the road; he again confirmed the attachment points of his bungee cords. As he started putting the pieces together, he began wondering about the logistics.

"But…what time are you guys gonna arrive there? Won't you be exhausted?"

"Man, we've all been adjusting our sleep schedules."

"Yeah, Reno. Staying up and sleeping later, man."

Bernie intervened on Keno's behalf.

"It's Keno, Jerr."

"Sorry, man…my hearing, all the loud music."

"It was Wavy's idea, man."

"Wavy? Gravy? He's still alive?"

"Yeah, man, Hugh's comin'."

"But don't you guys have jobs? Lives? How do you just change your sleep patterns?"

Jerry and Bernie looked at each other with a shared frown. Again, Bernie took the lead, this time with a knowing smile.

"Oh man, you can't fool us. We're like you, man…we don't work for the man, man."

Jerry followed up.

"No way, man. We're internet experts, we have our own gig, man. Bernie's the CEO and I'm the Chief Creativity Officer. That's why *I* need to do more acid…it's, like, part of my job requirement, man."

"Plus, Jerr, you lost your driver's license last year…so I'm *always* the designated driver."

"Bern, man, you say that like it's a bad thing…. Dude, you need to chill with all the harshness. Maybe, like, a little more mindfulness, huh?"

"Wait a minute, dude…*I* need to be more mindful? Man, *you're* the one that told Maharishi that meditating was like counting sheep."

"Dude, ancient history, man…that was like…eons ago."

Lola had been at the forefront of Keno's mind ever since Tijuana, but the two museum pieces who had picked him up were introducing so many interesting topics that Keno didn't know where to dig in. In particular, the "internet expert" thing had piqued his professional curiosity.

"Hey, Bernie, you said you were internet experts…what is that? Are you guys like programmers, or do you fix people's computers, or what?"

"No, man, nothing like that."

"It was really, like, Wavy's idea."

"But we ran with it, man."

They both stopped talking. Then, Jerry shrugged at Bernie.

"*You* tell him, man, he's one of us, right?"

Once again, Bernie made Keno really uncomfortable by taking his eyes off the black, empty freeway and looking back at him for too long.

"Keno, dude, you're not a narc, are you? The fuzz? Policeman?"

Holding his palms up and in front of him, Keno wondered about the turn of events.

"*What?* No way, man! Look at me…do I *look* like a cop?"

"But you wouldn't drop acid with us, man…"

"Guys, I'm a strict lacto-vegetarian," Keno lied. "I don't eat Jell-O."

The CEO considered the situation then nodded solemnly at his CCO. He took a deep breath and started explaining in a subdued voice.

"Dude, I guess we can trust you."

"Yeah, man, but you'll have to pass the acid test once we get there."

Keno nodded his head, happy for the temporary reprieve before Bernie started explaining.

"Have you ever been in a situation where you need, like, you know, an expert to vouch for you?"

Keno wasn't sure what he was getting at.

"Um, I guess so?"

"Man, if you hire us…we're that *expert!*"

"But, in what?"

"Man, that's the good part. *Everything!*"

Keno's confusion was obvious, so Jerry jumped in.

"Okay, man, let's say you're selling something, like, I dunno, tulip bulbs on the internet…and you wanna say your bulbs are the best, man, but you have no real proof to back you up. Dude, you just hire us and…*poof!*…we start an organization called, like, I dunno, maybe the Pacific Northwest Tulip Growers Association…and then, man, we award you our blue ribbon for Best Quality Bulbs Over the Last Three Years!"

"Man, like, we even build a Pacific Northwest Tulip Growers' Association web page that highlights your success!"

"And serve as board members!"

"And then everyone buys your bulbs!"

"Exactly."

Keno was speechless. Bernie continued.

"Or let's say you write a book, man, but it sucks and no one wants to read it."

"You hire us, man, and we start a trade organization called…umm… California Retail Book Sellers Cooperative!"

"Right? And we award you our, let's say…hmm…our Robert G. Freelander Gold Medal for Best Work of Fiction, 2008!"

"And then you use that accreditation to sell your book!"

"Yeah, man, you can even stick a little gold sticky thing on the front cover."

Keno shifted from speechless to incredulous.

"And people hire you for this?"

"Man, all the time. It's crazy, dude…we have three website designers working for us, *full-time*."

"Man, I think politicians are our best customers. They hire us all the time. Dude, those dudes make up more shit."

"Man, no one ever checks facts anymore."

"But…isn't that fraud?"

"No way, man! We never lie…it's…ummm…more like our expert opinions are for sale."

"But what makes *you* experts?"

"Dude, Jerry says I'm an expert, and I say Jerry's an expert! Plus, Jerr took a coupla creative writing classes at SF State."

Keno looked at Bernie skeptically, but he refrained from further challenging his hosts' business model. Bernie was hurt by their guest's lack of enthusiastic support.

"Dude, there's no government department that regulates experts."

"Yeah, man, it's like Vermont, ya know…live free and die?"

"Jerr, man, it's *live free* or *die,* and it's New Hampshire."

"Same thing, Bern."

"Dude, I told you a million times, it's not. Really, man, ya gotta stop sayin' that."

"Stickler, man…. I'm tellin' ya, man, it's like, gonna kill ya. You just need to let that shit go, man."

Gently shaking his head in resignation, Bernie started slowing down as they approached the Bay Bridge tollbooths. It was nearly three A.M., and all eight lanes were nearly empty. Keno was hoping to get dropped off at home, but he knew that would take them out of the way, and they were already late.

"So we're going through San Francisco?"

"Yeah, man, we always go through the Haight when we can."

"Yeah, man, just to reminisce, ya know?"

"Don't worry, man, we won't stop, we'll be in Muir Woods before four."

"We won't miss the concert, man…Phil will play at least until sunrise."

"Make sure those Jell-O shots are under ice, man."

"Hey, Keno, man, Jerry made a chocolate cake. Do you wanna slice, man?"

Keno leaned back, crossed his arms, and looked out at the lights twinkling off of inky San Francisco Bay. He decided he would leave the cake ingredients a mystery and just ride out whatever happened to him. It probably wouldn't kill him, and after being gone for six months, he figured one more day wouldn't matter. Knowing the morning would come fast and hard, he figured it was necessary to make a quick decision. His mind drifted back to Lola, and he wondered what she was doing right then, and whether a vegan chocolate cake was even worth trying. In the end he knew she was likely asleep, and he should pack away as many calories as possible. A long hike was likely ahead of him. With a resigned sigh, his diaphragm fought for shelf space alongside Bob Weir and Jerry Garcia as "Truckin' " poured from the speakers.

"Sure, guys," he answered. "A slice of chocolate cake would be great. Thanks."

As the west end of the bridge spit them out into the SoMa district in Northeast San Francisco, Keno luxuriated in his first bites of chocolate, flour, and sugar. He had never thought of himself as a big Grateful Dead fan, but the singing (intermingled with the pre-dawn street lights) wrapped him in its warm embrace.

Truckin'…

I'm a goin' home…

Whoa whoa baby,

back where I belong…

He started humming along with the boys formerly known as the Warlocks, as whatever was in the cake had him feeling pretty good for the first time in days.

CHAPTER 50 —

Procrastinundrum

"Scout!" Lilly exclaimed in to the telephone. "You're still in your apartment?"

Her daughter was in no mood to engage the battle.

"Mom, chill…I'm on my way out the door now."

"But you said you were gonna get an early start…seven A.M. at the latest?"

Sitting up in her apartment's Murphy bed, Scout wondered why she had picked up her mom's call. The drive was going to be hard enough without having to carry the burden of Lilly's disapproval the whole way. She had been holed up in her tiny Westwood studio since six that morning. It was now eight-thirty and she was still in her pajamas. She had been using her iPad to watch YouTube animal videos. Her whole pre-departure to-do list had been neglected because she couldn't commit to a starting point. She decided to change the subject.

"How's Dad doing?"

Standing with her packed suitcase in Elizabeth's Clearwater kitchen, Lilly was ready to head to the airport to fly back to the West Coast. Elizabeth was up and in her housecoat, bringing some water to boil.

"I don't know," Lilly said. "I've been visiting Elizabeth Barton in

Florida for the last few days."

"Dad's ex-wife?" She couldn't believe it! "What are you doin' there?"

"It's a long story…Scout, listen, no more procrastinundrum…you know what Dr. Blanco said."

Ever since her suicide attempt, Scout had been struggling to reengage with a normal routine. The scheduled drive to San Francisco had seemed, at varying times, as if it would be both invigorating and terrifying.

"Mom… I really wish you could go with me to this thing."

"I'm so sorry, honey, but I told you, I can't…I wasn't invited. You're the only one from Keno's family who was."

"Maybe you could be my emotional support animal?"

"Funny, but lately my wag has somehow gone missing."

"But, Mom, I won't know *anybody*."

"It's all right. I'll join you for a late dinner tonight at the hotel, and then we'll drive back to LA in the morning. Easy, peasy. You just have to make an appearance at the wedding and reception…. Scout, you can do this, but you have to get moving."

"Okay, okay, I'm goin', Mom."

"You're getting a late start, you'll need to take the 5…not the 101. Be careful. Bring some caffeine. I'll see you tonight. Love you, baby."

"Love you too, Mom."

Hanging up on her daughter, Lilly grabbed her suitcase and turned to Elizabeth, who was busy steeping tea for both of them. Switching the suitcase from right hand to left, Lilly stuck the now free hand in her host's direction.

"Elizabeth, it was such a pleasure getting to know you."

Elizabeth merged their palms with a gentle squeeze.

"Oh, Lilly, likewise. I'm sorry about eavesdropping, but what's *procrastinundrum*?"

"It's a term Scout's doctor uses, kind of a more nuanced take on Einstein's *options paralysis*. I think she defines it as the mistaken conflating of procrastination with freedom."

"Interesting…so…maybe like confusing the inability to act with keeping your options open?"

"I think so. Her theory is that in the beginning there is a mild euphoria that accompanies having a lot of options, and we're afraid that when we commit to just one we'll lose that good feeling of *possibility* along with all the other options."

"Hmm, I see. So the conundrum is that if we don't eventually commit to doing one of the options, we never do anything?"

"Exactly. And if we do commit we lose the ability, either real or imagined, to engage ourselves in all the other endless possibilities."

"Most of which are very low probability fantasies, but…thinking we may be able to do those things makes us…what was the term…*euphoric*?"

"Yep. Hence the conundrum between procrastination and doing. And it's not just big stuff…it can be things as simple as picking a restaurant for dinner, or your outfit in the morning. Unfortunately, for many people, including my daughter, the early euphoria starts to morph into anxiety if she can't commit, and then she just freezes."

"So we're afraid to commit to one thing for fear it won't be the right thing?"

"Yeah, exactly. So instead, we stay in our comfort zone, becoming spectators instead of participants…and we delude ourselves into thinking that inactivity is just a normal way to keep our options open."

"Like with young people and the internet?"

Lilly laughed.

"Or old people and knitting."

"Oh, no…you think so?"

"Just kidding. Dr. Blanco says it's not always bad…like anything, there just needs to be a balance."

"I guess if *look before you leap* can coexist with *he who hesitates is lost*, then there's room for procrastinundrum."

"Right? By the way, the ironic list goes on and on."

Elizabeth knew Lilly was short on time. She handed her a mug of Pu'er with a smile.

"Dr. Blanco sounds pretty smart…" She smiled warmly. "Your cab is here…keep the mug."

"Oh my God, look at the time," Lilly confirmed. "I have to hurry."

"Safe travels, Lilly. Thank you for everything."

"I'm not sure I really did anything. I couldn't even find Keno or Clay for you, let alone talk some sense into Lola."

A look of sadness and fatigue clouded Elizabeth's face.

"You did find some pieces of both…I'm sure, when the time is right…"

Lilly reached out and touched Elizabeth's hand.

"They're alive…they'll be home soon. It's the only thing that makes sense."

"God, I hope so."

Now it was Lilly's turn to smile warmly. "I'll let myself out."

"Please stay in touch, and let me know how Scout is doing…and how the wedding went? Oh, and hug Sam And Gus from me!"

"I will…I'll check in tomorrow…I've gotta go or I'll miss my flight."

"Bye-bye, Lilly."

And then, as an afterthought, Elizabeth whispered, more to herself than Lilly.

"Please greet Aloysius for me?"

CHAPTER 51 —

If the Horse Don't Pull, You Got to Carry the Load

He wasn't sure which came first, the splitting headache or the sound of the two men bickering. Either way, he knew he was awake.

"Man, did it rain last night?"

"Oh, jeez, no! Jerry, man…not again?"

"No way, man."

"Dude, I can smell it! You did! You peed yourself! You gotta stop gettin' so fucked up, man!"

"Man, Bern, I swear, I was practicin' moderation."

"Moderation? Are you shittin' me, man? Dude, you were so out of control…the whole bowl of Jell-O shots, half the keg, a lid, and then half the chocolate cake, and then…oh, man, that smell, fuckin' gross…and then you peed yourself, man…like you always do."

Bernie's description of Jerry's incontinence triggered a recognition in Keno's now wide-awake olfactory system that in turn compelled his stomach to consider catapulting the partly digested remains of chocolate cake, trail mix, Ritz crackers, apple, and burrito back towards their point of entry. Fortunately, the milk had already passed out of his stomach, its nutrients now inhabiting his circulatory system, where they were being delivered to whichever section of his depleted corpus had the greatest need. Keno was confident the ingredients in Jerry's chocolate cake were potent enough to light up all but the most indifferent urine test, and his nervous system was now suffering the consequences. He noted with self-congratulation that his board shorts were dry and his bladder full.

"Bern, man, I think I'm gonna do it. I saw it all clearly last night when I was trippin'."

"Jerry, man, how can you do something that explicitly requires *not* doing something?"

Somehow during the early morning hours Keno had gotten the pop-top of the van open, crawled up and into the cozy space, and fallen asleep. He guessed the voices were coming from the bench seat, which folded out into a bed below him.

"I'm gonna announce my candidacy, man…er, no…my… *availability*, man…if the people want me."

"Man, do you think you can change your corduroys first?"

"No, Bern, you're not listening, man. I want to be genuine, man, bring a…a tone of authenticity to the White House that's been sorely missin', man. Besides, I think my bladder problems can simultaneously capture the senior vote *and* Big Pharma."

A combination of sweat and cotton mouth compelled Keno to kick off the ratty old towels he had used to keep warm. The ripe smell of three mature men sleeping in such a small, enclosed space was strongly off-putting, with the aforementioned released urine serving as icing on the cake. Sensing the sun was high overhead, he reached up and put his hand on the warm ceiling, confirming his suspicions. He needed to get out of the van soon, or else his organs would start an involuntary evacuation process.

2009 - Still Out West (Mostly)

"Bern, man, the whole circus has turned into a marketing campaign."

"Jerr, man, do we have to go through this again? Everything in this country is sold, nobody does any real research, man…it's how our company makes money, remember?"

"But, Bern, man, our politicians are supposed to be thoughtful, humble…um, what's the term?"

"Public servants? Consensus builders?"

"Yeah, man, public servants *and* consensus builders…not megalomaniacal cult figures that spend two years campaigning and trying to sell us on their superhero powers."

"Jerry, I know, but…"

"Dude, the power is in the system…the three branches…checks and balances…all that Constitution stuff, man. The politicians are supposed to just manage the system, not become celebrity superstars."

"I know, Jerr, any monkey can sit in the White House and not fuck it up too much…even you."

Jerry, enraptured by his train of thought, ignored the insult from his buddy.

"Hey man, what's that chill song by the Eagles?"

"Man, you really need to change your trousers."

"C'mon man, you know the one I'm talking about."

With a resigned sigh, Bernie played along with his friend's vision.

" 'Hotel California'?"

"No…"

" 'Desperado'?"

"No…"

" 'One of These Nights'?"

"Definitely, no."

Keno couldn't take it anymore, his back teeth were swimming.

" 'Take It Easy.' "

"Yeah, man, that's it, 'Take It Easy.' "

Bernie was confused.

"What about it, man?"

"Dude, instead of doing all that fear-mongering and finger-pointing shit, I'm gonna remind everybody how good they have it…tell 'em to take it easy…not everybody needs cable and satellite in their SUVs, man… tell 'em to chill…sometimes shit happens, man…like kittens get stuck in trees or kids gettin' sick…but it doesn't always mean it's somebody's fault."

"Jerr, man, ya gotta go clean yourself up, man. It's unsanitary."

"Okay, Bern, but I only want the job if people want me to have it. I'm not one of those power-hungry, ego-driven dudes…you know me, Bern…I'm totally mellow. And you can be my campaign manager…and vice president."

Giving up on his immediate goal of getting Jerry out of the van, Bernie realized he had to let the conversation play out naturally.

"So…what, Jerr? You're just making yourself available and hope the people find you?"

"Exactly, man, maybe tell a few friends, the local paper, file some paperwork…"

"Dude, at least you'll capture the introvert vote."

"Don't laugh, man, there's a lot of us."

"Jerr, maybe you could wear a sandwich board and walk around Mission Beach? Like, maybe hope for some word-of-mouth that turns viral?"

2009 - Still Out West (Mostly)

"Dude, that's what Wavy said!" Jerry had a second thought. "Only I wouldn't be able to spend a lot of time on my feet 'cuz o'my arches and lower back, man...Bern, you know walking a lot is really bad for my Declaration of Independence, man."

Try as he could, Bernie was at an exasperated loss, "Man, your what...? Declaration of Independence?"

"Yeah, man, you know, my internal configuration...my composition?"

"Wait...dude...you mean your constitution?"

"Oh yeah, man...that's it...I always mix those two up."

Keno decided he couldn't listen to another syllable. He was trying to be polite, but he had to voluntarily relieve himself before either his stomach or bladder forced the issue.

"Make way, guys, comin' down."

"Reno, man...you've been up there the whole time?"

"Jerr, it's *Keno*, and he helped you with the Eagles song, remember?"

"Oh yeah, sorry, man. *Keno*, man, sorry you had to hear all that. I don't *always* pee myself, man."

Picking his way through the detritus from the previous night, Keno made purchase with the floor and slid open the side door. He made sure not to step on the exposed chocolate cake.

"No problem, Jerry...happens to the best of us, man. Hey, what was in that cake last night?"

"You know, Re—... er, Ke-no, the kitchen sink, man."

"Yeah, felt like it. I'm gotta go hit the head, guys...be back soon."

As he worked his way through the large meadow that separated their parking spot from the trees, he tried not to intrude on any of the triage being performed. There was an army of weathered hippies in the midday son, and if Keno squinted his eyes a bit the degree of disassemblage looked like the remnants of a battlefield. Hundreds of grey-haired bodies scattered around him on blankets or in sleeping bags, in various stages of undress, playing music, moaning, or chattering in soft voices. About a stone's throw into the trees, he watered the ground then stumbled barefoot back to the VW. Stopping a few feet outside of the open slider, he tried to gulp as much untainted air as possible before heading back in for his Zoris and Snickers bar.

"Hey, Bernie," he said, "are you guys leaving soon?"

"No, man…we're staying one more night."

"Yeah, man, Phil didn't make it last night, but he's supposed to play tonight."

"Yeah, man, supposedly got stuck at Marin General, waiting for his first great grandchild."

Keno looked over his head, through the light mist that filtered the midday sun. A chill was in the air, and he was antsy to get moving. He knew his home and family were just on the other side of Mount Tamalpais, in Mill Valley. The end to his odyssey was so close he could taste it. Before he started the long trek in his rubber Zoris, he had one more thing to take care of.

"Hey, guys, can I borrow a phone?"

CHAPTER 52 —

This Darkness Got to Give

He was just now showing up, and Lola was on the verge of a conniption. Elise had been welcoming when he'd arrived, but given the strained tone between the bride and groom, she had quickly taken her leave. Now the two betrothed were alone in Lola's bedroom, and it was clear both were uncomfortable. Already painfully squeezed into her modest wedding gown, Lola was struggling to make sure her bags were packed not only for the ceremony, but also the reception. And then, of course, a weird sense of loyalty required that they spend their wedding night at the Casa Madrona. She had a driver who would be taking her from wedding to reception to hotel, and he was on time, but everything else seemed to be falling apart. Her children had yet to appear. Trick was at the office. And she had something she'd been wanting to discuss with her fiancé for days.

"Wolfgang, *where* have you been?"

"I told you, I didn't get in from Miami until late last night." He was not in a mood that would allow him to accommodate her questions. "So I stayed at the airport."

"The wedding is in *two* hours! I've been trying to reach you for days!"

"Traffic everywhere was terrible, and I seemed to have gotten lost at every turn with that damn rental car GPS…and, my phone battery went dead, and I couldn't find a charger."

With skepticism Lola looked first at him—"I *told* you I would pick you up?"—and then at his casual wear: "Is *that* what you're wearing?"

"No, of course not!" Wolfgang replied defensively. "I have a tuxedo in the car. I thought I'd change at the church. And, last night…I knew you were busy, and I didn't want to…inconvenience you. Lola, this is just a small wedding, only forty or so people…why are you making it such a big deal?"

She examined him closely. Something between disappointment and disgust fluctuated inside her stomach. She wondered what had happened to all the chemistry they had had—why he no longer hung on her every word.

"There's something I need to talk to you about. I wanted to do it earlier, but you haven't been returning my calls, and you're just now showing up. It's a bit sensitive…"

Billy Idol's growl interrupted the moment. With an increasing frustration, Lola grabbed her phone off of the bureau. She hoped it was her boys with an update that they were on their way. Looking at her phone's screen, she lost it.

"I can't believe it! Another idiot spam caller!"

She hadn't slept in two days and was unsure about everything happening to her right now. Her hormones were racing out of control, and she was worried the stress of the last six months was prematurely pushing her into menopause. It all came out in a raging torrent, as she uncharacteristically screamed at her phone and the callers that she was sure were harassing her.

"Fuck you! Fuck You!! FUCK!! YOU!!!"

Then she winged the device across the room.

Wolfgang sat down timidly in a nearby chair. He had never seen this side of his future wife. It was unsettling.

"Are you...okay?"

Lola had to know—she had to look him in the eye and ask the question.

"Did you hire someone to kill my husband?"

"*What?* What are you talking about!"

"Keno's family thinks someone was trying to kill him. They think maybe you...and me."

"Lola, I have my flaws, but murder isn't one of them!" He shook his head in disbelief. "Killing Keno...? That's *insane*!"

She stared at him hard before realizing how out of control she was. Sitting down on the bed, she started to sob.

"I don't want you to see me like this..."

She buried her face in her hands for a moment then grabbed a tissue from the bedside table. It seemed like she barely knew the man she was about to pledge herself to, and yet they had set something in motion that now had a life of its own. It was as if she were tumbling forward in the clutches of a rain-swollen river and lacked the conviction or ability to swim free. The fact that her tears would require she redo her makeup only added to the whole mess. But her greatest fear was the gnawing sense that she was not marching towards the wedding chapel, but to the gallows. Right now, she just needed to be alone.

"My car is here now...I have to go or I'll be late...you're not supposed to see me...in my dress."

Wolfgang was struggling with his own problems. The walls were closing in on him...he was feeling asphyxiated. He knew his reputation as an immature wastrel was warranted, and he wanted to change, but this step just felt like too much, too soon. At that moment, the knowledge that his father judged him as lacking in fortitude fell particularly heavy on his conscience, and he yearned strongly for a drink. The knowledge that his parents approved of his plans to engage in a life of monogamy just made it all the more complicated. Preparing to make his escape, he reached into his pocket for his car keys and felt the pair of panties Debbie had secreted there, unbeknownst to him. The juxtaposition between past and future was visceral. The realization that his recent promiscuity lay hidden behind such a thin veil nauseated him. Through his nostrils he took a deep breath.

Steady old boy, he told himself. *One wrong move here and it all comes tumbling down.*

Getting up slowly, he made a move for the exit before pausing and offering all the reassurance he could.

"I'll be at the church at the appointed time."

And then, he left.

CHAPTER 53 —

680 Steps

Keno was bent over, breathing hard, with hands on knees at the intersection of Panoramic Highway and Muir Woods Road. He had made it to the ridge of the Coastal Mountain Range, and his quads and exposed skin were burning from the climb and afternoon sun. Now he had to decide whether to hang a left and hike a little farther up Panoramic Highway to the Dipsea Trail, or just keep going straight, over the top of the spine and down Edgewood. The latter route was shorter but more dangerous: it required walking on a road with several blind curves and no shoulder. With the idea that he could catch a ride, he had been avoiding the dirt trails thus far, sticking mostly to the narrow, twisting asphalt roads. But there had been several close calls with inattentive drivers. The Sunday traffic was heavy, but it seemed his disassemblage had been ineffective at attracting passersby. Keno justified the unanimous rejection by presuming that all of his fellow, disheveled, counterculture *compadres* were camped out at Muir Beach; either that, or the lack of a shoulder onto which the passing vehicles could safely pull over.

Overhead, a screeching hawk reminded him of how much the verdant environment had changed in just a handful of generations, even out here in restricted-use parkland. His imagination placed both himself and the raptor in the same spot three centuries earlier, a time when daily survival was a very different game. He wondered if he would have been the apex predator in his current state, or if the grizzlies and wolves would be the most feared hunters. Taking inventory, he realized he was woefully under-armed, his only weapons being his superior wits and half-eaten Snickers bar. The memory of the latter quickly installed food as a priority, and he finished off the gooey mess with two bites and a forceful lick of the wrapper.

As he considered what to do with the chocolate-covered plastic, the sound of a diesel engine laboring up the serpentine road cautioned him to grant wide passage. Glancing over his shoulder, he had to wait only a moment before the silver car came into view. He quickly stowed the wrapper in his mouth, straightened his posture, and hopefully stuck out his thumb. With the afternoon sun blinding him he couldn't see the driver, but he envisioned an elderly gentleman out for a Sunday spin in his cherished Mercedes. Still wearing the barely recognizable, red 49ers T-shirt, Keno hoped the man was a local football fan.

Not a likely rescuer, he acknowledged to himself, *but I have to risk it if I want to win the biscuit.*

He extended his thumb in a posture that implied a mixed plea of harmlessness and need.

As the car hurried past, he admired its aging lines and was surprised by the blurred profile of a woman occupying the driver's seat. Just as he lowered his thumb and prepared for the last climb up to the Dipsea, the car stopped in a gravel area fifty yards ahead, the engine still idling. At first he thought maybe something was wrong, but then an arm extended out of the window and urged him forward.

Keno started running jubilantly, as fast as his rubber flip-flops would allow. He made a deal with his screaming leg muscles that if they endured these final fifty yards—just half a football field—he would reward them with a long rest on a fine, leather-clad seat. He picked up the pace as the driver appeared to be the impatient sort. But as he ran, his right sandal began to disintegrate. The thong attachment between his big and second toes pulled free from the bottom piece of rubber. The tread and accoutrement separated. A moment later, all that remained was the upper rubber housing, resting on the top of his foot like a wishbone anklet. His naked instep felt the road detritus pressing sharply into his foot's calloused protection, and his stride slowed to a limp. The posture of the Mercedes-Benz 300 suddenly changed. He spit out the Snickers wrapper along with the words:

"No! Wait! Please! I'm coming!"

He reaccelerated, race-limping the final twenty yards. When he got to the car, the passenger window was just starting to descend. The woman inside conveyed a sense of urgency.

"Where ya goin'?"

Keno had a death grip on the aperture where the window had slipped down into the door, as if that alone could keep the mass of steel from leaving him behind. The fifty-yard sprint had left him gasping. He looked down at his damaged, unprotected foot while trying to recover his breath to speak.

"Mill Valley? Anywhere? Around The 2 AM Club?"

"Hop in, I'm in a hurry."

There was something familiar about the driver's voice…but that didn't slow Keno from immediately accepting the invitation. Like a Kardashian to the spotlight, he yanked open the door and nearly flung himself into the passenger seat. It wasn't until after he had pulled the seat belt across his chest and the Teutonic vehicle had started the downhill plunge, that the chance arose for Keno to examine the driver more intimately. The beginning of crinkles edging out from her eyes were the telltale signs of a woman in her thirties, and the driver's cadaver-like skin stood in stark contrast to the dyed raven-black bangs of a Cleopatra cut. Suddenly it hit him.

Is it possible? He could hardly believe it himself. *What are the odds?*

"Scout?"

The driver still wasn't sure why she had stopped for the bedraggled wayfarer—she thought maybe it was a karmic nod to her student hitchhiker days. But now that he knew her name, things were really getting interesting. Already hurtling down the Edgewood switchbacks, she could take her eyes only briefly from the road to glance at her human cargo.

"I'm sorry…do I know you?"

Now that he had the scent, the few extra syllables were all he needed to confirm his suspicions. Realizing most of his head and face were covered by an unkempt tangle of hair and beard, and that his frame was about twenty pounds lighter than it had been years ago, Keno wasn't surprised his half sister didn't recognize him.

"Holy guacamole! How weird is *this*? Scout…what are you doing up here? It's me, Keenan!"

The revelation was as unexpected as words from a pig. Scout was driven to such a level of distraction that she was nearly outmaneuvered by one of the hairpins. It took all she had to regain control of the car while not bringing it to a screeching halt.

"Keenan…*Barton*? But…but…*what? How?*"

Keno shrugged with a giddy smile on his face.

"Oh my god, Scout, I can't tell you how good it is to see you…and in Dad's old car! Sorry, I didn't recognize you at first, but you've changed your hair!"

Still working through all the implications of Keno's resurrection, Scout was struggling with who knew what.

"But...I can't believe this...where have you been? Everyone thinks you're dead!"

"Oh man, Scout, it's a long story, but basically I've been trying to get home...with no money or ID. Bummin' rides. What are *you* doing up here?"

Scout seemed really nervous, and he wondered what might be going on. He had no way of knowing how infinitely more complicated his presence had just made her day. Struggling with the sharp corners and the need to enlighten her recently un-marooned passenger, she decided to slow down and stay in the middle of her lane.

"Well, I've had some...difficulties...and I just spent an hour doing the walking meditation that Lola used to take me on...the Deer Park Fire Road out and back?"

"Oh, I love that hike...I just went by that trailhead... Wait, you drove up from LA just to take a walk in the redwoods? Why didn't you bring Lola?"

"Oh my God, Keno...have you...I mean...you must've talked to... anyone...since you...you...disappeared?"

Getting his first whiff that things might have changed during his half-year absence, Keno felt a slight trepidation starting to interrupt his cerebral revelry.

"Not really...I mean...I tried to call, but I didn't have a phone or any money...and when I borrowed someone's phone, no one picked up."

Scout wasn't sure how much to divulge, but she was convinced Keno should get to Lola before she promised herself to someone else.

"Keno, everyone thought you were dead. I'm not sure how to tell you this, but…I'm up here because…Lola's getting married"— she looked at her watch—"in a little more than an hour! In Tiburon!"

All of Keno's expectations for a warm family reunion plunged off a cliff in a burning wreckage of incredulity whose one passenger was the optimistic manic attack that had been driving him. Exhausted, his skeletal visage deflated under the pressure of his seatbelt and the news.

"Please, tell me it's not Trick."

"It's not Trick. It's some guy with money…from college…Wolfgang."

"Wolfgang? I don't remember Lola ever even mentioning him?" Keno's mind was spinning. "Scout, you have to get me there before it happens."

"I know, I know. But the traffic…"

Keno's mind started racing. His eyes scanned the car.

"Your phone! Where's your phone!"

"Eeeesh! Sorry! The battery died about twenty minutes ago and I brought the wrong charger!"

Cursing his luck, Keno considered the connection between karma and his recent infidelity. As Scout accelerated into the next turn, the Mercedes' tires rolled hard against the asphalt and strained to withstand the centrifugal forces. Inside the car, the repentant passenger resigned himself to the possibility that Fortuna might be punishing him.

"Scout, is there anything else I should know?"

Scout couldn't keep from smiling faintly as an inappropriate parallel drifted into her head involving a play and Mrs. Lincoln. But she repressed it.

"I don't think so."

CHAPTER 54 —

Old Saint Hilary's

Father Francis Wilder had been sitting quietly behind the altar for twenty-five minutes. His new hip felt fine, but the old one that had been serving him for eighty-two years was pestering. It seemed that long periods in chairs exacerbated the discomfort, but in this instance his sense of duty prevailed. Wondering what could be holding things up, he started contorting his torso to look behind him before a stabbing in his neck forced his head and attention back to their original position. While the sharp pain subsided to a dull throb, he followed the stragglers as they slowly filed in and chose sides in the partly filled landmark sanctuary. Watching the movements of the churchgoers, he was struck by his growing distance from modernity and, inversely, his increasing personal affiliation with the past. He reveled in the redwood intricacies of the surrounding walls, and the remarkable craftsmanship that went into the oak pews and amber windows. In contrast, he was indifferent to the predictable actions and chattering of the congregants, all of whom were younger than he.

A trick of the aging mind, he thought, *a change in prioritization to make the inevitable passing easier. That and, of course, the nagging deterioration and pain.*

The Carpenter Gothic architecture of the white, wooden building was something that he had always admired; but today, as he had approached the knoll that hosted the quaint, mission church, it had felt like he was coming home. While he walked up the steps towards the simple, four-panel entry doors, the wildflowers had sung to him from below like a chorus of silent angels shining in the sun. It all reminded him that the world was changing faster than his ambitions, and that, along with his arthritic joints, had him feeling tired.

While waiting patiently in deep contemplation, he realized that these were the times that he most often missed John. Usually during the quiet moments in between, often at night or before officiating at a ceremony, when some part of his body was articulating a pronounced pain. It was as if the real pain was an aching for his lost lover and the physical discomfort was just a manifestation.

In the name of their God, the two priests had witnessed the celebrations of myriad people traveling many crossroads. Each type of event had its own unique characteristics, but Fathers Francis and John had agreed that weddings were their favorite. The intrepid power of love—its ability to naively bind two people with a permanent vow and compel them forward against all odds—had captured both their imaginations. What some saw as wishful ignorance the two clergymen had viewed as shared grace.

Theirs had been a non-platonic relationship, but they had never let the romance interfere with their work. They both had felt a fiduciary responsibility, as shepherds to their flock, that required both compassion and discretion. This commitment to their parishioners was wrought not from iron, but from a shared faith in love as the divine guide. It was a wisdom that the two men had regularly reinforced in each other. Given the historical context, they both felt strongly that subtlety was necessary to minimize activating anything that might threaten the sanctity of their ministry.

As he sifted through his memory banks, recalling fondly the many good years, a growing specter started haunting from the shadows. He tried to ignore it…but that just gave it a better purchase, and he knew it would soon be front and center. And then, there it was…staring him straight in the face. The terrible ending with all the gory detail, and he not able to do anything to stop it. Unwilling to look away, he saw John clearly, poxed and emaciated, shriveling away to nothing in a hospital bed. It had been two decades last Christmas when the younger priest had been swept up by the invisible and sudden epidemic invading San Francisco. He was gone in a month, and in John's wake the elder priest's broken heart had never mended. Not breaking the established pattern, Francis silently prayed that when his time came, he would be granted the tender mercy of reuniting with his friend.

At the base of the steps, before the altar, a schoolmate friend of Samuel Barton's had been hired to play the harp. Finishing with Delibes' "Flower Duet," Valerie's fingers started delicately pulling Josh Garrels' "Lake Yarina" from the strings. As she slowly brought the notes to life, Father Wilder identified it as one of his favorites, and allowed the song to gently retrieve him from his reminisces.

In the front of the church, behind the chancel, a small changing room hid Wolfgang and Keno. What had started as an awkward conversation framed with disbelief and contention had evolved into a shared conspiracy. It seems that after the usual territorial hard-wiring had been defused, what remained were quite sympathetic interests. The final negotiations were still in progress, but both could see an agreement was approaching.

For his part, Wolfgang had found a path that allowed him to honorably dismount, and he was more than happy to facilitate in any reasonable way. In fact, he was already mostly out of the tuxedo.

"So, I'm not sure of the exact dimensions, but it seems you could just squeeze into this, and then ship the whole thing back to me when convenient? If that works? What size shoe do you wear?"

Keno, recognizing a great opportunity when it presented itself, and praying Lola would see him more as Prince Charming than Rumplestiltskin, was in a hurry to effect the switch.

"Size ten? Man, I am so grateful for your understanding. I realize this is all an incredibly awkward and unusual situation."

"Quite…and you'll tell everyone that upon presenting your claim, I realized there was only one honorable thing to do…bow out and let you and Lola try to patch things up? Despite my broken heart. Agreed?"

"Absolutely."

"If my parents confront you, please greet them for me, and offer my sincerest apologies for the expense and embarrassment."

"You're not gonna tell them personally?"

"I think there will be less combustion if I avoid them for a bit. I don't want to interrupt your moment. My father can be quite…forceful… when he feels I have disappointed him."

"Yeah, okay…I gotcha covered."

Wolfgang had already reestablished his legs as the occupants of his linen trousers and was new sliding his wool-covered feet into his cherished, burgundy boots. So close to completing the reinflation that he could taste it, he handed Keno the dress shoes like a postman would the mail.

"Here you go, black patent, size ten-and-a-half monkey shoes."

The jacket was a little tight in the shoulders, but with Keno's new, trim figure everything else was pretty close. In a perfect world, the trousers would have hung an inch shorter and offered a skosh more room in the fanny, but given the circumstances it all seemed good. As Keno slipped on the shoes, Wolfgang laid the tie and cummerbund on a nearby chair and made to complete his getaway.

Keno wasn't prepared for such a fast escape.

"Wait, Wolfgang…you're going now?"

"I know you think I've been tremendously decent about all this, but I'm not sure it serves anyone's interests for me to stay a minute longer than necessary. Salt in the wounds…clean breaks, and such…I hope you understand?"

Keno didn't, but that wasn't his focus.

"Umm, sure, okay."

Wolfgang could see Mr. Barton was very nervous.

"Everyone's waiting for you. You're already late. Remember, the bride is the painting…you're really more the frame. Strong and silent. Just walk out that door and stand stage left in front of the altar. Your boys will join you as groomsmen. They'll take their cues from you. It all should be a great surprise."

Keno took a deep breath, and nodded. This was the moment he had been waiting for…he had just never imagined it would be so public and full of ceremony. He wondered how much Lola and the boys had changed. For a moment, he worried they wouldn't recognize him, and his mind started racing for a razor or some scissors, but he caught himself and laid the whirring to rest. Either they would accept him or not, the time for preparation was over.

He whispered softly to Wolfgang's already receding back:

"Thank you."

CHAPTER 55 —

Not Forsaken

Elizabeth first heard the dog barking and then the muffled voices and knew something was up. Rising from her workstation, she hustled to the glass slider off the kitchen and walked out onto the small, screened back porch. Her sciatica started complaining, and she reminded herself to get to her yoga mat for some practice that evening before dinner. Without the interruption of walls and windows, the voices were now much clearer and more intense, and the barking more insistent. The words sounded threatening…she recognized one of the combatants as Roberto. Intuitively, she grabbed the aluminum baseball bat that she kept on the porch then limped out the screen door and around the corner, heading towards the small stand of papaya trees that sheltered the men.

"Last chance *amigo*, put down the machete and tell me what you're doin' snoopin' around here."

"No, *cabrón*, you tells me! *Yo* belong here!"

Now able to see the two men, she saw that one was indeed Roberto. The other man was not as tall, but with broader shoulders. She couldn't recognize him from behind, but something seemed distantly familiar about him. Roberto shifted his eyes from the man ten feet in front of him to Elizabeth.

"Elizabed! Run back inside and call da *policia*! Ees a bad man here! He hava *pistola*."

The thick stranger with short, cropped, grey hair moved like a dancer as he took two quick steps towards Elizabeth before pulling his eyes briefly from the machete.

"Mom, it's okay, I just caught this guy snoopin' around. D'you know him?"

"Me no snoopin'! I catch *you* snoopin'!"

There was only one person whom she didn't recognize that could possibly call her *Mom*.

"Clay?"

"Yeah, Mom, it's me."

Elizabeth wasn't sure whether to be angry, grateful, or simply dumbfounded. "Where have you been!"

"Ah, Ma, you know…around."

Roberto seemed shocked. "You knows ees *hombre*?"

"Boys, please, both put your weapons down, now!" Elizabeth commanded. *"Ahora!"*

They both suspected that the threat of the other man was more manufactured than real, so each man somewhat comfortably let down his guard.

"Roberto, Clay is my son. *Mi hijo*. Clay, Roberto is my…gardener."

Roberto sadly looked at the ground, which forced Elizabeth to reassess.

"And my boyfriend…*mi novio*."

The words had their intended effect. Roberto cheered up. Recognizing he wasn't needed, Clay started silently walking away, towards the side gate he had used as his entry point.

Elizabeth watched her son depart in bewilderment. "Clay, where are you going?"

"I have some stuff to do."

"That's ridiculous! I haven't seen you in over twenty years. Where are you staying?"

"I have a place."

"*Where?*"

"In my truck."

It was the straw that broke the matriarch's back. "Clay Barton, you'll stay with me for at least a meal."

"Ma, I really gotta go."

Elizabeth upped the ante. Gently.

"I can whip up a chocolate cake?"

Roberto couldn't take it any more.

"Ees no mi bisness, but when Mama say stay, you stay. You no know how long she be here. We's old peoples. All *mi familia* gone. Every day I miss. *Sabe?*"

Clay ignored everything, put his hand on the gate latch…and pulled.

"Clay, I know everything and I forgive you."

Clay stopped. He lowered his hand, but the shame of his tears kept him from turning. Through the fog he managed to mumble some words that Elizabeth barely understood.

"Mom, I think somethin's wrong with my head…"

Elizabeth took a deep breath and tried to control the strong emotions that were flooding through her. Collecting her thoughts, she decided the first step was to get her oldest son back, and then, if he stayed, she could later establish some ground rules. She carefully put together the next two sentences before releasing the words.

"Clay, you're welcome here for as long as you want…this has always been your home."

CHAPTER 56 —

Dreams

The early morning light had just cracked the surface of the sublime terrain. Like honey drizzled onto sandpaper, the sun's photons were spreading an orange glow across the surrounding desert. They were tracking an unmarked ribbon of asphalt that was leading lazily to the Pacific. The pocked surface of the road and the occasional slow-moving livestock required that Lola pay rapt attention. Keno, still mostly asleep, looked out at the landscape through the tiger-striped smears of the Bronco's windshield. Mesmerized, he watched the barren, cactus-studded topography undulate to the horizon without any regard for human existence. A desert chill overruled the old truck's inconsistent heater. Keno pulled his lightly quilted jacket tighter—crossed arms pushing hands into armpits. A familiar aroma drifted in from his left, and he started teasing Lola.

"My name is coffee. I am your master. You will do as I say."

Not proud of her addiction, she scowled at the comment but kept her eyes focused on the road. Her right forearm rested across her stomach, the wrist extending from belly with an overhand grip that allowed her fingers to lightly guide the steering wheel. Her left elbow pointed into the door armrest, supporting an upward-thrust left hand that gripped a large thermos of freshly brewed java. She frequently visited her lips to the aperture of the insulated container.

Keno, never having developed the coffee habit, liked to tease Lola about hers. Like a five-year-old, his creative genius often rested on the simple elegance of repetition.

"My name is coffee. I am your master. You will do as I say."

Lola decided to ignore him. Instead, she hoped his attention would soon redirect itself. But Keno's barely awake brain was captivated by the metronomic nature of the syllables. He found something soothing in the 5-5-6 count that he delivered in a computer-like automated voice. Of course he also enjoyed the dig at his wife that the clever message of servitude highlighted—not to mention the position of relative virtue implied by his abstention.

"My name is coffee. I am your master. You will do as I say."

"C'mon, Keno, give it a break. Besides, I don't see you volunteering to drive."

"My name is coffee. I am your master. You will do as I say."

Tired of his annoying mantra, Lola suddenly pulled hard left on the wheel, spilling an ounce or two of coffee on the dark towel in her lap while bouncing Keno's unprepared skull off of the passenger window. She wrote off the towel as collateral damage.

"Oh my god, Keno, that must've really hurt! I'm so sorry! Are you okay? Jeez, did you see that huge pothole! I barely missed it…it would've broken our axle!"

With his right hand Keno was already probing the rising knot on the side of his head. He then moved his fingers in front of his eyes to check for blood. Although he was looking straight ahead, his mind was suspiciously eyeing Lola. Deciding not to reward his wife for her questionable behavior, he mentally listed a few retaliatory options. His choice revealed more about his *preternatural laziness than anything else. Or maybe he was just childishly stubborn.*

"My name is coffee. I am your master. You will do as I say."

Lola looked over at him with a frown.

You wanna keep playin' this game, Mister? she asked silently. It's a long road, with a lotta potholes.

Just before Keno was ready to again let fly the 5-5-6 ditty, the throbbing on the side of his head forced him to reassess. He decided to keep quiet and return his gaze to the land of reptiles.

From a bush on the side of the road a jackrabbit burst into the illumination of their headlights before quickly disappearing under the front of the truck. They both cringed, waiting for the muted tha-thunk that never came.

"There must've already been a dozen like that! How do we miss 'em?"

"Those things gotta be soo fast!"

The exchange died as quickly as it had arisen. Soon Keno was daydreaming about their destination—San Juanico. A remote, small fishing village about two thirds of the way down the west coast of the Baja Peninsula, San Juanico was about three hours away from the nearest viable airport (which was in Loreto on the opposite—or east—side of Baja). During their first trip, years ago, they had quickly learned that the tiny pueblo had little in the way of infrastructure. Power, water, and internet, mostly nada. Gringo *surfers called the place* Scorpion Bay, *in reference to the long shoreline that ran in front of the town, which was curved like the tail on one of the venomous arachnids. Just to the southwest of the center of town sat a broad but squat headland that protected the bay from the large winter storms that blew down from the Gulf of Alaska. Jutting out from that formation were a number of rocky points, volcanic in origin, that captured sand and shaped the energy of incoming swell. These points conspired with a consistent bottom topography to* mold perfect, long-shouldered, right point breaks. With at least four different options, all within a short drive, Scorpion Bay was a surfer's paradise.

In his mind's eye, Keno first imagined smackin' the lip with his shortboard out at fourth point. When he grew tired of playing that tape, he switched to the one that had him reaching for a "cheater's five" off of his longboard at second. As the fantasy became particularly sensual, he noticed the beginnings of some timber in his nether region. He positioned his hands to hide the evidence. He was ashamed of being ashamed but didn't know how to get off of the merry-go-round. Lola interrupted his morning conundrum.

"They wouldn't sell me any Cipro."

His vacant stare required more.

"Yesterday. In the pharmacy at Wal-Mart."

Studying her face, he looked for a sign he could use for guidance. She gave him nothing. He reached in the door cup holder for his first bottle of kombucha, twisted off the top, and raised the opening towards his lips. First taking a sip, he then returned and tightly twisted the cap to preserve carbonation.

"That's weird, why not?"

He had just finished bottling the kombucha the previous evening, and the lime and ginger awakened his taste buds. Lola looked at him plaintively.

"My name is kombucha. I am your master. You will do as I say."

Keno smiled mischievously at his wife.

"Touché."

Having made her point, Lola refused to stoop to his level of childish repetition. She found her way back to the previous conversation.

"I guess Mexico is starting to tighten up."

"Makes sense, given the superbugs that are popping up everywhere."

"I think I still have some azithromycin."

"That's a 'Z-Pak? That should work for most stuff, right?"

"I think so."

"What are you worried about, baby?"

Lola felt vulnerable, being deep in the Baja Peninsula with no connectivity and no medical care. Like many women, after frequent or prolonged sex, she was prone to painful urinary tract infections. Ever since Keno had returned from his walkabout, there had been an impassioned amount of both. She didn't want to get stuck somewhere and not have access to a remedy, but she downplayed her fears with a shrug.

"Oh...you know...feces occurs."

He saw through the vague gesture.

"You have your pee-pee medicine?"

"Yes."

"Macrodantin?"

"Yes... but only a few expired pills."

"Don't worry, no sex for three weeks," Keno offered generously. "We'll just surf."

He was looking to score points in light of his historically strong libido and her historically challenged urinary tract. Not receiving any verbal credit for his act of thoughtfulness, he pressed for recognition.

"Sound good?"

She thought the offer gratuitous and less than genuine.

"Sounds to me like you're trying to weasel out of your responsibilities."

Happy with the silver lining embedded in her rejection, Keno let her comment die in the early morning silence. He looked out the window at a herd of goats grazing by the side of the road. As was often the case, they were shepherded by a rough-looking mutt—part dingo and part coyote—that took *her responsibilities for protecting the herd seriously. The dog glared at him, but the strange goat/sheep animals under her watch barely acknowledged the speeding truck passing through their midst. Lola slipped Fleetwood Mac's* Rumours *into the CD player and then pressed a few buttons.*

Now here you go again,

you say you want your freedom…

From the Bronco's speakers Stevie Nicks throatily exhaled the words to "Dreams," a song she had written over thirty years earlier, in Sausalito, in less than half the time it takes to bake a chocolate cake.

Well, who am I to keep you down?

Keno thought of something.
"Careful with your speed Lola, lotsa sleepy animals out here."
She turned and pantomimed handing him the wheel.
"You wanna drive, Mr. Know-It-All?"
"Didn't mean to offend…just the animals like to sleep on the warm pavement at night…when the desert gets cold."
"And who do you think taught you that? Maybe me? Not my first rodeo, cowboy."
Now it was Keno's turn to shrug. He could tell his kombucha was no match for the caffeine in her coffee. His mind wandered to the last time he was in Baja.

In the stillness of remembering what you had . . .

Another cluster of cows indifferently raced past his window.

And what you lost…

"I'm thinking about writing a book."

He had her attention.

"What about?"

"Just this whole crazy mess that just happened."

"Keno, you should! I bet it would be very cathartic."

Her enthusiastic support left him suspicious of her sincerity. He thought about his hike out from Irma's and decided he wouldn't be able to write about all *his* adventures.

"So *why* this *guy*… Wolfgang?"

"I told you, I was frantic…we didn't have any money, Keno. The boys were talking about leaving home."

"But you must've at least loved him?"

"I didn't have a choice! He was my only option. You had abandoned us, everybody thought you were dead!"

"Did you sleep with him?"

"None of us is perfect, Keenan," she mumbled.

He didn't know why he was pressing, it was as if the question controlled him rather than the other way around; despite his awareness that the path he was pushing them down would likely lead to an emotional train wreck of a conclusion.

"But did you sleep with him?"

Feeling like a cow being herded down a narrowing chute, she saw her escape in the form of a roadside outdoor kitchen.

"*There it is! Dahlia's Cocina! And it's open! How many breakfast burritos do you want? I'm gonna get two with* machaca *and two with* chorizo...*and I'm not sharing!*"

Before he could press the question further, she pulled over onto the dusty white shoulder in front of the wood-and-palapa structure and hopped out of the cab.

"You want the same?"

Keno decided he would let it die for now. Plus, he was really hungry.

"They're small, I'm big and hambre...three each, please!"

His mouth started watering in anticipation of the greasy, homemade Mexican sausage wrapped with egg and cheese in small corn tortillas. A few moments later, Lola was back with a paper sack of food.

"Hey, slide over to the middle, we're giving this young lady a ride to Constitución."

The door on Keno's right opened and he looked down on the top of a woman's blond head making ready to climb in and join them on the front bench seat.

"Calypso, this is my husband, Keno...he's not much to look at...but he won't bite."

Keno froze as Calypso threw a small pack up on the dashboard and then sandwiched him between herself and Lola. Their eyes locked for an awkward moment. She offered her hand and a knowing smile, as if they shared some secret.

"Hi Keno, you seem familiar...do I know you from someplace?"

His heart racing a million miles an hour, he had already lost his appetite.

"I...uh...don't think so?"

She laughed with a coquettish toss of her head. Her jaw was working a glob of Bazooka gum, and she first wet, then pursed, her lips before blowing a huge pink bubble at Keno. With a wink she deftly sucked out all the air without any gum sticking to her face..

"You don't seem like the type that would lie about anything. Maybe just a different life?"

Lola started up the car and the stereo came to life.

Players only love you when they're playing…

"Calypso, do you mind handing out some of those mini-burritos?"

"Not at all, Lola."

Pulling back onto the blacktop, their tires unleashed a cloud of fine white dust. Lola felt obliged to make small talk.

"Keno was just saying he wants to write a book, right Keno?"

Say,

women

they will come

and they will go…

"Really? That's interesting. About what?"

Keno felt his way forward like a blind man walking through a minefield. Calypso dealt everyone a burrito.

"Umm…sort of like some life observations wrapped in a fictionalized autobiography?"

Calypso placed her left hand on his lap and started brazenly searching through his loose fitting shorts. She turned towards Keno and fixed his eyes with a smile.

"No shit! Like surfing and sex and stuff?"

When the rain washes you clean,
you'll know…

Lola was happily singing along with Stevie. Keno glanced at her nervously, wondering when she would put a stop to the shenanigans. But she was somehow not aware of the below-the-belt activity happening just to her right. He squirmed his hips under the direct pressure.

"Kinda…I mean I haven't really figured…it…out…yet."

Having located him through the fabric, Calypso was now sizing him up by tracing the outline of his growing shaft with her fingertips. She looked up into his pleading eyes with an enthusiastic interest.

"This book you're gonna write…are you gonna try and get it published? Sell it and get a lot of money? Show everyone you're better than them? Maybe get some strange on the side?"

Lola turned to him with a playful sneer and a mouthful of egg and chorizo.

"Yeah, Keno, you gonna get a lotta money and strange? Prove you're special?"

Something very odd was happening, but Keno couldn't figure out the new rules. It was like the usual laws of physics had changed, and gravity no longer effected them. A very basic part of his brain wanted Calypso to continue with the intimate attention but the rest of him felt tremendously guilty about the unexpected massage. They were all so close that he knew it was just a matter of time before his wife caught on. Seemingly oblivious to Calypso's hands, Lola refocused on the road and continued singing along.

Thunder only happens

when it's raining...

Keno took a small bite of his burrito and then answered their weirdly forward questions.

"Well, I have some friends who can help me market the book."

Calypso used both hands to matter-of-factly unzip his shorts and reach inside. Keno cringed but couldn't put a stop to it. At the moment his arms seemed paralyzed. Somehow Calypso knew he was referring to the old hippies.

"You're gonna hire Bernie and Jerry to make up some reviews and fake awards that you can use to get people's attention?"

With no undergarments blocking her access, Calypso now had a firm grasp on his appendage and was blatantly bringing him to "up periscope."

"Umm...I was hoping they could help me with my web presence...if that's what you mean. The way you say it makes it seem like a bad thing."

Lola interrupted her singing to weigh in.

"You're gonna pay some friends to invent rewards and give them to you?"

Keno tried to dodge the question on technical grounds.

"Not paying for re-wards."

"What then?"

"A-wards. Pay for a-wards."

His angel was starting a slow, rhythmic massaging. At this point, Keno couldn't believe that Lola wasn't aware of the seduction occurring right next her.

"Keno, that sounds like fraud to me...why would you want to risk your reputation like that?"

"It's no different than celebrity endorsements. You think those guys actually use all that stuff? Everybody does this…it's how things are done."

"But Keno, you've worked hard to be an ethical, honorable man…at least the man I thought I knew? You don't need that kinda double-talk to try and sell your art. What do you want out of this, anyway?"

Calypso now had both hands fully engaged. Keno was slowly losing his ability to follow the conversation let alone speak. His simmer was heading to a boil and he was having trouble fighting the upwelling, yet he was terrified that at any moment Lola would see. To him, the heat in the truck felt like the desert had moved from first light to high noon in less time than it took to light a Molotov cocktail.

"He wants to show everyone he's better than them…get a lot of money and some strange…we've already established that…right, Freddy?"

Before Keno could respond, Calypso unashamedly rotated her hips one hundred and eighty degrees, straddling his thighs while placing her steamy mouth over his. Their tongues and saliva merged, and the tastes of bubblegum, chorizo, and tequila began to overwhelm him. He felt her firm breasts pressing into him. Like a hungry wolf enjoying the warm, fresh flesh of a bloody kill, he wanted more. Her clothes smelled like smoky mesquite, surf wax, and perfume, all rolled into one. He was starting to feel a flying-weightless sort of freedom as he melted into her. Things had never felt so good or so right…if he could just turn off his conscience, for a second, he thought he would be able to quickly reach that sacred, universally shared moment of procreation. Her right hand maintained its grip, guiding him under her bunched up skirt. Securing his scalp, her left hand grabbed a clutch of his hair, curved fingers tilting his head back and pressing his mouth up and into hers. He was glowing like the metal on the edge of a knife…and Lola didn't even notice.

Now here I go again, I see the crystal visions…

When the snake first started pushing out of her pack and onto the dashboard, Keno wasn't sure. Calypso's hair partially obscured his forward vision, and the fireworks in his brain were so intense that he didn't care about anything but the creature in his lap. Despite his imperfect view, when his ears registered the rattle he knew it was for real, and the receptors in his brain received a round of chemicals that elevated him to a new level of terrified awareness. He tried to warn Lola, but Calypso put a hand over his mouth and hushed him.

"Don't worry, she's with me...everything's gonna work out fine."

While focusing on keeping the truck away from the potholes, Lola was simultaneously noodling on the use of Bernie and Jerry for the marketing of his proposed book.

"Keno, I really don't think you should be doing that...it's just wrong."

The yellow, vertical slits at the center of the diamondback's eyes held him hypnotized as its thick, five-foot body emerged wholly onto the dashboard and began to coil. Somehow Calypso had willed open her blouse, and the look and feel of her naked breasts against his torso further sank the hooks. Forgetting the lessons of Icarus, Keno continued to push higher, convincing himself he could gorge on the she-devil, just this last time, without attracting the notice of Lola right next to them. His physical yearning was now so feverish he forgot about the snake and just focused on the body entwined with his and the need for release. Like a man falling into the grasp of propofol, Keno was warmly incapacitated, yet at the same time horrified by what would happen if his family found out what he was acquiescing to.

Dreams of loneliness

like a heartbeat drives you mad...

Her mouth full of burrito, Lola kept on with her sloppy singing, still *dramatically unaware of all the threats swirling around her. Ignoring Lola, Calypso was now grinding on Keno fervently, pressing her tongue deeper into his mouth while the snake kept cadence. The desert heat was pouring into the truck. Saltwater ran in rivulets from Keno's skin. He was unable to control Calypso's movements and only moments away from climax.*

Rounding the corner at high speed, Keno saw the massive Brahma bull a split second before Lola. He screamed as loud as he could, trying to warn her, but his cries felt impossibly muffled. He tried yelling again, but the words stuck in his mouth like a wet Nerf ball. Finally, Lola realized the danger all around them and pulled hard on the wheel while slamming on the brakes. The Bronco hurtled sideways towards the flimsy guardrail that fronted the steep embankment. The snake opened its mouth and revealed her descending fangs. Leaning to one side while separating her mouth from Keno's, Calypso unleashed a shrieking howl while pulling back hard on the handful of hair. Keno's throat lay exposed to the lunging serpent.

And what you lost—
and what you had—
and what you lost…

As Keno's eyes took in the smoke-stained ceiling of the cab, he reflexively threw up his arms to ward off all the incoming calamities: the hulking, two-thousand-pound bull; the serpent's glistening fangs; the long, sheer drop-off of the cliff. But his movements, like his screams, were muted. A flash of his boys popped into his head…he reached for them, but the image disappeared. His last thought was one of profound emptiness.

"Ke-no! KEENAN!! Wake-up! It's okay, I'm right here."

Keno slowly surfaced from the nightmare. Sweat soaked the rumpled sheets. His heart was bouncing against his ribs like a tiger caught in a cage. He could still hear himself trying to scream. He kept his eyes closed and focused on catching his breath. The first thing he noticed was her scent. He luxuriated in its familiarity, comforted by the smell that had insinuated itself into his heart and soul without ever offending. Forcing his eyes open, he saw the redemption—his best friend—Lola—hovering over him, concerned and shaking his shoulder. She stroked his forehead and looked tenderly into his face, trying to discern any clues to his hauntings. In spite of his fogged, transitional state, he thought she had never looked more beautiful. At that moment he realized he was probably as close to home as he would ever be.

"It's OK, honey," Lola said. "You fell asleep in the boys' room…"

He looked around. On a shelf to his left, books were stacked alongside a violin that his younger son, Gus, hadn't touched since eighth grade. A few "participation" trophies stood scattered on bureau tops, commemorating Sam's athletic indifference. Close behind Lola, a poster stood tacked to the wall: Four young men stared out at him, the word *Coldplay* the only hint as to their *raison d'être*. Off to the right, a contemporary Rock diva he recognized as Rihanna reclined in a revealing pose, her feet in stiletto heels leading her long, naked legs up a barely visible wall.

He looked beneath him and realized he was lying atop the covers of one of the room's two symmetrically placed twin beds. He remembered that during quieter moments, ever since returning from his odyssey, he had been drawn into the quarters of his two children. Often, he simply lay down in either Gus's or Sam's bed and reflected. He wanted to absorb everything about his progeny that was still available to him. He had regrets from situations that were now long past—thoughts on how he would parent his two boys differently…if Fortuna would only give him the chance. Sometimes he would cry, sometimes he'd just fall asleep.

Usually he did both.

"It's all right…you're home now. You just had another bad dream."

Nodding his head, Keenan fought back the tears. The dappled, late afternoon sun danced across the bedroom floor. It seemed to be a perfect Marin County Sunday, not a leaf out of place. But he wasn't sure what he wanted at that moment: solitude, or the comfort of Lola's companionship. Noting his apparent indecisiveness, his wife did what she had always done.

"Move over, I'm comin' in."

He slid over a few inches on his back, making room for her to lie down next to him. A tiny upwelling of desire pushed through his melancholy as her warm body contacted his.

"Boy or girl?" she asked.

"Girl," he answered, embracing the passive stereotype.

Turning away from her, he rolled onto his side. She closed the small gap, wrapping her arms around his shoulders while "spooning" her body against his from behind. A few laggard songbirds sang to them from outside the second-story window.

"Wanna talk about it?"

"Not yet."

And then, a few minutes later.

"Maybe."

"I'm here."

"It's just, I don't know…so complicated…so much stuff…and it's all happening so fast."

"I know, baby."

"Maybe I'm going crazy."

"Probably."

"Just when I think I've got it figured out, it changes…I change…you change…the kids leave."

The pinging sound of Keno's ringtone interrupted their moment. He reached over and grabbed his phone. Lola resented the intrusion but tried to keep the emotion from destroying the moment. As Keno picked up the phone, his knuckles grazed an old baseball glove he had passed down to the boys. He couldn't recall them ever using it.

"It's my dad. I should take it."

Lola nodded, got up, and pulled her own phone out of her back pocket. Keno sat up on the edge of the tiny mattress.

"Hi Dad…I have you on speaker and Lola is in the room…so none of our usual pornographic banter."

Aloysius' voice came through loud and clear. "Oh, darn! You know I always come to you for my prescribed daily dose of pornographic banter…KIDDING! HI LOLA!! MERRY CHRISTMAS!"

Lola was trying to hook her phone up with one of her boys's Bluetooth speakers so she could dial up her favorite playlist. "Hi Aloysius!" She called out. "MERRY CHRISTMAS!"

"Full disclosure," Keno's father continued, "I've got Paul and Roshan with me…I've got you on speaker too…we've all been playing Pickleball!"

"Hi Paul! Hi Roshan!" Keno greeted. "Y'all're in Florida?"

In the background of Aloysius's phone, he heard Paul and Roshan compete for bandwidth. Their voices sounded flush with exercise-induced enthusiasm.

"Hi Keno! Hi Lola!" Paul said.

"Yeah, we just got back from the Y!" Roshan chimed in.

"The Y is open on Christmas Eve?"

"For the over-sixty crowd, Pickleball is a form of worship!"

"What's Pickleball?"

Aloysius' voice overrode the other two.

"It's like if ping-pong and tennis had a baby."

Lola successfully connected to the single speaker and started softly playing some music. She tried to picture Roshan, Paul, and Aloysius playing a court sport.

"And Paul can play? In his wheelchair?"

"Yeah, I can play! I stay at the kitchen line mostly…and I'm ambidextrous, so I can reach a lot of balls. I just need a fast partner to cover the rest of the court."

Like a whisper in the distance, Clarence Greenwood started singing from the speaker.

Been left for dead…

"And I'm his fast partner!" It sounded to Keno as if Roshan had grabbed the phone from Paul. "Who'd a thunk I'm a natural at something called Pickleball? We just crushed Al and Lilly!"

"To be fair, it was our first time playing…" Clearly, Aloysius felt the need to defend his prowess as an athlete. "And Lilly's not much of an eye-hand coordination athlete."

A, E, I, O, U…

Lola shuddered at the memory of the last time she had spoken to

Lilly. It was the day before the wedding and she had been melting down.

"Lilly is with you?"

"No. Not right now. She took Elizabeth out to the late Mass. Those two are like peas in a pod."

Roshan's voice cut in eagerly.

"Tell us about the wedding? Scout says it was the most emotional event she'd ever witnessed?"

Lola responded first.

"I was totally surprised…I mean it was pretty amazing…"

Then Lola remembered the confused looks on the faces of Wolfgang's family and friends, and the complicated explaining that was later required in the absence of the scheduled groom.

"Well, at least for half the church…"

Keno had never been happier than when he had approached the altar from the changing room and saw his boys' faces light up with recognition, despite all of the unkempt hair. By the time a trembling Lola had marched down the aisle and taken her place across from them, it had become obvious that she recognized him. The amount of endogenous morphine transmitted to their brains at that moment had pushed them all to a place just south of heaven.

"Probably the most magical moment of my life, " Keno recalled.

Lola remembered the sad look on the face of the dry cleaner when she brought in her wedding gown a few days after the event. "I cried so much that the tears washed a gallon of mascara onto my dress."

And then Keno caught himself.

"Right up there with the births of the boys and our first wedding."

Then, just to let Lola know he hadn't completely gone off the deep end of the sentiment pool: "And, of course, the Forty-Niners winning the

Super Bowl the first time with Joe Montana."

As expected, the obligatory eye roll and shoulder punch from Lola.

Roshan's voice joined the disapproval.

"Keno! You're such a bonehead!"

Like the mischievous little boy he was, Keno relished the flimsy joke, allowing himself a smile for the first time that day.

"Sorry! I couldn't help myself."

Lola was secretly happy to see a glimpse of playfulness return to the morose old man who had recently occupied her husband. Thoughts of the wedding had triggered her brain to pursue another topic.

"How's Scout doing?"

Paul fielded the question, as he and Scout had developed a connection through painting.

"Lola, she's doing really well. She met a boy at your wedding."

It took a moment for the words to register. *"What?"*

"I know, crazy right?"

Keno thought about the stunning coincidence that had allowed him to derail the Wolfgang train. "No way!" he said. "If she hadn't driven by and picked me up when she did I don't know what would've happened. And *then* she meets a boy?"

Aloysius had to state the obvious.

"A lot of strange coincidences in this world…"

"Anyway, things seem to be hot and heavy, because she got a job and is moving up to the Bay Area to be near this guy."

"No. Way."

"Way. *And* she's painting regularly. She says the creative process is very therapeutic."

Lola held a warm spot in her heart for Scout.

"Awesome. So we'll get to see more of her, I hope?"

"Well, she'll be in the South Bay starting as an admin with some tech start-up, but I know she'd like that. I think she doesn't want to be a pest, with all that you've been through."

Lola made a mental note to reach out.

"That's silly," she said. "She's never a pest. I'll call her after New Year's."

"I'm pretty sure she'd like that," Paul said.

Since his return from his Mexico banishment, Keno had been having trouble catching up with the many developments taking place with all the family. He mounted the next inquiry with a small spring in his verbal step.

"Dad, how are your knees holding up?"

Aloysius matched Keno's spring with some verbal bounce of his own. "Really good! Lilly's got me on this new anti-inflammation diet. No nightshades, no dairy, no grains, no peanuts…and especially no sugar! That and the PRP treatments seem to be keeping the pain at bay!"

" 'PRP'?"

Over the previous two days, Paul and Roshan had already heard enough of Aloysius' proselytizing.

"Bye guys, we gotta go!" Paul said.

"Rosalita's got a sitter waiting!" Roshan explained. Keno and Lola bid them *adieu*. "Hug Rosie for us!" Lola added.

"Merry Christmas!" Paul said.

"MERRY CHRISTMAS!" Keno and Lola returned in stereo.

"PRP," Aloysius said, returning to Keno's question. "Platelet-rich plasma. They take out some of my blood, spin it in a centrifuge, isolate the good stuff, and then inject it back in to my damaged joints."

Keno shook his head and whistled into the phone. "Wow…That's a thing?"

"Oh yeah, all of the fogies are doing it. Hey, enough about me, how are you guys holding up?"

Keno raised his eyebrows as John Mellencamp queued up on the speaker.

A little ditty, 'bout Jack and Diane…

He looked at Lola. She took the lead.

"Good, good…well, a little rocky with the boys…but…Keno's got the business back on track…and I think Gus is coming home soon. Fingers crossed. He was supposed to be here tomorrow for Christmas, but…"

"They're both still in Cartagena?"

"Somewhere in Columbia…we think Cartagena…we don't hear from them much."

"Lola is worried to death about them, Dad…" Keno explained.

"Not 'to death'…I just think they're a little young…"

"I think it's probably good for them to grow up, just a little, on someone else's dime."

Keno and Lola had had this discussion several times before and held opposing convictions.

"Keno, Sam went on a semester abroad and never came home! Two weeks later, Gus withdrew all his college savings, dropped out of high school and tramped after him…"

"Dad, I think Sam has a girlfriend and a job waiting tables. He and Gus share an apartment. At least they're upgrading their Spanish."

Aloysius wasn't picking up on the dynamic.

"Lucky Sam! I hear the Colombian women are gorgeous."

Lola cringed. *Just like Aloysius to totally miss the point*, she thought.

Having a good idea of what she was thinking, Keno decided to change the subject.

"How's Clay doin'?"

There was a pregnant pause.

...long after the thrill of livin' is gone.

"He left."

"Oh no! What happened?"

"Elizabeth just got tired of him hangin' out and smokin' weed all day. He wouldn't go for help, kept breaking all the appointments with the docs. She told him he needed to find a job. Not a pretty situation."

"Where'd he go?"

"Not sure…maybe living on a friend's boat up in Pascagoula…or Spanish Fort…but we haven't heard from him since he left. Elizabeth thinks he may have a girlfriend in Calexico who tolerates him."

Another long silence.

"Keno," Aloysius said, "we all tried really hard. Towards the end he was drinking a twelve-pack nearly every day on top of the weed. All those chemicals…alcohol, THC…his brain…just a mess."

"Dad, you don't have to explain. I understand."

"No, you don't, Keno…it was horrible…I only saw him for a coupla days…your Mom tried for a month. The whole story that someone had put out a contract on you? We think Lilly was right…it was all a distraction, a…a…Deschutes Pivot…so he could come home as a bit of a hero…but he changes his facts so often we'll probably never know for sure. He literally wakes up in the middle of the night, screaming, at least once a week."

Lola looked at Keno and sadly shook her head. Her husband wasn't ready to give up.

"Dad, is there any hope…anything we can do?"

As an old dog, Aloysius had some experience with learning new tricks.

"I believe there's always hope. Miracles happen."

Thinking that was a nice note to end on, Lola tried to deftly shift gears.

"Aloysius, it sounds like you're back together with Lilly?"

Aloysius' voice had turned dark while discussing his oldest child. Now, it brightened considerably.

"Well, not really a full-time starter…yet. She's sorta plugging me in as middle relief for now. She's still seeing that crazy, Indian, toe-stubber, but at least she's giving me a tryout when he's not around."

Now it was Lola's turn to raise her eyebrows.

"And you guys are all good with that?"

Aloysius laughed.

"Haven't you heard about the STD epidemic that's plaguing nursing homes?"

Both the youngsters cringed.

"Oh, Dad! TMI!"

A sense of urgency filled Aloysius' voice.

"Guys, I gotta go. The girls just pulled into the driveway and it's my night to do the dishes."

"Bye, Dad," Keno said. "Love to Mom!"

"Bye, Aloysius!" Lola chimed in. "Hugs to Lilly from us!"

"Merry Christmas!"

"MERRY CHRISTMAS!"

And then they were alone.

Looking down at Keno with a sympathetic smile, Lola shrugged. Remaining seated on the edge of the bed, he turned off his phone and placed it on a shelf behind them. She sat next to him then put her head on his shoulder.

"Well, that should've cleared everything up for you!"

"Like mud."

"Our parents are really getting old."

"I don't know how he does it."

"You mean the breathless enthusiasm at his age?"

"Yeah."

"I can see him prancing around Clearwater…"

"Tam-o'-shanter rakishly askew on his head…"

"Singing Christmas carols and endlessly testifying about his new diet to anyone who will listen."

"And platelet-rich plasma…eesssshhh, sounds painful."

"Right?"

"It's just amazing…his enthusiasm, the ability to change and try new things, his sustained love for women and just…just…life."

Lola lightly pushed Keno's hand away from her breast.

"Yeah, well that libido thing seems to be genetic. And what about your mom? Starting yoga and a new career in her sixties?"

"In computers!"

"Crazy!"

"Right?"

Lola's thoughts returned to her father-in-law's seemingly boundless energy levels.

"Maybe he's taking testosterone?"

"Who?"

"Your dad?"

"Maybe"

"You don't know?"

"I guess I never thought to ask. He's really open about some stuff, and really private about others…unless he's drinkin'."

"I think he likes to keep the question alive."

"I don't think he even thinks like that. He just does."

Considering how unusual his family was, and what they had just put Lola through, Keno realized it was time. He had been trying to apologize to her since the wedding but hadn't been able to find the right words. Turning his eyes to her, his earnestness captured her full attention.

"Lola…I…I know I don't say this enough, but I need you to know…I really, really, really am grateful for you…I think…without you…I'd a… well…I just really need you and…you know…thank you for staying with me all these years…and…um…you know, always fighting for…us.…"

Watching him try to overcome his linguistic and emotional challenges pushed Lola to the edge of tears. She noticed the early rumblings of desire bubbling up from within.

Keno wasn't sure why the words were such a struggle, but he finally forced out the most important ones.

"God, I…umm…really…just…you know…love you so much.…"

Her hands found their way to the crown of his head as she ran her fingers through his recently cut hair; then, like a blind woman, she used the pads of her digits to delicately explore the contours of his face.

"Thank you, sweet, brown-eyed man. Sometimes I need to hear that."

After completing the tracing of his mouth, she quietly waited a bit before turning away and amplifying Jeff Tweedy's voice by fiddling with the volume on her phone.

Jesus, don't cry,

you can rely on me, honey . . .

Keno wasn't done with his sharing.

"What am I gonna do when they die? My parents?"

"That's a cheery thought on Christmas Eve."

Keno shrugged. At his side once again, Lola encircled his waist with both her arms and squeezed tight.

"Ahhh, baby…you know…same as always…one foot in front of the other."

"I mean, I don't even know what I believe anymore. When I was little, I used to think life only had meaning within the context of an afterlife… heaven or hell…consequences for your actions, and all that stuff… and then I thought that immortality meant there was no value to existence, that the finite nature of our days is actually what gave them worth."

I'll be around,

you were right about the stars...

Each one is a setting sun.

"Now I'm just confused."

Feeling like a teacup in a vast ocean, he realized that his time with Lola was probably taking him as close to belonging as he could ever hope for. As if to confirm his thoughts, she reached her left hand up and silently put it over his heart. Instinctively, his fingers gripped hers for stability.

Still feeling melancholy, he set his head back down on Sam's pillow, his back to her. He kept ahold of her hand. She once again conformed the front of her body to his back, hoping her silent presence would bring him some peace. As he welcomed the press of her body against his, he whispered a silent prayer of gratitude for their physical chemistry. He hoped their mutual desire would never be exhausted.

Our love,

our love is all of God's money...

As they spun away from the sun's dwindling light, one of the birds outside continued its twilight serenade from the trees. An open window allowed the room to start losing its heat, and Lola involuntarily shivered in response to a breath of cool air.

"I's a gettin' cold, baby."

"You's a shiverin', baby."

Their intimate *patois* was something that had naturally developed decades ago. Like many longtime partners, they comfortably slipped into the dialect during those moments when conversation was necessary but predictable.

"Whut we's a dewin' for dinner?"

"I'n a know, whut you wanna do?"

"Now don' start 'at again."

Lola had hoped the familiar patter would help lighten Keno's mood.

Our love,

our love,

our love…is all we have.

Still feeling unresolved, Keno looked out at the darkening sky, where the first stars were beginning to reveal themselves. He listened to the music and let the moment sit for a while.

And I'm wonderin'

where the lions are…

He thought about the magical Christmas stories he had heard growing up—Santa Claus and the Three Wise Men—and was saddened by the realization that they no longer brought any sense of mystery or wonder.

"What do you think happens, baby?"

Lola was thinking about her dad.

"After death?"

"Yeah, but bigger…the whole thing…I mean…does anyone have a clue?"

Pretty confident the question had no legitimate answer, Lola rested with it for a bit.

Through the open window she heard the whispers of the emerging bats and swallows as they hunted the early evening insects. She yearned to know whether her offspring were safe. She wished she could inject some of her hard-earned wisdom into the boys as easily as she had their childhood vaccines. She mourned a career that had not been seen to fruition. She wondered if her mom and dad were suffering…if Wolfgang ever missed her…and whether or not she had remembered to set out any hamburger to thaw. She thought about the deepening lines on her face and hoped Keno wouldn't join the bloom when it abandoned her. She contemplated her death…whether or not the funeral would draw any attention, or if she would just be left to drift away, a puff of smoke in the wind. She felt the heart beating through his chest and took solace in knowing that she had at least one witness.

….they got me thinkin' about eternity;
some kinda ecstasy got ahold on me…

Caressing his shoulder through his shirt, she felt him subtly push his hips back into her. Nearly imperceptibly, she returned the message. Moving her hands lower on his body, she finally decided to answer his question. She let the worries die as she gathered a breath and told him her simple truth.

"I's a girl and you's a boy…an' dat's all der is."

But he was already asleep.